Panthers
in the Skins of Men

Panthers
in the Skins of Men

Charles Nelson

A Meadowland Books Title
Published by Carol Publishing Group

To Mike DeRaddo
and
Cliff Pritchard

who extended kindness and offered amusement
to a wide-eyed youngster

told the boy wonderful stories
introduced him to strange people

and are remembered with affection

"I have . . . seen among the flowers the wild eyes
Of panthers in the skins of man . . ."

—ARTHUR RIMBAUD

Panthers
in the Skins of Men

Prologue

I plodded out of the jungle. Disdaining a shower, I flopped upon a gritty blanket. A jarhead peered into the tent. "Strom! The chief wants you."

"Not another patrol!"

"No," croaked Chief Froggi. "Instructions come down from Battalion Headquarters. They wanna know where you prefer to stand duty after Nam. You ain't leaving soon enough to suit me." The Bullfrog and I enjoyed a mutual antipathy. "You get three choices." He handed me a printed form. I expressed astonishment that the chief had refrained from filling in the blanks: an isolated weather station in the Antarctic, a patrol boat traversing the Bermuda Triangle, and a doomed submarine. "I thought about it." A flick of his tongue snared an unwary fly.

The raucous calls of jungle birds and the clarion curses of muddy marines made the compound a bedlam; perspiration soaked my reeking greens. I imagined the hush of snowflakes. Colorful Mod clothes. Civilians giving no thought to carnage. I printed "New York" and "Boston." A third choice? "Any navy bases between those cities?"

"New London, Connecticut. Submarines."

A memory surfaced on the *Thresher*, which hadn't. "No submarines!"

"They wouldn't let a candyass like you aboard one noways." Chief Froggi expectorated a large yellow hawker.

Dull eyes fixed on me and blinked. "Big base in Newport, Rhode Island."

Fashionable Newport, summer home to Cornelius Vanderbilt and Janet Auchincloss. Music festivals. Regattas. Caucasians. "I'll take it."

And got it.

Before I could embark for the States, a Viet Cong bullet smashed my right elbow, so I missed the Jazz Festival. I missed the America's Cup. I missed a New England autumn and the first days of winter. I missed Janet Auchincloss.

The wound sent me to a naval hospital in New Orleans, forty miles from the old plantation. Military surgeons progressed from discussing the amputation of my arm to a self-congratulatory prognosis of a full recovery. Three operations transformed a shattered mass of incessant pain into a steel-and-plastic artifact that ached only during inclement weather.

Throughout five dreary months, my maternal grandmother drove to New Orleans twice a week for lengthy visits. She sat by the bed in which I lay attached to traction—a steel pin holding my elbow together—inspired by my immobility to recall the highlights and the despondencies of her life in repetitive, compulsive, neverending monologues.

My family had scattered and I'd grown away from high school friends; my social life embraced the recuperating men in nearby beds. I listened to their histories and offered an expurgated version of mine; contact assured, I could choose between building my days around pesthouse gossip or losing myself in literature. The hospital library offered westerns, mysteries, science fiction, and military memoirs. My intellect, like my body, softened with disuse.

My old pal, Paul, flew from Colorado for a weekend visit. "How ever do you while away the hours?"

"I endure physical therapy and look forward to meals."

"You are wasting days that could be used constructively."

12

"Do you grasp my situation?"

Paul grimaced. "I never figured you to wallow in self-pity."

"Should I enroll in correspondence courses advertised on matchbook covers?"

"Not a bad idea." Paul nodded at a devastating marine of Russian descent whose bed stood next to mine. "If nothing else, a plethora of attractive young men surrounds you."

"I'm hardly set up for seductions."

"In the old days, no mere bullet could stop you from rapine and mayhem." Paul studied my face. "Here?" I grinned. "Sisters among the orderlies?"

"I try to avoid fairies even under duress."

He sighed. "You're such a homophobe."

I indicated a couple of rugged-looking grunts across the aisle. "We pretend to ignore one another as we abuse ourselves." Paul shook his head. "It passes the time."

A week later, the mailman dropped off a package that enclosed five books: The Assimil Method of learning languages. Should I learn to speak French, German, Italian, Russian, or Spanish? Nothing if not game, I set aside an hour a day for each language. A month passed; a box arrived, filled with novels in five languages. Paul had a knack of stirring one's ambitions.

My term of trial finally ended and I emerged from the hospital, free to enjoy thirty days of leave. My grandmother booked passage on a ship cruising the Caribbean; for three weeks, I lay in the sun and listened to Mom prattle. Tan and sturdy, I spent a week with my sister in Ohio before flying to New York City.

Between planes at Kennedy Airport, I strolled around the main terminal. A leering stewardess whistled. Emboldened by her concupiscence, I entered a door marked MEN. A tall, dark, and handsome TWA navigator followed and stood next to me at a urinal. Satisfied with each other's wares, we met outside. The Birdman indicated the sling covering my

13

right arm and the medals pinned to my navy blue middy blouse. "New in town?"

"Just flew over the rainbow." The young man glanced about the terminal; no one hearkened to us. "So . . . here we are: strangers in the night."

His eyes sparkled. "Did you leave your heart in San Francisco?"

"I'm wearing it on my sleeve."

He flashed a roguish grin. "Waiting for someone to pluck it off?"

"Would you mind?"

"Follow me."

Ten minutes later, bellbottoms around my ankles, my body jackknifed over a sink, I gazed at a reflection of the grunting flyboy behind me in the mirror of a restroom serving Air Liechtenstein. The outer door of the restroom opened; Smilin' Jack disappeared into a cubicle. Two middleaged mechanics entered. As I struggled with one arm to pull up my bellbottoms, they broke into hearty guffaws. Noting my purple hearts, one slapped my bare ass. "Enjoy yourself, kid. You deserve it." They urinated and left, still chuckling.

The Devil Dog of the Air emerged shamefaced from his hiding place and led me to the Air Damascus terminal, where we continued our lubricity. After six months of relative chasteness, I felt back in the swing of things.

I flew to Boston, rode the MTA into the city, and trudged along an icy sidewalk towards the Greyhound bus station. A good-looking hustler of Mediterranean descent stood on a corner, just jeans and a tight t-shirt protecting his muscular torso from a freezing wind. I set down my sea bag and my travel bag. "You out for business or pleasure?"

"Business," he snapped, while looking me up and down, "but for you—pleasure. Got the dough for a hotel?"

"I'm steeped in poverty to the very lips."

The fancy man paused, checked me out again, and picked

14

up my sea bag. "My car's down the block."

He drove to a lumberyard closed for the night; snowclad boards served badly as a love couch. The hustler drove to Beacon Hill and rented a squalid room at a seedy hotel. Although I enjoyed the session, nothing in my bag of tricks could bring him off. Defeated, I arose from the sagging bed. "I dislike embodying a cliché, but this sailor's got to catch a bus."

The hustler flogged a limp log. "Put on my jockstrap." I obeyed. "Walk around the room." Three steps to a stained wall, three steps back. "How did you hurt your arm?"

"It was a dark and stormy night."

"I'm serious."

"So am I. Riding in a helicopter outside DaNang. My elbow stopped a bullet."

"That's not my fantasy."

"Sorry."

"I like football players."

"Pro or college?"

"College."

"I played safety at Central Louisiana. During my sophomore season, after a come-from-behind victory over the top team in the conference, we stripped to our jockstraps in the locker room, hoisted the quarterback on our shoulders, and carried him to the showers. Old Beau yelled 'If you really want to render me honor, the whole team would kiss my precious.' One of the tackles, drunk with victory, whooped, 'Why the hell not? He deserves it.' Next thing I know, we're lined up. . . ." The rent boy dropped me at the bus station, incapable for a few hours of selling his wares.

The Newport Naval Base lay along an icy shore of Narragansett Bay. Long gray ships floated through the mist under a slate sky. A damp frigid wind blasted the red brick hospital and barracks. Automobiles splashed dirty slush upon unwary pedestrians. Recollecting the sultry jungles of Vietnam, the prospect heartened me.

So did the First Class Hospitalman in charge of Personnel. "Get out of here! Go home! Come back after Christmas!"

Greyhound carried me to Manhattan. I checked into a YMCA on the East Side and considered my options. No battle-scarred veteran of a foreign conflict would call friends to whine, "It's Christmas Eve, and I'm alone in this big cold city"; inviting pity would tarnish my image. It would be bad manners to discommode anyone's holiday arrangements. I walked up Fifth Avenue to gape at shop windows. After supper in a Greek restaurant near Penn Station, I bought a bottle of Scotch and a quart of eggnog. Feeling sorry for myself, I returned to the YMCA.

In the lobby, an agitated young naval lieutenant spoke into a telephone receiver. Sandy hair. Blue eyes. A halfback's build. I slipped past without his noticing me.

Hurrying to my room, I pulled my good arm from my middy blouse, wrapped it in a bandage, and thrust it through my extra sling, which I slipped around my neck. I rode an elevator down to the lobby, where the disconsolate lieutenant sat on a sofa. I sat in an easy chair across from him. "Forget to mail a letter to Santa?"

He looked up. "Pulled duty Christmas Day."

"Never realized that officers get shafted, too."

A huge sigh. "We put in port yesterday. Three months at sea. I had five days of liberty coming. Planned to fly home. Another officer got sick."

"The best laid plans of mice and men. . . . Where you from?"

"Toledo, Ohio."

"I played ball for the Mud Hens in '65." (Toledo's professional baseball team.)

He stared. "What's the name?"

"Kurt Strom."

"You played shortstop!"

"Badly. The manager should have left me at third base, where I approached mediocrity."

16

"Never! I saw you play. The Tigers might have won last year with you on the team." I agreed. We talked baseball for a few minutes. "Will you play after your enlistment is up?"

I shook my head. "My arms got racked up pretty good."

"How?"

"In Nam. A rescue flight on a chopper."

"Bad deal."

"Could have been worse. A friend bought the farm."

Concern creased his face. "I'm surprised you're out of the hospital."

"After five months! Give me a break!" He indicated the slings. "I'm in transit from New Orleans. A top orthopedic surgeon in Boston will work on my arms."

"How do you get around?"

"I'm traveling with a marine who wanted to spend Christmas with his girl in Yonkers. He's my hands, I'm his brains."

"He left you in the lurch?"

"I insisted. He stepped on a mine near Chu Lai. Lost a leg. Hasn't been laid in six months. So what are your plans for Christmas Eve?"

He sighed. "I don't know a damn soul in New York."

"I've got the makings for eggnog in my room. How about joining me?"

The lieutenant communed with himself. "Why the hell not? It's not as if I have anything else to do."

I sat on a chair; the lieutenant lounged upon my bed. We talked about his family, his college career, and his fiancée. A second drink carried us through several horror stories about Nam.

"After all that, I suppose you consider it a Christmas present just to be alive."

"You bet, although I'd like to look in my stocking and find a shapely elfette eager to scrub me under a hot shower."

"Wouldn't your bandages get wet?"

"They'd dry. After two days of traveling, I feel like

17

something the cat dragged in."

He studied my slings. "If you don't mind my asking, how do you manage to shower?"

"Can't, unless someone helps me. Takes the suppleness of a contortionist just to undress myself."

The lieutenant nodded. "I've been guzzling your booze. A fair exchange."

"What's that?"

"You get undressed. I'll go to my room for a towel." Ten minutes later, we stood under adjoining nozzles in the shower room. Careful to keep my slings dry, I let water splash over my back and legs. The lieutenant soaped my washrag and applied it to my face. "You'd probably prefer a nurse to do this."

I gazed into clear blue eyes. "Be nice, but it hasn't happened." He lathered my back. "I've had to depend on corpsmen, and they're lax." Carefully avoiding the slings, he washed my chest. "Tell you the truth, no one's bothered to wash my private parts for three weeks."

The lieutenant stared. "You're kidding!"

"Wish I was."

"You should complain."

"Sure. 'Hey, admiral? Nobody will scrub my balls for me.' I feel enough of a freak." The lieutenant hunkered and thoroughly washed my lower body. My precious reacted. "Sorry."

"Why?"

"Putting you to all this trouble."

"No trouble."

"Getting an erection."

The lieutenant blushed. "I suppose it's been a while. Lift your left foot." His own member swelled slightly; the embarrassed officer turned his back to me and scrubbed that well-knit body. Precious raged. My Samaritan reached for a bottle of shampoo and said gruffly, "Bend over." As he washed my hair, I gave thought to lunging at his pride, yet

18

despite its semi-swollen state, such ardency seemed bad timing. Nor would lunging heighten eroticism. Nonetheless, opportunity seldom knocks twice. This man enjoyed intelligence and a moral upbringing. A formidable adversary. I decided to wait.

The lieutenant unlocked my door, set the key on the dresser, and turned to say goodbye. I spoke quickly. "Silent night, lonely night."

"Yeah. Well. . . ."

"I spent last Christmas in a foxhole while our base got mortared. I swore that if I survived, this Christmas would be spent among family and friends. So much for good intentions. One more drink before turning in?"

He regarded me compassionately. "Sure."

The lieutenant washed out the glasses and we drank straight Scotch. Both of us wore only towels; I didn't let him see me studying that robust body stretched across my bed. "When do you report back to your ship?"

"Tomorrow at fifteen hundred." (Three PM). "How about you? Got a girl?"

"She sent a 'Dear John' letter just before I got hit."

"Tough."

"She was nice enough to see me in the hospital. Tried to explain why she dumped me. I didn't care. I just wanted a handjob."

The lieutenant chuckled. "Talk her into it?"

"No, dammit, and six months have passed since I've been able to extend my arm enough to reach old Precious. My grandmother visited every day. I was about ready to ask her for a hand."

"You'll have those slings off soon."

"Two more operations. Three more months of casts and slings. Way up here, even my grandmother can't visit."

"Rent a call girl."

"On Christmas Eve! That seems tasteless."

"When you get to Boston."

19

"Right! I could thumb through the Yellow Pages for Dial-A-Slut and invite her to the hospital. She and I would perform for the amusement and edification of a nurse, two corpsmen, and thirty other patients." The lieutenant appeared crestfallen. "It's not as if the idea doesn't turn me on."

"Maybe one of the nurses . . . some dark night."

"Nurses drop their drawers only for doctors . . . and a lieutenant or two."

"Yeah. Sure."

"It's ironic. In Nam, I endured voluntary celibacy for nearly a year. Now the condition has turned me maudlin."

"Christmas Eve. You're far from home."

"I've always considered myself an average guy. I wanted to make the major leagues, serve my country, and marry a nice girl. The American Dream. Normal as blueberry pie. Yet in the shower room, when you . . . touched . . . my private parts, I almost went through the ceiling. I didn't want you to stop."

He blushed. "That's as intimate as I've ever been with another man."

"A little more such intimacy, and I could bear a dismal holiday."

The lieutenant laughed. "I'm feeling guilty for not jerking you off. Holy Cow! Believe me, if I were a female, I'd be glad to help you out."

"I'm past caring who or what gets me off."

He realized my seriousness. "I . . . uhh . . . it goes against my . . . It's not my thing."

"To be blunt, I sure wish it was."

"I've never handled another guy."

"Twenty minutes ago, in the shower room."

"Just helping you out." I laughed. Surprised, so did he. "My dad warned me about the weird people who hang around a YMCA." He became grave. "You haven't set me up, have you?"

I tried to appear perplexed. "Huh?"

The lieutenant rose, took the glass from my hand, and set it on the dresser. His towel bulged. "I can't believe I'm doing this."

Home was the sailor, home from the sea. . . .

After Christmas dinner at Tad's Steak House, I attended a double feature of Hayley Mills movies on 42nd Street; the theater was packed. I spent the night with a lonely German sailor ungiven to cleanliness.

When I returned to Newport, the First Class Hospitalman in charge of Personnel said, "Get out of here! Go home! Come back next year."

I'd become a yoyo. In New York again, I checked into the Enlisted Men's Club, a trio of five-story brownstones on Manhattan's East Side, where a bed cost two dollars. Repenting my Yuletide diffidence, I called an old friend, Francisco the Model.

"Kurt! You're back!"

"Closed my eyes, clicked the heels of my sequined combat boots, and cried, 'I want to see no more yellow Munchkins, I want to see no more yellow Munchkins, I want . . .'"

"Click them again and come down for dinner. The Big Apple's been waiting for a worm like yours. By the way, I'm invited to the best New Year's Eve party in town. If you're wearing one of those uniforms with a red stripe running down blue trousers, you can serve as my escort."

I disappointed Francisco by wearing my navy dress blues, which he'd seen before; we attended revels in Greenwich Village. During my convalescence, I had suspected my physical appearance forever displeasing to others. An attractive florist dissuaded me from that notion, cajoling me into accompanying him to New Jersey. Why not? I'd traveled farther with less anticipation.

21

January 1968

Blaring inanities assaulted my raging hangover. I opened bloodshot eyes. At the foot of a sofa bed, purple people stood on green boats sailing down a yellow river. *The Martian Chronicles?* No. Mine Host, the florist, watched the Rose Parade. All those flowers.

Unable to tear himself from the television, the florist pointed at a sauce pan sitting on a hot plate. "Make yourself some coffee." Instant Sanka. I looked futilely for a Danish or hot cross buns. Burnt toast. The parade passed by. "I gotta go see my family in Camden. I'll drop you at the bus station."

How embarrassing! "Would you believe that when you mentioned living in New Jersey, I assumed an apartment in one of those cities across the Hudson, never dreaming our destination to be Atlantic City?" He grunted. "To be honest, I'm financially unable to afford bus fare if it runs more than three dollars."

"Hitchhike."

I glanced through a grimy window; snow fell, soft and thick. "Bad day for an outing." Another green boat sailed by.

The florist knit his brow. "I'll drop you at a Howard Johnson's along the Turnpike. You can get a ride there."

Fair enough.

I drank three cups of the restaurant's coffee and trod

warily down an icy ramp leading onto the New Jersey Turnpike. As cars passed by, I tried to recall the events of the previous night, no easy task considering the vodka I'd consumed. A state patrol car stopped; a handsome trooper with magnificent posture checked my identification. "You can't wait here for a ride."

"Where can I wait?"

"At an entrance ramp."

"The closest?"

"Three miles."

"Quite a hike!"

"No pedestrians allowed on the Turnpike."

I couldn't stay, I couldn't leave. What a choice! I unbuttoned my peacoat and exhibited the sling. "Can't fly with only one wing."

The trooper noted my medals. "I'll give you a lift."

We waited for a dispatcher to check if I were a wanted man. "Makes me nervous to ride in a police car. I had a real bad experience once." The trooper cocked an eyebrow; needing no further show of interest, I expanded my repertoire with another tall tale. "My family owns a beach house on the Gulf of Mexico. A couple of years ago, I went up to think over the pros and cons of enlisting. One morning, I struck up a conversation with a girl on the beach. A schoolteacher from Atlanta. Not really pretty. Cute, though, and a body like Natalie Wood's. She planned to leave for home at noon and dreaded the long lonely drive. I had nothing else on tap, so I offered to keep her company. She accepted."

I felt ridiculous, telling this story to a man I had no hope of seducing. It did, however, pass the time.

"Traveling north, we talked about everything under the sun except sex. We reached Atlanta and her apartment; within five minutes, we're naked and on the floor. Afterwards, we dress. Have a drink. Her roommate strolls through the door. A stewardess for Delta Airlines. Blond,

23

wearing that tan uniform. Stunning. She sniffs the air, smells the sex, and stalks back to the bedroom. Doors slam. Drawers crash. The schoolteacher hurries to join her. The stewie's pissed. The schoolteacher's pleading, comes back to the living room acting nervous. Mixes fresh drinks. Rearranges some pillows on the floor.

"The stewardess stalks in wearing a tiny blue peignoir and looking dynamite. She lays on the floor and gives me one of those looks: 'You can gawk all you want, rube, but you ain't touching it.' The teacher sits on the floor beside the stewie, holding her hand and apologizing. She rubs the stewie's fingers. Her wrists. Her arms. The peignoir is open and the teacher's caressing the stewie's breasts. She bends over and kisses the nipples. Licks them. Licks the stewie's belly. Her pussy. My knees shook, I couldn't catch my breath, I have never wanted any woman more than I wanted that hard sexy blond, who's staring at me, meanlike. Finally, she growls, husky, low in her throat, 'Come on down, tiger.' "

The dispatcher denied my having earned a criminal record, so the trooper opened the back door of the patrol car. I climbed inside. "They were Lesbian ladies, but took on a man once in a while. I stayed with them three days, all of us sleeping in the same bed. The third night, the schoolteacher wakes us up by throwing a fit, screaming that me and the stewie had been messing around while she's asleep. Wasn't true, but she raised so much hell, I had to leave their apartment at one AM."

The trooper's good looks and quiet masculinity must have unnerved me. Had I been telling the story correctly, I would have situated the family beach house on Long Island or the Jersey Shore and the dykes' apartment in New York or Philadelphia, hinting at a possible rendezvous were the trooper amenable. But out of practice, I based the skeleton of the story on fact: I had met a cute (male) schoolteacher in a restroom of the Atlantic Public Library, he had seduced his lover on the floor in front of me, the blond lover had worked as a ramp rat for Delta Airlines, and the teacher did throw a conniption fit during the night. Now I had to conjure up a reason for feeling ill-at-ease in a police car.

"I decided to thumb home and caught a ride with a man who had already picked up a little hippie with long blond hair. Two hours later, the hippie and I are standing alongside a dark highway outside Macon. A car stops. The Georgia Highway Patrol. A young trooper sits behind the wheel; his partner, a fat fiftyish frog-type, orders us into the back seat. 'We'll carry y'all to a better ramp.' As the car speeds along the highway, the fat trooper starts hassling the hippie. 'With that purty yaller hair and lil as you are, we figgered you was a gal, didn't we, Jake? We figgered a gal might give us a lil liplock. You oughtta git a haircut. We good ole boys, but there's them might pick you up ain't so pertikaler. They might want a lil liplock and not give a good shit you ain't no gal. They might make *you* give them a liplock, ain't that so, Jake?' The Frog turns around and shines a flashlight in the hippie's face. 'You sure do got purty lips. I don't mind tellin' you that I'm gittin' a whopper lookin' at them purty lips. Turn off the next exit, Jake.'

"'Why?'

"'Jest do as I say!' Jake turns off at the next exit. Three miles done the road, the fat cop directs him to turn and park on a dirt track. Swamp noises all around us: Frogs croaking, owls hooting, gators bellowing. . . . The fat cop says, 'You boys carryin' dope?' We said we weren't. Froggie climbs out of the car and opens the back door. 'Git on out and strip off them britches. We gotta search you for dope.' The young cop searches our discarded clothing; Froggie jiggles his crotch and waddles up to the little hippie. 'You got purty lips, boy. You lak a gal. Jes lak a gal. You ain't no boy. You truly a gal, ain't you?' The hippie denies the gender change. The fat cop knocks him to the ground. 'Admit you a gal.' "

(The New Jersey state trooper drove past an exit ramp,

raising the slightest of hopes. Never to my knowledge had I bedded a policeman.)

"Froggie kicks the hippie in his stomach. 'Say you a gal.' The breathless hippie admits his femininity. The Frog smiles. 'I figgered you was, didn't you, Jake? This purty lil gal ain't got no pussy, though. Sure makes me feel turrible, knowin' how good it would feel puttin' my whopper in sumpin' warm and wet.' He kicks the hippie again. 'You sure you a gal?'

"'I'm a girl! I'm a girl!'

"'You one of them gals lak to give liplocks?' The silent hippie receives another kick. 'I ain't gonna ast you agin.'

"His head bowed, the hippie replies, 'I like giving . . . liplocks.'

"Froggie grabs him by the hair and turns the boy's tear-stained face upwards. 'What you say?'

"'I like giving liplocks!'

"'Well, hot damn!' Froggie unbuttons his pants and pulls out a tiny crooked penis. 'If'n you lak givin' liplocks, ah can't find it in my heart to deny you the pleasure. Go to it, gal. Give my whopper a liplock.' The revolted hippie stares. The Frog slaps him twice. 'Lissen, gal! Ain't nobody to know if'n we shoot both your asses and leave you here in the swamp. You jest do what I say. I ain't tellin' you agin.'

"The hippie draws a deep breath, opens his mouth, and swallows the whopper."

(The New Jersey state trooper passed another off-ramp. I felt like Scheherazade: One Thousand and One Exits.)

"After the fat cop shoots his wad, he pulls out and swats the hippie across the face. 'Faggot! Okay, Jake, your turn.'

"The young cop had watched the hippie's performance with seeming embarrassment. 'Ain't really my thing, Cal.'

"The Frog draws his pistol. 'Pull it out, Jake. No way you gonna tell nobody 'bout this.'

"'It's atween us, Cal.'

"'If'n you git blowed, you ain't gonna tell nobody I did.'

26

" 'I won't tell nobody.'

" 'Dadblamed right you ain't, 'cause you gonna shoot your gun in this here gal's mouth or I'm gonna fill your ass with bullets from a real gun.'

"Jake realizes the fat cop means business, so he pulls out an honest-to-goodness whopper, big as a coffee pot and hard as Stone Mountain. The hippie's on his hands and knees, retching. 'Cal, I don't want no barf on my uniform.'

"The fat cop points the pistol at me. 'Git on it, boy.' "

How to make my acquiescence palatable to the New Jersey state trooper. "I conjectured that my last night on earth had arrived. I lacked any yearning to end up a rotting corpse in the Okefenokee Swamp. And I'd sworn to try everything once. Jake was nice-looking. Appeared clean. What the hell! Afterwards, they let us dress and drove back to the highway, dropping the hippie at one exit and me at another. I hid behind a billboard till light, scared they might come back."

The trooper drove without speaking. Five minutes passed; then he turned off the highway and into a truckstop. "How about a cup of coffee?" As we entered the restaurant, I tried to maneuver behind the trooper to check his legs and ass, but policemen prefer to assume the rear position. We ordered coffee. The trooper pulled a pen and a notebook from his shirt pocket. "South of Macon, Georgia. Cal and Jake. You recall the date?"

"What?"

"The month and year?"

"I'm not going to swear out a complaint."

"A bad cop ranks with the lowest forms of life. Those creeps don't deserve to wear a uniform."

"Nevertheless, I like mine, and reporting the incident would get it stripped off me."

"You were a victim!"

"No nevermind to the military. Whatever the circumstances, I participated in a perverted act. Goodbye

27

Honorable Discharge. Farewell VA benefits. Hello disrepute."

"Those assholes might be forcing a young boy into sex right now. They might even kill someone."

"If I learned anything in Vietnam, it was 'Look out for Number One!'"

The trooper gestured at my medals. "Takes honor and courage to pick up three purple hearts."

"More an uncanny knack for being at the wrong place at the wrong time. My reporting two corrupt cops could only wound me again. I don't like getting hurt."

The trooper set down his pen, and a strong, well-shaped hand encircled his coffee cup. His face would have sent Michelangelo scuttling to the marble quarries: healthy skin, Prussian blue eyes, a straight nose, full lips, good cheek-bones, a strong chin. Thick curly dark hair. Broad shoulders. He spoke in a low baritone. "I'm disappointed."

"I've just spent five months in a hospital, ace. I interrupted a promising baseball career to serve three years in the Navy; a fucked-up elbow has pulled the curtains on my ever making the major leagues. My mother died last year, and my stepfather stole the savings I'd entrusted with her; I need the GI Bill to finance the rest of my college education. You're asking me to throw away what little remains, aware that no one will take my word over that of two cops." The trooper sighed, and to my relief, put the notebook in his pocket. I could return to the hopeless task of trying to seduce him. "So, I've relieved myself of a sordid moment from my past, and you've given me a ride. What now?"

"A piece of pie." We went with the season and ordered mince. He asked about the purple hearts. As I told the story behind each, he listened well and asked good questions. "When are you due in Newport?"

"It doesn't seem to matter. Because I'm short of cash, I'll probably catch a bus up tomorrow."

"Your gear?"

"Stored in a locker at the Enlisted Man's Club."

"Like spaghetti?"

"Love it."

"I'm off in an hour. Wait here and I'll take you to Newark. My family always holds a New Year's Day bash."

I watched him leave the restaurant. He had great legs, a nice ass, and a lithe athletic walk. I pulled *The Garden of the Finzi-Continis* from my pocket.

The trooper returned at three-fifteen. As we drove west, I said, "I'm sure glad you're honorable. I feared a spooky case of dejá vù when I climbed into another police car."

"You don't expect every cop to be like those assholes?"

"People are funny. A sailor giving you head might have been the furthest thing from your mind, yet my having done it before . . . to a state trooper . . . and never reporting it. No one would know. Easy enough to suggest that I repeat the episode."

"Can't quite imagine myself even thinking such a shitty thing."

Where there is no hope, there is no endeavor.

He drove to a residential neighborhood of two-story frame houses with small backyards, one house crowded with two dozen Italo-Americans. The trooper handed me over to a tall ample woman who filled a plate with spaghetti, handed me a glass of red wine, and set me at the kitchen table. As she and I chatted, several dark-haired children trickled into the room and stared at me. The woman touched my hand. "They've never been so near a man who looks like an angel. My sister-in-law will be here soon. She'd crawl over broken glass on her hands and knees for your smile."

A stout woman of fifty flew breathlessly through the door. She clasped her hands together and raised her eyes Heavenward. "An angel! Gina, I'd crawl over broken glass on my hands and knees. . . ." She pulled a chair against mine and watched me eat.

Two glasses of wine later, the trooper, wearing civilian

29

clothes, rescued me from the Cobra Woman and two tots who had crawled onto my lap. "Some of the kids went sledriding. I don't bring them home, they'll stay till midnight. Wanna come along?" We strolled over sidewalks strewn with ashes to a large park. The trooper allowed half-a-dozen exhuberant children one last ride down a slope. He pointed out three as his and two as his brother's; then he leaned against a tree and lit a cigarette. "Aunt Francesca likes you."

"I could tell."

His smile faded. "This is Ma's last bash." His eyes filled with tears. "Cancer."

"I admire her for not allowing it to intrude upon the party. Everyone seemed to be enjoying themselves." The kids reached the top of the hill. "She's a nice lady."

"The best." He moved away and stood alone.

After dropping off the children at his parents' house, the trooper and I carried fresh linen to a carpet shop a few blocks away. "My brother's place." A narrow flight of exterior stairs led to a small room furnished with a sink, a double bed, a lamp, and an easy chair. Dog-eared *Playboys* littered the floor. Nick plugged in an electric heater and made up the bed. I sat on the chair, wondering what he planned. Another reference to homosexuality would have caused suspicion in a Kallikak, so I said nothing. Nick smoothed out a blanket, sat on the bed, and lit a cigarette. "Tell me the truth."

"Huh?"

"Ma said you have nice manners."

"So?"

"Nobody with class would tell a stranger what you did, especially a policeman. At first, I thought you might be high on something or maybe got hit in the head during Vietnam. Wasn't sure what to do with you. That's why I stopped at the restaurant." I said nothing. "I can usually tell when people lie. About being wounded—that was true?" I nodded.

30

"Figured. A liar would have made himself a hero or a victim. You just shit your pants and tried to save the wounded."

"I dare do all that may become a man."

"Then why tell me about those screwy cops in Georgia? That wasn't manly."

"I hoped it might get me into your pants."

The trooper blinked. "Did it really happen?"

"Made up the story as we drove along the Turnpike."

"What did you expect me to do?"

"Ask if I enjoyed serving a highway patrolman."

His eyes narrowed. "You wanted to blow me?"

"Still do."

He laughed mirthlessly. "You have a thing for cops?"

"I have a thing for dudes with dazzling exteriors, particularly one with the sexiest walk I've ever seen on a man."

He shook his head. "Can't do it."

"More's the pity."

"A guy like you . . . Chicks go crazy over your type."

"Straight men don't, and that's the challenge."

He frowned. "Something I said or did make you figure I'd go for it?"

"On the contrary, but you can't kick a guy for trying. You're one hell of a beautiful man, buddy."

He stood and walked to the door. "Nutty way to start the new year." He turned and smiled. "See you in the morning."

Oh that my head were waters, and mine eyes a fountain of tears.

Early the next morning, Nick returned to the carpet shop and drove me to the Newark bus station. Before I could get out of the car, he handed me ten dollars.

"I can't take this."

"You'll need it for bus fare."

"I can thumb to Newport."

"Not with that arm in this weather."

31

"The arm's fine. I wear a sling merely to protect it."

"Take the money!"

"Give me a name and address so I can return it."

"I don't think so."

A pall settled between us. "I'll accept it only because I'm broke and the Navy has screwed up my pay record in the past. If you ever need a favor, I'm at the Newport Naval Hospital. William Kurt Strom, Hospitalman Third Class."

We shook hands, "Go get 'em, sailor."

The next day, I reported for duty. My arrival perplexed the First Class Hospitalmen in charge of Personnel. What ever could he do with a corpsman returned from Nam? I'd enjoyed authority as a field medic and attained a practical expertise surpassing that of the nurses under whom I would work on the wards. It seemed unlikely that I would grovel beneath the tyranny granted nurses by their officers' bars and too likely that I would sneer at their flustered incompetence. The First Class decided I would work in a department unencombered by bitches wearing starched white. "You have a choice: Supply, Personnel, or the Laboratory."

A job in the Supply Shed would have meant lifting and toting, too much of a strain on my damaged arm. Personnel would have occasioned my prying into the records of other sailors, an engaging vocation, but clerical work included the utilization of such sissy skills as typing and filing. Throughout my scholastic career, I'd received abysmal grades in Biology and Chemistry; nevertheless, I asked for the lab. I knew it would please the Navy if I worked at the job for which I was least suited.

I began as a leech, drawing blood from the arms of naval personnel and their dependants. I pricked the fingers of pregnant women and the heels of jaundiced newborns. I drew blood from a handsome young captain who had been informed five minutes earlier that he suffered from terminal leukemia.

Weekend liberty began Friday at fifteen hundred hours. I

rode a bus to New York and rented a bed at the Enlisted Man's Club. As I entered my room, the soldier sharing it brushed past without speaking. Eyeglasses completed his homeliness. I rummaged through the drawers of his bureau and found a diary. It lacked grammar and style. A recurring entry: I'm so horny.

I crossed town for a date with my fiancée, who had just returned from a Christmas visit back home. I'd met Jane through my sister when they attended Tulane University. A big honey-blonde with soft clear skin and the body of a primitive fertility goddess, Jane amused me with her penchant for murmuring delicate sarcasms in a dry-martini voice. Over the years, we had dated occasionally, but without passion; then, during a thirty-day leave after Mother died, Jane broke my cherry and I hers. We planned to marry after my graduation from college.

Kissing on the sofa led us to the bedroom. While Jane brushed her teeth, I examined a tube upon the nightstand. The package illustrated defenseless little sperm being enveloped by a white flood of foam. My precious barely functioned.

When Jane's roommate returned from a date, I left for the Club. Entering my room, I switched on the overhead light. The horny soldier lay nude on his bed. The body appeared hard. So did his unmentionable. He jerked a blanket over himself. I undressed, switched off the light, and crawled into my bed. Recalling the soldier's homeliness, I doubted that his lust had been slaked, so I attempted conversation. He grunted and rolled over. No matter. I disliked dipping below my standard. Still, it had been a slow night.

I spent Saturday with friends and Sunday with Jane at the Museum of Natural History. That evening, a long line of sailors waited at the Greyhound terminal for the last run to Rhode Island; I chatted up a sandy-haired little boiler technician who proved amenable to sharing a seat. Two giggling females screeched their excitement at finding themselves on

33

a bus otherwise filled with sailors and kept everyone awake by exchanging inane badinage at the top of piercing nasal voices. I considered euthanasia, but navy dorks eventually plugged their orifices. The resulting silence allowed everyone to doze, including the boiler tech. I covered our laps with my peacoat, which hid a roving hand. Stealthy fingers unfastened six of his bellbottoms' thirteen buttons and slipped into the opening. When they grasped a slender hardness, I realized that the boiler tech was awake and little inclined to hinder me. Glancing warily at sailors who slept across the aisle, I ducked my head under the peacoat. All around was darkness like a wall.

At Newport, I fell into a routine. When not serving night duty, I awakened at six AM, performed my ablutions, and made my upper bunk so an inspection party could bounce a quarter upon the blanket. From seven to three, I drew blood from out-patients, leaving the Leeching Room only for lunch and to tote a metal basket filled with tubes and needles through pale-green corridors to draw blood from in-patients—some accepted my leeching fearfully, others with ennui; a few patients attempted wit, Lord bless them, crying, "Here comes Dracula!" After work, I crossed a little bridge to Coasters Harbor Island, where I worked out at the base gymnasium. At five, I returned to the hospital for supper. Then, changing into civilian clothes, I walked downtown.

Saturday afternoon, Jane greeted me with eyes aglow: old friends from Tulane had produced a daughter. We argued about names for our children; Jane held strong family feelings and wanted to honor her parents, Walter and Lillian.

Jane believed that I had arrived in New York that morning; actually, I'd checked into the Enlisted Man's Club on Friday. A long-legged air jockey with dark hair and an attractive face shared my room. When he stepped out to use the john, I stripped quickly. He returned to catch me abusing Precious before the mirror. "Sorry, ace," I lied, "I

34

thought you'd gone." Embarrassed, he grabbed his overcoat and left.

I dressed and roamed the upper floors of the Club. Finding no one remarkable, I braved the cold to cruise Third Avenue. A slinky Latin invited me to his apartment and urged me to spend the night; he wanted to sleep with Precious in his mouth. I declined the offer. What if he ground his teeth? Besides, I had business at the Club.

The air jockey slept. I knelt between our beds and slowly eased my hand between his sheets; my fingertips inched up a hard thigh. They reached an opening in his cotton shorts and touched hair. They explored a long soft unmentionable and gently tugged it through the fly. Then kneaded it into hardness.

I retrieved my hand and began the lengthy process of folding the blanket away from his body. The sheet followed. I stood and leaned over the exposed airman. Several minutes of rapture ensued. He awakened; I leapt into my bed. He sat up, looked about groggily, and lay down, pulling the covers over his body.

I waited for his breathing to become regular and repeated the procedure. He awakened during rapture, glanced at me, and covered himself. I waited and tried again. He accepted the situation.

My old pal, Paul, expostulated over such caprices. "It's rape!"

"He eventually enjoyed three orgasms."

"I'm aware of your technical proficiency. It's rape."

"He was sensitive enough to know that he owed me."

"Owed you!"

"He caught me before the mirror, which invaded my privacy and set up a sexual bond between us. A fair-minded person would comprehend our intimacy."

"Bullshit! It's rape."

"I don't force them. If they continued to sleep, they'd be none the wiser."

35

"But they do wake up and find themselves compromised."

"Their subsequent reactions fascinate me."

"A polite person would ask."

"Etiquette books include no chapters on 'How to Gracefully Offer Fellatio'; one cannot present the pleasures of a blowjob without sounding tawdry. Should I ask and be declined, usually because of an outdated Old Testament morality, further acquaintance would be uncomfortable. And having been declined, it would be dreadful manners should I persevere. Better by far to help them avoid the trauma of choice."

"Sex without choice is rape."

"Many people fantasize about being gently raped by a clean attractive stranger."

"You should advertise that sucking vacuum of a mouth in the entertainment pages of newspapers with large circulations."

"Who reproves the lame must go upright. Paul, most women dislike performing fellatio. Those who do perform the act usually lack accomplishment."

"How ever would *you* know?"

"A rational deduction. A woman lacks a man's apparatus, forcing her to depend upon imagination; history confirms my cynical view of women as creative artists. Most women consider their partners satisfied by orgasms inside vaginas; few realize that men also have erogenous zones. A man, usually as untutored, cannot, or embarrassed, will not instruct a female partner, too many of whom consider sex as an unpleasant obligation to be endured as seldom as possible. In search of elaboration, men go to prostitutes, who sacrifice refinement to speed. The exquisite sensations produced by an imaginative and enthusiastic cocksucker will never be felt by the majority of mankind. To make a choice in the matter, a man must know what he will miss by abstention."

Paul sighed. "So many gays would hop into bed with you at a glance. Leave the straights alone."

"Should I limit myself to less than one per cent of the desirable males in these United States?"

"Studies show that every third man experiences homosexuality at some time during his life. That should be enough, even for you."

"I can't be everywhere at once, and that's how many times most of those men hop the rod."

"Studies show that every sixth man adheres to homosexuality."

"Subtract the chicken hawks who prefer young boys, geriatric queens enamoured of the elderly, dinge queens into blacks, rice queens into Orientals, and femme queens into girlish types. Such people have shown little interest in me, nor do I sustain desire for the genres they esteem. Nor am I inflamed by uglies, fatties, drearies, and the religious."

"Somebody's got to love them."

"That's what mothers are for. I shall continue to begrudge them my affection until I, too, am fat and bald and old and ugly; meanwhile, I value attractive masculine men with sexy walks. Unfortunately, too many hide in closets, emerging only occasionally for furtive quickies. Others get snapped up by wives and lovers. Of all the hunky men I meet during the routine of my life, I would vouchsafe one in a thousand as amenable to immediate coupling without intrigue."

"Most gays don't demand intrigue. And they're safe!"

"Oh, Paul! You're becoming a bourgeois midwestern housewife. The peril intensifies the pleasure. My knees tremble. I can't catch my breath. Fever and chills alternate in consuming me."

"Sounds like malaria."

"I enjoy the hunt and the kill. I revel in the danger."

"Sex with gays is relaxing, friendly, and fun."

"At its best. Yet I've encountered tension, hostility, and boredom. Too many gays refuse to expand limited repertoires. And to those fairies accustomed to promiscuity, I'm just another trick, likely to be forgotten within a week."

37

"No one could forget you."

"Too easily. A straight man would be likelier to remember our coupling. I might be unique within his experience."

"You are certainly unique within my experience."

"Because you surround yourself with limp-wristed queens wafting towards eternity while chirping about opera, recipes, and drapes."

"At least they can form sentences. I'm surprised that some of your tricks can count their fingers and toes. They're beneath you, Kurt. You lie down with dogs, you get up with fleas."

"And you with sequins in your hair. I utilize more of myself seducing straights. Gays demand little beyond my outward appearance."

"Which is remarkable."

"As long as I'm physically acceptable, I could be a moron without character or personality."

"You prefer straights without character or personality. You told me so."

"Don't twist my words, Paul. I desire the archetype: the soldier, the sailor, the policeman, the fireman. . . ."

"Et cetera, et cetera, et cetera."

"The outer man fulfills my fantasies. The inner man's ordinary yearnings, limited ambitions, and trite concerns diminish him. I have trivial yearnings of my own. I desire strength and adventure."

"Conan the Barbarian is a fictional character."

"Say it isn't so!"

"You could delve into the soul of a particular man and find adventure enough for a lifetime."

"I have yet to meet that man."

"How ever would you know? You're a butterfly, flitting from one trick to another, sipping a bit of nectar from each. It will not always be summer."

"Is that an image you conjured up all by yourself?"

"How can I make you understand that seducing straights

is wrong?"

"You can't. The world is made up of predators and grazers. Now let me finish telling you about last night."

Jane and I spent Saturday afternoon touring the Museum of Modern Art. She prepared supper (Spanish omelets) in the small one-bedroom apartment (kitchenette in the living room) that she shared with a roommate, an actress; Rachel had gone on a date, so Jane and I made love. Although her vagina felt comfortable, it lacked the friction necessary for my orgasm; unsatisfied, I returned to the Club.

The air jockey had moved out, and a cheerful strawberry-blond soldier occupied his bed. We chatted for a few minutes before switching off the light. As the man slipped off to Dreamland, I counted five hundred, marked his even breathing, and began the execution. He slept lightly, and it took an hour of tactile probing to prevail over his elusive movements. Yet he said nothing to dissuade me. Why? "I didn't want to hurt your feelings." Consummating fellatio usually fulfilled my ambitions, but occasionally, I made tentative gestures toward further procedures; the soldier delighted me by expanding my overture into an opera of five acts. Why ever had he acted shy? "I was afraid I might like it."

"Did you?"

He reached across me for a cigarette, rubbing his thigh against Precious. The next day, I returned to the workaday world of the Navy.

My daily rounds took me throughout the hospital and two outlying wards, gaining me a familiarity with patients and personnel. Every fourth day, I stood duty, which demanded my presence in the lab all night. When inundated with emergencies, my duty partner and I sometimes got no sleep. Nevertheless, we were expected to work at full capacity the next day.

Following one such thirty-six hour stretch without sleep, I trudged to the barrack I shared with two dozen other corpsmen. A radio blared. I politely asked the radio's owner to turn down the volume. Lardass ignored my request, which I repeated.

"I don't have to turn it down till 'Lights Out' at eleven."

"You won't have a radio at eleven, because I'll have thrown the goddam thing into the bay. Turn it off!" Although I had regained full use of my arm, it remained at a fraction of its former strength. Outweighing me by forty pounds, Lardass could have pummeled my body into the ground. But he didn't know that. And veterans of the Vietnamese conflict had earned a reputation for violent behavior. I yanked the plug from a socket and swaggered back to my cubicle. From that time, Lardass kept a quiet environment.

I'd always abhorred fisticuffs.

As a child, a skinny, bespectacled sissy and tall for my age, I was continually forced to defend myself against older boys who resented my reputation as the brightest student in the tough Pennsylvania coaltown where I attended elementary school. I lost almost every fight.

My teens passed in a quiet southern college town. Popularity depended upon good grades and athletic ability, neither of which I possessed. (I'd hoped to be liked, a prospect closed to an effeminate prodigy; I held my wrists rigid, let my mind atrophy, and permitted Mother to convince me that I ranked between a simpleton and a nitwit.) I labored unskillfully on my stepfather's plantation in Louisiana and my grandparents' ranch in Montana. While attending college, I began a regimen of exercise that further developed my peasant frame. The four summers I spent playing professional baseball increased my vigor. In spite of a propensity for uttering caustic gibes, I'd never been physically challenged as an adult.

In Vietnam, a marine offered a possible explanation. "I like to fight, but I'd never mess with you or McGrath."

I could sympathize with his fear of McGrath, a lean mean

redneck from the Mississippi delta. But me? "I'm a pussy, Sweeney. I loathe personal combat."

"Don't make no difference."

I mentioned Tennessee, two hundred and thirty-five pounds of solid muscle. "He's stronger than I."

"Mebbe. I doubt it. He's dumb. You ain't. He's slow. You're fast as a snake. You're the type goes blind during a fight and don't feel no pain. You'd go for the throat. Fight to kill. You scare the hell out of me, Doc. Like, underneath, you're a fucking animal."

More poodle than mastiff, I'm afraid. (Sweeney, like Tennessee, now moved restlessly among the shades on the far side of the Styx. McGrath, whose savagery enthralled me, caught a bullet in his neck and lay permanently paralyzed in a veterans' hospital.)

The beast of the jungle received a telephone call from a Nick Esoldi. Who? "Do you have the right Kurt Strom?"

"If he gets picked up hitchhiking by weird Georgia crackers." The New Jersey state trooper! "My sister goes to college in Boston. Wanted to furnish her room with some stuff from home, so I brought it up in the van. I've never been to Newport, thought as long as I knew somebody . . ."

"I have duty in the lab this weekend, but you're welcome to drop by."

Nick arrived carrying several cartons of Chinese food. "Thought you might be homesick for an Oriental meal."

I opened a carton. "Oh, wow! Last time I relished moo goo gai pan was the day Pearl Buck kicked Mother Goddam off the Shanghai Express. By the way, here's the sawbuck I owe you." My duty partner sat riveted to the bunkroom boob tube, so I hosted my handsome guest in the Leeching Room. "Frankly, I'm surprised to see you again."

"Want the truth?"

"Think I can handle it?"

The trooper rolled an empty tube back and forth across the table. "I kinda admired that cock-and-bull story."

41

"You should be used to the machinations of libertines, good-looking as you are."

He blushed and ducked his head. "I'm an old man now. Four kids and another on the way. Thirty-five next birthday."

"My sister and her girlfriends agreed that thirty-six is the ideal age for a man. He's established in a career, mature enough to be interesting, and still in possession of a taut, healthy body."

"Write down their telephone numbers." Nick looked me straight in the eye; he expected the truth to whatever question he was about to pose. "Why did you admit being . . . gay? I wouldn't have known."

Tough question. "You're too savvy to fall for trickery. You'd been decent, bringing a viper into the bosom of your family. I liked you and wanted to part honestly, if not as friends. Oddly enough, I've never before admitted my perversity to a straight."

"I could have turned you in. Still could."

"I realize that."

Nick lit a cigarette—against the rules, but who was around to protest? "You're like the guys in South Orange; their dads are big-time lawyers, executives, professors . . . WASP types. Drive sports cars. Go to Ivy League schools."

"The 'In' crowd."

He nodded and cleared his throat. "Even before I married, I never run across much high-class pussy. The chicks I dated in school—they worked as secretaries or receptionists till they got married. Cops don't get close to nobody but waitresses, nurses, and prostitutes."

"No need of finesse. They will or they won't."

"If they will, it's hard to turn down, and then you got trouble. It sounds kind of shitty, but you want them available when you're horny and invisible when you aren't."

"Women reject such an attitude."

"Right. When I married Rosemary, I made a

42

commitment. Fine. The chicks know how it stands. Two dates later, they love me. Want me to leave my family. After that, they sulk and bitch and cry. I got drama enough at home."

"Many snazzy dames in Manhattan prefer freedom. Models, actresses, career girls . . ."

"Don't have the time or money for wooing, even if I knew where to meet them. Besides, snazzy dames don't go for dumb cops."

I laughed. "Why do people want what they can't have. Almost every queer in New York would give up half his income for a relationship with you."

He almost snarled. "I can't fuckin' stand queers."

"And here we sit."

Nick smiled apologetically. "No, you didn't bat your eyes or stick out your tongue or offer me money. You used psychology. Sort of plucked my strings. I appreciate you going to all that trouble."

"And you're here to reward me. All right, I can get an hour off. We could slip into an empty barrack and . . ."

He looked horrified. "No! Nothing like that! I mean . . . from a couple of things you said, I got the idea you know your way around Manhattan." I reckoned this a gauche attempt to meet, through me, some high-class gash. Had he forgotten my perversity? "I'm real interested in psychology."

"You imagine my line with women as a sophisticated marvel to study and emulate?"

He nodded, relieved. "Something like that." Boy, had he dialed a wrong number!

"During four seasons in the minor leagues, I spent many nights in tanktown diners listening to cops talk about their work. No occupation boasts better storytellers."

The trooper slammed his fist on the bloodletting table. "Then how come nobody wants to listen."

"Most people find it difficult to keep their footing on this whirling planet. Insecurity leads to self-absorption."

"Everybody wants to talk about themselves."

"People need to feel they're important, either as part of a group or in a relationship or as unique beings. The reality of others holds little interest, unless useful or competitive or threatening."

"What about you?"

"Mother trained me to listen politely to another's story, but I'm too selfish to suffer fools gladly. I'll listen to you if it gets me into your pants. . . ."

"Not a chance!"

"Then you should either interest me or say goodbye."

A couple of customers dropped in for blood tests. Nick watched my partner and me perform our duties. I could keep my eyes off the sexy trooper only by concentration. Joy would enter my life while caressing that splendid body. Ah well! For the moment, I'd enjoy the novelty of being pursued as a conduct to fine pussy.

We talked for several hours about Nick's family and his work. He seemed reluctant to leave. "You'll let me know when I start boring you?"

I spoke truthfully. "I'm not sure you could."

Nick smiled and stretched. "I feel comfortable."

"In a room furnished with two plastic chairs and a bloodstained table, reeking with the ambience of fear and pain?"

"I get turned on by the damnedest things."

"I'm hanging by my nails until you tell me the damned things you mean."

He swelled with the power given him by my desire. "You going to college after your hitch?"

"Yeah. Probably major in World Literature."

"I kinda always wanted to go. Maybe study psychology."

"You get excellent on-the-job training. Why settle for secondhand information out of books written by people whose experience usually comes from other books?"

"I don't know the words."

"Jargon merely reinforces the psychologist's sense of superiority. In an era when God is dead, people still need ritual words. I compare students of psychology unfavorably with astrologists, numerologists, and witch doctors."

"A really good psychiatrist might change your mind."

"He'll never get a change to examine it. A good friend picked up his address book and crossed out the names of everyone who paid for professional counsel. Having met many such self-absorbed whiners, I must respect his decision."

"Don't you ever feel insecure?"

"Sure. I lack the training for this job. I fear my arms will never be symmetrical. I maintain friendships with people whose sophistication surpasses mine. My failings as a son and brother worry at me. Did marines die in Vietnam because of my blunders? Does my queerness show? All I can do is put forth my best effort."

"It's a pretty good effort." He stood. "I better go."

"At midnight! There's an extra cot in the bunk room. Get a good night's sleep and start off fresh in the morning." Nick stiffened. "For crissake, I'm not going to violate you with my duty partner in the same room. You wouldn't get home until three AM." He relented. I was honorable.

Nick's visit increased my need for companionship, no matter how momentary. Whenever the marquees changed, I joined the naval personnel that constituted the sparse patronage of Newport's two movie palaces.

One evening, a tedious comedy lost my attention. Looking around for diversion, I spotted a likely prospect sitting alone in the balcony. I bought popcorn at a concession stand in the lobby, climbed the stairs to the balcony, and plumped down near the sailor. He had a cute snub-nose profile. "Good movie?" I asked.

"A dog!"

"Beg pardon?" I moved to the seat next to his and hearkened to a repetition of his critique. I offered popcorn.

45

Eventually, my hand pressed against his bellbottoms. He drew a ragged breath, but didn't move. My hand slid across his lap. He watched the screen with rigid attention.

Back at the barracks, my bunkmate presented me with a gift. He'd noticed the negligence with which I treated my contact lenses. (I never soaked them as prescribed. At night, I removed the tiny plastic orbs and set them on a shelf in my locker; in the morning, I licked the lenses and stuck them in my eyes, a habit that, combined with my avocation, could have led to gonorrhea of the eyeballs.) Langman had bought a lens case and a cleaning kit. Grateful, I allowed him to fondle my purple hearts. I even condescended to accept an invitation for supper the next evening at his grandparents' farm across the bay.

A nice-looking, well-built kid with a swarthy complexion, Langman had just received orders for Nam and seemed eager to learn all he could from someone who had served there. During the ferryboat ride and a five-mile hike through the snow, I told him a series of horror stories that would have set Poe aghast.

Langman's grandmother pressed double servings; his grandfather filled us with tales about World War One. I declined a third piece of pie and rubbed my belly. "I am so stuffed with your outstanding cuisine, I'll roll back to the ferry."

Granny responded quickly. "Why don't you both spend the night and catch the boat in the morning?" I smiled my acceptance. "Good! Donnie, why don't you show Kurt the barn?"

We looked at the barn. It was full of hay. A cow mooed. Langman noticed me shiver. "You must be used to warm weather."

"A hundred and thirty degrees in the shade." The germ of a plot formed, so I shivered again.

"Let's go back to the house. You don't want to catch pneumonia." I shivered uncontrollably. "You all right?"

"I caught a recurrent fever in Nam from the bite of a Lao-Tse fly. It's not contagious," I hastened to add.

"Should we go back to the hospital?"

"I'd be in the cold too long."

"Grandpa's car has a heater."

"Better if I took a hot bath."

I luxuriated in the tub while a concerned Langman watched from the doorway. "This happen often?"

"Last time I visited Jane in New York, I caught a chill while ice skating."

"What did you do?"

"What the doctor ordered. We hurried home, stripped, and jumped into bed. A half-hour of rubbing our nude bodies together, the shivering stopped." I held my breath, ducked under the water, and emerged with another sequence. "I really got scared the first time it happened."

"When was that?"

"New Year's Day, while watching the Rose Bowl with a buddy. At half-time, we ran outside in our shirts to play catch. I got chilled. Started shivering. My buddy called a doctor who had served in Nam. He recognized the Lao-Tse syndrome, told my buddy to immerse me in a hot bath. Then Nick and his wife stripped and got in bed with me."

"Naked?"

"No better way to warm me up, according to the doctor."

"A guy!"

"A buddy, who didn't want me to die."

"You're not shivering now."

Because I couldn't dream up a logical progression of spurious events and shiver at the same time. "Water's hot. Soon as I get out of the tub, the shivering will start again."

"I'll turn down the covers. Dry off real good."

I crawled nude into bed and looked up helplessly. "The doctor said I could fall into a fatal coma."

"What should I do?"

"I gotta get warm. The ice skating almost chilled me as

47

much, but Jane rubbed against me until the shivering stopped." Langman sat on the edge of the bed and rubbed tentatively, a sheet and two blankets between his hands and my body. "The combination to my locker is in my wallet. Get Jane's number from my address book. Call her after I'm dead and say I loved her."

Langman kicked off his shoes, and fully-clothed, slipped under the covers. "Should I call an ambulance?"

I shivered. "Too late."

"It's my fault. I should have told you how far we had to walk from the ferry."

"You didn't know." I could afford to be kind. "No one will blame you."

"I feel so bad."

"Your clothes keep your body heat from reaching me."

Langman shucked his shirt and pants. His big hands rubbed my back, stopping modestly above my buttocks. "Better?"

"I'd hate to have survived Nam only to die like this." I skinned up his t-shirt. As he pulled it over his head, I whisked off his shorts and pressed against him. "Rub! Rub! I'm going under!" His body burned. A fair fire makes a room gay.

Langman's ardor surprised me, but it would have diminished had I mentioned my eosinophil count. During a slack afternoon in the lab, another tech and I drew each other's blood several times to learn where the needle hurt most. (The back of the hand.) I examined my blood sample under a microscope and counted twenty-four eosinophil cells per hundred. A normal count ranged between two and five. No one had ever seen a count higher than twelve, and astounded co-workers made slides of my blood for their collections. We studied the lab manual. I had either leukemia or worms. Bacteriology studied my droppings. No worms. Ohmigod!

A doctor in the Emergency Room counseled against

48

despair. "Everybody comes back from Vietnam with worms."

"I've been back for six months and had dozens of blood tests. None showed parasites." My future looked black until I recalled dining in a small cafe on a back street of Port-au-Prince during the cruise with my grandmother.

The doctor handed me a spongy red wormpill the size of a ping-pong ball. "Lie in bed and wash this down with water."

I disobeyed the order by swallowing the pill at a drinking fountain in the barrack. It seemed as if a globe of ammonia burst in my esophagus. Ten hours later, I awakened in my bunk with a shattering headache. The Master-At-Arms had found me unconscious on the floor beside the fountain. I left for New York that weekend with an eosinophil count of five.

My roommate at the Enlisted Man's Club was so ugly, I dashed into the icy slush outside. Stopping by the USO to case the joint, I noticed a list of Broadway and Off-Broadway shows chalked on a blackboard; a volunteer explained that theater managers offered free tickets to ser-vicemen and their dates so they could fill the houses of fail-ing productions. I called Jane, who worked at menial jobs while looking for openings in costume design; a lame excuse stifled her wonder at my presence in Manhattan on a Fri-day, and she hurried to the USO. During the months that followed, we sat in the best seats of the worst shows in town.

Saturday afternoon, I enjoyed lunch with an old friend and made a date to meet another friend at midnight, when we would go barhopping. The evening stretched before me. A gruesome roommate seemed an anathema, a barful of fag-gots an ordeal, and streetwalking cruel and unusual punish-ment. Should I call Nick, as he had urged?

In the past, friendships with unyielding straight men had driven me to despair. I enjoyed Nick's company, but I desired him too much. Oh well! Whenever did I say that I

49

was wise? I called. We agreed to meet at a coffee shop near the Newark bus station.

Conversion quickly descended to 'My Wife Doesn't Understand Me.' "We went steady through high school. While I was in the army, she worked as a receptionist. When I got out, we married. Rosemary looked good then: slim, pretty, dark eyes always dancing, hanging on to every word I said. She's heavy now. Complains about her back. Her feet. Everything."

"Four kids and another on the way. . . . You can't expect her to have the smallest waist in three counties."

"We don't talk anymore except to worry about money. Stevie's bike got stolen and he needs one for his paper route. Gina's got to have braces. Should we buy a new furnace? My days off, I fix whatever the hell broke during the week. Saturday nights we visit my folks, Sunday nights hers. I come home from work to hear the kids hollering and fighting. We never go anywhere. Not even a movie."

"You can understand why REST IN PEACE is engraved on tombstones."

"I used to talk about the job. Rosemary would sit there like she was listening; then, right in the middle of a story, she'd break in with, 'Do you think I should make new slipcovers for the sofa?' Piss me right off!"

"Women lack concentration."

"Tell me about it."

"Has to do with bearing children. The little vampires never suck up enough attention, demanding that Mommy applaud every action and fill their burgeoning personalities with stories and activities. Against this continual onslaught, Mommy holds tenuously to her list of priorities, forced to limit them as she spends her days being drained. Daddy's lucky if the list includes a good dinner and a relaxed roll in the hay."

Nick's eyes narrowed. "How do you know so much about it?"

50

"My sister has two little boys, and I've had buddies that marriage robbed of their youth. In some ways, life ends for many women at the birth of their first child. What about friends?"

"Who has time for friends?" Nick stared out a flyspecked window. "My brother—he's wrapped up in his work. A couple of guys on the force. We talk about the job. Gets old. The single dudes go hunting and fishing, carry on about new cars and hot women. Can't get into that."

"You mentioned several affairs."

"Did I?" Nick appeared startled. He lit another cigarette and sipped his coffee. "I got my first piece at fifteen when a buddy and me screwed a nigger whore in Jersey City. Cost us four dollars. Then we heard about Big Red, the easiest lay in Hoboken; she'd put out for a pack of cigarettes or a forty-five record. We'd drive over to Manhattan, check out the fancy stuff, shit our pants at the thought of trying for any, and come home to Red. Christ, she was ugly!" He shook his head. "In the service, you meet lushes, sluts, and hookers. Never could keep it up for loose women. So I married a virgin. Great! At first. Nothing fancy—Rosemary don't like that. It was all right."

"Your first extramarital affair?"

He sighed and studied the red-and-white checked tablecloth. "After Joey—he's our second—Rosemary wanted to hold off. We're Catholic. Can't use protection. One night, I had to accompany some accident victims to the hospital. While the doctors worked on them, I started talking with an inhalation therapist. Good legs. Sexy voice. Nice skin. We had a thing for five years, off and on. She wanted to get married. Don't think she ever has." Nick lit another cigarette; I marveled that nicotine hadn't stained his perfect white teeth. "Nothing else that lasted more than a year. Waitress in a doughnut shop. A nurse." He gazed at me defiantly. "Wife of a burglar I put in jail." His broad shoulders sagged. "Sounds pretty cruddy, don't it?"

51

"I doubt that many men feel pride in every facet of their sexual history."

Nick tapped an ash off his cigarette. "I always envied guys like you. Good-looking athletes with money to spend on cheerleaders and majorettes. Talking easy with rich chicks. Getting into all that blonde snatch." That's me to a T. "I remember one stud in high school. Cool dude. Tall. Handsome. Quarterback on the football team. President of the Key Club. Lived in a big house overlooking the park. Money out the yang-yang. Every girl in school would have spread her legs for him." Nick's jaw set grimly. "My buddies and me hated the son-of-a-bitch." He chuckled mirthlessly. "We talked about getting him drunk. Make the fucker blow us; then, we'd piss on him." Such nasty boys. "Never did it." He leered. "You look a lot like him."

"I'd be happy to provide vicarious revenge. What do your buddies look like?"

Nick snorted and changed the subject to the failings of the New Jersey judicial system. An hour later, he gazed into my eyes. "What do I stand to gain?" Huh? "Letting you do your thing."

"Relief. A sensual experience. The satisfaction of making a wounded veteran happy."

"Not enough."

"I could save a few dollars. . . ." Nick grimaced. "Lessons in abnormal psychology?"

"I get enough of them at work." He grabbed the check and stood. "Gotta go."

That night, my Uncle Ralph insisted that I accompany him to his "Very Favorite Bar," a hustler hangout; I found little amusement among the soulless. The next morning, I prepared for brunch with Francisco the Model and a pair of giddy composers. Gruesome had checked out, as had almost everyone else; nonetheless, I stood in the shower, erect with unreasonable anticipation. I glanced up to see an attractive sailor staring at me. He grinned, embarrassed. "Uhh . . . do

52

you know what time it is?"

Sure, buddy. Let me check the clock under the faucets. Eager for acquaintance, I rinsed off and grabbed my towel. The sailor had disappeared. I was left to wonder about his interest and his availability.

Doubts are more cruel than the worst of truths.

February 1968

Fifteen people worked in the laboratory: two pathologists, a medical service lieutenant, a civilian secretary, two retired lifers, and nine corpsmen. The other lab techs had attended college before entering the Navy; they viewed askance the experiment of on-the-job training. My utter lack of knowledge concerning theories and procedures could have led to my becoming the company scapegoat, a position I feared fit when a hot-tempered lifer charged into the Leeching Room, screaming about a tube of congealed blood. Instead of delivering the tube with a violet top to Chemistry immediately after leeching, I'd set it with a dozen others, unaware that the white crystals inside the tube caused the blood to jell within minutes.

Fortunately, I made no other outstanding errors. I learned to count blood cells in Hematology, examine pee in Urinalysis, conduct tests in Blood Chemistry and read VDRL samples (venereal disease) in Serology. I abhorred Bacteriology (shit and spit) and the PAP smears (pussy cancer) of Cytology, both manned by First Class perverts who loved their jobs. Like everyone else, I found it difficult to draw blood from obese Negresses, who patiently endured my stabbing at invisible veins rolling within enormous brown arms.

My bunkmate, Langman, avoided me, apparently spending his off-duty hours in another barrack or at his grandparents' farm. I missed his shy hero worship. I should have known better than to initiate sex with another corps-man.

Did I learn from the experience?

A barrackmate who worked on the Neuro-Psychiatric (NP) Ward invited me for a couple of beers. During our conversation, he made several unsubtle references to homosexual patients on NP awaiting dishonorable discharges. The soft blond tech lacked the insouciant manliness I preferred, but alcohol turns dogs into foxes. As we climbed a wooded hill above the bar, I took his hand to pull him over an icy ledge and didn't let go. We enacted the two-backed beast in the snow.

I'd always approached a new environment with good intentions. "I will make straight A's this semester." "I will be brave and fearless in Vietnam." "I will keep carnal contact with fellow servicemen to a minimum and will never indulge with a barrackmate." How terrible is constant resolution!

I vowed to spend the weekend reaping iniquity at the Enlisted Man's Club, but Friday night, I roomed with a squatty lump that expressed an unrequited longing for a weekend buddy with whom to go juking. I escaped to the billiard parlor and blatantly cruised a stalwart soldier who obviously classified me as something lower than an amoeba. Patrolling the upper halls, I espied a beauty with ebony hair and noted his room number; an hour later, I trespassed into his room and began "Creepy Fingers," but he awakened just before rapture and successfully defended his honor. The frigid canyons of Manhattan proved desolate. The lump snored.

Unable to sleep, I carried a cup of coffee to the night clerk's desk. "May I join you?"

The sallow clerk smiled and closed a paperback mystery. "How's it going?" he boomed heartily, in a fruitless attempt at manliness.

"Bad," I replied gloomily. "I'm so horny, I could fuck a

goat."

The "Approach Bestial" disconcerted him for a moment. "Lots of women in New York."

"The better dismiss servicemen as hayseeds. The worser want money I don't have."

"The Club holds dances every Saturday night. Some nice girls come."

"They want romance. Flowers and candy. I just want something warm and wet to stick my pecker in."

A pause. "Lots of queers in New York."

"Give me an address."

He glanced around a reception room empty but for us. "Ever been down in the basement?"

The desk clerk had undistinguished looks and a gimpy leg; nonetheless, I was occasionally inclined to brighten humdrum little lives. Fifteen minutes later, while pulling up my trousers, I asked if he'd serviced any other military at the Club.

"No," he replied, affronted.

"Really?"

"I said 'no'!"

"But you've wanted to?" He nodded reluctantly. "Afraid?"

"I guess so." He waited at the bottom of the cellar stairs.

"You work the desk every weekend?"

"Yeah, I have to get back to it." He fiddled with the light switch.

"What hours?"

"Six PM to six AM. You ready yet?"

We ascended the stairs to the lobby. To the clerk's annoyance, I sat next to his desk. "Tomorrow night, I want you to put me in a room with a hot number."

His eyes widened. "You're queer!"

"As a pilgrim to Sodom." I could sympathize with his disappointment. "I'll seduce him, if possible, and you can have sloppy seconds."

"You must be nuts."

56

"I prefer 'fiery' and 'passionate.'"

His astonishment subsided. "How do you seduce them?"

I had no intention of describing my tacky "Creepy Fingers" routine. "With an infallible technique handed down for generations from uncle to nephew."

"They go for seconds?"

"Usually. Let's try it. These guys are available. Why not enjoy them?"

"I'd hate to lose my job."

"An unlikely denouement. If you want the best, you must take chances."

"I can't believe straight men would let a . . . us . . . you know."

"These boys swarm to New York in hopes of getting laid. City girls won't give them a tumble. Rejection depresses the ego. They're lonely. Horny. Far from home."

"Just because they're horny doesn't mean they'd go for . . . queer stuff."

"I assume that you enjoyed yourself in the basement."

"Sure, but . . ."

"How ever can you be reluctant to enjoy yourself again?"

"You made it easy."

It was my aura of instant availability. "Every Friday, those military men inclined toward domesticity and routine hurry home or remain on base. The adventurous sally forth, usually willing, perhaps subconsciously, to experience new sensations. Separated from family and friends, egoes deflated by the anonymity of the military, they arrive in Manhattan with the sophistication of newly-hatched chicks. We stand ready to help them psychologically and biologically."

"What?"

"Our desiring them inflates their sense of self-worth and our relieving them mitigates the congestion in their testicles."

"I don't know . . ."

"Put me in a room with a hot number. If I can't seduce

57

him, it's no skin off your ass. If I can, it's fun and games."

Leaving the desk clerk to his task, I toddled off the next day to see Jane, who had replied to an advertisement in *Variety:* Dresser Needed. A renowned Nipponese actor-director planned to produce a Kabuki play Off-Broadway and needed someone to help his wife care for the elaborate costumes they had brought from Japan. Watching a rehearsal, I recognized the play as one I'd seen in Tokyo during R&R (a week's vacation from Vietnam for "Rest and Relaxation"). To my mind, presenting Kabuki on a small stage with Occidental actors in front of serious-minded Gothamites robbed it of glamor and bravado. I did enjoy seeing Jane's efficiency and the burgeoning friendship, in spite of language difficulties, between her and the traditionally-dressed wife.

Jane stayed at the theater for a second rehearsal, so I went back to the Club, where the desk clerk basked in his efficiency. "A lieutenant in the army. He's real handsome."

I knew from my baseball days that one praised a man before criticizing him. "That's great!" A blush. "I thought officers weren't supposed to rent your beds."

"He got his wallet lifted at the bus station and doesn't know anybody in New York. I loaned him five dollars and gave him an empty bed. Told him to wear civilian clothes."

"Good tactics. He has enough money to eat, but not enough to woo a female."

"Think you can get him?"

"I can only try. Officers condescend to enlisted men, a sub-human species sometimes too eager to serve their masters in the goddamnedest ways."

"Sexually?"

"I like to think so, but can offer no evidence. A lieutenant has yet to become jaded, although he'll be conscious of power, situated as he is between the gold braid of higher-ranking officers and us lesser mortals. Yet our man must forego his rank this weekend and pretend to be an enlisted man, an animal that performs raunchy acts in dismal settings. Perhaps he'll believe that among the proletariat, aberrance is the norm."

Half-baked rhetoric led to my usual strategy: "Creepy Fingers." The cool, handsome lieutenant proved as susceptible as the most gullible marine private. After rapture, I turned him over to the desk clerk, who marveled Sunday morning as we drank coffee. "What if he tells?"

"He won't."

"If he did?"

"I would say that I awakened to find him groping my precious and reported the incident to you. Has the Club a policy for faggots?"

"I'm supposed to inform the groper that another complaint will get him ejected."

"Fearing the end of his military career, he twisted the story to blacken me. As he never saw you, the room dark during your impropriety, you could confirm my report, which makes him the pervert."

"That's not very nice."

"The dude cooperates twice; then he blows the whistle. The armed services has little need of another irrational officer."

The desk clerk nodded. "Where do you go on Sundays?"

"Lunch with my fiancée, a stroll through a museum, dinner with a gay friend, and a meeting in New Jersey with a sexy straight beast whom I'm determined to seduce."

"Will you?"

"I'm always doubtful, especially with this one. See you in two weeks." The day went well and I determined to nudge Nick into a decision. I longed futilely for several heterosexual corpsmen at the hospital; I had no business letting another straight upset my weekends. We met in that same seedy cafe. "Where does Rosemary think you are?"

"Here. She saw you at my parents' New Year's Day bash."

I shrugged apologetically. "So many strangers . . ."

"And so many dumpy Italian women. She remembers you. No one else had blond hair or wore a sailor suit."

"Why do we meet?"

"For years, I've been talking about going to college. Study psychology. Never will. Rosemary knows it's a dream. Anyway, I told her that your brains got scrambled in Vietnam, that you gotta talk about some of the things that happened over there. Makes me feel good to help. I never did anything in the Army. Played horseshit war games. Nothing that mattered." A bitter look came over Nick's face. He glanced at me and smiled tightly. "Christ, I envy you."

"Ever stopped to think how much I respect your life? A worthwhile job and a settled future. Four beautiful kids. A wife who cares about you."

"A worthwhile job? Chasing down drunk drivers and spaced-out hippies. How the fuck can you take pride in a job when every guilty piece of scum you arrest is back on the street within hours because of crooked lawyers and wimpy judges. Goddam kids never stop squalling. My wife don't care what she looks like." His face convulsed with rage. "Know how many times I've been laid in the past two years? Six. Six goddam times. Three a year. Once every four months. My life ain't nothing, Kurt!"

"What do you want, buddy?"

"Christ, I don't know. Wouldn't make any difference if I did."

"What do you envy about my life?"

"Freedom."

"I still owe the Navy eight months."

"Yeah, but most of the time, you're free."

"The way I see it, you want to have your cake and eat it too."

Nick sighed. "The impossible dream."

"Not necessarily. Suppose you continue your lifestyle, but give up one evening a week to have adventures with me." Nick regarded me with suspicion. "You're too good-looking

60

not to enjoy sex. It's a sad waste. I'll introduce you to my friends, who are amusing."

"What kind of sex?"

"We'll start with guys. . . ."

"No way."

"Nice guys, Nick. Straight, with virgin mouths and asses."

"I don't want sex with guys."

"Ever try it?"

He knit his brow. "Not really." I wondered what that meant.

"I firmly believe it important to understand who I am and what I'm capable of doing. I love the power of seduction. I'm half-nuts from wanting you."

Nick stared. "You like me, don't you?"

"Scares me just how much."

His voice turned harsh. "Maybe you'd like to show me." He stood. "Let's go."

We drove to his brother's carpet shop in silence. Nick plugged in the heater, plucked a *Playboy* from the floor, and sprawling in the easy chair, opened the magazine to the centerfold. I fell to my knees and pulled off his shoes.

Humiliating? No. At the least, I could partially satisfy curiosity and a yearning; sensual experiences with other tall, lean, pale Italo-Americans, however, made me hopeful for more. Romantic and gentle lovers, those I'd known considered experiments in depravity as lessons in the important study of sex. I might lose Nick's respect should I serve him without reciprocity, but I had faith in his heritage and my technique. Within half-an-hour, my faith was rewarded.

Nick's capitulation warmed me through the following two weeks, particularly while standing duty with my tutor, a lab tech whose yellow wrinkled face was disfigured by several large moles: He looked like the offspring of Witch Hazel and the Abominable Snowman. An inveterate and malicious talebearer, the Yellow Yeti kept me up on hospital gossip and lectured me incessantly about our work and life in general. He held rigid opinions on a myriad of subjects. He lacked charm in face, form, and personality. I spent every third weekend with him. Sixty-three consecutive hours.

The Saffron Snowman seemed hellbent upon inspiring me to seek a career in his field. Intensity set on HIGH, he bustled about the lab with me tagging along meekly in the swishing wake of his baggy bellbottoms. He treated the most trifling tests as top-priority emergencies and rejoiced in his authority. He hated me out of his sight.

The lab filled one wing in the basement of the "H"-shape hospital. Other wings housed X-ray, Physical Therapy, and nursing offices. The Emergency Room stood in the crossbar. Three floors of wards lay above us.

One evening, I eased away from the Yellow Yeti as he argued with a newscaster on the duty room boob tube and wandered into X-ray. A fellow I'd met in Chu Lai had arrived a week earlier, the second survivor of that conflict to be stationed at the hospital. A prematurely-aged nervous Nellie with knock-knees, he was Molly Goldberg entertaining Adolf Eichmann. "I'm married now! I don't do those things anymore!" Did I ask? He'd been a shadow on a dark night during a black month. I rationalized my lousier lays as stepping-stones to wisdom; nevertheless, I wished God would exile the fuckers to Neptune.

Vietnam seldom intruded upon conversation or in memory; when it did, I preferred to reminisce about the more pleasurable interludes. Sometimes, however, pain wracked my plastic elbow and brought back the bad times. One afternoon in the gym, I added weight while benchpressing and failed to lift it. The bar lay across my chest. My arm throbbed.

"Need some help?" Someone stood over me, his features blurred by the tears of my frustration.

"Please!"

The barbell clanged into its frame. "You should work out with a partner."

"I know. Thanks." I sat up, cradling my elbow and hanging my head.

"Your arm looks good. Another month or two, nobody'll notice the difference."

"I used to be so strong."

"Vietnam?"

I nodded. The unseen stranger hunkered next to me. "What happened?" No one else in Newport had asked. I'd accepted the role of a man without a past, but the merest inkling of concern unleashed the horror of that night and its aftermath: a rescue chopper careering through a monsoon to pick up the charred bodies of marines doomed to die; the guard, a friend and occasional bedpartner, falling from the helicopter into a dark jungle six hundred feet below; the agony of a shattered elbow; oblivion in the black-velvet womb of stolen morphine; murky memories of a desperate escape from indifferent medical care in Nam with the hope of reaching Cincinnati and a sister who loved me; awakening from a coma in a stateside hospital to the voices of surgeons discussing the unlikelihood of my survival even were they to amputate the injured arm. . . . I finished my monologue and glanced at its victim, shocked to see a magnificently-built creature whom I had worshiped from afar for a month. Ashamed, I apologized for being a bore. The man stared at me, shook his head, and stood. "Let's hit the showers."

I learned that he was a SEAL (Sea, Air, and Land) teaching several courses at the Naval War College. What little I knew about those intelligent ferocious men filled me with awe: Comparing a SEAL with a Green Beret was like comparing a Canadian Mountie with an Eagle Scout. Only a couple of hundred men made up the two branches (Atlantic and Pacific) of this elite corps, la crème de la crème of American manhood. I showered with the SEAL, whose body would have won him an honored place in Valhalla.

I returned to the barracks atremble. My plans for the

63

evening had included a movie, but however could I sit through someone else's fantasy? For five months, I'd read too many books in a hospital while life passed by outside.

A list of places declared OFF LIMITS TO NAVAL PERSONNEL hung above the Master-at-Arms' desk. Scanning the names of dens filled with sin and temptations, I noted that a gay bar operated in Newport. Hoping that my barrackmates adhered better to taboo, I donned my snazziest civilian clothes and hurried downtown.

I sat on a stool near the darker end of the bar and ordered a beer. It cost double the going rate; I had come to the right place. A butch curly-haired blond occupied the next stool. We no sooner exchanged aliases than he asked if I had a room. I didn't. He grimaced and considered our plight. "We could make it behind the bus station. How much money do you have?"

Impertinent lad. "Four dollars."

"I don't go for less than twenty." Our acquaintance ended, and he set about charming a portly gentleman on his right. I guzzled my beer.

A smooth baritone voice sounded on my left. "Could I buy you another?" A sleek darkhaired man flashed white teeth. "To drown your disappointment." I stared. "Couldn't help overhearing."

However had a crummy hustler blinded me to this? Wow! I accepted the beer. "Navy?"

"Civilian. An actor." On vacation? "I've been cast as a commander in a training film." No commander ever looked this good. "Shooting at the School of Naval Warfare." Refreshingly honest or perilously naive. "Would you like to read the script?" Those white teeth set off a Caribbean tan. "It's in my motel room."

Overdeveloped calves and a misshapen penis marred his physical perfection, but the amiable actor was cuddly and I enjoyed myself. He lived in Manhattan with a jealous lover of long duration. "Kirk couldn't come, but he wasn't about

64

to let me turn down this job. It's been three years since I've fooled around." I felt like the other woman.

My bunkmate, Langman, announced that he had married a WAVE. He'd met her in August at Hospital Corps School. Their sole date had occurred in October. An exchange of Christmas cards constituted their entire correspondence since graduation in November. Immediately following the Night of Shivers, Langman mailed a letter of proposal. She accepted by return mail. He left for Maryland Friday evening, married the WAVE Saturday afternoon, and returned to Newport Sunday. The following week, he would leave for a thirteen-month tour of duty in Vietnam. My astonishment must have shown. "I love her," he muttered sullenly.

Every morning, a middleaged woman greeted me by whining, "Here comes Dracula!" I would swallow my rising gorge, deny myself the pleasure of stabbing her to the bone, and try to alleviate her tension with chat. The woman's husband out to sea, she was lonely, ailing, and afraid. She reminded me of Mother, whom the angels had so lately taken to Heaven, where she was probably raising Hell.

The woman died on the operating table during a D&C (dusting and cleaning a woman's reproductive organs). One of the pathologists asked me to assist at the autopsy.

The pale nude body lay piteously upon a slab. The pathologist slit it from neck to crotch and removed organs that I weighed. The Yellow Yeti sawed off the top of the skull; when he skinned down the face, the hair looked liked a beard. Almost gagging at the pervasive odor of formaldehyde, I noted a resemblance between the woman's body and Mother's.

Friday, the actor invited me for dinner and a romp; afterwards, we drove to New York. When I entered the Enlisted Man's Club, the desk clerk looked up, aghast. "I didn't think you were coming. The doubles are filled."

"What's left?"

"Four triples."

65

I accepted the challenge. While waiting for the desk clerk to choose my roommates, I heard water running in the shower room. A little air jockey lathered himself. Although he could claim no outstanding attributes, slick clean skin inflamed my libido. "I've often wondered," I lied, "how the foreskin is attached to an uncircumcized penis." He appeared startled, but pulled back his prepuce. I dropped to my knees for a closer inspection. I took him in hand. I gave new meaning to 'a hand-to-mouth existence.'

He pulled me up. "Let's go to my room."

I had satisfied my curiosity and hoped to move on toward bigger and better things. He gazed at me with pleading eyes. Well, I'd started it. He braced a chair against the door of his room and reached under my towel. Dismayed, I watched him perform. A faggot!

I cooperated with diminishing pleasure until, beyond endurance, I pleaded an imminent rendezvous with Jane.

"Will you come back tonight?"

If the airman saw me skulking about the Club, his feelings would be hurt. "Yeah, but Jane will probably have fucked my brains out."

"I'd like to see you again."

"I'll be as drained as the heroine of a vampire movie."

"Please!"

The dreary little thing lacked looks, pride. . . . "I won't be back till late."

"What time?"

Jesus! "I don't know."

"Midnight?"

"Perhaps."

"Meet me in the lobby at twelve. We'll go to that new dance bar on 72nd Street."

What fun! To avoid the airman, I had a choice of hiding in a drab triple or chancing frostbite on the frigid streets of wintry Manhattan. I opened *Peregrine Pickle*.

Two hours later, I turned the last page. On the lookout

for Rudy the Airman, I slunk down to the lobby. A brawny blond paid for a bed and ascended the stairs. I watched him out of sight before turning to the desk clerk. "Buy me one of those, daddy."

"Bought and paid for and yours if you can get him."

"In my room?"

"All night long."

After an appropriate interval, silhouetted by a light across the air well, I writhed upon my bed, making spectacular ado with Precious. Having set the stage, I prowled the room restlessly and settled upon the unoccupied bed between mine and the blond's. He thrust a knee from under his blanket. I reached out tentatively and touched the knee. He lay unmoving. I slid my hand under the blanket and caressed a hard hairy calf. A muscular thigh. A thick erection. I plunged into rapture. He grabbed the iron rail behind his head with powerful hands. Forty minutes later, that strong young body arched with ecstasy.

I'd no sooner crept into my bed than the third musketeer entered the room, a sailor with dark hair, fine features, and a lean body. I wondered how to approach him. "Creepy Fingers?"

I heard scratching sounds under the newcomer's blanket that continued, faint but persistent, for some time. Was he jerking off or tending an itch? I could hardly ask. After ten breathless minutes, he left the room; I waited a suitable interlude before following. Bare feet showed under the door of the last stall in the john. I entered the adjoining stall. Standing upon the toilet seat, I peered over the partition. He scratched a lovely itch.

The queer airman entered the john and saw me. His mouth opened in horror. I motioned him away, but his anguished cry, "What are you doing?" alerted the scratcher. I ducked and scuttled to my room.

As promised, I met Rudy at midnight. The delighted air jockey chattered incessantly despite my hostile silence.

At the bar, I became enamoured of a graceful hunk with excellent legs, which set me between the horns of a dilemma. I could return to the Club with Rudy, who might press for a rematch that I intended to decline, or I could admit preferring the hunk's perfect teeth and masculine carriage to the airman's lesser wares. Either choice would hurt the little fellow's feelings. Why ever did I care? Maybe I could sneak away. No, even while dancing with someone else, Rudy watched me, smiling wistfully whenever he caught my eye.

At closing time, a bright white light revealed the pallor of perspiring queens. The hunk suggested that we retire to his apartment.

"I'm here with a friend," I said reluctantly.

"A lover?"

"Hardly." I pointed at Rudy, who watched us.

The hunk studied him. "I'm not into trios."

"He's in the Air Force," I confided hopefully.

The hunk looked me up and down. "My roommate owes me one."

The four of us walked to an apartment three blocks away. When the hunk led me into a bedroom, leaving Rudy with a plump, homely banker, the airman appeared stunned. In the morning, I left for Jane's without seeing him.

Jane worked as a temporary in the subscription department of *Commentary* magazine. "An Isadore Steinberg complained that his last three issues hadn't arrived. The subscribers' index lists the surname and the first and third letters of the given name. In this case, we had cancelled a duplicate: STEINBERG, I-BLANK-A at the same address, but those three issues had been mailed. I called to tell him. 'Sure, my wife, Ida, gets her copy, but what about mine?'"

Jane and I ate in an Hungarian restaurant and attended a matinee. Two hours remained before she had to be at the theater for the Kabuki play, but I said goodbye at her door. "Aren't you staying?" Women! Not only must you wine and dine them, you gotta fuck them, too. Troubled by Jane's disappointment, I returned to the Club.

"The blond's checked out," said the desk clerk. "You still have Old Scratch."

"He's tainted. I keep thinking of ringworm and scabies."

"The guy was jacking off! No rash! No itch! He's a hot number."

"The picture in my mind's eye cannot be altered." I started up the stairs.

"Hey! You got a message from Nick Esoldi. Wants you to call before eight."

My heart leaped. I felt gratitude toward those who shared their bodies with me, but I refused to allow myself the optimism of a second chance at them; most were strangers who quickly disappeared from my world. Nick had been fabulous in the sack: his responses gratifying, his technique unerring. His body glowed with health. He had no effeminite mannerisms. I'd left New Jersey, certain that I would never see him again. I couldn't believe that he wanted me to call.

"Hello."

"Kurt Strom here. Nick?"

"What's happening?"

"Absolutely nothing."

"Wanna talk?"

"Sure."

"I'll meet you at the bus station." An hour later, I disembarked to find the trooper waiting. "Interested in a beer?"

We climbed into a brown van. "Didn't think I'd see you again."

Nick shrugged. "Thought you realized I made a commitment."

Bright lights flashed in my brain. A roaring in my ears transported me to a different plane. After a minute, I could speak. "Reckon you want a few psychology lessons."

Nick smiled. "I reckon." He parked near a blue-collar bar and we sat at the back in a dark booth. My buddy had something to say, so I waited silently, basking in the pleasure of his company. He lit a cigarette before speaking. "I figured the best thing to do is to be honest with myself and with you." He closed his eyes and ran a hand across his forehead. "I hated what we did." Iron bands constricted my chest; I couldn't breathe. "No, what I hated is how much I liked it." My lungs functioned. "How much I like you." Someone played another Country-and-Western song on the jukebox. "I knew it was coming. Like I was putting myself in the path of temptation. Didn't intend to do anything myself, though. Christ, what you can do with your hands and mouth!"

"Please don't regret it, buddy."

"Kinda hard to think of myself as a queer."

"Impossible for me to think of you that way."

"Yeah, well . . . All my life, I've believed that faggots are scum."

"You aren't a faggot."

"I sucked dick, man. I'm willing to do it again. What else can I call myself?"

"Any dude who can get it up for a chick can get it up for a guy."

"Bullshit!"

"Before the night is over, I'll prove it."

"How?"

"I don't know."

Nick laughed. "Those wheels are always grinding."

I was given to concentrating on whomever I talked with, so I paid little attention to the bar's other customers until Nick left the booth to use the men's room. The clientele ran to middleaged men wearing shabby clothes, but one young man caught my eye. Black-Irish . . . handsome . . . good legs . . . He looked out of place in a sports jacket. A few minutes later, he took his turn in the john. As he came out, I nodded and waved a half-ass salute. He took a few steps forward, the better to peer into our murky corner. Shaking his head as if to clear it, he staggered a bit as he came closer.

"Sorry. Thought I knew you."

I smiled again. "No, but you could. Bring your drink over and join us."

He grinned. Devastating. A convival man among strangers too weary to strike up conversations. He sat next to Nick and offered each of us his hand. "Terry Scanlon."

We introduced ourselves; within three minutes, I revealed that I made my living as a psychiatrist. "Nick's a patient."

"No kidding!" He turned to Nick. "You give him a good recommendation?"

"The best!"

"No kidding! You figure out what makes people tick?"

"Terry Scanlon. Grandparents: shanty Irish, parents: lace curtain. You have an interest in math, but never went to college. You work a blue-collar job. Older brother's successful. You can't live up to him."

"Pat's an electronics engineer. I wanted to be an accountant. Manage a warehouse instead. Hey, he's good! Tell me more."

"You had a date tonight, maybe with a girl who wants to be a virgin on her wedding night. Or you had a fight with your fiancée."

He nodded. "She wants to get married, but we can't live like she wants on my salary. You sure I don't know you?"

"Part of my job. You don't screw around on your girl, but the evening's still young. Wouldn't meet any chicks here, so you're safe, but if anything comes up . . ."

"What do they call men witches?"

"Warlocks. No, it's the way you talk. Carry yourself. Dress. The bar. The neighborhood."

"Guess if you know what you're looking for . . . You guys live around here?"

"Nick does. My office is in Manhattan."

"Making money hand over fist, I'll bet."

"Not yet, but I plan to."

71

Terry turned to Nick again. "Hope he isn't robbing you blind."

Nick replied by lighting a cigarette. I'd seldom worked with a partner before and didn't know what approach to use. "Actually, maybe you could help. Nick has a problem." Terry stared curiously at my buddy. "He's thinking about committing suicide."

"No kidding! Why?"

Good question. "You don't mind my telling him, do you, Nick?"

The trooper's mouth twitched. "Go ahead."

"Nick's an executive for Standard Oil. Married. Four kids, another on the way. Last year, he flew to Houston on business. Had to stay over, so he called an army buddy, a pilot for TWA. They painted the town red, reminisced over old times. The pilot was too drunk to drive home, so he stayed over in Nick's hotel room. During the night, Nick woke up. The friend was sucking his dick while he slept."

"No kidding!"

"Nick never let on he was awake, but it felt so good, he let the pilot finish. Nick's a real man. It's obvious. But since that night, he's come to believe that no man would let another fellow blow him, and if he can't be a man, he'd rather be dead."

Terry looked at Nick. "You really think that?"

Nick sighed glumly. "Yes."

"I've tried to tell him that a hard cock has no conscience, that a lot of real men have let other fellows blow them. He doesn't believe me."

"I can sure think of worse things."

"What are you drinking?" I bought beer for Nick and me and a double Scotch for Scanlon.

The Irishman shook his head. "You're serious? You really thinking about suicide 'cause a fag gave you head?"

Nick looked solemn. "No real man would have let him."

"It's not like you were expecting it. You were asleep, for

goodness sake."

I spoke sternly. "This can't go on, Nick. You have a lovely wife and four children who need you. I can't speak for Terry, but I don't look down on you for what happened." Terry agreed. "I hope you consider me a real man, and Terry appears to be one, too. Neither of us would suffer torment because . . . Damn, that jukebox is loud. It was a mistake meeting here. I can't hear myself think."

"My wife is home," said Nick firmly. "I wouldn't want her to know this."

"She's gonna wonder if you jump off a bridge. Maybe we should go to my office. I can't leave you alone tonight." I looked at Terry. "You're good for reinforcement. Would a trip into Manhattan be a hassle for you?"

Terry beamed. "I got a better idea, if it's all right with you. My apartment's just around the corner. Nobody's there. We can get a bottle and talk all night, if you want."

We accepted the offer, and I bought a fifth of Scotch at a nearby package store. Terry had furnished his apartment with a mixture of odds and ends that added up to clutter. He talked about his background, which included a year in Vietnam with the Air Force. We traded war stories. Nick interrupted. "Kurt played baseball for the Detroit Tigers."

"No kidding!"

"They brought me up for a cup of coffee. My biggest thrill came when Whitey Ford struck me out in Yankee Stadium." I shrugged. "It paid my way through college."

"A celebrity in my apartment!"

Our host awed, the moment had come to strike. "All right, Nick. It's time to shape up. You've talked with Terry and you know me. Both of us Vietnam veterans. Both of us athletes." Terry downplayed his high school football career. "I consider myself completely heterosexual, but I'll admit there have been times . . . in the jungle . . . in a lonely hotel room . . . if a dude offered to blow me . . . I might have accepted. Terry?"

"A guy gets horny . . . You never know."

Nick rejected the argument. "Easy to talk."

"And hard to prove." I cogitated a moment. "We had a series in Indianapolis. I overslept and missed the team bus. Saving every dime for school, I couldn't afford the fine I'd have to pay if I was late for infield practice. A cab cost too much. A city bus took too long. I thumbed it. Guy picked me up, offered to take me right to the ballpark if I let him blow me. Our first series in Indianapolis, I didn't even know where the park was. I let him."

Nick frowned. "Didn't fuck up your mind?"

"Not really. I'd already decided I wanted to be a psychologist. Figured it best if I knew as much about myself as possible. Gotta admit that the dude's mouth felt damn good. How about you, Terry?"

He shook his head. "Nothing to tell. Sorry."

"If you were in the same situation?"

"Maybe. I don't know."

Nick stood. "I gotta go."

"Sit down! You're a great guy, Nick. The world would be a darker place without you."

"We ain't getting anywhere with this."

"Sit, please! God! If it were my bag, I'd suck off Terry in front of you just to prove it has nothing to do with being a man."

Nick sat and crossed his arms. "No, you wouldn't"

Terry stared at him. "You're really serious, aren't you? About killing yourself?"

The trooper's lips tightened. "Yes, I am."

Concern creased my brow. "Nick, I've bared my soul and told you that I would blow Terry in front of you. If Terry knew you better and realized what a waste it would be if you killed yourself, he'd probably blow me, wouldn't you, Terry?"

"Hell, yeah!"

"Talk's cheap."

74

"It's the fucking truth! Watch!" I moved to the sofa where Terry sat and knelt between his legs. "Watch, goddammit!" Surprised, Terry offered a token objection, but quickly leaned back to enjoy it. As I worked, I eased off his clothes, revealing a muscular body with a lovely hair pattern. I stood and removed my clothes. "Just to show you ain't nothing unmanly about it, Terry's gonna do the same for me." Inexperienced teeth scraped Precious. I beckoned Nick over, undressed him, and had him take my place while I took care of the Irishman. Later, I straddled Terry's face while Nick eased up a dark tunnel. When we finished, Mr. Scanlon staggered into the bathroom.

I smiled, "Satisfied?"

Nick washed himself at the kitchen sink. "Shock Theater! How did you know that he'd let us stick it to him?"

"I didn't."

The trooper dressed. "Want to stay at the carpet shop?"

I peered into the bedroom. Terry sprawled across an unmade bed. "I'll spend the night here." Blue eyes flashed. "You gotta take me the way I am."

Nick pulled on his jacket. "Right." He left the apartment. I turned off the lights and lay next to Terry. Neither of us slept much that night.

In the morning, the Irishman looked at me over his coffee cup through bloodshot eyes. "Give yourself heart and soul to your work, do you?"

"I think we convinced Nick that he's a man."

Terry sat back gingerly on a sore behind. "I should hope to Christ so."

Back in Manhattan, I made the mistake of mentioning Nick to Paul, who began interrogating me. "Are you falling in love with him?"

"Don't be ridiculous. He's just a trick."

"Yet you're planning to spend more time together."

"Maybe. Nick's good company and the best sex I've had since McGrath."

75

"Who's that?"

I replied reluctantly. "A marine in Nam."

"The one who tried to kill you?" Paul reached for my hand. "You have a compulsion to charm straights into loving you against their will. You play dangerous games, Kurt."

"Should I spend more time at a bridge table or on a shuffleboard court?"

"History repeats itself. Do you plan for the trooper to kill you?"

"What a silly thing to say?"

"How will you drive him to it?"

"The nagging auntie, herself without fault."

"I love you, and I want you to be happy."

"Believe it or not, I'm content. Just spreading myself around so if lightning strikes . . ."

A busy mind dispels shadows.

I spread myself around the hospital, too, becoming friendly with several patients, a couple of corpsmen, and even a nurse. I enjoyed a special rapport with the children on Pediatrics.

When obliged to drain blood, the other techs enlisted the aid of corpsmen or nurses to hold the children's arms. They would murmur soothingly, "This isn't going to hurt," although it did. The child would jerk, the needle would slip out of the tiny vein, and a blue hematoma would form. This meant an injection in the other arm of a by-now hysterical child.

Not this vampire.

I would wave aside offers of help and chat with the child before getting down to the nitty-gritty. "I gotta take some blood now. You choose the arm." The children enjoyed the power of choice. Tourniquet tightened and needle poised, I intoned darkly, "This will hurt, but if you move, you'll die." The children turned to stone and my tubes filled with blood. No hematomas. No hysteria. So fearful of dying that they felt no pain, the children asked for me by name and refused to let anyone else do their leeching.

The SEAL joined his company for maneuvers in the Arctic. Although our acquaintance had gone no further than casual gymnasium chat, I missed those huge muscles straining to press four hundred pounds and jerk three hundred-and-fifty pounds. I pictured his stalking polar bears barehanded.

Because I stood duty Thursday, the medical service lieutenant let me off Friday at noon. The actor had completed filming, so we enjoyed lunch and a final romp before driving to New York. While waiting for the desk clerk, who started work at six, I wandered through midtown Manhattan and happened upon a paving crew at work. A muscular blue-eyed fellow handled the jackhammer. Shutting off the drill to ease his broad shoulders, the worker glanced my way. We stared. I smiled. He winked and pointed at his thick wrist. He opened and shut his hand three times. Fifteen minutes. Rat-a-tat-tat.

The driller led me down Third Avenue. "My apartment ith thikth more blockth. My lover will like you." An Indian struck a lanquid pose on the sofa. "Thee what I brought for you." The Chippewa smiled, revealing the loss of two front teeth. "I'll lick hith ballth and ream hith ath while he blowth you." Suddenly, I felt very tired.

I lacked prurient thoughts about Indians: their broad flat faces, their fleshy hairless bodies, and their little purple peewees; unfortunately, I was incapable of the rudeness necessary to cancel our session. The Chippewa spoke once. "I've been to bed with my father and six of my seven brothers." I raised no clamor for details.

Someone knocked at the front door. The Chippewa grabbed a flowery robe and wafted out of the bedroom. I heard voices. The driller's head lifted from my nether region. "Ith Don. Heeth an Inca and thraight ath a board. We're dying to have thekth with him." The Chippewa led the Inca into the bedroom. An elegant, masculine,

77

incredibly beautiful Inca. My prejudice against redskins vanished.

The Inca had a presence the Sun God might have envied. Leaning against a wall, he handled our nudity with aplomb and acknowledged our introduction with a silent smile.

The driller lacked such manners. "Thee what I'm going to do to you thumday?" He resumed reaming me. The Inca yawned.

He declined an invitation to take my place and said, with only a trace of an accent, "I want to buy six lids." Business prevailed. I showered, dressed, and made going-away sounds. The Inca glanced at me. "Would you like to smoke some reefer in my flat?"

The driller glowered. "We'll go with you."

The Inca shrugged. "Forget it."

The driller and the Chippewa dressed so they might accompany the Inca and me outside to ascertain that we walked in different directions.

The desk clerk gave me a choice of roommates. "A marine on his way from Vietnam to guard an embassy in the Middle East: brown eyes, brown hair, good face, wiry body. . . . A tall blond sailor named Waslewski . . ."

"No Polacks!"

"Why?"

"They have pointy peckers."

"What?"

"Men of European and African descent have penii crowned by heads larger than the shafts. A Polack's pecker tapers to a point."

"I've never heard that."

"Nor have I, and it could be an unfair generalization, but I've showered with half-a-dozen Polacks, each exhibiting a pointy pecker."

Shrugging off another of my eccentricities, the desk clerk continued. "The third is my favorite. A soldier from Evansville, Indiana. Dark red hair, gray eyes, and a cute smile."

The soldier looked like a choirboy. He fell from grace.

The desk clerk joined me for breakfast. "Do you think it was his first time?"

"Unless they tell me differently, I always pretend it is."

"Don't you wonder?"

"Most assuredly. If Heaven were to my taste, I would sit before a movie screen to watch the life stories of everyone I've known, in and out of the Biblical sense of the word. Simultaneously showing on a second screen would be each life story had I never existed."

"You must know thousands of people. Could be a bore."

"We're talking about eternity. You want boring? My grandmother's idea of Heaven includes an angel to whom she could tell her life story over and over." A smartly turned-out marine marched briskly into the coffee shop. "My God! What's that?"

"You turned him down for the choirboy."

"Would it be much trouble to move me into his room?"

"Not at all. Think you can get him?"

"Won't know till I try."

That afternoon, I dropped by the costume shop where Jane worked part-time. She stood emergency duty. "A commercial for toothpaste. The producer needs costumes for thirty-two actors by Monday. Six years of studying design, and I'm sewing teeth. This will take all weekend. Sorry, dear."

I wept crocodile tears and wondered how to seduce the marine. No game of "Creepy Fingers" would suffice. The Marine Corps trained its men to hate queers, and violence simmered just below the surface of those who returned from Vietnam. I felt little desire to wake up with my throat slit.

After attending *Fortune and Men's Eyes*, I returned to the Club, entered my room, and switched on the light. "Jesus!"

The marine jumped out of bed into a crouch. "What?"

"Sorry, ace. You look just like my best buddy in Nam. The spirit and image."

The marine relaxed and reached for a pack of cigarettes. I checked his strong lean body for scars. A slice below the kneecap: a football injury—I liked that. Tiny blue pits in his thigh: shrapnel—proof he humped the boonies. A small pucker above the right nipple: a bullet through the lung, most likely—a corpsman might have saved his life; the marine would be grateful and his subsequent hospitalization might have reinforced the mental passivity so prized by military officers.

The grunt recognized the cadeceus and the ribbons on my uniform; conversation elicited our having served in the same regiment and our common abhorrence of a medal-hungry colonel. During an hour of chat, I mentioned his "double" several times. Eventually, he expressed curiosity. "Tell me about your buddy."

Glad you asked. Tales filled with derring-do established my buddy as the pride of the marines. "When his tentmate got blown away by a landmine, Barry moved into the back of the First-Aid tent with me. One day, I came from a shower; Barry was sifting through some Japanese fuckbooks. I looked at them, couldn't help getting turned on. Barry reached over and starting stroking my pecker. No way I go for queer shit, but you know how it was over there: the women dirty and diseased, razor blades up their cunts . . . It had been so long since I'd had decent pussy. I leaned back and closed my eyes. A warm mouth enveloped Old Precious. It felt so good, I had no inclination to push it away.

"Barry expected me to return the favor. No fucking way. I called him a goddam fruit and ordered him out of my tent. Kept my distance for the next week, knowing Barry felt bad. Then I got to thinking: Barry's my buddy. A good buddy. Saved my life twice. A lot of grunts took care of each other. Helped each other get their gun. Bad as it was on the lines, this wasn't right, putting my buddy down. I'd about decided to make it up when Barry bought the farm during a firefight. He died believing that I hated him for being a queer. I'll never, ever forgive myself." Tears ran down my cheeks. God, I was good!

The marine nodded sympathetically. "Nam did funny things with people's minds." He put out his cigarette.

I switched off the light and crawled into bed. "Thanks for listening, ace. I . . . I never told anybody else. They wouldn't of understood. They'd of thought Barry a queer. He wasn't."

"No problem."

We lay in the dark. "Some bad things happened in Nam, but nothing sits heavier on me than putting down Barry. It haunts me." A huge sigh. "I want it to end. I relive that day in my mind and do what Barry wanted. Doesn't work. I've never done it, so I can't imagine what it's like. I've got to do it someday, so I'll know what it's like. Then I can satisfy Barry, at least in my mind, and put his ghost to rest." I was crying again and the jarhead couldn't even see me. "While I was in the hospital, I took weekend liberty with a buddy, a marine with a racked-up leg. We tore up the French Quarter and crawled back to our hotel. I respected the marine. A great guy. Remembering Barry, I come mite nigh to asking the dude if I could blow him. Get it out of my system. Nobody'd even know. And he'd probably of let me. But he didn't look like Barry." I let that sink in, hoping the jarhead hadn't fallen asleep. "When I saw you, it was like, 'This is the guy. He looks like Barry. He's been to Nam. Knows how things were. Tell him the story. He'll let you do it. Pretend he's Barry. Don't have this hang over you all your life. This dude will let you pretend that you're making your buddy happy.'"

A short silence. "What are you trying to say?" I made the offer in terms even a grunt could understand. "I really look like him?"

"The spittin' image."

Reflecting a few moments, he threw off his blanket. "Go to it, doc."

81

Later, I felt honor-bound to tell the desk clerk, but he agreed it would be callous to strive for sloppy seconds. "I still can't believe he did everything."

"He didn't want me to feel queer."

"But he's straight, right?"

"I'd bet my balls."

"How do you do it?"

"I try to make perversity seem reasonable."

"How do you decide what will seem reasonable?"

"I trust my instincts."

Instinct is intelligence incapable of self-consciousness.

March 1968

A sadistic electrician must have wired Pathology. To reach the light switch, one had to pass by a refrigerated locker (reefer) that often contained bodies, the autopsy slab, and shelves holding jars filled with diseased organs and deformed embryos.

My mentor, the Yellow Yeti, informed me one night that a dissected corpse lay on the autopsy slab awaiting transferral to the reefer. I opened the door to Pathology and peered into the darkness at a lump covered by a sheet. "Turn on the light!" ordered the Yeti.

"Let's not forget in your arrogance that I outrank you."

"Then you should be the one smearing spit and shit in Bacteriology."

"Watch my dust!" I was halfway across the room when the door slammed shut behind me. An eerie moan resounded against the walls. The corpse sat up.

I reached the switch within a heartbeat. The Saffron Snowman, whom I'd suspected of being humorless, slid giggling down the wall to the floor. Another tech, a mealy-mouth little redhead, cackled on the slab.

Scorning peasant humor, I avoided my co-workers after hours. In the balcony of Newport's grander movie palace, a lithe seaman accepted my advances, but in the restroom, a brawny sailor tried to kick me in the face under the partition between our stalls. At the gym, a trim ensign watched from the next row of lockers as the product of my spermary splashed upon a concrete floor; a doughty captain interrupted a similar display in the shower room. "That's a good way to get booted out of the Navy and a sure way to Hell!"

Considering it best to stick with like-minded companions, I tripped to the gay bar downtown. Two middleaged drearies offered felicity. I declined. They offered mammon, coming on so strongly that I fled the establishment. Trudging home to *Roderick Random*, I passed the bus station, which had closed for the night. A sailor huddled in the doorway. I woke him. "It's freezing! You'll die!"

He mumbled incoherently. I lifted him into the light of a streetlamp; around thirty-five, he had the youthful looks of those protected by the Navy from life's vagaries. Rejecting my initial impulse to haul him to the YMCA, I hailed a cab, which dropped us near the hospital at the unguarded back gate, and carried the sailor to the night barrack, a small annex with windows painted black and crammed with bunks for the corpsmen who worked the eleven PM to seven AM shift. No one used it at night, so I undressed the lifer and lay him on a bunk. He feigned sleep throughout my ministrations, but as I made ready to leave, he mumbled, "Thank you. Thank you so much."

The Yeti and I endured a hectic duty weekend, catching only snatches of sleep. Monday, a sympathetic medical service lieutenant released us at noon, and I decided to crash in the night barrack. Wielding a flashlight, the Master-at-Arms (MAA) led me to an empty bunk. As usual, I fell asleep when my head hit the pillow.

I awakened with Precious under oral attack. Unable to see in a room dark as a wolf's mouth, I grabbed the phantom fellator by the hair and dragged him into the hall. The Master-at-Arms! "You goddam son-of-a-bitch! How fucking dare you!"

The rodent cringed under my onslaught. "I'm sorry."

"You asshole!"

84

"I don't know what came over me. I swear I'll never do it again."

I lifted him against the wall with one hand. "You've been fucking around like this for months, haven't you? Years! Don't lie to me."

"I . . . can't . . . breathe."

I banged his head against the wall and dropped him. "I ought to kill you." He groaned, his narrow face white. "We're marching straight to the admiral's office."

"Please! I have two years for twenty." Retiring honorably after twenty years of military duty entitled the sleazeball to free medical care, half-pay, and other benefits for the rest of his unnatural life.

"You don't belong in this man's Navy. I'm going to report you."

"Please! I'll do anything."

I deliberated. "Give me a sheet of paper." He pulled a wallet from the pocket of his middy blouse and tore a page from a tiny address book. "A pen." He produced one. "Write 'I, HM1 — —, suck the peters of sleeping sailors in the night barrack."

"The hell I will!"

"Then I'm marching you in my underwear to the admiral's office." I scorned pleading eyes.

"Who are you going to show it to?"

"No one, if you concede a few points. Write!" He transcribed my dictation, which was stupid; I had no witnesses and he could have denied my accusation. Sheep can't handle fear. "Sign it!" He obeyed. "Let's go to your apartment." The MAA lived in a small suite behind the game room. Handy . . . private . . . I made myself at home. "Number One: My name will be stricken from the clean-up squad." (Twice a month, I had to sweep, mop, wax, and buff one of the barracks; the corpsmen who hadn't served in Vietnam could do that job nicely.) The MAA agreed. "Number Two: I will make occasional use of your apartment. Let's say once a week." He frowned. "I'll let you know ahead of time and I won't abuse the privilege." He glanced at the damning confession I held in my hand and nodded. "Number Three: Tell me if you've sucked . . ." I named six sexy corpsmen for whom I yearned.

"I don't know."

"What do you mean, you don't know?"

"It's dark in the night barrack."

"You don't know whose dong you're gobbling?"

"No."

"That's sick, man. Some ugly dudes soil those sheets."

He waxed indignant. "I don't 'gobble' ugly dudes."

"How do you know?"

"I turn out the lights every morning. I know who sleeps where."

I felt like the prosecutor who tripped up Oscar Wilde. "What about those six men?"

Two worked in Supply; a third was head corpsman on the NP ward. "They don't stand night duty."

"The other three?" He hung his head. I demanded circumstances. How many times? Did they awaken? Did they ejaculate?

"Why do you want to know all this?" asked the MAA suspiciously.

"Pernicious information is my hobby."

I planned to ponder the placement of this information during my next duty night, but several emergencies kept the Yeti and me hopping until early morning. Three Navy wives went into labor, so we had to type-and-crossmatch six pints of blood. We set two pints in the reefer for each woman, should an emergency occur. Two of the confinements involved the Rh factor, an incompatibility of blood types between mother and child that occurred in many second pregnancies. This kept us in the Blood Bank for quite a while.

An automobile accident involving a drunken officer sent us

to Chemistry for a lengthy, difficult test measuring the amount of alcohol in his blood. Just as we prepared to retire, a corpsman called to tell us that a patient had died on his ward; we waited until a doctor pronounced the old man dead and the corpsman wheeled the corpse downstairs. At four AM, we finally fell into our bunks. At six, the Yeti, half-asleep, turned off the alarm clock. When the other lab techs arrived at seven, they awakened us, and we hurried to the wards for morning blood drawing.

Because her patients ate late breakfasts, the head nurse on SICU (Surgical Intensive Care Unit) went to the admiral, who handed down new orders: 1. Morning blood drawing would begin an hour earlier at five, and 2. Four techs would make rounds instead of two. No matter that we already stood the worst duty in the hospital or that morning rounds had never before occurred later than scheduled. The pathologist in charge of the lab failed to protect us and let the order stand. To my amazement, none of the lab techs complained, accepting an unfair retribution with apparent equanimity. As the new man, I could say nothing.

The afternoon of our debacle, I returned to the barracks, tired and irritable. While standing at the urinal, I glanced behind me. A golden Irishman sat on a toilet abusing himself. (I wondered who coined that connotation.) O'Hara was one of the supply corpsmen whom I hoped to seduce, somehow. I watched the Irishman shoot off upon the toilet seat, wipe himself, and leave the restroom, blushing. Suddenly, I was wide awake and happy.

Felicity made me goatish, so I deemed a weekend in New York most necessary. I checked into the Enlisted Man's Club, learned that my roommate was a "dynamite" soldier from Idaho, and walked to Yorkville for supper with friends. Three hours later, filled with Wienerschnitzel, Apfel Strudel, and Gemütlichkeit, I ambled down Third Avenue, several bottles of Heinekin beer warming me against a raw March wind. As I passed a long line of people standing outside a movie theater, someone called my name. Irving Oysterman!

I had enjoyed a short affair with Irving two years earlier. My infatuation seemed ridiculous now. How ever could I have considered a giddy creature given to namedropping as a potential life partner? Had Vietnam matured or disillusioned me?

We'd parted on unfriendly terms, but Irving seemed to hold no grudge and paid my admission to an arty British film about Armageddon. I thought it pretentious, but Irving raved over its symbolic significance. As we strolled down Third Avenue, he invited me to a party. "Tonight. You must come."

"Thanks, Irving, but there's this dynamite soldier from Idaho. . . ."

He shot me a withering glance. "There will be rich and famous people at the party. *Interesting* people."

Few people could interest me more than a dynamite soldier from Idaho; nonetheless, I decided to check out the party. I could always leave.

Decorators, hairdressers, and jewelry salesmen prattled around the hors d'oeuvres. Irving rushed from one to another, compulsively dropping names. I didn't wonder who started the game "Stars of Stage and Screen Whom I Have Known in the Biblical Sense of the Word." Faggots slandered men and women who, surely, never descended to intercourse with such twits. After an hour of nonsense, Irving turned to the corner where I quietly sipped a martini. "Kurt, have *you* ever 'known' anybody famous?" Aha! Irving did harbor resentment.

"I was working the counter at Child's Pancake House on 59th and Third," I said, ignoring gasps that suggested the position comparable to sweeping up the turds of Brahma bulls in Calcutta, "when two women and a man entered the restaurant, sat down at my station, and ordered ice cream. One of the women wore a lemon suit lined with black fur;

she had lovely orangish skin. As I scooped out coffee ice cream, I recognized the woman: Barbra Streisand! I told the manager, who peered closely at her and played 'People' on the jukebox. Streisand grimaced and snapped, 'Let's get the hell out of here!' and the trio left the restaurant. That's the closest I've ever come to balling a famous person."

A dreadful silence made me envy Onan, who suffered a kinder fate when the earth opened to swallow him. No one deigned to approach the "untouchable" except an attractive butch talent agent who invited me to his apartment. As he ejaculated, he screamed nasty names and tried to strangle me. Appalled, I threw him off easily. As I dressed, he sobbed, "I'm sorry. Please stay." Fat chance.

The "dynamite" soldier from Idaho slept soundly, but half-drunk and bummed out on sex, I fell upon my bed and passed out. In the morning, I dialed Irving's unlisted number. "Why ever did you let me leave the party with a psychotic?"

"Oh, Kurt, he's had such a tragic life. Did you know he almost married ____ _____?" Irving's voice squeaked with awe. I recalled seeing snapshots in *Photoplay* of the psychotic and a wide-eyed starlet scrambling about the foundations of a house under construction. A sentence of her interview stung. "I've finally met a man in Hollywood who is neither married nor gay." A few months later, I read that she'd dumped her career and entered a religious order.

Great Jane disgusted me at dinner. She ordered an avocado salad and a pizza covered with little fishies. We attended *Don't Drink the Water.*

That night, the soldier from Idaho asked incredulously, "Do you like doing that?" I did it again as proof. After the second cumming, he repented his accessibility and reported me to the desk clerk. I changed rooms; within an hour, a robust sailor awakened before rapture and protected himself manfully. In the shower room, a brawny flyboy took offense at my proposition and threatened to detach my manhood. In the game room, a pair of strapping marines objected to my blatant cruising and discussed tearing my body from limb to limb. It was a general union of total dissent.

Because Mother and my sisters confided their experiences with few inhibitions, I knew that having a vagina resulted in the aggravation of menstruation, the danger of infection, the discomfort of pregnancy, and the agony of childbirth. Hairpies, however, sure did attract men. Francisco the Model told me about two ugly queens who underwent gender changes in Denmark, returning to Manhattan as grotesquely tall and even uglier women; hunky men swarmed about them. I considered myself presentable, yet I underwent the Labors of Hercules to seduce straight men. Because I had no pussy, I was labeled with derogatory nomenclature, suffered rejection, and contorted myself into undignified positions. Oh well! At least I could go swimming whenever I wanted.

Sunday evenings, Greyhound ran several buses to Providence, Rhode Island, where sailors changed to buses destined for Newport on one side of the Narragansett Bay or a large naval base on the other side. I sat next to a good-looking sailor, who dozed. Saturday's children having impaired my confidence, I took more time than usual to explore his bellbottoms, but I'd set the stage for rapture when the bus turned off the Connecticut Turnpike to disembark passengers in New London. The sailor stood, buttoned his bellbottoms, and walked down the aisle. I sat alone to Providence.

A two-hour wait for the next bus to Newport did nothing to alleviate anger at my caution, the diffidence that faltered. I saw no hope of redemption in the dreary collection of sailors waiting with me, so I took a corner seat and sullenly opened *Tristram Shandy*. A handsome young man of Black-Irish extraction and wearing civvies sat beside me. "When does your bus leave?"

"Eleven."

"Prefer a ride?" The "prefer" labeled him a student at Brown, or more likely, the Rhode Island School of Design.

"I've already paid for my ticket."

"Take you right to your door."

"What's the price?"

"No money." Silence. "I've heard that sailors are always horny."

"Wouldn't doubt it."

"How about you?"

"What's your angle, buddy?"

A pause. "I'm gay."

I stared with revulsion. "A cocksucker!"

He nodded, preparing to flee. "I'm real good," he reported earnestly.

"You like doing that?"

"Yeah, I do. I really like it."

"Why me? I ain't no queer."

"You're the epitome of machismo."

I couldn't help laughing. "What will you do if I turn down your offer? Come on to another sailor?"

He glanced about the terminal. "Nobody else worth it."

We agreed like bells; we wanted nothing but hanging. "It's not my bag." Disappointment clouded his face. "But I've always said I'll try anything once."

As so many Irishmen that I've bedded, he looked marvelous, talked tough, and acted butch, yet proved unremarkable between the sheets. I enjoyed his physical splendor, but for wild, delightful, uncorrupted sensualism, I preferred an innocent-looking southern boy or a tall lean Italian.

Afterward, I feigned wonder. "I can't believe I did those things."

He assumed a world-weary attitude. "Most sailors do."

"You're joking!"

"Soldiers, hitchhikers . . ."

"They do everything I did?"

"Some of them. Most are trade."

91

"What's 'trade'?"

"They prefer fellatio."

During the ride back to the bus station, the student continued my education. He had scoured New England for pick-up spots that I committed to memory. For once, I'd found where it was at before they moved it.

I returned to the stolid taciturn patients and the whining, complaining patients of Newport. I enjoyed working in the lab, but always welcomed a chance to visit the wards, especially Maternity. Following months of swollen ankles, aching backs, and hemmorhoids, the young women seemed ready for bear. They leered and muttered lewd proposals, jesting, of course, their pussies too sore for adultery. "Hey, Kurt! Wanna know how it feels to have a baby? Take your mouth and stretch it over your head."

I should have thought some of the mothers hated me for their babies' sakes. Every day, I pricked the heels of jaundiced newborns, squeezing enough blood from each to fill twenty tiny capillary tubes. The infants screamed. I felt like an ogre.

The other lab techs deserved my respect for their capabilities and the pride they took in performing well, but we had little in common. Nor had I made friends among my barrackmates. Accustomed to revealing only a small part of myself, I couldn't help wishing for a buddy, someone with whom to share an evening or two of chat. When I heard that another corpsman had arrived from Nam, I decided to make his acquaintance.

Rumor had him a bitter, unfriendly fellow who stayed to himself in a small room over the MAA's apartment. I knocked at his door. "Come in." He reclined on a bed, nude, a hefty uncut schwantz draped across his thigh.

Anecdotes about the daily life of a corpsman proved a dead end, and he showed no interest in other topics. A rough complexion and a stocky body robbed him of any claim to beauty, but his brutal masculinity fascinated me. A reliable tale about a pair of bisexual ladies caused a thick hardening that he made no attempt to hide. I confessed to a curiosity about foreskins. "May I look?"

I rose from my chair and moved slowly to the bed. He allowed me to look. I took it between my fingers and skinned back the prepuce. He stared at me, his eyes empty.

Two night later, I visited him again. He looked up and frowned. "Beat it!" I assumed that he meant "Leave."

Fuck him! I would go where I was wanted.

My twenty-sixth birthday fell upon the Ides of March; Nick called on the fourteenth to extend a dinner invitation. "I'd like you to meet Rosemary and the kids."

"Sorry, buddy, but I'm booked all weekend."

"A busy social life." Did I detect a note of jealousy?

"Old friends. Friday, I'm dining with two middleaged men whom I met five years ago. Saturday, I brunch with Francisco the Model, and I've promised the evening to Jane."

"Sunday?"

"Jane and I plan to visit her aunt in Dobbs Ferry." Silence on the other end of the line. "Why don't you come to Vince's Friday evening. He would adore you."

Nick lowered his voice. "I'm not interested in meeting faggots."

"Vince is a warm generous man and delightful company. I'm offended by your insult, which could hardly pass for a birthday gift, even in New Jersey."

Silence. "Time and address?"

Vince lived in a shabby ground-floor railroad flat packed to its dingy ceilings with the dusty accumulation of a lifetime. I rang the doorbell, a buzzer sounded, and an apricot poodle bounded down the hall into my arms. Vince fried chicken wings in oyster sauce. "Hello, baby. Where's the glorious policeman?"

"He'll be along. You've prepared my favorite dinner!"

"Happy Birthday! We'll open a bottle of my homemade

93

blueberry wine and belatedly celebrate your return to the land of the living. How's your arm?"

"Same size as the other. I no longer look like Igor the Hunchback."

"You never did, baby." The doorbell rang in a shave-and-a-haircut rhythm. "That'll be Ralphie."

A tall heavyset man wearing denims entered the kitchen and embraced me, never removing the cigar from his mouth; then he held me at arm's length and gave me the once-over. "Is that a new outfit?" My sister, Karen, had sent me a blue sweater and a pair of gray slacks. "It's gilding the lily, but you look wonderful. Then again, I've always said you'd look good in nothing at all. Vince! Whatever you're cooking smells absolutely scrumptious."

Nick arrived a few minutes later, stunning my old friends. Vince circled the uneasy trooper. "So this is the infamous Nick. Kurt's told me about your juicy dago cock. You sure can pick them, baby."

We ate dozens of chicken wings before carrying our coffee into the living room. Ralph told the story of our meeting. "I'd been out of town for several months and returned to New York deeply depressed. Rumor had it that Vince had taken up with a fabulously sexy baseball player, but people do exaggerate and I knew only too well of Vince's affinity for dreary things wearing eyeglasses." Vince protested; Ralph shrugged. "Vince insisted that I come by Christmas Eve to meet this beauty out of old legends. 'You'll kill yourself if you don't.' When Kurt walked through the door, rockets burst, lightning flashed, and a star danced, under which I was reborn. Ever since, he's been the delight of my life, continually rejuvenating these tired old eyes."

Flattery, of course, and I loved it. Vince and Ralph usually entertained me for hours with monologues about New York of the forties; both, however, employed good manners and set about drawing out Nick. We learned that the trooper had worked Vice during his first three years in law

94

enforcement. "Downtown precinct. Every new man started out as a decoy."

"Entrapment?" asked Vince softly.

"Yeah. Prostitutes . . . fags . . . uhh, homosexuals. Had to patrol public bathrooms. I hated it. Standing at a urinal with my pecker hanging out."

"A subject worthy of Caravaggio," murmured Vince.

"What exactly did you do?" I wondered.

"Glared daggers at anybody who came closer than three feet."

Ralph smiled. "Not likely to make many arrests with that attitude."

"That's what my partners said. Had to let the faggots play with it." Nick spoke bitterly. "Never once got a hard-on."

"The sound of disappointed sighs must have carried across the Hudson," Vince opined. "Every young cop goes through this?"

Nick nodded. "Kind of an initiation."

"Queers play with their cocks?"

"Suck them, too, according to my partner. Not everyone. A lot of the guys."

"Police watch each other get blowjobs?"

Nick shrugged. "I never did. The guy that trained me knew my dad. Wouldn't have fucked me over."

"How did you make arrests?"

"In public bathrooms. My partner hid in one of the booths. Cracked the door to watch. Sometimes I was wired for sound. A few places had two-way mirrors. We sat behind them and waited."

"An unwilling audience to sordid doings."

"Made me sick sometimes. Nothing against you guys, but watching old men sucking and fucking each other, making indecent proposals to young kids. We had a quota to meet, but we tried to arrest mostly slimebags." Apparently, we slimebags looked askance on such harsh punishment for a bit of fun. "Hey, they wanna make it, let them do it at home. I

95

wouldn't want my sons walking in on that crap." We couldn't fault his reasoning. "Couples of times, I worked with partners who left me hanging. I'd stall the fags long as I could, but my partner didn't come in, I'd leave. One cop I hated would let the fag work his prick all the way up; then, he beat the shit out of the poor guy. Same cop made the whores blow him for free." Nick's mouth tightened. "Seventeen years on the force and he's still on Vice, always meeting his quota. After a couple of months, I subbed on the narcotics squad. Showed an aptitude for sniffing out dopers. Never had to work the sex squad again. Three years later, I transferred to the state police."

When Vince and Ralph began trading anecdotes about their favorite tearooms (men's restrooms) along New York's subway system, I suggested to Nick that we leave. My old friends glowed; I could receive no better birthday present than a night with the handsome trooper.

Nick had parked nearby, but seemed reluctant to unlock his car. I suggested that we walk to the park adjoining the mayor's mansion, which overlooked the East River. As we ambled along the promenade, Nick broke a silence that had lasted several minutes. "I'm really pissed that you told anybody about my job."

"I always keep Vince and Ralph informed of my activities. I never dreamed that you would make a commitment. When you did, I called both and advised discretion."

"If it leaked out . . ."

"These are honorable men. They will never breathe a word."

Nick sighed. "They seem to like you."

"They've never asked for anything except my delight in their company."

"Can I ask a question?"

"Of course."

"Why do you hang around with losers?"

"Vince and Ralph enjoy many friends and like their jobs.

96

Both served their country during World War Two and each pursues an active sex life. Neither has much money, but they share what little they have."

"They hang around public bathrooms like the fags I used to arrest."

"Those women you fucked before you married—did you rescue each from a dragon while riding a white stallion?"

"I didn't meet them in sewers."

"And the whole world's wired to your ass? Queers should search for potential bedmates only in bars given the Nick Esoldi Seal of Approval?"

We turned around and retraced our steps. "Do you pick up guys in public bathrooms?"

"Not in New York, but playing ball in small towns, I had a choice of abstinence or ruining my liver in straight bars while waiting for someone to drink himself into nonchalance; yes, I occasionally cruised local johns. I'll admit to an aversion to the smell of offal and the grim numbers who seem to thrive amidst flatulence; nonetheless, I couldn't help hoping to mollify my loneliness with the gentle relief of another's care."

"Maybe you should try lying sometimes. That disgusts me."

"It disgusted me, too."

"Why do you hang around with older guys?"

"They talk so naturally about cocksucking that the stigma is removed."

"You got a brutal mouth."

"Figuratively speaking. Ralph and Vince make me feel as if my presence enriches their lives, and less self-centered than my peers, they strive to amuse and inform me."

"Old dudes talking about sex all the time . . ."

"Middle-aged prurience seems undignified from this side of forty."

"Their lives are so dead-end."

"Lilies of the field." I leaned against a railing and gazed

across the East River. "Who am I to judge whether friends live up to my sense of their potential? Far better to appreciate them as they are and profit from their examples." I knew that Nick studied my profile. "My German grandmother maintained an old-country tradition: A birthday celebrant should receive something for the inside, something for the outside, and something for the soul. Vince fed me a favorite meal; something for the inside. My sister sent these clothes: something for the outside. Ralph offered to treat me to a Mae West double feature for the elevation of my soul, but I preferred nirvana to occur in a Newark carpet shop with a devastating state trooper."

A fat queen walking his Schnauzer passed by, cruised us blatantly, and stopped six feet away, ostensibly to let the dog make doodie. "I didn't get you anything."

"How about a couple of yummy hitchhikers?"

The fat man fingered his crotch. I waited for Nick's reply, sure to be negative, perhaps explosively so. "Maybe someone at the entrance of the Turnpike. If not, soldiers coming in from Fort Dix." He cuffed my arm gently. "Guess it's time to mosey on down the trail."

A hundred yards from the Turnpike tollbooths, Nick pulled over beside a couple of good-looking youths carrying knapsacks. I opened the side door of the van, and they crawled inside. "Where are you headed?"

"Fort Lauderdale."

"Spring Break?" They nodded. "Where do you go to school?"

"Tufts."

"We can get you to the other side of Baltimore."

"Great!"

"Got any dope?"

They grinned broadly. "Sure!" One fished a plastic bag from his knapsack.

Nick pulled a pistol from under the dashboard and flashed a badge. "You could get ten-to-twenty in Jersey for carrying.

Down on the floorboards." The trooper turned the van around and drove towards Newark. The miserable youths could see nothing of our route; no identifying signs marked the back of the carpet shop. We led them up the stairs to our *chambre de l'amour*. I strip-searched the students while Nick lit the heater and rummaged through their knapsacks. He held up a second lid. "You're in big trouble, men."

The nude youths said nothing. One shivered. "You cold or scared?" I asked.

"Both. May we put our clothes back on?"

"Your drivers' licenses give the same hometown. You been friends long?"

"Since the fifth grade."

"You're both nineteen. Ever seen each other naked before?"

"Sure."

"Ever seen each other with a hard-on?"

"No sir."

"Come off it. All kids compare sizes. See how far they can shoot their loads."

"No sir. We never have."

"Sit down on the bed. No, leave your clothes on the chair." We could force them into sex with each other; I wanted Nick to see them make it with some degree of willingness. "My buddy here and I are like that. Best friends since junior high. Know each other's families. Heard every story the other has to tell. Although we've balled the same chicks on a number of occasions, we've never seen the other in action. We talk about sex, but I don't really know how he does it. We're together eight hours a day, five days a week, and spend a lot of free time at each other's houses.

"Last month, we worked Vice. Had to arrest faggots in public restrooms. We met our quota, but I felt guilty. Always knew I loved my buddy like a brother; watching faggots suck each other off, I realized that I wanted to love him that way, too. Last week, I told him. Almost destroyed

99

our friendship. Luckily, he's a free spirit. Said we would make it for curiosity's sake. Thing is, he's worried that only queers would blow each other. I said anybody might, given the right circumstances. He said 'Prove it and I'll do anything you want.' That's why we picked you up." Neither of the students seemed to understand. "I'm gonna take care of my buddy and he's going to take care of me. You guy will do the same thing."

One youth's member swelled slightly; the other asked, "What if we don't."

"You'll take a chance on serving ten-to-twenty for possession, and believe me, you'll be well-taken care of in prison, regularly gang-raped by brutal hate-filled blacks."

"We could tell your chief that you approached us."

"Think anybody would believe you?"

The boys looked at us, then at each other. "What do you think, Brent?" The other youth nodded and tried to cover his burgeoning member. The first boy looked down, shot a surprised look at Brent, and gazed into space. His unmentionable began swelling.

After watching Brent bring his best friend to a climax, Nick took the youth's anal cherry. The best friend had his turn. For the next few hours, we performed in various combinations, stopping only to wash ourselves at the sink.

At one AM, we dropped the boys near the Garden State Parkway and returned to the carpet shop. Two lids of marijuana sat on the floor. "Why didn't you let them keep the grass?"

The trooper spoke professionally. "Highway patrols up and down the Atlantic seaboard watch for the stuff. Those kids get stopped, they might talk about us. Dope's stupid at any time, but carrying it while thumbing fifteen hundred miles. . . . I'm going to throw it out."

"Maybe not."

Nick gazed at me curiously. "Thought you weren't into this shit?"

100

"I'm not. But it could come in handy." Silence. "I feel like a hypocrite. When I was a kid, a playmate who lived at the bottom of the hill had lots of neat toys and gadgets. His father used his position as a gym teacher to confiscate students' belongings and bring them home for Jared. I didn't envy Jared the toys so much as I disapproved of the way he got them." I thought a moment. "I hate waste. Let's leave the lids alongside an entrance ramp. Make some hitchhiker feel lucky." Nick chuckled and nodded. "So what did you think about that little episode?"

"I'm trying not to."

"Whatever happened to your deep interest in psychology?"

Nick bundled soiled linen and sat on the stripped bed. "Will they talk about it?"

"I long to know. I would wager they'll mention it just once to confirm their heterosexuality, asserting that they performed those disgusting acts only to avoid prison, but they've experienced each other intimately to several climaxes. I like to think that during a slack season, one might suggest repeating the procedure and the other agree. What would you have done in such a situation?"

"Don't know. Never been in it."

"Oh, Nick! A psychologist must sympathize with the problems of his patients. Imagine yourself a teenager, picked up with your best friend by perverted cops."

Nick cogitated. "I really don't know. How about you?"

"A different case. As a horny gay teenager, I probably would have loved it. My best friend, however, might have chosen death."

"I never messed around. Knew guys that did. Just never turned me on."

"No circle jerks during puberty?"

"Sure. Everybody does that. But none of us get down to dirty stuff. Some of the hoods in high school went fagbashing. Said they needed money, but we figured they got

101

blowjobs, too."

"No curiosity?"

"Nah!"

"You've never had any homosexual experiences?"

"Working Vice would turn even you off. Scumbags whining and crying and begging for mercy. . . . Trying to bribe us. Slimy faggot scumbags."

"Yet you made it with me."

Nick shook his head. "Just going along for the ride."

I spent the night alone in the carpet shop. The next morning, a piercingly beautiful man knocked at the door. "I'm Nick's brother, Mike. He'll be over in half an hour. Want some coffee?"

Mike's dullness exceeded his looks, but as "Uncle" Ralph always said, "A pretty boy is never boring." His philosophy might have been challenged by Mike. Subjects certain to interest Italo-American carpet layers—colors, texture, pizza—failed. Sports. Travel. I conversed with an amiable sponge. But those long eyelashes shadowing deep blue eyes. Hairy muscular forearms. A slinky masculine walk. I could have talked with him for hours.

As Nick drove into Manhattan, I remarked upon Mike. "He's not very vivacious."

"No," said the trooper shortly.

I changed the subject.

Nick parked under the West Side Highway and we walked to the charming cul-de-sac in Greenwich Village where Francisco the Model lived in a very smart apartment. Now nearing middle age, our host had been renowned for two decades as one of Manhattan's great beauties; his photographs advertised clothes and luxuries in every magazine. An illiterate celebrity chaser of crude upbringing, the generous Latin threw amusing parties, shared my appetite for vicious gossip, and delighted in finding me bedpartners among the triumphant.

Using the excuse of my birthday to hold a brunch, the

gregarious model had invited a dozen sparkling guests. Our entrance interrupted a game of "Botticelli." "Are you a German playwright who shot his noble mistress before committing suicide?"

"No, I am not Kleist."

Distracted by our arrival, Francisco hadn't heard the question. "Who is Kleist?" he whispered.

"The Chinese Messiah," I replied.

After handing Nick a drink and setting him between a rising young Off-Broadway actor and a Harvard law student, the Latin bade me follow him into the kitchen. "He's divine! Rough trade?" I shook my head. "Dios mio! Isn't anyone straight anymore? Where did you find him?"

"Howard Johnson's. They have twenty-six other flavors."

"You complement each other well. Do I see the beginning of a love affair?"

"Just a fling. He's sensational in bed and likes to play games."

Francisco's eyes glittered. "Will you share him?"

"He's not into queers." The model's eyebrow lifted. "Don't push it, and you might succeed."

"I marvel at your lack of jealousy."

"The last person for whom I felt jealousy was you, my amigo."

Francisco caressed my cheek with a finger. "Whores like us are better sisters."

"At twenty, I couldn't comprehend that."

"You've forgiven me?"

"You broke my heart. I wouldn't have missed that experience for the world."

Francisco pulled a tray of scones from the oven. "I invited the elegant blond for you. A Danish baron with millions from beer. I suppose you're not interested."

I had noticed the noble Dane. "Nick's leaving early. And it is my birthday."

As Francisco had invited the more masculine among his

103

acquaintance, Nick felt comfortable, although their wit and intelligence astonished him. I walked the trooper to his van. "Enjoy yourself?"

"Sure is different from the crowd I run around with."

"Women in the kitchen talking about babies; the men discussing automotive parts." He nodded. "Everyone liked you."

"I didn't say much."

"You didn't have to."

Nick blushed. "I made a commitment."

I nodded. "Bless the day!"

Hamlet stayed in a suite at the Plaza. I'd had more fun in the carpet shop.

That evening, Jane and I went on a double date with her roommate, Rachel, and a stranger. After souvlaki and baklava, we stopped by a West Side nightclub. As a fat colored queen moaned "Memphis in June," I dropped my napkin under the table. Retrieving it, my hand brushed Rachel's shapely calf. I apologized. "I didn't mean to."

Jane's best friend leaned against me and whispered violently, "Oh, Kurt, I wish you had." So much for honor among women.

Rachel had been furthering her sexual education with a married man and issued complete reports to Jane after every session: The man could boast of technical proficiency, but lacked the pizazz of Rachel's fiancé, who attended medical school in Boston. I wondered what Jane told Rachel. Not much, I'm sure. While the adulterers cuckolded wife and fiancé in the bedroom, Jane and I made abortive ado on the living room couch.

I returned to the Enlisted Man's Club and seduced my roommate, an easygoing air jockey from Wichita, Kansas. When the clerk slipped upstairs for sloppy seconds, I watched the desk. A disconsolate little soldier knocked at the door. "Every YMCA is filled, and I can't afford a hotel."

"We're filled, too, but there's an empty couch in the

104

library." Considering the literary aspirations of most service-men, I inferred that he would sleep undisturbed. The desk clerk and I compared notes about the airman before I tip-toed in the library. The little soldier awakened during rap-ture. Half the men so compromised eventually capitulated; most of the rest growled and turned over. The soldier proved the tenth man. He threatened to kill me. A Chihuahua snapping at a Doberman Pinscher. Owing him dignity, I retreated.

Two more lab techs joined the duty roster, one a Jew from New York who seemed amused by all I said or did. He invited me to dinner, although his wife obviously disliked me. Wives usually did, and I'd never understood why. My manners were exemplary. I listened attentively to their inane babbling. In this situation, I harbored no lust for the husband. Perhaps the snippy little brunette resented my learning over dessert about their lovemaking. "Last night," recalled my co-worker, "we experienced our first mutual orgasm."

A blond NP tech with whom I'd coupled in the snow had married; he invited me to meet the "Little Woman," a hard-bitten dyke if ever I'd seen one. I was driven to their house outside town by Montchanin, head corpsman on the Neuro-Psychiatric Ward and an impossible dream. I'd taken a fifth of Scotch for a wedding present; the malevolent dyke served it to me in a mug. During three rubbers of bridge, she kept refilling the mug while the others sipped beer. I spent the shank of the evening outside in my shirt-sleeves, making angel wings in the snow.

On the way back to Newport, I stretched across the front seat with my head snuggled in the handsome Montchanin's lap. After a futile effort to dislodge me, the stud gave it up to concentrate on the icy winding road. As I reached for his zipper, I passed out. I awakened the next morning, undressed and in my bunk. Oh god, that man should put an enemy in their mouths to steal away their brains.

105

The Yellow Yeti took a month's leave, so I stood duty with a tech who resembled a death's head. The Skull's pitted face and pale knobby body would have dismayed a leper, but one day he joined me at the lab's urinal. His unmentionable could have won prizes.

As he'd followed me into the restroom and visually measured my Precious, I thought it his place to make a pass. He didn't. The Skull planned to marry in a month, which confused the issue. I waited until he slept to take his manhood and my military career in hand.

Someone knocked softly. I jumped up, threw a sheet over the Skull, and opened the door to a tearful WAVE holding a newborn infant. "It's not dead! I know it's not dead!" She threw the infant at me and ran away. I put the body in the reefer and returned to the bunk room, where the Skull stirred restlessly. The spell had been broken anyway.

The next morning, the Skull invited me to spend the following weekend in Vermont. "You can bunk with my brother. He's retarded, but a real sweet guy. You'll like each other." Uncertain as to how soundly the Skull had slept, I considered the prospect too kinky to accept.

"Why not?" said Paul grandly. "He probably has a big dick, too."

"I could celebrate no triumph by seducing a retard."

"I can't imagine it a triumph to seduce someone with a pale knobby body who looks like a death's head."

"Neither his body nor his face interested me. His unmentionable happened to be a thing of beauty."

"Ah ha! You admit that you're a size queen." Having vanquished me, Paul settled back in his chair.

"I've attained content with three skinny inches, although an overendowment can quicken my interest. Yours, too, if I rightly recall an ex-lover with a gargantuan appendage."

"I prefer to rejoice in the entire person, both body and soul."

"I prefer to keep the two apart. Paul, I'll have sex because of a bewitching smile, a hairy chest, or a cowboy stride. In my salad days, I had sex with nondescript types merely because they asked me. Should I demand physical and mental perfection, which smacks of hypocrisy, I might have remained a virgin to the grave. The Skull had a lovely penis. Should I deny myself the pleasure of admiring that beauty because the rest of him appeared unpreposing?"

"You rationalize."

"Could I exist otherwise? I admire the paintings of Goya, Vermeer, Masaccio, Renoir, and Klee, who paint dissimilar subjects with varying techniques. Must I enjoy only the work of one to the exclusion of the others?"

"What a ridiculous simile!" Paul tapped his foot in irritation. "Fate gave you a remarkable physical presence and an enquiring mind of some intelligence. You should seek others of such ilk."

"I would never deny you those fluttering, posturing wimps whom you find adorable despite their repelling vapidity."

Paul swelled like a toad. "Go back to your Skull and enjoy an affair lasting decades. I couldn't care less."

"I don't want an affair!"

"Yet I continue to hear of a New Jersey state trooper."

"A married state trooper with four-and-a-half children. I'm little more to him than a passing enthusiasm. An object of curiosity. Never underestimate my sense of proportion."

Paul's harsh laughter elicited no offense. 'Tis impious in a good man to be sad.

My old pal's admonitions couldn't halt my nefarious activities. Every morning, an alarm clock rang in a cubicle across the aisle. It belonged to a tall redhead with great legs who jumped from his bunk to turn off the alarm, a morning pisshard jutting through the fly of his drawers. Tiernan was the first of the Master-at-Arms' conquests in the night barrack whom I planned to seduce.

I filled a bag with gear from the laboratory, usurped the MAA's apartment for the evening, and invited the good-looking redhead to step into my parlor. "A report has crossed the admiral's desk that at least three men have been fellated while sleeping in the night barrack. You have been identified as one of the men."

The green-eyed Tiernan replied coolly. "Not me."

"The admiral knows that you didn't instigate the action and stopped it when you realized what was happening. He's interested in the identity of the phantom fellator, not in hassling the victims."

"You've got the wrong victim. I don't know anything about it."

I had the right victim. The MAA reported that Tiernan had awakened and cuffed him soundly. "This pervert reflects badly upon the tight ship run by the admiral. Theoretically, you could receive a dishonorable discharge that would haunt you for the rest of your life. You would lose the GI Bill, VA benefits. . . . Prospective employers would be told you're a homosexual. So would your family."

"I don't know anything about it."

Had the MAA misinformed me? Plunging ahead, I said, "Homosexuals have a gland in their throats that craves semen. Unless this craving is sated, the gland secretes corydon cells into the brain, which leads to Proustomania." I paraphrased what my best friend had told me in high school. Horrified by his ridiculous theory, I had felt consoled at the same time: A queer like me couldn't help himself. "The homosexual maintains his sanity by fellating other men. During an act of fellatio, corydon cells enter the penis being sucked and lodge in the suckee's vas deferens. Scientists in Australia have developed a test to isolate corydon cells from the suckee's sperm and match them to the homosexual's saliva. It's called the 'Melbourne Method.'"

"What if I refuse?"

I might have been the one who received a dishonorable discharge. "At the very least, you would climb to the top of the admiral's shitlist. You'd probably receive orders for

108

Vietnam. I went to Nam with eight hundred other corps-men. Only two hundred and sixty lasted the year."

"Why are you doing the test instead of a doctor?"

"Because I'm a lab technician who served in Nam, where men without women performed bizarre acts. Having learned to revere grace under pressure, I would never censure a man for indulging in occasional deviance. The average doctor, conservative if not small minded, might feel that the victims should be discharged from the Navy along with the pervert. With nurses humping their legs at every opportunity, doc-tors don't know what it is to be horny."

"Why do you need sperm? Why can't you examine the suspect's saliva?"

Had I mentioned a suspect? Sometimes, these arias of improvisation confused me. "The corydon cells secrete only during fellatio. We must match the saliva in your sperm with that of the suspect's."

"What kind of test is it?"

Upon the beside table, I had set two tubes holding dry chemicals, a bottle of alcohol, cotton swabs, sterile towels, and sterile gloves. "I need a sample of your sperm in this tube."

He glanced at the bathroom. "That where I'm supposed to do it?"

"No! The 'Melbourne Method' calls for a sterile catch." (An uncontaminated specimen.)

"No big deal. I could do it."

"Any contamination could give an inaccurate reading. I have to do it."

"You gonna watch me beat off!"

"Oh, for crissake! I see you with a pisshard every morn-ing." I locked the door and turned around. Tiernan gazed miserably at the bed. "Hey, buddy! It's not as if I've never done it."

"I got a *Playboy* in my locker," he said hopefully.

"Take off your uniform." He obeyed. "I won't look until

109

you're ready."

A minute passed. "I'm embarrassed."

I opened my eyes. Tiernan lay on the bed, fingering a limp log. I sighed with exasperation, kicked off my shoes, peeled off my whites, and set to work on Precious, which erected within seconds. Tiernan tried again without success. "Close your eyes and think of pussy." Nothing happened.

I told Tiernan about those lesbian ladies, who now lived in Boston. He listened attentively. "I'm ready now."

"Wait! This must be a sterile catch." I poured alcohol on a cotton swab and cleaned his penis, breaking another taboo when I held it in my hand. By the time I'd wiped the test tube and set it on a sterile towel, he had gone limp. I sat on the bed, my hand resting on his leg. "Better try again." I helped by lightly brushing my fingertips across his thighs and testicles.

"I'm ready."

I could tell. I cleaned him once more and held the tube against the opening of his urethra. "Ejaculate."

"I'll have to work it up again."

"Don't touch yourself! You'll contaminate the sterile field."

"If I don't touch myself, I can't ejaculate."

"Ain't this a bitch!" I manipulated him with my gloved hand.

Two minutes passed. "Why did you stop? I was just about ready to shoot."

"I'd better tell you something. When you asked why I was doing the test, I didn't tell you the whole truth. I'm another of the victims. I tried to do my own test, but . . . Would you help?" Tiernan glanced at a throbbing Precious and shrugged, his tumescence undiminished. As he pulled on a pair of sterile gloves, I crawled into the bed. We lay in a sixty-nine position and took each other in hand. He caught my semen in the tube; his would be absorbed by my diges-tive system. I apologized for such inexplicable behavior. "It's

110

been two weeks since I balled my old lady. I was really hot."

He nodded. "What'll we do now?"

I smiled ruefully. "We try again."

He grimaced. "Let me take a leak first."

This time, Tiernan lay back, eyes closed and hands cradling his head. I began with prolonged rapture. Tiernan accepted my ministrations with a frown, but didn't urge me to hurry. Immediately after I collected a specimen, he dressed and left without saying a word.

Later that week, I hosted a well-formed corpsman from Orthopedics. The dark-haired Reynolds had awakened while the MAA manipulated his unmentionable; the corpsman's surprised cry had frightened off the sneaky rat before he could proceed to fellatio. The virginal sailor protested any carnal contact, so I convinced him that the "Melbourne Method" would prove his innocence. An hour later, he left the apartment lacking the sun-clad power of chastity.

Jane visited Newport that weekend. I rented a spacious room with an ocean view at the beginning of Cliff Walk. A cold wind rattled our windows.

Travel brochure proclaimed Newport to be the most interesting small town in America. A tower supposedly built by Vikings stood near the country's oldest Jewish cemetery. Houses dating from colonial days clustered around the port. The town's greatest splendor occurred during Victorian and Edwardian summers.

Cliff Walk meandered for three miles above crashing waves and through the backyards of magnificent summer cottages, replicas of French and Italian chateaux that would currently cost thirty to fifty millions to build. Haunts of the very rich. Jane and I had walked halfway when she turned her ankle; I offered to carry her back to the hotel, but my fiancée insisted gamely upon continuing to the end. A heavy drizzle soaked us on the way back.

After supper, my Precious functioned for a few minutes,

111

but drooped too soon. Jane tried artlessly to raise it. Mortified, I pleaded weariness and pretended to sleep. Jane sewed.

Sunday evening, I put her aboard a Greyhound. As I strolled towards base, a white Pontiac stopped beside me. A Portuguese with dark curly hair and a foxy face beckoned. When I approached the car, he patted the empty seat beside him.

The interior of the car smelled like perfume. A queen! He pulled into traffic before I could get out. Shit! Staring through the windshield, he unrolled a whopper. Hating to pass it up, yet still on the limp side of randiness, I admired its size and shape. He pulled my head into his crotch. "Suck it!"

Maybe he wasn't a queen. I fancied his authority. I performed.

Following his climax, he pulled the car over. "Get out!" I walked for twenty minutes before recognizing a landmark six miles from the naval hospital. Rain began to pour.

A moral, sensible, and wellbred man will not affront me and no other can.

April 1968

An outbreak of German measles occurred at the Officers' Candidate School. The next morning, I arrived on an outlying ward to find a dozen young men victims of the malady. A good-looking ensign fainted when I injected the needle; feeling contempt for his pusillanimity, I slid my hand into his pajamas for a quick feel.

After breakfast, I entered the Medical Service Lieutenant's office to announce my exposure to contagion. "I shouldn't be leeching pregnant women." The lieutenant brushed off my objection. "You ever seen those pictures of little kids wearing thick glasses and hearing aids!"

The lieutenant smiled blandly. As I refused to leave his office, he stared at papers spread upon his desk. I waited. He shuffled the papers. I stalked to the bunkroom. Fifteen minutes later, the secretary knocked at the door, opened it, and peered at me. "People are waiting to have their blood drawn." I glared at her. Half an hour later, word came down that I was to exchange jobs with the tech working in Urinalysis.

The "Melbourne Method" succeeded with the third of the MAA's boys from the night barrack, a wiry little Scot, butch and remote, who transmuted into cuddly amiability. (Awakening with the MAA slurping about his unmentionable, McDade had merely pushed him away with a warning.) I continued to be tantalized by four unsullied men, including

113

the muscular SEAL; he had returned from the Arctic and dazzled me thrice a week in the gym.

Thursday afternoon, as I pored over a slide of urine, the Yellow Yeti tapped me on the shoulder. "You got a visitor up front. That civilian."

Nick! "You have duty tonight?"

"No."

"I'll get a motel room."

"Great! I'm off at three. Come see my office." Nick sat beside the microscope and I taught him how to read a slide. A plan occurred to me. Speaking softly to frustrate a nosy lifer working Chemistry, I asked, "Wanna play a game?"

My trooper smiled wolfishly. "Sure."

"During your years as an undercover cop sniffing out drug dealers, you had to play scenes by ear, right?" Nick nodded. "Good at it?"

"I hate to brag . . ."

"You are Captain Vince Nicholas, Ph.D. in Psychology from Rutgers, stationed at Annapolis."

"Got it."

I reached for my telephone. "You're going to request an interview at nineteen hundred hours with Graham Montchanin, Hospitalman Second Class. He's head corpsman on the Neuro-Psychiatric Ward, home of the fruits and the nuts."

"Thought that was California."

"They're everywhere, buddy."

Montchanin agreed to the meeting. "What's he like?"

"Good-looking, well-built, sensitive, and intelligent. Patients respond to him, corpsmen like him, doctors trust him, and nurses despise him. Probably the outstanding enlisted man on base. Although he seems amiable, I've been too shy of his magnificent looks to further our acquaintance."

"Shy!" Nick snorted. "I watched you with those dudes at Francisco's bash. They were all good-looking, rich, and sort of famous, yet who was it they looked at?"

114

"I walked in with the sexiest man they'd ever seen. Everyone wondered what you saw in me."

"More a case of vice-versa."

"We're a mutual admiration society."

"Every guy there flirted with you, and you never noticed."

"I noticed. Perhaps after years of fending off importune passes by unsightly queens, I've learned to invite intimacy on my own terms."

"When you went back to the party, I'll bet every guy there invited you to dinner or something."

This was one sharp cookie. "Only because they hoped to meet you through me."

Nick nodded with satisfaction. "I felt tongue-tied. Out of my depth. Must be nice to feel secure wherever you go."

"You're kidding! In high school, I stood in awe of upperclassmen and the popular kids; if one condescended to speak, he got a reply half-strangled by the sense of my inferiority. The strangulated replies continued in college, where I was the only outsider among students who had known each other for years. I've never talked easily with teachers, professors, doctors, officers, bosses. . . . A couple of major leaguers spoke to me during spring training; I could only grunt."

"You have a gift of gab the Irish would kill for."

"To be shy is to be self-absorbed and bad-mannered. One discomforts others. And diffidence will never get me into a hunky dude's pants."

After work, I led Nick on a tour of Newport. At supper, we elaborated upon our plan. I watched Nick light a cigarette. Such a masculine guy! I sighed with content. "Why did you come up?"

"Rosemary and me had a fight. She took the kids to her sister's. I rattled around the house—it's my day off. Decided to pack a bag."

"Must have been a whopper of an argument."

115

Nick shrugged. "The house was closing in on her. This gives her an excuse to sit and bitch with her sister about their lives."

"And their husbands?"

"I got some bad habits that annoy her. Smoking most of all." He blew a smoke ring.

"Does Rosemary suspect that you're playing around?"

"She don't give me any, so what's her gripe." He shook his head. "She'd never guess the things we do."

"I can't quite believe it myself."

At five minutes to seven, I saw Montchanin's car pull into the motel parking lot. I left my vantage point across the street and approached Nick's room, expressing polite surprise at meeting the NP tech.

Nick opened the door and bade us enter. "At ease, men. Take a seat." As he grabbed the only chair in the room, Montchanin and I perched gingerly on the bed. We listened while Nick spoke of a study that would prove or disprove the theory that homosexuals were unfit for military duty. He supervised the committee, with two psychiatrists and an intelligence officer working under him; two enlisted men were needed. "A lab tech and a neuro-psychiatric tech. Each of you would be transferred to Washington, raised in rank to First Class, and given a generous expense account."

Montchanin demurred. "I leave next month for Vietnam."

I hadn't known that, but Nick detoured well. "Do you want to go?"

"I've almost convinced myself that it would be to my advantage."

"Your orders could be changed. Think it over."

I spoke. "Sir, this study sounds like a long-range project."

"Two years."

I had to keep the trooper on his toes. "My enlistment is up in six months."

He scowled. "Your tour of duty can be extended for eighteen more months. You will be adequately compensated.

What are your plans after the service?"

"College.'"

"Montchanin?"

"College, sir."

"Both of you could attend classes at Georgetown, a fine university. All expenses paid." Neither Montchanin nor I could think of any reasons to decline the offer. "Excellent! Now, getting down to brass tacks, have either of you ever had a homosexual experience?" We chorused our negatives. "This is off the record."

"Sir," I said meekly, "the Navy is not above entrapment. If I've had a homosexual experience, and I'm not saying I have, why should I chance a dishonorable discharge by telling you about it?"

"I'd hoped to have men on the committee who would feel free to speak openly."

"Begging your pardon, sir, but speaking freely, have you ever had a homosexual experience?"

"No."

"The other officers on your committee?"

"Not to my knowledge."

"You expect to study homosexuality without ever having experienced it?"

"We have books, tapes, films, interviews. . . ."

"Isn't that like studying soldiers in combat while watching newsreels?"

"Not exactly." Bemused, Nick glared at us; suddenly, I realized that he had forgotten the rest of our scenario. Could he improvise? A long silence followed.

"You don't have a homosexual on your committee?"

Nick looked at me blankly. "No."

"A delicate subject. In the wrong hands, leaked to the press, the study could be political dynamite."

"Yeah."

"Why were we chosen?" No reply. "Montchanin has a good reputation and he's obviously a handsome guy. . . ."

117

Nick recalled the dialogue. "That's why. We figured faggots would come on to dudes that look like you two." Not exactly the right dialogue, but close enough. "Have they?" I nodded. So did Montchanin. "Tell me the details." Silence. "How do I gain your confidence?"

"By convincing us there's no hidden camera or tape recorder in this room."

Nick stood and walked to the window, staring at the parking lot for a minute. He drew the drapes, locked the door, and turned to face us. "Strip!"

"Sir?"

"Strip down to your skivvies."

Montchanin blinked. "Is that an order, sir?"

"You're goddam right it's an order, stud. Snap to it!" We removed our uniforms; Nick tore off his civilian togs. "Should any cameras or tape recorders be hidden in this room, I am . . . Captain . . . Vince Nicholas, United States Army . . . Navy . . . standing nude in a motel room with two enlisted men . . . take off your skivvies, . . . who are also nude. I am head of a committee that . . . uh . . . will decide whether faggots should be in the Army . . . Navy . . . Marine Corps or the Air Force . . . the military. Every man on the committee will . . . uh . . . perform unnatural acts . . . so they'll understand faggots better. I ain't somebody to ask my men to do something I wouldn't, so I'll start. First, I work myself up. Second, I fall to my knees in front of Strom, a medic. I blow him some. Now I blow Montchanin, another medic." Ten minutes later, I leaned against the wall, gazing down at Montchanin's bobbing head while Nick opened a tube of K-Y lubricant.

Montchanin dropped me at the front gate of the hospital, where Nick picked me up ten minutes later. We drove to a bar near the docks. "Sorry about forgetting my lines."

"Experienced actors rehearse plays for a month or more. You had an hour to improvise your role. Hey, it worked!"

"Sure did. Thought you said he was smart."

118

"You would have convinced Doubting Thomas."

"I'm wondering how many of my friends messed around with other guys."

"A shame that the mind is so private. What's the difference between making it with a man and making it with a woman?"

"No comparison."

"Details."

"Christ, Kurt!" Nick sat back and looked at me with exasperation. "I ain't used to anyone asking my opinion." He lit a cigarette. Another, half-smoked, lay propped in an ashtray. "A woman's made for fucking. Everything about her is soft. It's natural."

"A man?"

"More of a head trip. Men got tight assholes and it feels great getting head, but . . . I'm not all hot and bothered. I like the idea they're virgins. Putting it where no man has been before. I don't have to worry about V.D. or getting them pregnant or feeling guilty for not loving them. The women I've balled . . . if I wasn't around, they'd have balled some other dude. Rosemary would have fallen in love, married, and had kids, even if I never existed. These guys—Montchanin, Terry from Newark, the hitchhikers from Tufts—they might not have done these things except for me and you. Unless they're raped, women choose who they ball. We chose these guys." Nick motioned for the bartenders, who refilled our glasses. "I don't much like giving head and nobody's going to put it up my ass, but . . . I like using my brain to get my rocks off. I like using psychology. Only thing, I kinda wish I knew these guys before . . ."

"Perhaps we should seduce somebody you know."

"I ain't shitting in my own backyard."

"What about your high school superstar?"

Nick gazed at me searchingly. "Think you could work something up?"

"You know where he is?"

"I could find out."

"Do that."

Nick smiled. "You really dig this."

"Turning my fantasies into reality? Of course. Inspired, I'll return to the barracks and fill a slim volume with poems."

"You look as good as I've ever seen you."

"A fine dinner, great sex, a couple of beers with a dynamite buddy. . . . One of the best evenings of my life. It really turned me on to watch you go down on Montchanin."

Nick reddened. "Wanted to see the difference between you and somebody else."

"Was there?"

"Well, sure. I like you."

"You'll be taking it up the ass next."

The trooper's face closed. "Never."

I backed off and attacked from another direction. "Did you enjoy servicing Montchanin?"

"Felt strange. Your skin's smooth; he's hairy. Not built like you. Not so muscular. Not like a statue. Smaller prick. Spongier. I didn't mind. Nobody forced me." He coughed. "I kept thinking about getting into that tight ass."

"Ahh!"

The trooper appeared worried. "You push buttons I never knew I had. How did you know?"

"While stationed in Boston, I developed a passion for a bartender in a small gay bar. Terrific guy. Happy Jack. Denizens gasped about the length and breadth of his unmentionable, but no one could prove intimate contact. One slow night, we talked for hours. Like you, Jack's easily amused; after the bar closed, he invited me home. He had the prettiest cock I'd ever seen. Eminently suckable. But he held back. Couldn't ejaculate. He asked me to cease and desist, but I began a fantasy about horny baseball players."

"Sounds interesting."

"I've jerked off to it a couple of times. Anyway, I spouted

my monologue and stroked his unmentionable. Didn't work. I consider masochists boring because they usually demand fantasies for their titillation, but I enjoyed spinning yarns for Jack. I started another tale: He is asked to lecture a junior high gym class on masturbation; Jack describes the process, strips, and shows the boys how it's done. As I spoke, Jack thrashed about on the bed, almost screaming when he popped his load. Afterward, he asked how I knew, admitting a compulsion that sent him to ballfields and swimming holes where adolescent boys gathered, sitting in his car with the door open while he masturbated. Extremely self-destructive—the boys could have reported his license plate—but if they watched, he experienced ecstasy."

"You pushed his button."

"How did I know? We'd never mentioned sex in the bar."

"Did you see him again?"

"You bet. Jack was the most amiable man I'd ever met."

"You become lovers?"

"Would have been nice. Jack liked to make people comfortable. I enjoy comfort. He cooked like Julia Child's nephew. I amused him. Bed worked."

"Why didn't it happen?"

"Monogamy shrivels my soul. I'd pick up guys in the bar where Jack worked and return after a round of sex expecting to go home with him, my face flushed, my eyes starry. He understood, I think. Even approved. It didn't bother him, because I wasn't his type."

"What did he like? Lizards?"

"Older men. Daddy figures. His father abandoned the family when Jack was twelve. At fifteen, he moved in with the middle-aged man who seduced him. Cleaved to the man for twenty years, until 'Daddy' humiliated Jack by flagrantly two-timing him with a new youngster. When I met him, Jack was marking time while waiting for another older man who could take care of him."

"How did you feel about Jack exposing himself to kids?"

121

"It's easy to disparage another's compulsion. At thirteen, I would have been thrilled to see Jack pounding away for my benefit, knowing a masculine good-looking guy could be queer, too, instead of identifying with lisping sissies in school and the toothless old men at the parish courthouse."

"I guess faggots don't have role models."

"Batman and Robin."

Nick had to think a moment about that. "Montchanin could talk."

"Never get anything without taking chances; besides, he's in just as deep. I would deny the episode. No use worrying."

"How do you work it alone?" I explained the "Melbourne Method." "You didn't get into their asses?"

"Couldn't contrive a scenario that included buttfucking."

"Tiernan looks good, huh?"

"Flawless, except for a small birthmark on his right buttock."

"Hey! It's past twelve. Better get you back to the barracks."

At two AM, a Navy captain shook me awake. "Rise and shine!"

"Nick?"

"Shh!"

"You could go to jail for wearing that uniform."

"No shit!"

"Where ever did you get it?"

"Stole it."

"Stole it!"

"Where's the redhead with the green eyes and the pretty ass?"

"Tiernan? Now? Jesus, Nick! I have to get up at five."

"Then I'll take him alone and tell you about it later."

"The devil you will! He's across the aisle in the top bunk."

Rubbing sleep from our eyes, Tiernan and I followed Nick out a back door and through the rear gate to his van. He drove to the motel. Considering our earlier session, Tiernan must have been worried. We followed Captain Nicholas into his room and stood at attention. Nick circled us threateningly. "I'm with Naval Intelligence, assigned to surveillance following reports of drug dealing here in Newport. Suspicion fell upon a couple of men with access to the Master-at-Arms' apartment, so we set up a hidden camera that automatically took pictures whenever anyone entered it. Guess whose pictures got took?" Nick sat back in the chair, a diabolical smile playing about his lips. "The pictures came out real clear. For instance, Strom has scars on his forearm, elbow, rib cage, and buttocks. Am I right?"

"No sir."

"Bull! You lie! Strip!" Nick gloated over my scars. "Tiernan. A birthmark on your butt." Tiernan nodded. "Let's see it. Strip." Tiernan stood bareass. "You two have a choice. Deny what you did, and not only will I assure you of dishonorable discharges, I'll send copies of each photo to your families and to every girl in your high school yearbooks." Nick reported later that Tiernan paled so visibly, he thought the sailor would faint.

I cleared my throat. "What's our alternative?"

"Well . . . Those pictures were kind of interesting. My wife doesn't like giving head. You hear what I'm saying?"

"Yes sir."

"If my old whopper gets some relief, I might find it in my heart to tear up the pictures and flush them down the toilet." I looked at Tiernan, who swallowed and nodded. Nick opened his legs. "You first, Red."

The following afternoon, Nick drove his van aboard the ferry that crossed the bay. I sauntered on deck, looking for a likely prospect among a couple of dozen sailors hoping to hitch rides west. A tall SeaBee with muscular arms straining against his middy blouse swaggered to a rail and stared at the water. Nick and I converged on a point five feet away. He wore the captain's uniform, so I saluted.

Nick spoke gruffly. "Going to New York?"

123

"Yes sir."

"Need a ride?"

"Yes sir."

Nick looked past me at the SeaBee we stalked. "How about you, sailor?"

"I'd appreciate it, sir."

The ferry crossed the bay. Nick led us to the van and we disembarked. The trooper passed around a pint of peach brandy; after several minutes of three-way chat, Nick said, "Feels good to get out of Newport."

The SeaBee agreed. "Sure does."

"Going home to see your girl?"

"Yes sir. Allentown, Pennsylvania. We got engaged last month."

"Great! See your family. Eat some pussy. Am I right?"

The SeaBee decided not to take offense. "Yes sir."

"How about you, doc? Glad to leave Newport behind?"

"I'd fuck a dromedary to get out that pesthole filled with whores and faggots."

Nick glanced my way. "We must run in different circles."

"Thames Street. Last weekend. Hit the bars. Met a chick. Nothing special. She had a hole. Invited me to her motel room. I must of been drunker'n I've ever been, 'cause I passed out before we got down to any action. Woke up, my wallet's gone and a dude's copping some head from me. Christ! I open my eyes all the way, see another dude zipping up his pants, leering at me. Said, 'You'd better wipe off your chin,' and leaves. The fucker had pronged my mouth while I slept."

Nick whistled. "You know him?"

"Nah!" I stared malignantly at our passenger. "A SeaBee. Good-looking dude. Pissed me right off."

"What did you do?"

"What could I do? Let the other guy cop my load and got the hell out of there. Two weeks pay gone. I'm heading for New York stone-broke, but I had to put some distance between me and Rhode Island even if I have to sleep on a park bench."

Nick offered me five dollars. " 'Least you can eat."

"Thanks, ace, but I pay my own way. If I'm that foolish, I deserve to suffer."

"You could earn a few bucks."

"How?"

"You seem more upset about losing your money than sucking off another fellow."

"I served in Nam. My sergeant and a couple of other marines—whenever we stood perimeter watch together, we helped each other out."

"What do you mean?"

"Too dangerous to mess with women. They put razor blades up their snatches, for crissake! Only way to get our rocks off was with each other. No big deal."

"Might be worth money to some guys to have you help them out."

I studied Nick's profile thoughtfully. "Like . . . how much?"

"Ten dollars."

"You?"

"Unless I'm too old and ugly."

"Nah, it ain't that. How about twenty?"

"Sure."

"Pull over."

Nick drove into the countryside and parked in a copse of trees. We joined the uneasy SeaBee in the back of the van. "Want me to wait outside?"

"Hell, no!" cried Nick. "He does a good job, I'll slip him another twenty to take care of you."

The SeaBee watched with furrowed brow. Whatever his predisposition, the action turned him on. Nick pushed me toward the sailor. As I prolonged rapture, the trooper slid behind the handsome youth. "No, man! That's too heavy."

Nick spit on his hand. "You gotta try everything once."

125

My firm grip on the SeaBee's testicles decided him to oblige.

We dropped the kid at the entrance of the Lincoln Tunnel and continued on to the Village. I returned Nick's forty dollars. "Tell me how you stole that uniform."

"Son-of-a-bitch deserved it."

"I'm waiting on pins and needles for the story."

"After I dropped you at the barracks, I decided to have another beer. Sat at a table, noticed a captain, drunk and disorderly, with a nasty mouth. A couple of civilians sitting down the bar got disgusted and left. The barmaid turned her back, the captain pocketed the civilians' tips. Couple of bucks. I flashed my badge, told him to follow me to the men's room. When I read him the Miranda, he started blubbering, begged for another chance. I refused, said I'd have to arrest him, but at the moment, was tailing a drug dealer. Ordered him to stay in the men's room. He swore he would. I didn't believe him. Told him to take off the uniform, that I'd hold it till I was ready to take him in. Then I dropped two dollars on my table and blew the joint."

"You stole his uniform!"

"He was an asshole."

Francisco the Model treated us to dinner at a new "in" restaurant; then we dragged the trooper into Julius, a Village establishment that opened when Noah danced naked. Years earlier, I'd entered its premises with my heart thumping in anticipation; now the stifing crowd annoyed me. Nick's looks made him the star of the evening, so Francisco stood with us long enough to establish our association before joining some friends. Nick had no craving for stardom. "Everyone's a fag, and they're all staring at us."

"Appears you would bring top dollar on the open market."

"I could give a shit. Let's get out of here." We said goodbye to Francisco and walked towards Washington Square. "Kurt, I don't want to meet any more faggots. I ain't worried about my masculinity and I don't have any secret desire to be like those guys and I sure don't want in their pants. I like learning psychology from you. Maybe I could learn from Francisco or Vince or those fruits in the bar, but they make me uncomfortable."

"You dislike being mentally undressed, grossly propositioned, and lasciviously groped." Nick stared. "The ugly fat bald man next to you."

My buddy laughed. "You don't miss much."

"Now you know what an attractive woman endures."

Nick threw himself upon a bench and cogitated. "Never thought of that. Okay, I'm a quick learner. No more bars." We watched people pass by: students, queers, village characters, village idiots . . . "I'm not a hypocrite. I never put gross moves on a chick, even when I was a kid."

"Really! You're Italian."

"So's Pinocchio. You see him pinching the Blue Fairy?"

I'll be damned! The Dago had wit, too. "Next lesson."

"No fags!"

"You seduce a guy by yourself."

"How?"

"Use your imagination."

Nick considered. "Won't be fun without you."

"Break the ice and we'll make it a threesome."

He gazed at me defiantly. "You're on."

We drove to the Enlisted Man's Club. The desk clerk reported that I shared a room with a sensational soldier from North Carolina. I gave Nick directions and sent him upstairs. The desk clerk gaped after him. "That's the butchest, sexiest man I've ever seen."

I tried to avoid smugness. "Nick's a bit of all right."

We chatted for twenty minutes before my buddy reappeared. "Play it straight. Expect me when you see me."

I entered my room and switched on the light. The soldier sat up quickly, blinking, his eyes red. He'd been crying! What ever had Nick done? Eighteen or nineteen, the youth had wholesome All-American good looks: sandy hair, blue eyes, wide shoulders, a broad chest, good arms. . . . A blanket covered his lower body, but I could depend upon the desk clerk, whose limp made him a connoisseur of good legs and macho walks. The soldier regarded me suspiciously. "Who are you?"

"William Kurt Strom of the United States Navy. Home port: Bonifay, Louisiana. Currently stationed in Newport, Rhode Island. If this is Room Four-Oh-Two, your roommate for the weekend." I glanced at the empty bed apparently rumpled by Nick. "Don't they clean up between customers?"

"Someone else was here," my roommate stated glumly.

"The number on the door matches the number on my receipt. Where is he?" The soldier shrugged; he looked so forlorn, my heart went out to him. "Probably a drunk," I conjectured blithely. "Realized he was in the wrong room and left."

I remade the bed and undressed. Immediately upon my switching off the light, the door opened and closed behind me. A hand pushed me onto the soldier. "Either of you move, I'll slit you from ear to ear."

What ever was Nick up to? "We won't."

"Shut up! Don't make a sound. Okay, real slow, get under the covers." I obeyed, huddling against the soldier's long warm body. Nick tore the covers off us. "Both of you, real easy, pull off your skivvies." We obeyed. "Now, you do everything I say, or I'm gonna gut you."

At first, the soldier lay limply passive; it took all my expertise, under orders from Nick, to work him up. His erection accomplished, it proved sufficient for the duration. Nick and I took gentle care of the soldier, all things considered.

An hour passed pleasantly. As I cornholed the soldier, Nick slipped quietly from the room. Unable to resist several more deep thrusts, I finally stopped and whispered, "I think he's gone." The soldier said nothing. I pulled out and switched on the light. The soldier lay sprawled across the

bed, his lovely derriere shining. Gazing at that splendid ravished body, I almost felt shame; this was someone's little
boy. I broke the silence. "I got wounded three times in
Nam." He turned over and looked up, covering his crotch
with his shorts. I exhibited my scars. "Each wound occurred
during an action that killed several men. I saw marines get
their arms, legs, and heads blown off. One of my best
friends, a man of constant action, will never walk again. At
one time or another, thirty men of my acquaintance died. I
saw the bodies of three or four hundred marines who had
been alive hours, sometimes minutes earlier. Somehow, I
survived.

"That man had a knife. He was obviously crazy, making
us . . . do that stuff. We could have fought him, but he
might have stabbed us." I pointed at the scars on my
forearm and rib cage. "Stab wounds. Hurt like a bitch.
After spending five months in a hospital because of my
elbow, I felt little desire to go back on account of some nut
stabbing me. I almost lost my arm in Nam. Tonight's cowar-
dice may have besmirched my honor and bruised my pride,
but my body remains whole and undamaged, other than a
sore asshole. I will put this out of my mind and continue to
enjoy what's left of my life." I sat on my bed. The soldier
stared blankly at the door. "Hey! Snap out of it!"

He slung long legs over the side of his bed and held his
head in both hands. "He was here before."

"The drunk!"

"He wasn't drunk."

"He buttfucked you before I got here?" The soldier
winced. Good for Nick!

"I thought about killing myself. Go up to the roof and
jump off."

Why the hell couldn't they take it in fun? "Oh, man! No
crazy queer is worth offing yourself."

"I . . . I didn't want to die."

"You show good sense. Let's hit the showers."

Ten minutes later, we returned to the room, towels wrapped around our midsections. Darby had outstanding legs and a great walk. "Should we report this to the desk clerk?" He seemed alarmed. "We'd have to explain how one dude controlled two big men, even if he carried a knife. I've gone through too much grief to end up with a dishonorable discharge, but I'll abide by your decision."

"Maybe better to forget."

"Good!" I hung the towel on a rack and lay nude on my bed. "The worse part was being humiliated, forced to have sex with an unknown soldier instead of making love to a good-looking woman. To brood about this would be unhealthy. It might become a festering sore that could send me whirling into a depression." The soldier flopped upon his bed. "I'll be damned if I let that bastard fuck my mind, too. I'm going to make the best of a bad situation."

"How?" he asked dismally.

How indeed! Trusting to intuition, I rattled on. "I don't know about you, but I've never before had sex with a man."

He groaned. "That makes two of us."

"I'm going to pretend you're my buddy. We came to New York on weekend liberty, rented a room, and painted the town red. Back in the room, drunk, we wrestled around and got carried away. We enjoyed each other's bodies, doing what that bastard forced us to do."

"It's hard to forget he forced us."

"Sure it is, but that bastard had you contemplating suicide. Forget him."

"I can't."

"Okay, let me approach a compromise from a different direction. No pretending. The truth." I wouldn't have uttered the truth if it was forced down my throat with a crowbar. "When I entered this room tonight, I felt horny. Out to sea for three months, I'm awarded unexpected leave, so I come to New York. My girl doesn't answer her phone. No idea of where she's gone. I'm horny and hope for a room

130

to myself so I can jack off. No dice. You're here. All right, I'll wait till you're asleep. Buddy, I was one lonely, frustrated sailor.

"An uncontrollable situation forces me into sex with two men. Ugh! P.U.! Other guys! To my amazement, I turn on. It's difficult for me to say, but I enjoyed . . . the things we did." Darby stared at the floor. "Admit it. The sex felt good. You turned on. I was there."

He said fiercely. "What do you want, man? Yeah, it felt good. I turned on. But . . ."

"You wish we hadn't been forced into it?"

"Truly."

"Want to beat that crazy dude?"

"Oh man, he's probably long gone, and I ain't never ever coming here again."

"Forget him! Okay, I didn't shoot my gun, and I don't think you did either. Am I right?" I'd made certain that he hadn't. "I am hornier now than I've ever been in my life. You're a fine-looking man with a great physique. Under different circumstances, we might have been friends." He nodded. "To erase the memory of that creep, we should . . . repeat those acts we performed under coercion. Get our rocks off. Make what happened a good experience." The soldier looked at me incredulously. "Drain the poison from our memories." He shook his head. "Okay, I've embarrassed myself for no reason." I feigned embarrassment. We lay back in silence, he staring at the ceiling, I at his excellent profile. I stood. "Can we shake hands and sleep friends?" He raised up and extended his right hand. His eyes widened at my rampant Precious. "Told you that I was horny." I brushed my teeth at the washbasin, aware that he stared. I rinsed my mouth and turned. "Hard to believe this big old thing fit in that little hole." His towel lifted in the middle. "The offer holds." He said nothing. I switched off the light and sat on the edge of his bed. I placed my hand upon his towel. He trembled. I slipped my hand under the towel. His

131

hand grazed my knee.

Nick played gin rummy with the desk clerk. "About time. I gotta go home."

I warned the desk clerk off the soldier—"He's emotionally unstable"—and walked Nick to his van. "I thought we used silver tongues, not steel blades."

The trooper laughed. "Aluminum. The identification tag from my key ring."

"You did real good, buddy."

"I did better than that. I cased the joint, figuring you would take a while with that soldier. Found a drunk taking a shower. Nice-looking blond. He stared down at me, surprised-like, while I took care of him."

"I'm surprised-like, too, that you took care of him."

"Got me into a tight ass. Don't think the scene held much for him, though, drunk as he was. Probably thought I came out of a dream."

"Or a nightmare."

"His wet footprints led to Room Three-Two-Six. You might like him."

"So you enjoyed yourself?"

"Three cherries."

"Three?"

"The soldier, the drunk, and a marine in the library."

"A marine in the library!"

"The desk clerk put him there after the place filled up. I planned to jaw with the grunt till you came down, but one thing led to another. . . . You known how it is."

"Not exactly."

"Told him about waking up with a queer blowing me, beat up the queer, still horny when I left the room, wished I'd let the queer finish, I'll finish it now, I'm embarrassed, pull yours out and join me. . . ."

"Great tactics!"

"One of your stories."

"Thought I recognized it."

"Scares the hell out of me to know I'm a closet sociopath."

I asked the desk clerk about the drunk in the shower. "Navy. Good face. Slim boyish body. Gave him a 'B.'" The desk clerk had adjusted to my rating system: A–Handsome, B–Goodlooking, C–Average, D–Strictly from Hunger, and F–Total Disaster. "Only a 'D+' for his buddy. Short and dark. Greek, I think. Butch, though. Hairy. So ugly he's cute. Swanson and Kratsas."

I slipped into Room Three-Two-Six. A wet towel hung at the end of the bed nearest the door. Blond hair against a white pillowcase. The drunken sailor slept heavily, so I crawled into bed with him. Alcohol relaxes the sphincter muscle; I'd penetrated him to the hilt before he awakened. Although he soon lapsed into the arms of Morpheus, his weak protests had awakened his buddy, who peered at us. He arose, switched on the overhead light, and watched. "That's heavy."

"Wanna try it?" Of course, he wanted to try it; he was a Greek, for crissake! And in no need of foreplay. I fantasized the ugly creature into Achilles and foreplayed anyway. "He a good buddy?" Kratsas nodded.

I eased out of Swanson and watched the Greek take my place. The blond awakened when Kratsas became rambunctious. "What's happening?" He twisted his head around. "Kratsas! What the fuck are you doing?" He tried to pull away, but the Greek pinned him to the bed and ejaculated with loud groans. When he left for the shower room, I performed rapture upon the blond, who complained, "This has to be a bad dream," while holding my head with both hands.

Kratsas returned and watched for a while, his short fat unmentionable becoming ramrod straight. He moved to Swanson, who sighed and orally accepted his friend.

Following a short conversation, the marine in the library offered no objection to a physical therapist giving him a massage, a token objection to my attaining rapture, and a strong but futile objection to being used as a woman. I reported my successes to the desk clerk, who satisfied himself with Swanson.

The next morning, my roommate ignored my cheerful bon mots. "Hey, Darby, you aren't regretting what we did?" Silence. "That's a bummer, man." He said nothing. I tore off his covers and grabbed his testicles. "Move, and I'll crush them." He lay still as a wild fawn. I gently brought him to a point where his sensuality betrayed him.

After calling Jane, I joined Darby for breakfast in the coffee shop. "What are your plans for the day?"

He answered sullenly. "Sightseeing."

"The Statue of Liberty, the Empire State Building, and Radio City Music Hall." He blushed. "Do them tomorrow. I've got you a date with a snazzy actress."

Rachel whimpered when I introduced Darby; the blasé redhead recognized a hot "goyim" under a bashful "Aw shucks" exterior. I guided everyone to the best cheap attractions in New York: the ferry across the harbor to Staten Island (five cents per round-trip), the Cloisters, a medieval monastery with lovely gardens and a good view of the Jersey Palisades (free), and the Bronx Zoo (free), where the carnivorous animals gamboled with their cubs in the spring sunshine.

To celebrate Rachel's first professional acting job, I treated everyone to supper at an excellent Mexican restaurant in Brooklyn Heights. (Four deluxe specials and two pitchers of beer cost ten dollars, including tip.) Rachel dug into an enchilada. "Touring the hinterlands in Camel Snot and The Smell of Mucous. Yuck! My luxurious auburn tresses will be covered by a wimple and my shapely legs will be hidden under a nun's habit. Provincial audiences will see only my pointed nose. This is my big break?"

We strolled along the Esplanade (free) while watching the sun set behind the Manhattan skyline. A subway (fifteen cents) carried us to Times Square, where we picked up free tickets for *HMS Pinafore*.

After the show, the girls invited us to their apartment for a nightcap. Although Saturday was Jane's night in the bedroom, I suspected Rachel capable of a quickie on the couch. She deserved compensation for Darby's unsophisticated company; on the other hand, he'd been an eager audience for her vivacious chatter. I suggested a stroll up Broadway, hoping that the actress lacked the turpitude to drag the soldier into a dark alley for a brisk upright. We kissed our dates goodnight at their door and walked towards the Club. Darby grinned broadly. "This has been, no lie, the greatest day of my life." It certainly had begun well.

As we showered, I discretely scrutinized Darby's body, unable to detect any flaws. We lay in our beds and exchanged pasts, his, I believe, unexpurgated. It would become more titillating on the morrow; while Jane and I visited another of her aunts, Rachel would prepare Sunday dinner for a soldier.

I arose to brush my teeth. After I finished, I switched off the light and leaned against the door. "Darby," I croaked, "we've committed sodomy three times. Would it make us queers if we did it again?"

"You'd have to put a knife to my throat." I grabbed my toothbrush and held it against his carotid artery. He chuckled. "I reckon I'll just have to give in."

Jane's aunt lived in New Rochelle, so I carried my travel bag; following lunch, I hitchhiked along U.S. One to the ferry landing across from Newport. I'd hoped for a groovy driver, one for the road, so to speak, but a garrulous middle-aged woman picked me up. She had designs upon me. "Last week, I picked up a sailor who kept staring at my legs. He scared me. Do you think there's any reason to stare at my legs?" She pulled up her skirt to mid-thigh. "He just stared and stared. I thought he was going to rape me. Mother told me that if a man planned to rape me and I couldn't get away, to try and enjoy it. Do you think I was

135

over-reacting to a man staring so at my legs? Do you think I have nice legs?"

Even were I tempted, recalling the urine samples that women turned into Urinalysis would have defeated Precious.

I enjoyed working in pee. Every morning, I collected several dozen bottles containing urine samples from a table outside the large sunny room I shared with Blood Chemistry. I numbered the chits wrapped around the bottles with a red crayon. After pouring a few grams of urine out of each bottle into a corresponding tube, I placed the tubes in a spinning machine. This separated liquid from the sediment that I examined under a microscope. Men's urine usually appeared clean except for a few harmless crystals. (Several samples containing sperm arrived daily from the NP ward; I delighted in noting such evidence of self-abuse on the patients' chits.) Women's samples stunk and were glutted with matter: hair, string, the red cells of menstruation, the white cells (pus) of infection. . . .

Thursday, Nick drove to Newport, and we secured the services, if not the affections, of the "Melbourne Method's" other two victims. Like Montchanin and Tiernan, they could deny us nothing. I saw Reynolds and McDade many times that summer; they always averted their eyes. A rematch with each would have pleased me, but I could think of no way to do it without Nick and more pseudo-blackmail; I preferred that each recollect our session as a frolic. They might never experience such intimacy with other men. I wondered what they thought.

Nick's excuse for the trip was to pick up his sister in Boston and take her home for the weekend. After McDade left the MAA's quarters, my buddy said, "It's so easy. Do a lot of fags play these games?"

"I imagine so, although most stick to a particular scenario. Usually, transactions are aboveboard: a gay man offers money, a ride, a meal, or a woman for another's favors. The powerful dangle jobs in front of their victims. I

136

have nothing to offer, so I must resort to trickery and deceit."

The trooper smiled. "I went to a parochial school through the sixth grade. The nuns held up saints and angels as perfection, what we would be like if we didn't have dirty thoughts or do dirty things. My mother thinks you look like the Archangel Raphael come to Earth." He reached over to squeeze my knee. "I get a taste of Paradise watching a perverted archangel tear off a piece of ass."

Nick dropped me at Boston's Greyhound station, where I checked my gear in a locker. The USO provided coffee, doughnuts, and cut-rate movie tickets, but no hot numbers. I partook of the first three items before walking to Sporters Bar in search of the latter. My old pal, Paul, had introduced me to Sporters, which embraced college students, young professionals, and the usual fruit flies. A squatty Lebanese with thick glasses and a bad complexion shouldered up to pontificate upon weighty matters; I escaped to the side of a skinny little queen, a type usually full of gossip. The queen obliged me by talking about the most newsworthy event of the past year.

Three prominent members of the Boston Red Sox American League baseball champions had visited the bar one evening and stayed for two hours. Fear or awe kept everyone from approaching the attractive athletes, so the queen couldn't tell me whether they'd entered with idle curiosity or prurient interest. I had heard rumors about the pitcher, but the trio left the bar together. For my own piece of mind, I hoped they had been sightseeing.

This night's star, a bruised, thick-featured professional hockey player, made a grand entrance with an effeminite little boyfriend on his arm. Neither he nor anyone else stunned me; nevertheless, I hated to waste money on a hotel room. A dark aggressive fellow approached me with sufficient flattery, so we left together for an apartment filled with mirrors. He walked out of the bathroom holding a bottle of amyl nitrate and wearing an intricate network of leather straps. Sex was an ordeal.

Saturday afternoon, I rented a room at the Parker House and walked to the Back Bay station to meet Jane's train. I listed the sights: the Museum of Art, the Public Gardens, Bunker Hill. . . . Jane shook her head. "I want to walk across Harvard Yard."

"Not much to see."

"All my life, I've wanted to walk across Harvard Yard."

I would have been a hypocrite to decry another's peculiarities, so we rode the MTA to Cambridge and walked hand-in-hand across Harvard Yard. We climbed and descended Beacon Hill. We strolled through the Public Gardens. We dined in Chinatown and attended a play. At the hotel, Jane emerged from a bath and attacked me, her clitoris swollen to the size of a Vienna sausage. I proved woefully inadequate to her expectations.

Sunday, we attended the afternoon concert at the Isabella Stewart Gardiner Museum. Jane clung to me at the train station. She looked so pretty. I wished that I . . . could satisfy her.

After waving goodbye, I hurried to Sporters. A horde of chattering fruit flies picked at the remnants of brunch. An elegant gentleman of quality stood alone in a corner. I assumed the drawl of a well-bred Louisiana planter and introduced myself to the extremely handsome young man. "I'm meeting a friend," he stated abruptly.

"If you're saying that because I'm not your type, I'll leave. If you'd like someone with whom to talk until your friend comes, I'd enjoy it."

He replied with silence. I bade him adieu and found my own corner. During the next hour, I shook off several drearies, aware that the dark-haired patrician watched through clear gray eyes. He bought another beer and eased through the crowd to a spot two feet from me. Without looking at him or committing him to a tête-à-tête, I uttered casual observations; before another hour passed, he had learned the basic facts of my secular past. He overcame his shyness to divulge his recent return to the States after eighteen months in Greenland as an electronics engineer, planning to buy a schooner with his savings. He warmed to the subject, and I got an inkling of the differences between a schooner and a kayak.

Although I regretted giving up an "A+," I had a bus to catch. I thanked the beauty for a pleasant evening and took my leave. I had walked a block when I heard steps behind me. The engineer pulled abreast. "Guess we're going the same way."

"Lucky, isn't it?" A natural aristocrat would never ask my destination. "I'm headed for the bus station." Were thoroughbreds aware of plebeian modes of transportation?

We walked a block in silence. "Would you like a ride?"

"Sure." He had parked his car several blocks from Sporters, so that no one could link him with a gay tavern. The aristocrat dropped me at the terminal; I retrieved my travel bag from a locker and waited for the bus.

Someone sat in an adjoining chair. I looked past *Middlemarch* at a pair of lean shapely legs. The gentleman of quality! I closed the book. As we talked, he watched my reactions to the servicemen and hustlers pacing the station. I appeared oblivious. "When does your bus leave?"

"Twenty minutes."

"Would you like a ride to Providence?"

As we neared the city of renegade Puritans, I broached the lavender topic; he'd winced when I touched on the subject at Sporters. "Any opportunities for sex in Thule?"

Disgust tinged his voice. "Eskimo women."

"Ah! The tang of whale blubber. Any sex between men?"

"No!"

Were he a tad less handsome, a little less aristocratic, a wee bit less masculine, I wouldn't have put up with his diffidence for another minute. "It's not such a bizarre

139

question. We met in a gay bar."

"I'm not gay!"

"I didn't think you were. That's why I never made a pass."

He drove through Providence towards Newport. "Are you gay?"

"As a sailor, I've learned to adapt."

He mulled my ridiculous statement. "Everybody at Thule had his own room. Two electricians got drunk and flopped in the same room, fully-dressed, one on a chair, the other on a bed. They were shipped back to the States on the next plane."

His tale of visiting a glacier carried us into Newport. I stared a his fine profile. He blinked self-consciously. "Would you like me to make a pass?"

He cleared his throat and swallowed several times. "What do you mean?"

"Have you ever had sex with another man?"

His hand clenched the steering wheel. "No."

"Would you like to?"

He wiped sweating palms on his trousers. Anguish hoarsened his voice. "I don't know."

"Take a left at the next light, and we'll talk about it."

At dawn, I raised my head from his lap and looked out the window. We had parked at the county dump.

Pathology was the dumping ground of the hospital, and I entered it three times that week to assist at autopsies. I decided that dead bodies were repulsive, especially hydrocephalic newborns with large purple heads that burst like rotten pumpkins when opened and splashed unwary corpsmen with a rainbow of gore.

The father of one monster wanted to see the infant, but the pathologist refused him access. The father, a captain, went to the admiral, who sent word to open the reefer. Two months later, I learned that the staff psychiatrist was treating the captain for a nervous breakdown, the officer unable to touch the mother of such a creature.

I stood weekend duty with my mentor, Yeti the Yakker, whose monologue began Friday afternoon and ended Sunday night, interrupted only by sleep, when he snored.

That week, I performed ten times the usual number of pregnancy tests. Part of the Atlantic Fleet would soon pull into port after six months at sea, and adulterous wives worried. Their boyfriends called, pretending to be doctors. "I'd like the results of Mrs. _____'s rabbit test."

I responded truthfully. "I can't supply that information without the permission of my commanding officer."

"Mrs. _____ is in my office now. Give me the results and I'll clear it later with your C.O."

"I'll obtain his permission and call you back immediately."

"My number is . . ."

"I'll look up your number in the directory, doctor."

Huge sigh. "Never mind."

They never fooled me. The proper application of a physician's knowledge deserved my respect, but if a layman pretended to be a doctor, his voice should have echoed with pomposity. A verbal command from God could hardly have sounded more patronizing.

One evening, Montchanin joined me for supper in the hospital cafeteria. While trading uneasy conversation, I aired an intention to attend a movie. Montchanin proposed driving me downtown; instead, he drove out Ocean Drive and pulled onto a shoulder overlooking the Atlantic. Rain spattered the windshield. Montchanin pushed back his seat. "I haven't received any orders for Washington."

Uh oh! "Neither have I."

We watched waves crash against the rocks in front of us. "I suppose it's time to get ready for Vietnam."

"You'll hear from Washington."

"Sure, I will." Montchanin glared at me. The sea raged. "After what we've done, there shouldn't be any secrets

141

between us." I agreed. "Tell me the truth. There's no study."

"I don't follow you."

"That guy was no captain."

"Really! I thought so."

"Jesus, Strom! The game's over!" I feigned innocence. "Okay, we'll play it your way." He grabbed my hand and pressed it against his crotch. "You give me head, I'll know the whole thing's a hoax. You keep your hands to yourself, I'll wait for orders to Washington." When I started to unzip his trousers, the sailor knocked my hand away. "Why?"

"I couldn't let you believe a fairy tale. How did you know that captain didn't pull our names out of a hat?"

"For a reluctant novice, you performed too well."

Ocean spray splattered the windshield. "You pissed?"

"Damn straight!" He ignited the motor and drove towards town.

"Plan on ruining my reputation?"

"I'm thinking about it."

"You'd look foolish."

"I'm leaving in a couple of weeks. You ought to be stopped."

"You have no witnesses and I would deny everything."

"Who was the captain?"

"A friend."

"Why did you do it?"

"You have the fatal gift of beauty." He snorted. "We figured you'd be worth it."

A mile of silence. The capable, assertive, masculine corpsman asked in a shy, strangled voice. "Was I?"

"You'll marry a lucky girl."

His momentary return to adolescence gave way to thoughtfulness. "In a way, it's kind of flattering."

"You're a handsome man, Montchanin. I'm surprised that no one has hit on you before." How did I suddenly know someone had? Hmm. I'd like to hear that story. "Sorry

142

about the Washington angle. Such trickery is despicable."

"Do you really feel bad about it?"

"I've beat my teeth and gnashed my breasts. I've gone to confession daily and murmured a thousand 'Hail Marys'. I considered throwing myself from the rim of a volcano into a lake of boiling . . ."

"Stow it!" A corner of his mouth twitched. "I'm more interested in combat fatigue and battle trauma than the posturings of fairies."

"I wish you luck, buddy."

"Kissing me off? No way, Strom. You owe me. For the next two weeks, I'm going to pick your brains about Nam. You will be at my beck and call. Your ass is mine."

"Wouldn't be the first time."

He pulled against a curb, his face dark. "There will be no more of that shit! Get out!" I felt incensed and offended until I realized that Montchanin planned to attend the movie with me.

The NP tech kept his word. Every evening, we met for supper and spent several hours talking about my experiences in Vietnam. I'd just about run out of material when, on Thursday afternoon, my phone rang. "HM3 Strom?"

"Yes."

"Captain Vincent Nicholas here. Your uncle, Commander Carl Strom, asked me to look you up when I arrived in Newport. Would it be possible to meet for lunch."

"Sure. I'm free at eleven-thirty."

"Fine. I'll wait outside the front gate of the hospital."

Good old Nick! Always the cop. Not a bad idea around the hospital. A quivering mountain of maidenly flesh, our middle-aged secretary, listened to every conversation on the laboratory party line. Five minutes after I hung up, the Medical Service lieutenant strolled into Urinalysis. "Strom, why don't you take the rest of the day off?"

"Annie the Wop has spread the word, huh?"

"Umble Uriah" rebuked me with a smile.

143

I changed into civvies and met Nick at the hospital gate, suggesting that he drive to a secluded bird sanctuary beyond the city beach and park in a bee-loud glade. As the trooper climbed into the back of the van, I grabbed a pair of handcuffs that hung below the dashboard. During our ado, I slipped them on his wrists. Nick was instantly wary. "What are you doing?"

"Removing an inhibition." I turned him onto his hard flat belly.

"I don't . . ."

"Shut up!"

He suffered my gentle entrance. "I don't like this at all." Contrary to my usual pattern, I ejaculated within a minute. We dressed in silence and drove to a diner. After the waitress took our orders, Nick lit a cigarette. "Are we going to talk about this?"

"The first time I balled a man, I came inside him. It never happened again."

"But you . . ."

"Until today."

"But . . ."

"I've so feared that the length and breadth of Precious would hurt the bottom man that I couldn't concentrate on my own pleasure."

"You've had guys that love it. Francisco. You said he could take seven in a row."

"You can clap your hands inside Francisco's ass. I need friction." The waitress brought coffee. "You staying over tonight? I know this great little bar. . . ."

"You've had virgin asses before."

"None that belonged to gorgeous hot-blooded Italians."

"Anybody else, I'd kill them." Nick's eyes narrowed. "You like me, don't you?"

"Who could doubt it?"

His jaw set grimly. "You don't give an inch."

"I just gave you eight inches."

"Let me tell you something, Kurt. This was a first for me, and I hated it. I hated every second. But my ass is yours, and yours alone, whenever you want it."

"Maybe after the third race at Santa Anita. Okay, I assume that you came up for the two corpsmen in Supply."

"Yeah. Right. That's it."

"Good. Before I changed out of my uniform, I called the Supply Shed and arranged for Smitty to meet us in the MAA's apartment at seven and O'Hara at ten. The gear we'll need is in my locker. I'm a dead duck if the brass holds a locker inspection."

"Likely?"

"Be the first since I arrived; corpsmen are considered trustworthy. You brought your fake uniform?" He nodded. "I hope you don't mind, but Montchanin will join us for supper." I explained our sudden friendship.

"Could be interesting to get acquainted."

"You might enjoy bedding him again." Nick shrugged. "I owe you."

"Goddam right you do! Where's the john? I feel like my insides are about to fall out."

I had told Montchanin all I'd learned as a field medic in a hostile jungle, treating sick and wounded marines and how to avoid booby traps; as a corpsman on a surgical intensive care unit, watching over seriously-wounded marines just out of the operating room; and as a cut-rate doctor in a Vietnamese village, working with a platoon of marines to improve the rustics' life style. We'd arranged to meet for that evening's lesson—NEVER VOLUNTEER FOR HELICOPTER RESCUE FLIGHTS—in a pizza parlor near the base. Nick's presence surprised my new buddy, who sat silently through the meal. Conversation eventually turned to sex, and I bragged about Nick's and my rape of the Enlisted Man's Club. Our promscuity diminished the NP tech; I supposed that he had hoped himself unique.

A third round of beers appeared before Montchanin

145

spoke. "I've always considered sex as something private between two people. Maybe that's why I fell for your act. Do you always work together?"

"No. Our partnership is recent. I've always been a loner."

"Is it easier working alone or together?"

"Six of one, half-a-dozen of the other. It's more fun with Nick along and he can verify the seductions. I have friends who refuse to believe they happen."

"You've done this often?"

"Dozens of times. Different scripts. They don't always come off, but it passes the time."

"Why?"

"Why did they fail? Because I didn't trust my instincts or lacked the time or place."

"Why do you seduce guys?"

"It's fun making it with hunky dudes."

"Does it fulfill you?"

"Does a day at the beach fulfill you? Or a night at the theater? Surfing? Mountain climbing? Maybe it's the universal urge to create. Most people aren't artists, so they compensate by developing an expertise in some field. I may create nothing but havoc, but I enjoy a talent for seducing attractive straight men."

"Does this satisfy you?"

"Partially. Having possessed the body, one desires a conduit to a man's memory bank."

"So you feel thwarted?"

"Only if I miss out on the body."

"So you're examples of the Don Juan syndrome."

"Not exactly. I believe that Don Juan and Casanova seduced women with words of love. I never do that."

Montchanin nodded. "They were homely men, which you two very definitely are not."

Nick spoke. "Ridiculous as it sounds, Kurt thinks that he's ugly."

"Mother's doing. 'When I married your daddy, I hoped to

have good-looking children. Another dream shattered. Look at Kurt.'"

"She said that?"

"Mother always was one to call a spade a fucking shovel."

"She must have had problems."

"Many."

"You two . . . It seems a waste."

"Would you consider a dude who successfully seduces a series of beautiful women to be wasting his time? I'm surprised, Monty. As a prospective psychologist, you should be able to adjust your viewpoint."

He shook his head. "You guys are something else. I'd enjoy seeing you in action."

"Remember Washington?"

He blushed. "With somebody else."

"We've planned an operation for tonight."

Nick growled.

"What kind of operation?"

"No details unless you're in with us all the way."

"What does that mean?"

"You gotta do anything Nick says."

"Including sex?"

"Nothing you haven't already done."

Montchanin considered his participation. "I'd rather just watch."

"All or nothing at all. Like the song."

"I don't think so." Too bad. "What about you, Nick? Why?"

"I've been giving that some thought. My job's frustrating. I do it good, but rules and regulations make everything I do seem worthless. My wife and me raise the kids together, but we don't have much else in common; we sure don't have any fun together. Screwing around with other women gets to be a hassle. I like knowing what makes people tick." He looked down at his glass. "It's Kurt. He's so goddam much fun. His brain's always whirling, but if I ask a question, he shuts

147

everything down and gives me his full attention. Nobody's ever done that for me without wanting something."

"What do you want from him, Kurt?"

The question startled me. "His company, I guess. Nick knows how to show a girl a good time."

Montchanin bit his lips. "No pain?"

"None."

He took a deep breath. "Okay. What's the plan?" I described the "Melbourne Method."

"Nobody would fall for that."

"I'm batting a thousand with it."

"Who's the victim?"

"Smitty and O'Hara."

"Two!"

"One at a time."

"Christ, Strom! Those are mean dudes."

"Sweet meat must have sour sauce."

"I don't like them."

"Who does? Describe their physical appearance."

"Smitty's of medium height, well-built, a good-looking cuss."

"O'Hara?" (The golden Irishman, whom I'd caught abusing himself.)

"Handsome face. Muscular. Okay, I get the picture. They have such nasty dispositions. How can you touch them?"

"With fervor. They're both clean; I see them in the shower room after work. As for their personalities, I realized long ago that one can't eat every meal at the Four Seasons. By the way, may I ask you something?"

"No secrets between us."

People disliked my probing their psycho-sexual histories. "You've made it with another guy. Where and when?"

Montchanin jerked back. "How did you know?" He frowned. "My first semester of college, I got stuck with a bozo of a roommate. A total fuck-up. Everybody made fun of him. Put him down to his face. One night, I woke up and

148

heard him crying. Hated to ask what was wrong, but I did. He laid his troubles on me, said I was his only friend. Some friend: I'd already made arrangements to move in with somebody else." Montchanin cleared his throat. "The bozo said he'd dreamed of fellating me. Asked if he could. Begged. I felt so guilty, I let him. Didn't really like it. Too mortified, I guess, and he wasn't much good. His teeth scraped my penis. I couldn't bring myself to touch him."

I hoped the bozo appreciated Montchanin's generosity. The NP tech ranked high among the ten sexiest men that I'd met in the military.

We drove to the barracks in separate cars. Nick seemed doubtful. "Him being there could make your supply guys clam up."

"Consider it a challenge. I'd like to see Montchanin perform spontaneously. He's straight, right?"

"You're the expert. You tell me."

"He is. We've got something very important going for us: Montchanin is honorable, and we're probably the most dishonorable people he's ever met."

"I resent that."

"I'm looking at it from his point of view."

"He could be warning the supply guys right now."

"He's trustworthy. And he's sincerely intrigued by our shenanigans. Unlike the average psychologist, immersed in statistics and interested primarily in his own personality, Montchanin studies other people that he might help them and for his edification. It's another boon that he isn't promiscuous."

"How do you know?"

"He's determined to like us, in spite of our shitting on him, and it's because we had sex together. Lacking a compulsion for anonymous encounters, he must salvage his pride by knowing us better. Only friendship can assuage his uneasiness."

"You've talked about this?"

149

"Hell, I doubt that he's delved that far into his psyche. You realize, of course, this is supposition."

"We'll see."

Smitty arrived promptly at seven. Dressed in the captain's uniform, Nick introduced himself as the officer in charge of the Newport Shore Patrol. "One of the doctors here at the hospital saw you behind the Dental Clinic last Tuesday with some faggot giving you head." Actually, Smitty had spent Thursday night in a bar downtown and staggered back to the barracks half-conscious, according to what I'd heard him tell O'Hara Wednesday morning. He denied the doctor's accusation. Nick described (badly) the "Melbourne Method," which would prove or disprove his guilt. "Strom here will perform the test."

Smitty indicated Montchanin. "Why's he here?"

"My assistant, an NP tech, who will decide whether you're a crazy faggot or not. Okay. Strip."

"In front of everybody?"

"We're all men."

Aghast, Smitty set his strong jaw in stubborn defiance. Nick painted a black picture of life after a dishonorable discharge tht reduced the supply corpsman to quivering terror. He stripped and lay on the bed. Montchanin spoke. "Is it necessary to humiliate him?" Nick raised his eyebrows in an "I-Told-You-So." I glared at the NP tech, who wavered. "I mean, what if he's innocent?"

"That's extremely doubtful. I recognized him from the doctor's description. Get to work, Strom."

"I can't do anything until he ejaculates."

"You ain't hard yet, Smith? Beat it!"

The supply tech looked up with anguished eyes and wailed, "I can't."

"Why not?"

"All of you in the room."

"We have to be here. Maybe it would help if you two guys beat it, too. Strip!"

150

"Huh?"

"I ain't got all day. Strip and get on the bed beside Smith." I obeyed with alacrity. Montchanin refused until Nick glared at him with hard eyes and said coldly, "I strongly advise you to join them. Hurry up! This faggot shit pisses me off." The NP tech stripped and climbed on the bed, where we lay side by side—The Three Little Bares. "Get 'em hard." The incorrigible Precious arrived first at the post; Montchanin, probably to his astonishment, finished a length behind. Smitty never got out of the starting gate. "Help him, Strom."

"What?"

Nick grunted with impatience. "Help him get it up. Play with his balls." That didn't help. "Fantasize about pussy, Smith. Montchanin, beat it for him." The NP tech hesitated. "Beat it!" He performed awkwardly. "Lick his balls, Strom. That'll do the trick. Lick the shaft. That's it. Hmm. Maybe it only turns Smitty on if he does the licking." Nick dropped his pants, climbed on the bed, and straddled Smitty's face. He rubbed his unmentionable against the supply corpsman's lips, which parted. Montchanin eased off the bed and stood watching.

Nick stripped and took Smitty from the rear. I worked on his front. Lying on his side, Smitty faced Montchanin's swollen member. The NP tech moved forward. Smitty lifted his head to accept him.

We never utilized the "Melbourne Method." As we'd gone beyond the bounds of the experiment, Nick decided that the doctor's allegation would be reported as mistaken identity. Agreeing to keep the episode to ourselves, Smitty and I returned to our barrack, leaving the others to use the MAA's bathroom. Smitty showered, dressed quickly, and left for town with the intention of getting very drunk, not bothering to confer with O'Hara, who played pool in the game room. I toweled off and returned to the apartment.

Montchanin worried. "Will he tell anyone?"

151

"Would you?"

"If I didn't want to serve in Vietnam."

Smitty and O'Hara are reserves with less than three months of active duty remaining. No worries about Nam."

"Why did Smith do it?"

"Momentum."

"But to be used anally!"

Nick spoke. "A lot of so-called straight dudes seem to dig it up the ass. I'm far from understanding the urge myself," he glared at me, "but all the men Kurt and I have seduced together went for it like guineas for opera."

"Why? A penis inserted into the rectum gives pain."

"Not always," I retorted, "and the pain is often supplanted by physical and psychological pleasure." Nick snorted. I ignored him and gazed at Montchanin. "Let's use you as an example. Age?"

"Twenty-four."

"Upper middle class, although your parents aren't educated and come from the lower middle class. Small town for three generations. I'd like to say that your great-grandparents were immigrants, England maybe, but I think I'm wrong."

"Scotland and Canada."

Nick grinned. "I love it when Kurt does that. How right is he?"

"Dad started off as a truckdriver; now he owns a fleet of trucks and three garages. I was brought up in a little town outside Philadelphia. How. . . ?"

"All those years playing baseball. I met a lot of people."

Nick laughed. "Kurt never forgets a goddam word anybody says. He also hears what you're not saying, reading between the lines. Sometimes he tells me what I don't even know I'm thinking." Nick looked at me thoughtfully. "Maybe that's how you convince some of these dudes to pull out their peckers."

Montchanin stared. "You should work on NP."

152

"Crazy people depress me. Education?"

"Three years of college."

"Ever ball a girl in high school?"

"No. I wanted to, but always dated nice girls who believed sex came after marriage."

"College?"

"Two girls my freshman year; then I met my fiancée. My ex-fiancée.

"Why did you enlist?"

"Broke up with her."

"You ball anybody on the rebound?"

"A couple of party girls. Nothing serious."

"When was the last time?"

"About three months ago. A WAVE. No one since I got my orders for Vietnam." He blushed. "I guess most guys would fuck their brains out with Nam staring them in the face."

"You're too honorable to subject any girl you cared about to your imminent demise. Okay, here we are in the present: horny, slightly fearful about the future, and lonely among those of lesser intellect. Do you feel threatened by the homosexuals on the NP ward?"

"No. They're sad. And stupid for getting caught."

"Do they come on to you?"

"Sometimes. It's boring. I'm not interested."

"Suddenly, you're thrust into a sexual situation with us."

"Like being shot out of a cannon."

"How did you feel about us when we entered the motel?"

"I respected Nick as a high-ranking officer and you as a corpsman back from Nam. You survived experiences I wondered about. Tell you the truth, I wanted to know you better, but you seemed so cold and arrogant." He looked at Nick. "One of my roommates works in Personnel. Kurt's name came up in a conversation. Corky had looked at his record, said Kurt made perfect scores on four of the seven Navy entrance exams. About one man in a thousand makes

153

even one perfect score."

"Why did you take off your clothes?"

"An officer ordered me to."

"Not good enough."

"Well, you took off yours, and it seemed natural to follow your lead."

"What did you think while you stood naked?"

"My skin tingled. Whatever went down seemed out of my control."

"You liked being passive?"

"Liked it? No. I just waited. I had no expectations."

"What did you think when Nick went down on you?"

"An officer is sucking my prick. Hot damn!"

"Psychological pleasure?"

"I hardly felt it, I had such a sense of power."

"When I went down on you?"

Montchanin paused. "That night you got drunk and made angel wings in the snow, I thought . . . in the car when you put your head in my lap . . . that you were making a pass. At first, I was surprised; then I got pissed. Finally, I decided to let you go ahead. That's when you conked out."

"To my sorrow. Did you put me to bed?"

"Yeah. Felt funny undressing you." The NP tech blushed. "Afterwards, I sat by your bunk watching you. Wondering what you knew that I didn't. About Nam. Women. Even drunk, you looked . . . perfect."

"With all my scars!"

"They make you interesting. They're barely noticeable, Kurt."

Nick chuckled. "Doofus here thinks he looks like Frankenstein."

Montchanin smiled. "Hardly. One night, I was . . . this is embarrassing . . ." He drew a deep breath. ". . . I was masturbating, and I dreamed you did go down on me that night in the car. Couldn't climax to a gay fantasy, so you turned into Miss Woofter, the new nurse on MICU, and that

154

brought me off."

"I refuse to let my transformation into a peroxided bitch dismay me."

"She dyes her hair!"

"Roots as black as her heart. Moving right along, what did you think while you survived us?"

"About physical things. How big you both were. How silky a penis feels. How well it fits. The texture of your skin surprised me."

Nick interjected. "All those muscles and the skin is so soft."

"Like a baby's ass. Did I think anything? Yeah. Like my privacy was gone. With a woman, I wanted intimacy. With you guys . . . like I stood in a window. Bare."

"A loss of innocence?"

"No, I was too curious. I knew I didn't have to do it, but I didn't mind."

"When Nick penetrated you?"

"I expected it to hurt more. It did feel uncomfortable at first."

"You tensed up."

"I relaxed pretty quick when Nick hit my prostate. It helped a lot that he used his hands so well."

"An expert."

"Incredible. When you did it with me on my back, I . . . pretended that I was a woman. Some of the things we did felt so good, I committed them to memory for the next time I balled a chick."

"After we separated?"

"Alone. I felt lonely. My butt ached with emptiness. I was disappointed when Nick kicked us out. I'd got used to your body warmth and your smell. I guess I wanted to spend the night."

"Did you want to do it again?"

"Not really." Montchanin smiled sheepishly. "I remembered it, though, Gave me hot flashes. I remembered every

155

bit of it."

"You appear to be the type that would maintain control during lovemaking, desirous of making the act pleasurable for the woman." He nodded. "A man must take care with a woman, conscious of his strength and her frailty, solicitous of his weight upon her, heedful of the depth and violence of his thrusts. A sensitive man avoids offending a woman by not expressing inclinations such as buttfucking. He is hesitant to ask if he can lie back and lose himself in sensation while she fellates and reams him, caressing his erogenous zones orally and tactilely. Unless a woman suggests it, a man is denied the pleasure of passivity."

"I've experienced passivity once, and it was limited."

"Nick and I allowed you to be mindlessly torpid, to lie back and receive strong men who could accept your weight and your violence, men who welcomed your grosser inclinations. You could drop your inhibitions, ask us to supply any sensation, and rut like an animal."

"Am I bisexual?"

"Given a choice, which would you bed: a handsome man or a beautiful woman of similar acquaintance and charm?"

"The woman. Every time."

"A bisexual would waver. Why did you want Smitty to blow you?"

"I identified. In the motel, when you were using me . . . I wanted total degradation. I wondered if Smitty felt the same way. The power appealed to me, knowing I could force him to take it."

Nick interrupted. "It's almost ten. The golden Irishman is due."

I looked at Montchanin. "You staying?"

"Might as well be hung for a sheep as a lamb."

The phantom doctor had seen O'Hara accepting fellatio two weeks earlier. The Irishman declared innocence, and none of Nick's interrogatory tactics could budge him. Failing to seduce O'Hara might have led to his mentioning our

156

assembly to Smitty, endangering the naval careers of both Montchanin and me. Nick was hip. "Let's go search your locker."

O'Hara paled. "Why?"

"You don't cooperate, I'll bust you for dope."

"What do you want?"

"The 'Melbourne Method.'"

O'Hara stripped, revealing an erection. An exhibitionist! I wondered if the scene in the barracks head had been staged. Surely not! The dude was straight. Christ! I had enough difficulty trying to understand my own perversions.

Nick turned to me. "Strom, you were addicted to morphine. You and O'Hara friends?"

"No."

"Aww, I'll bet you're very good friends. Strip."

"Huh?"

"I'm gonna make sure you're the best of friends."

"What's this all about?" wondered O'Hara.

"Shut up! Okay, Strom, on the bed. Head to crotch. You're gonna be real good buddies."

"Hey, man! No!" O'Hara sat up and reached for his shorts.

"Let's go search some lockers." No one moved. "You gonna cooperate?" O'Hara pondered; then he eased back on the bed. "Montchanin, scuttlebutt has it that you balled one of your patients."

"Not true."

"A pretty little nurse with peroxided hair. A schizophrenic manic-depressive with sado-masochistic nymphomania."

The NP tech almost giggled as he joined in the game. "She'd been discharged from the ward."

"Nevertheless, she was your patient and you fucked her. The Navy don't like that. Grounds for dismissal. Strip."

O'Hara was soon acquainted with the textures of three unmentionables.

After he left, I congratulated Nick upon pushing the right

157

button. The trooper shrugged. "The dude walked in full of bravado, obviously scared shitless. When I hung the queer rap on him, the tension vanished. He's a buddy of Smitty, who was too easy, not the type to let us shaft him unless a bigger screwing was in his future. Had to be narcotics, either in the Supply Shed or their lockers. Kurt mentioned never having locker inspections." Nick stared at me with reproach. "I'm surprised you didn't pick up on it."

Nick had been urging me to think about a career as a policeman. "Well, I don't know about anybody else, but I have to be up at five. Nick can crash in the night barrack."

"I'm wide awake," said the trooper.

"So am I," said Montchanin.

"Indeed! Then you can keep each other company."

Friday afternoon, Nick offered to indulge my interest in college boys thumbing home for the weekend. We drove along the Boston–New York Turnpike, passing several hitchhikers before seeing two worth the game. They crawled into the back of the van. Clean cut, good teeth, well-nourished bodies, attractive faces . . . I wondered whether Long Island Italians would strike a chord within Nick.

The youths majored in Business at Boston College, preparing for law school. I announced my presence as a hitchhiker, too; Nick portrayed himself, an off-duty policeman with a loathing for criminals. "We put our lives in danger every day so you shysters can get scum off on technicalities or bleeding-heart judges can give them lenient sentences. The country ought to build prisons underground and just stick the cocksuckers in a deep dark hole."

The students politely refused to argue, but appeared willing to discuss the issue. "What about rehabilitation?"

"No such thing. Ninety-five per cent of criminals have something missing in their brains. They turn into assholes when they're little kids and they'll die assholes."

"The loss of freedom seems punishment enough."

"Bullshit! The scum get treated like royalty. Decent

158

people put up thousands of dollars for court costs, not to mention forty or fifty thousand per asshole for building and maintenance, guards, food, clothing, color televisions. . . . Their victims get nothing but grief. Now the assholes want conjugal rights. Sailors serving their country, ship's out to sea for six months at a time. No women aboard. They sleep in bunks stacked three or four high. Don't get shit for pay. They ain't got color televisions."

I acted jittery, talking loudly and my movements spasmodic. "They got it a lot better than guys in stir."

Nick glanced at me. "What were you in for?"

"Nothing, man. I didn't do nothing." I had to have done something. "I borrowed a car. The owner's pissed I been dorking his old lady, so he calls in the law and says I stole it. Got thirteen months, man, and I didn't do nothing."

Nick sighed heavily. "Sure, buddy. Nobody ever does."

"It's bad in jail, man."

"Should be worse."

"What could be worse than a dude holding a knife to your throat while six of his buddies prong you? Six! Ever get it up the ass, man?"

Nick glared at me. "I heard that punks get to like it."

"Oh, man! You fucking pig!" I pulled Nick's revolver from under the dashboard, afraid that he'd left it loaded. The van swerved violently. It was loaded. "Turn off the next exit. You dudes in the back. Stretch out on your bellies and don't move. We're gonna see who's a punk." We looked for an isolated spot, no easy task in southern Connecticut, but finally parked behind an abandoned gas station. Forcing Nick into the back of the van at gunpoint, I saw a coil of rope, which he used to tie the hands of the college boys. "Okay, trooper, pull off their britches." Nick obeyed. "You're gonna see what it's like in stir, when you ain't got no pretty sweet pussy. I'm gonna make you dork some nasty ass. Get it up."

"Please. I'm married."

"Get it up or I'm gonna blow it off!"

159

"Yes sir." Nick got it up and dorked some nasty ass. I put the handcuffs around his wrists and pulled down my pants.

"Now I'm gonna show you shysters what stir turned me into—a cocksucker." I showed them. "Now it's your turn." With Nick's hunting knife at their throats, the youths showed me what stir would turn them into; then, they showed each other. For a finale, I stuck his undershorts in Nick's mouth and ordered the boys to turn him into a punk. Nick's ass was no longer mine alone.

I drove to Manhattan, parked the van on a quiet street in Greenwich Village, and threw the keys to the handcuffs in the back. "See you later, punks. Viva Avila!"

Francisco was at home, so I had no need to wait next to a door buzzer marked "Avila." A few minutes later, Nick entered in a fury checked by the model's presence. A martini calmed him. "They grabbed a subway to Grand Central after I convinced them that reporting the incident could embarrass all three of us. I promised to catch up with you and get even, which is the truth." He shot me a meaningful glance.

"They messed up mentally?"

"Nah! Guineas dig sex. Never let it interfere with their home or their church; besides, they ain't gonna feel guilt for something they couldn't control. I told them the experience might help them understand the criminal mind better. One of the little smartasses asked if he was any good as a . . ." Nick recalled our host, the biggest gossip between Hell's Gate and the Statue of Liberty.

Francisco chuckled. "Kurt told me that both boys fucked you."

Nick glowered. "You told him that?" I nodded, smiling. The trooper stalked out of the apartment.

Francisco shook his magnificent head. "God protect me from such a destructive love."

"Love! No, just a curious straight dude indulging a passing fancy."

"I wasn't speaking of Nick, my amigo."

Saturday evening, I called the trooper to ask if a dinner invitation issued Thursday still held. "I guess so." Sunday at four-thirty, he met Jane and me at the bus station, three of his kids in the car.

A month from delivery, Rosemary was huge and looked a weary fifty. As she and Jane made woman sounds in the kitchen, I wandered into the backyard, where the children whooped and Nick tinkered with the engine of the van. He ignored me. "Fixing it up to sell? Rid yourself of a bad memory?"

Nick set a wrench in the toolbox and wiped his hands on a greasy rag. "I don't want to have anything more to do with you and your faggot friends."

"Francisco will tell no one. Considering our relationship as something pure and terrible, he'll save the story for the day when one of us kills the other."

"He better start practicing it."

"Bothered by damaged pride?"

Nick threw the rag into the toolbox. "Why do you shame me?"

"You should comprehend the humiliation a queer must endure."

"I dig it."

"You arouse my lust and my curiosity. Only two persons of my acquaintance continually surprise me, whose essence remains a mystery. You and Paul. And Paul has never been more than a friend."

"I'm more than a friend!"

"Goes without saying. You're my buddy, ace." Nick smiled tentatively. "My asshole buddy."

Table talk focused on babies. Both women watched me surreptitiously; I assumed that Rosemary had asked Jane just how crazy I was. Later, the lady of the house and I made idle chat while washing dishes. Jane strummed a guitar in the living room, softly crooning "Un Bel Di" from *Madame*

161

Butterfly. Nick played outside with the kids.

It pleased me to speak about the trooper, so I told Paul about our torrid Thursdays. My old pal expressed concern that I would interfere with a happy family. I protested. "Our adventures release his tensions, which can only make his home life more pleasant."

"What if he's caught doing those things you do, which I consider most likely."

"He does them only with me, and I'm careful."

"Careful! I scan the headlines daily for your name."

"You tend to wallow in sensation."

"These episodes might cease if you'd stop fighting what you feel for Nick."

"I'd rather squander my brief infatuations upon the unworthy."

"Be serious."

I was serious. "Love ends, Paul. I don't like pain."

May 1968

Montchanin stopped by the lab and invited me to supper at his apartment. Good conversation carried through spaghetti and several beers. He picked up a pair of empty bottles. "Want another?"

"Where are your roommates?"

"Both have duty till eleven."

"Three hours. I'm loath to chance putting an end to a pleasant evening by making a pass."

Montchanin smiled. "Might enhance the evening." An hour later, he watched as I tried tactilely to commit the feel of his body to memory. "Will you tell Nick?"

"Sure." I ran my palm across a hairy chest. "Did you enjoy talking with him after I'd gone to bed?"

"Yeah. He wanted to know about my work. The courses I took in college."

"Psychology courses?"

"Yeah. Would you have been jealous if . . ."

"Absolutely not. I like both of you and wish you the best. Jealousy is an adolescent emotion of the insecure."

"Yet you love Nick."

"Is it that apparent?"

Montchanin nodded. "The way you watch each other when the other isn't looking. Nick said he worried about it, but decided he'll just ride the crest of the wave till you disappear. Why won't you make a commitment?"

163

"Nick's already tied down with a family; I couldn't fetter him with more chains. My past dictates nonchalance: Whenever I love someone, I get sloppy and lose him. Better to cloak my affection with fun and games."

"You don't want to be hurt?"

"No, I don't. So . . . how have you rationalized the sex with Smitty and O'Hara?"

"I try to see them as guinea pigs in an experiment. At first, I tried to fantasize the situation by substituting women for those jerks, but I'm not into rape. Guess I'm a romantic. I like this." He looked down at me. "The gay patients on NP call their sexual partners 'tricks.' Am I just a trick to you?"

"I define a trick as a brief encounter with no future. As an appellation, it eliminates the possibility of friendship."

"You think we can be friends?"

"Sooner or later, straight men always feel contempt for homosexuals."

"Surely you trust Nick."

"I trust no heterosexual on that subject."

Montchanin sighed. "Do you have many tricks?"

"After every meal." His body smelled as good as it felt. "During my youth, I plunged into promiscuity with a vengeance, considering every trick a potential lover, that special person with whom I could bond and become a complete person. I fell in love on every corner and out of love before I crossed the street."

"You don't strike me as a shallow person."

"I'm a Pisces: The Babbling Brook. Over the years, I've made friends, but one moves on and too many slip away. Even one's attachment to his family weakens. One becomes a superfluous man."

"Sounds lonely."

"I hold continual conversations with my other selves."

"Steppenwolf?"

"Right. Oddly enough, I'm happy. The doctors in Louisiana said few men could have survived my trek from

164

Vietnam. They gave credit to my constitution, but remarked upon my 'enormous will to live.'"

"In all our talk about Vietnam, you've never expressed bitterness."

"I enjoyed myself. War is a grand adventure."

"But you were wounded three times! Had friends killed!"

"Goes with the territory."

"You sound callous."

"Hardly. The shadows of those who have gone before me will always darken my days."

We lay quietly for a minute. "I'll probably never do this again, but for the rest of my life, I'll feel shortchanged because my friendships with men will lack this final intimacy."

"On the other hand, you and your friends will never be struck dumb by a mutual embarrassing memory."

"I'd like to have known you in Vietnam. Seen you playing baseball. Met your family."

"That's why fairy godmothers bestow imaginations."

I caressed a "hot spot"; Montchanin sighed and closed his eyes. "Twice in an hour and I'm still charged up."

"The third time may prove the charm."

He groaned. "This is a lot nicer than with Smitty and O'Hara."

"That was head sex. This is sensual sex."

"When you and Nick make it alone. . . ?"

"He's a gentle and considerate partner with a natural flair for lovemaking. When you reach the point when you must be touched in a certain way or die, he touches you in just that way. Every time. I'm mechanical. Man-made. I had to learn from scratch. Experimentation. Blunders. Always disgusted the first time that I tried anything, yet compelled to try again until the act became pleasurable. I made a determined effort to learn how to kiss after a high school date informed my sister that I smooched like a wet dishrag. An impatient queen pulled away as I fellated him. 'Better learn to watch those teeth, honey.' Heeding a dirty joke, I learned how to be fucked by moving my ass in rhythm: Hit that apple with my left hip, bump that orange with my right hip, grab that banana, and grind that coffee. I marked how a man performed on me because it was probably what he preferred having done to him. I've a bagful of techniques, and to learn each, I've bedded legions of unmemorable tricks. It seems ironic to be considered cold and arrogant when I try so to make other people feel good."

Montchanin stroked my hair. "You are the most vital person I've ever known. I'll appreciate the distance between Newport and Vietnam."

"I lie here bemoaning that same distance."

"I don't want to be gay."

"You're not."

"But I like this!"

"I like pizza, but I'm not Italian."

Two days later, Montchanin left for Combat Training School at Camp Lejeune, North Carolina.

I dispelled gloom by scurrying to Manhattan, where the desk clerk put me in a room with a good-looking sailor. By the time I recognized a sister, his conquest was imminent. Adding to my boredom, he lacked experience. "I want you to teach me everything!" he gushed, suddenly girlish. "I want you to take my anal cherry."

God help me! "This ole Precious of mine might bring you pain."

"I don't care. I want it to be you."

I'd barely begun when he asked me to stop. "Just relax."

"It hurts!"

"Only because you expect it to. If you relax, it will feel real good."

"If you don't stop this minute, I'm going to scream."

Goddam faggot! The greater the difficulty, the greater the glory.

I showered and stalked downstairs to reprimand the desk

clerk. Anxious to correct his error, he pointed at a burly butch beast in the coffee shop. "A Marine Corps recruiter. Lives here in a single."

"Background?"

"Vietnam. Refuses to wear his Purple Hearts and his Silver Star."

I carried a cup of coffee to the recruiter's table and engaged him in conversation. A few minutes later, he invited me to a nearby bar, where he drank eleven tumblers of straight Scotch to my two beers. "When I flew into San Francisco, some little hippie chick come up to me with a flower in her hand. I thought this was sure nice. Then she screamed, 'Murderer!' and threw dog shit at me. Made me feel real bad."

"How can you care what some dumb cunt thinks?"

"You weren't there. Made me feel like all the pain . . . my buddies getting killed . . . worth nothing."

"I served my country, which is honorable. Those who loved me worried about my safety and my wounds. Why should I care what some self-righteous, semi-ignorant little college sophomore thinks? Just pity the boring creep that she'll marry and make unhappy."

He shook his head. "You weren't there."

I endured three hours of a maudlin monologue before half-carrying the handsome marine to his room at the Club. I undressed him, revealing a strong hairy body. Had the faggot been half as relaxed, he might have learned a lot.

I might have learned a lot had Jane been able to tell me how to work on her body. Too shy. Both of us. Oh well, I supposed an affair with a battle-scarred warrior enchanted her. It would have me.

Three costume designers under whom she'd worked on temporary jobs recommended her, each unbeknownst to the others, as shop supervisor of a prestigious summer theater. (Jane had not applied for the position, unaware of an opening.) She would build costumes: construct the patterns and

167

piece the material together. She would also keep the costumes clean, pressed, and in repair. It seemed unrewarding to labor on another's creations; at Tulane and Yale, I had seen several shows dressed in Jane's stunning designs. Nevertheless, she felt the job a big step toward Broadway.

"I have to leave next week and will be gone all summer. Oh, Kurt! We'll be separated for so long."

"It's the break you've been waiting for. I'll still be in Newport when you get back."

"Will you live in New York when you get out of the Navy?"

"I want to finish college."

"You could attend Columbia or NYU."

"Lacking both money and brains? I've already been accepted by Evangeline." (A second-rate college in my hometown.)

"You'll be so far away."

"If I live with my grandmother, the GI Bill will cover everything but tuition."

"We could live together. I'd help."

"You're barely making it now, and your parents would disapprove. And how much studying could I accomplish amid the distractions of Manhattan?"

"I want us to be together."

"You turned down the Milwaukee job because of me. In four years, you'll have made it. We can marry then."

"Stop it, Kurt!"

"What?"

"Believing you're stupid."

Among other epithets, Mother had called me a big dumb Swede. Although I was only one-eighth Swedish, I'd believed her. My grades in high school proved my stupidity.

"I don't understand."

"You've already finished two years of college. It will take only two more years to get your degree, not four."

"After graduating, I plan to travel in Europe for a couple

168

of years."

"What?"

"Spend a month or so in England, a month in France, a month in. . . ."

While preparing supper, Jane guzzled four gin-and-tonics and put in a long-distance call to her parents. I could hear her side of the conversation through the bedroom door. "If he thinks I'm going to wait while he gads about all over the world . . ." I pulled on my jacket and slipped out of the apartment. Women are such ugly drunks.

The Enlisted Man's Club held its weekly dance on the second floor. Every Saturday, local girls served as hostesses to appreciative servicemen. I'd never attended, but the desk clerk reported the galas to be successful. "Lots of engagements and marriages. We used to have two hundred military and fifty girls. Pretty girls, nice, too. Now we're lucky if five girls come."

Curious, I dropped in to see why. A quartet of homely females with fixed smiles stood around the punch bowl. On the other side of the room, three dozen Filipinos giggled. No Caucasian males were present.

The desk clerk seemed depressed. "A pair of them checked in last month. A dozen turned up the next week. We have ninety beds; this weekend, Filipinos fill sixty."

"The Yellow Peril. Next weekend, you'll have a full complement."

"They're all Navy. Your shipmates."

"Stewards. They serve the officers by waiting tables, shining shoes, making beds. . . ."

"The parties are ruined. The girls don't like dancing with them and the white guys hate them."

"Odd how attractive Oriental women can be while the men look like beetles and grasshoppers."

"You ever make it with one?"

"A Eurasian that I met in front of the YMCA in Newport. Well-dressed kid around eighteen. Snotty. Probably the son

169

of an officer. Dispiriting sex. During R&R in Tokyo, I enjoyed looking at young Japanese businessmen, each wearing a dark suit, his sharp-bony face inscrutable; naked, however, their hairless bodies appeared fleshy or disjointed. In Chu Lai, I appreciated a badly-wounded patient, a Korean captain with blue eyes, white teeth, a hairy chest, and sexy legs. A stunning Amerasian from a brutal nation. Unfortunately, he had a twisted swollen purple cock."

"So you didn't?"

"No. They're uncircumcized and have a fishy odor. What's my roommate like?"

"Nothing special. Because of the Filipinos, I've had to turn away forty Americans, including the soldier you and Nick raped. Sent him to the 47th Street YMCA."

I erred. My roommate instilled no passion within me, but I made a pass anyway. He hurried downstairs to report a predatory faggot; I gathered my belongings and spent the night on the floor of a room shared by eight zips. Accustomed to crowds, they ignored me.

I awakened early and strolled over to the YMCA. Darby shared a room with a fat soldier who was game for anything except leaving us alone. The three of us spent the afternoon exploring Little Old New York south of 14th Street, a tame way to cap a lousy weekend. I couldn't get back to Newport soon enough.

The Yellow Yeti had taken over the training of a new tech, a six-week reserve fresh from laboratory school, so I stood duty with the lab's sole WAVE. A porcine woman with thin hair and an ungainly walk, she slept in the WAVE barrack while I spent the night alone in the lab. Comforted to know that her expertise was available should I have needed it, I opened *War and Peace*, planning to enjoy the solitude. Ten minutes later, two corpsmen carried in one of my co-workers, a Polack who had overdosed on pills and liquor after an argument with his wife; they put him on the lower bunk and extracted my promise to watch him.

170

The Pole had a wiry body, tiny features, and prominent teeth. He had bowed legs and wore eyeglasses. He looked like a blond Jap. He did have a cocky attitude and a swaggering walk, but his tight white pants appeared soiled at the crotch and his fingernails had black rims; on the other hand, a long bulge stretched along his thigh. I might have been tempted were I certain that he'd bathed since screwing his snippy little wife, who had turned in a filthy urine specimen.

The SEAL would leave for the Mediterranean Fleet in six weeks. Alas! No scenario for a seduction came to mind. All my ruses involved dishonor, and the glorious hunk would choose death first. Probing for weaknesses, I could intuit only his thwarted patriotism; he wanted to serve in Vietnam. His buddies scattered to the four corners of the globe, the SEAL seemed lonely and irked by his assignment to the War College. Then the actor sent a postcard informing me of his return the following week to finish the training film in good weather and I learned that an old friend was back in New York. I sent off a couple of letters.

Dear Nick and Rosemary,

   Mother taught me to send bread-and-butter notes immediately. Blame a rebellious youth and spring's awakening for my tardiness. I've yet to taste an Italian dish that repelled me, and your ravioli enhanced my infatuation. Your culinary skills could probably make anchovies, cooked carrots, and rice pudding digestible.

   Jane and I left your house marveling at the beauty of your family. Gina will be a knockout, and as Jane exclaimed, "The boys ain't chopped liver!"

   She's gone to North Carolina. A job in costume design. I'd hated seeing her only intermittently; a separation of four months dismays me into thoughts of razor blades and hangman's knots.

   My best buddy in Newport, a Navy SEAL, leaves town next month. We exercise at the base gym and run seven

171

miles around Ocean Drive whenever possible. He says very little and I must talk for both of us. All that time together, and I don't know the guy.

Here at the hospital, sadistic doctors insisted that several tubes of blood be drawn everyday from Ginny, a long-term patient on Pediatrics. The pale, cranky nine-year-old demanded that only I leech her. Cancer finally extinguished Ginny's little light. Another tech subbed for me at the autopsy.

If you can hire a babysitter Tuesday night, two tickets await you at the box office of the Minnie Maddern Fiske Theater for the opening night performance of *Bake and Fry*, a musical starring, among lesser talents, my old love, Diana Durland, who will expect you backstage after the show. It might be a lonely dressing room; I've heard through the grapevine that the show is in trouble. Nevertheless, Diana's always good. Expect to attend the cast party—Off-Broadway types that crept through Alice's looking-glass by way of Sodom, Gomorrah, and Oz.

Relentlessly,
Kurt

My dear Diana,

You owe me, bitch. Two tickets . . . opening night . . . Nick Esoldi . . . take them to the cast party . . . you'll like him . . . a lot.

A Navy SEAL resides nearby whom I must have. Perhaps you and Nick could come up on an off-day. Do you know anyone in Newport with a house? My plan is too elaborate for a motel room.

Ran into that hideous bulldagger you used to date. Angie Lichtenfelder. Love her name! A restaurant on Second Avenue. Headed for Radio City Music Hall to ooze over the Rockettes. Is that the Sapphic equivalent of cruising for rough trade?

Up yours,
Kurt

172

Monday, on my way to the gym, I passed a WAVE. I smiled, said "Hi!" and walked on.

"Corpsman!" The WAVE's voice halted my progress. "Why didn't you salute me?"

"Why should I?"

Her sharp chin lifted indignantly. "Do you see these bars? I'm a lieutenant."

"Really! I didn't know WAVES had officers."

"Your training leaves a lot to be desired."

Depends upon how you looked at it. In Vietnam, my training had saved a few lives. I apologized. "Sorry, ma'am. From now on, I'll sure watch for bars on ladies' uniforms." She reached into her navy-blue shoulder bag for pen and paper. Damn! She planned to write me up, a punishment that could confine me to barracks for a weekend of sweeping, mopping, waxing, and polishing. I tried to look regretful. She glared at me. "Lady, I just got back from a year in Vietnam and five months recovering from wounds in a stateside hospital. After all that, you're not going to rob me of a weekend liberty for something this dumb?"

She asked for my identity card, continued writing her report, and snapped it into her bag. We saluted smartly and went our separate ways. I felt like a penguin.

Worried that such nonsense might be taken serious by the admiral, a pussywhipped old wimp who would make my humiliation an example to other untrained corpsmen, I went to the MAA; he said not to worry. I resented adding a search for tiny silver bars on a cunt's shoulders to the picayune irritations of my life in the military.

One of the lab techs, a sirupy little redhead, accosted me at dinner and demanded that I go drinking with him. Astounded at his effrontery, I could dream up no good reason to avoid the excursion, so he led me to a high-priced bar by the docks. His insipidity cloyed quickly. The junior lab pathologist entered the bar, and the redhead insisted that we join him. The Navy frowned on fraternization between

173

officers and enlisted men. I slipped out of the bar, leaving the redhead chatting inanely, snuggled up to an uncomfortable captain ever deeper in his cups.

Wednesday, I called the effervescent Diana, who had spent a year touring the U.S. in *A Streetcar Named Desire*, *Mourning Becomes Electra*, and *Picnic*. "Darling!" she said, "I feel absolutely dreadful about not visiting you in the hospital. I'd devised a marvelous scenario. An enchantingly handsome actor in the troupe would portray a physician and I asked the costume girl to work up a dazzling little nurse's outfit that emphasized the old balookas. The actor and I would sneak into the hospital and seduce you and whomever you lusted after, within reason, of course, but the actor caught the clap in Shreveport, and while waiting for his faucet to stop dripping, I met this giddy little dyke in the French Quarter who never hushed her mouth and the next thing I knew, I'm in Birmingham, which was like Little Nairobi, and I met the most charming jigaboos who talked all mushymouth and had thick untiring tongues and Atlanta was another story altogether, certain to make your Precious stand ramrod straight and I'll climb aboard and die of ecstasy upon a hairy telephone pole. How are you, darling?"

"Fine."

"Nicky says your damaged arm has regained its fearful symmetry and that none of your hideous scars detract from the beauty of my favorite Adonis."

"The wop insists upon exaggerating my qualities. I'm coming to see your show this weekend."

"Too late. It closed after one performance. A dreadful piece. I'll never appear in another musical, no matter how many solos they give me. Fairies who tinkle piano keys and trip the light fantastic should be sent to Never-Never Land and fed to the crocodiles. Oh darling, if you'd seen me as Blanche. She broke the hardest hearts from coast-to-coast. Poor Tennessee."

"Rosemary in *Picnic*?"

174

"More broken hearts. A critic in Fresno called me a 'six-hankerchief Duse.'"

"*Mourning Becomes Electra?*"

"Chorus, indistinguishable among a smelly brood of bitches and sluts. Hated the show. I could tell you stories about the tour that would shrivel your testicles into chick-peas."

"When can you come up?"

"Thursday. Nicky's bringing me. As you *demanded*, I left two tickets at the box office. After the show, and darling, five minutes into that travesty, an orangutan would have recognized a disaster, two simply gorgeous men showed up at my dressing room, each more beautiful than the other, and so masculine, although compared with the boys in the chorus, Truman Capote is a macho man. The cast party would have been a wake without them. The lavender lads stared flagrantly, licked their lips lasciviously, and lisped lewd proposals. As I devised a plot to get them both in bed . . ."

"Who was the simply gorgeous man with Nick?" I wondered.

"A little bit snappy, aren't we, darling? Not to worry. His brother, Michael. I assume it was his brother. I'd adore finally seeing your eyes green with jealousy."

"Did Michael have eyes of Prussian blue?"

"Aren't they lovely? Several of the chorus sluts dragged him off to a better party—my dear, is he really as boring as I suspect—so I told him that Nick would be waiting in my humble flat. Lured into my trap, Nicky stood firm against my wiles. He looks like the Archangel Lucifer before his descent into Hell. I threw myself at him, slithering from sole to crown, but he refused me, sweetly explaining his true-blue fidelity to some washed-out tramp from the Jersey bogs. Constancy from a friend of yours! I didn't believe it for a minute and finally proved that an act of fellatio from the distaff side could rival your expertise. As he manipulated my

175

marvelous mammaries with gaping wonder, we traded tales of Strom. I wondered myself at your ability to inspire such passion in a glorious Latin. He loves you, Kurt. Wherever did you meet two straight longshoremen and whatever have you done to them?"

Longshoremen, huh? "Nothing to Mike, whose beauty masks the soul of a turnip. I'm teaching Nick how to play games."

"Lord help him, although I cannot censure you a whit, he's quite divine in bed. So is Michael, according to three of the trollops in the chorus. Very very well-hung. By the way, I'm playing a season of classics this summer in Cleveland. Lady Macbeth, Emilia again, and Millament in *The Way of the World.*"

"That play confuses me at the beginning, in the middle, and near the end."

"It does everyone, darling, except the most pretentious English professors, but I simply must do it. Can you come? There must be someone in Cleveland who could charm us both. Isn't it terribly German?"

"That's Cincinnati."

"Don't you think I'm still too young for Emilia?"

"I breathlessly await your Cleopatra."

"Oh happy horse that bears the weight of Antony! Nick could make his debut playing opposite me. Does he enjoy the docks, unloading fish and refrigerators? Don't they attack each other with grappling hooks? Is he Mafia? If I wore a black wig, do you think I could do the Anna Magnani part in *The Rose Tattoo?*"

Before we began playing Diana's favorite game, "Roles You Think I Should Play," I changed the subject. "Where will you stay in Newport?"

"I have a choice, darling. After Michael, reeking of contaminated snatch, rolled in to drag Nicky home, I made some calls. A Baroque gatehouse on the Dochmius estate . . ."

176

"San Façon?"

". . . rented by a waspish dilettante who would never perform a sordid act himself, but has salivated at my escapades, or a rustic cottage overlooking the bay owned by two spinsterish sisters who make the most severe pottery that they paint dun and who pretend that neither of them is at all interested in tonguing my little jampot. I do hope you choose the wasp, who will demand only a detailed report, so if all goes well, you and Nicky should thank him personally. He'll be creaming his Brooks Brothers undergarments at the sight of you, but he's too uptight and asexual to make a pass. The Sapphic sisters may strum up their courage, and I really haven't the inclination after my flop to endure their mournful wooing. And should your walrus . . ."

"He's a SEAL!"

". . . do something macabre, the ladies would be unable to fib about knowing a girl like I. The hornet can prevaricate without pause, having declared for fifty years that he's human."

"The gatehouse is fine."

"What part do I play?"

"A communist spy."

"Oh, Kurt! That's so tacky."

"The illegitimate daughter of Eva Peron and King Haakon the Ninety-Sixth of Norway."

"I love the Eva Peron."

"The Baron von Richthofen?"

"I'd be distracted by thoughts of Snoopy."

"Manolete?"

"I'd never pass as a full-blooded hot tamale."

"Raoul Wallenberg?"

"Perfect. Trading information with the Soviets to release him from the Gulag." We worked out a few details, Diana uttered vicious critiques of actresses currently appearing on Broadway, and I finally ended a long-distance connection that cost me two weeks' pay.

My friend, the actor, agreed to take part in the production, but admitted a weakness for improvisation; I spent the better part of Wednesday evening at work on a script. Thursday afternoon, the actor took a break during a camera set-up and entered the gym wearing his navy drag. He strolled over to the mat where the SEAL and I worked out. "Commander Barrymore of Naval Intelligence. May I speak to you in private?" I hoped fervently that the SEAL hadn't watched any of the filming, but he struck me as someone with little interest in "The Arts." We withdrew to the locker room. The actor affected a confidential tone. "A beautiful Soviet spy has been seducing officers of the Atlantic Fleet to gather information on NATO strategy. We must learn the exact information she has obtained so that we can falsify papers, which will fool the Rooskies. We need your help."

I let the SEAL speak for both of us. "What can we do?"

"We have learned that the woman exhibits nymphomanic tendencies, especially when confronted by pairs of muscular young men. Apparently, the Rooskies have pictures of such young men in Intelligence, so we must use outsiders. The two of you have been recommended by a high-ranking officer to take part in a clandestine operation." The SEAL nodded. "As she always seduces two young men at the same time, you must get invited to her room. While you keep her busy in bed, our man can sneak in downstairs to locate and photograph her dossier. I cannot impress upon you enough that the operation must be conducted with the utmost discretion. Your best friends may be among those compromised by this woman, and they might warn her. Are you willing to undertake the mission?"

The SEAL stood ramrod straight. "Yes, sir." I agreed.

"Good. The beautiful Soviet spy lives with a man, a Roumanian communist. He usually guards the dossier, but we've learned that he goes upstairs to watch while the woman has sex with pairs of muscular young men."

Such perversity shook the SEAL. "I'm not a ladies' man,

178

sir. Are you sure . . ."

"Do you love your country, mister?"

"Yes sir."

"You *will* succeed with this mission. The two of you must shower, dress in civilian clothes, and drive to the restaurant she frequents. Hopefully, she will invite you to her house. Once there, you will perform as she wishes, whether or not the conspirator watches or even takes part in the sex. We *must* photograph that dossier. It can be of international importance." On paper, my script had seemed on the level of *The Hardy Boys Meet Mata Hari*, but the actor made it sound good. "Remember, to give our man the time he needs, you must do everything she and her cohort ask. Everything!"

"Yes, sir."

"Okay, get dressed. And good luck. Strom has a reputation with the ladies, which should help." I had the grace to blush. "Tell no one. The Pentagon considers this more important to national security than any operation currently underway in Vietnam." He turned on his heel and departed.

After a quick shower, the SEAL and I jogged to his barrack; I waited in the parking lot while he changed. On our way to the hospital, we drove past the film location, where the actor stood illuminated by bright lights. My heart skipped a beat, but the SEAL was too preoccupied to notice. "I better tell you that . . ." The confession came hard for him. ". . . I'm not much good with women. I like them. God, how I like them! It's just . . ."

"You're the quiet type. A lot of women go for that."

"Nowhere I've ever been."

"Thought you had a girl back home."

He nodded. "Real nice girl." We drove across the bridge to the mainland. "Not very exciting." We stopped at the hospital barracks so I could change into civvies; when I returned to the car, the SEAL seemed perplexed. "He never told us the restaurant where we're supposed to meet the chick."

179

Son of a bitch! The actor had forgotten that part. "The Viking Hotel."

"I don't remember him saying that."

"The man at the front desk just handed me a note. Said 'Viking Hotel.' Apparently, the commander called on our way over."

"Got the note with you?"

"I ate it." Ice water ran through my bowels. Why ever did I do these things to myself?

We drove to the motel and ordered dinner. The SEAL seemed more nervous than I, "How will we recognize her?"

Damn the actor! He had forgotten to describe Diana. "As she's a foreigner, she'll probably look exotic." Diana entered the dining room wearing a tight black cocktail dress and a large picture hat. A veil covered her face. Smoke trailed from a violet cigarette at the end of a long green holder. "I think that's her," I opined.

The actress tottered on six-inch heels to the table nearest ours. Seated, she lifted the veil and studied us through a scarlet lorgnette. "Vot beeyootivol yunk men!"

We dipped our heads shyly and shoveled food down dry throats. The SEAL nudged me with his elbow and muttered, "Say something."

"What?"

"You're supposed to be good with women."

"The commander said that, not me."

"I'll go to the head. You get something started."

I watched him leave the dining room; he had a great butch walk. I turned to Diana. "You look like the Whore of Babylon."

She smiled sunnily. "Why ever do I feel typecast? Speaking of types, the walrus isn't mine."

"The SEAL!"

"Musclemen have little between their ears or their thighs."

"I've showered with him; it's nice, if average. And don't believe for a minute that he ain't bright."

180

"He's too macho."

"You like Nick."

"Because Nicky is so graceful. The walrus, like most macho men, appears awkward and brusque and is probably a premature ejaculator. Ah well! I promised you a gift, and if a walrus is what you want, a walrus you shall have. Does he understand that I don't accept *la pénètration*?" Diana believed that contraceptive devices inhibited her orgasms.

"You call the shots."

"I may make an exception again for Nicky. Sitting next to him during that long drive, I flowed a quart." She indicated the menu. "Must I eat dinner? I'm on a stringent diet."

"A small salad?"

"Fine. Let's get this over so we can catch up."

"I have to seduce you."

"Do your damnedest, darling."

The SEAL returned. Diana flashed cryptic smiles. I didn't know how to seduce women; why ever had I written that into the script? "Ma'am?"

"Da?"

"How can we talk you into joining us? Just sit here trying to look stud, show you snapshots of our dicks, or ask if you like it mean and greasy?"

The SEAL growled.

"I hof nefer been zo inzulted." Diana turned away indignantly; then, she giggled. "But az da peniz zed to da poozy, you haf talked me into it." She joined us.

"You speak with an accent," I noted. "Where ever are you from?" The SEAL kicked my leg under the table.

"Argentina."

"Ah!"

I could think of no more questions. Diana flashed cryptic smiles. The SEAL ate. "Vould you like to zee my bedroom?"

"Yes, ma'am."

"You come. A yoke, no? Ha ha ha!" We rode in the SEAL's car; Diana's chatter obliterated sane thought. We

181

entered the gatehouse and climbed the stairs to the bedroom. Blue and gold Rococo: a gay descendant of Tiepolo must have furnished the room. "Unsip me, pleaze." The SEAL obliged. Diana's undergarments had been ordered from Frederick's of Bucharest. "Now I unsip boz of you."

Everyone naked, the SEAL and I joined Diana on a massive four-poster. Nick entered, also dressed in black. He looked like a Mafia hitman. "Who's that?" I wondered.

"My hozpunt. He likes—how you zay?—to vatch." The SEAL's unmentionable went limp. "Vill you make me da hot?"

"Sure. How?" I asked brightly.

"Lick on hiz schvantz."

"Huh?"

"Lick on your friend's dinkalink. It makes me da hot to vatch."

I looked at the SEAL, who seemed in pain. "Well, as they say in the Navy, 'Anything for our country and a beautiful woman.' Right, buddy?" He nodded imperceptively, his eyes closed.

Diana watched, smiling. "Ah, dot makes me a leetle da hot. Now, da udder vay." We looked uncomprehendedly at her. "Dummkopf! Da udder vay. He licks on your dinkalink."

I flopped onto my back. The SEAL didn't move. I smiled artlessly. "Anything for a beautiful woman, huh, buddy? And our country?" The SEAL sighed deeply and performed for America. "Hey! Watch the teeth!"

Nick had stripped and lay beside Diana, caressing those enormous breasts. The actress stroked her clitoris. "Ah, I bekin to get da hotter." Nick sat up and ran his hand over the SEAL's backside; the sailor looked behind in alarm. "Ah! Dot's vot makes me da hottest, vatchink my hozpunt put hiz schvantz in da rozy hole." The SEAL glared at me, near rebellion. I hummed "America the Beautiful"; he closed his eyes and accepted Nick, who took no little time penetrating the rozy hole. When my turn arrived, I comprehended the difficulty; the SEAL's ass was as hard as iron and tighter than a miser's grip. Diana diddled her clit, crying, "Da hottest! Da hottest!"

Thus, two hours passed. When we left the gatehouse, I asked the SEAL to drop me in town. "I need to think about this." Ten minutes later, I met Nick and Diana near the entrance of Cliff Walk; we strolled its length under a full moon. The actress giggled. "Kurt makes it all so complicated. A simple seduction emphasizing my fabulous bazooms might have accomplished as much."

"Don't flatter yourself, Bernhardt. Without logical elaboration, we would never have stretched da rozy hole."

"I expect to be rewarded with this gorgeous Latin."

"A bunk awaits him in the night barrack. Nick doesn't find you attractive."

My buddy, the longshoreman, snorted. "Bullshit! Diana beats any *Playboy* centerfold. You're so . . . voluptuous."

"Some women sew. Others cook. I volup."

"Before you ravish each other on the Vanderbilts' lawn, we must plan our next venture."

"Christ! The SEAL wasn't enough?"

"For any normal pervert," murmured Diana, "but Kurt . . ."

"Nick wishes to wreck vengeance on a high school classmate."

"Ahh!" exclaimed Diana.

"Did you research the subject?"

Nick cleared his throat. "He's a lawyer in Manhattan. Top firm. Makes fifty grand a year. Married to a congressman's daughter. Plans to go into politics. Short of holding him at gunpoint, it's impossible, Kurt."

As we strolled along Cliff Walk, I wracked my brain for a plan. My friends, arm-in-arm, threw amused glances at me. "What would a well-to-do lawyer need for a political career?"

183

"Lots and lots of lovely money."

"Patronage. What sort of corporation could we represent?"

Diana played this game well. "When you said 'patronage,' I immediately thought of a millionaire."

"Nick's friend might be honorable, so it would have to be a disinterested millionaire."

"One whose name he knows, but inaccessible to him socially."

"Any millionaire getting married this summer?"

"Janet Auchincloss."

"Really! Too well known and a little too close to home."

Diana named an English duke and an American heiress. "From all reports, he's nasty besotted lech."

"The heiress?"

"Push her face in dough, you'll bake monster cookies."

"She get around much?"

"Raised in a Belgium convent. Spends most of her time fishing in Scotland."

"How do you know so much about her?"

"Met the hag at an Amazon ball in Paris. She wanted to bury that pitted face between my lovelies."

"Nick's friend likely to know of her proclivity?"

"Doubtful. Even I was surprised."

Nick worried. "Wouldn't you need some sort of reference to even meet him?"

"I'll use my own name."

Diana explained. "Kurt's stepfather is one of the wealthiest men in Louisiana. Long lineage. More 'begats' than the Bible."

Nick looked at me wonderingly. "I didn't know that."

"Doesn't mean I have a pot to piss in. My sister's best friend has worked her way through medical school as the mistress of a businessman, the scion of an aristocratic New Orleans family. I'll call Jock and ask him to give me a reference." We sat on a large rock at the end of Cliff Walk and gazed at a moonlit sea. "Jugs, do you know a beautiful brunette who would be willing to take part in a raunchy quintet?"

"You and Nicky and me?"

"And Nick's bête noir."

"Is he really a beast with a black soul?"

"Au contraire."

"I know just the person."

"Nick, did you bring the captain's uniform?"

"In the van. Just got it out of the cleaners."

"You can use it tomorrow to get me off work; then we'll drive to New York for a meeting with your buddy."

Diana shuddered. "I don't even know your plan, but I'm working up an exquisite orgasm at the prospect."

The next morning, Nick laid a mountain of bullshit on "Umble Uriah." "Commander Carl Strom . . . Kurt's uncle . . . hasn't seen him in fifteen years . . . inspection tour of Boston . . ." I got the rest of the day off, and after stopping to thank the actor and borrow his extra commander's uniform, rode to New York with Nick and Diana.

My executive secretary (Diana) set up an appointment with Buchanan Gilbert. We wondered if the lawyer would recognize Nick.

"He never knew I existed."

"Will you be able to erect? Old Belle Poitrine didn't wear you out last night?"

"I tried, darling. Oh, how I tried!"

A stunning Negress swept into Diana's apartment. "Rushed here from dance class. Gotta shower." She studied Nick and me. "Fine." She disappeared into the bathroom.

"You asked for a beautiful brunette," said Diana ingenuously. "Her name is Louella."

At three-thirty, the four of us sat in a well-appointed suite high in the Pan Am Building. A sleek secretary ushered me into Gilbert's office. He came around the desk to shake my

185

hand. Tall. Impeccably dressed. Imperially slim. Handsome as a movie star. "Commander Strom?" (I wore the actor's extra uniform.) "Please have a seat." We sat. "As I understand it, you're here about the marriage between Edythe Van Slyde and the Duke of Sandition."

Experts at logic and prevarication, lawyers could prove my most formidable opponents. And to feign aristocracy at the same time! "I'm against it," I drawled. "Edythe holds no illusion about this being a love match. A plain American heiress and a European nobleman—the stuff of Wharton, James, and the tabloids. Edythe is fully aware of the Duke's reputation as a libertine. She cannot hope for fidelity; she does expect discretion." I wondered if Gilbert had received an invitation to the wedding. Doubtful. He had attended a public high school.

"May I ask your relation to Miss Van Slyde."

"Cousin by marriage. We grew up together. My family's plantation in Louisiana. Her family's enclave on the Hudson. Newport and Palm Beach. May I speak confidentially?"

"Of course."

"I'm quite fond of Edythe. Despite her unfortunate appearance, she is sensitive, kind, and loyal. The Duke is sadistic, amoral, and weak. He'll hurt and embarrass her."

"Yet she will be the Duchess of Sandition."

"Edythe has a taste for politics and philanthropy; instead, her millions will enrich an impoverished, useless, selfish family."

"Where do I fit into all this?"

"I'm hosting a stag party for the Duke that will create a scandal, forcing Edythe to call off the wedding. Such interference sounds presumptuous, but good men abound who would marry my cousin and make her happy. Until that occurs, Edythe will involve herself in politics. She has heard of your ambitions, checked your background, and would heavily support your first campaign. No strings."

"That's very flattering."

186

"Edythe is practical. She believes you would be an excellent candidate." I wondered to what office he aspired. "Edythe wants to know nothing about my plans, but she did insist that I disclose them to an impartial observer, worrying that the stag party may be in dubious taste."

"Is it?"

"Most assuredly. Edythe wants a candidate whom she can trust. An honest man whose taste and discretion would be tested by acting as an impartial observer in this situation."

"What are your plans for the stag party?"

"At its climax, we'll put on a tawdry stage show. The Duke will be invited to take part. If he falls too far into licentiousness, the scandal will cancel the wedding."

"Tell me about the stage show."

"Better than that, we'll act it out for you. The performers are waiting in the outer office."

The lawyer looked at his watch. "I don't know . . ." Click! Click! All those millions. "How long will it take?"

"Half-an-hour at the most."

He nodded. "Let me make a couple of telephone calls." He escorted me to the door. "I won't be five minutes."

As I entered the waiting room, my crew stirred restlessly. "Darling, I'm drenched with anticipation," whispered Diana. "Did he fall for it?"

"Can't tell. He's making phone calls."

"What could he learn?"

"Nothing about me that you didn't mention over the phone. I'm worried that he might know Edythe Van Slyde."

"Unlikely. Gilbert and his wife are parvenu. He's probably postponing appointments."

The secretary picked up a telephone receiver. "Yes, sir. Thank you." She smiled at us. "Mr. Gilbert will see all of you now." As we entered the lawyer's office, his secretary covered her typewriter and pulled her purse from a drawer.

Gilbert gazed appreciatively at Diana, who wore an emerald cocktail dress, and the Negress, who wore an

187

orange sheath. Both looked likely companions to a pair of naval officers. After introducing everyone, I set the scene. "Two hundred guests will attend the stag party: the Duke's buddies from England and the Continent, several Broadway and Hollywood actors, and the Newport-Palm Beach crowd. Oh, the Prince of _____." I looked at the lawyer. "You, of course, will receive an invitation." Gilbert's face twitched involuntarily; who among us is not a starfucker? "I will play the part of the Master of Ceremonies, an actor who couldn't be here, nor could the actor whose place Captain Nicholas will take. You'll stand in for the Duke, if you don't mind." Gilbert nodded. "Ready?"

The lawyer smiled. "Ready."

"Gentlemen! Earlier this evening, I heard a startling confession from the Duke's uncle, Count Bellevue, who admitted under prodding that no one had ever told the Duke the facts of life. I promptly asked the Duke if this were true. 'Do you know the facts of life?' 'Absolutely, old chap. Babies come from belly buttons.' Such ignorance appalled me, so I called some friends to teach our bridegroom a few things. Ladies, will you bring the Duke forward?" Diana and the Negress led Gilbert to my side. "May I introduce Milady Castlemaine?" Diana performed a ladylike striptease to my humming of "An English Country Garden." I gestured to the Negress. "Princess Shalimar of Lower Nubia!" She stripped to a sexy rendition of "Swing Low, Sweet Chariot."

Diana took over the narration, pointing out her body's erotic parts; the Negress demonstrated various techniques upon each part. I introduced Nick. "The Earl of Jersey." The women undressed him. Diana pointed out his genitalia. The Negress demonstrated.

Nick and Louella moved to a couch, where they made love. Diana slithered around Gilbert and me, unbuttoning my uniform and removing his tie. He protested when she tugged at his suit coat. I said, "The Duke would permit this much without objection." The lawyer nodded, his forehead wet with perspiration. His vest followed.

Diana unbuttoned my shirt. "I must press my luscious breasts against your manly chest." I allowed the action. She turned to Gilbert. "You too, ducky." He stood rigid, staring past Diana at the couple on the couch. They rose and glided towards us. Louella kissed me; Nick unbuttoned my trousers. After Diana loosened Gilbert's belt, the four of us eased him onto the thick rug and removed his pants and shoes.

"Oh no!" he murmured, when he realized that I performed orally upon him. When Diana straddled his face, he obliged her, but murmured, "Oh no!" when she moved aside and Nick stuck his unmentionable in the attorney's mouth. Nick arose and Gilbert buried his face between Diana's breasts, the fingers of one hand moving in and out of her vagina. "Oh, no!" he murmured, when Nick took him anally. I took my turns at his mouth and ass, as did Louella, who strapped on a huge black dildo to ravish him anally. Nick took another turn while I brought the stricken man off. As we washed ourselves in the private john, Gilbert lay on the floor, an arm across his eyes. I don't know if he saw the Negress slip two fifties from his wallet; he hadn't moved when we walked out the door.

None of us spoke in the elevator or crossing the street to a restaurant. Everyone ordered a steak, including Diana, diet or no diet. After the waiter left, we sat and looked at one another. A minute passed. Another minute. I smiled at Nick. "Sated with revenge?"

He shook his head. "Heavy, man. Jesus Christ!"

Diana fanned herself with a napkin. "Kurt, darling, I know you seldom repeat your ruses, but I experienced three orgasms. We must do this again."

The Negress flashed white teeth. "I love fucking over honkies." She studied me. "You're good. You and Diana do this before?" I nodded. "Who started it?"

Diana smiled. "Kurt, of course. I went through a period

189

of lusting after young mothers. Kurt craved humpy daddies." A dreamy look crossed her face.

"You get many?"

The actress returned from the past with a happy sigh. "A
baker's dozen of couples. I've worked with professional
actors for a score of years, since I was fourteen. I've never
seen a better improvisator than Kurt. No living actor has his
range. I'd love to work with him on stage."

I protested. "Diana's better. She can talk both men and
women into servicing her without reciprocation."

"We're both good, darling. Now, are we doing this again?
I leave for Cleveland at the end of the month. Kurt?"

"Thanks to Nick, I've had everyone on my hit list. Anyone
here holding a grudge?"

The trooper glanced at each of us before speaking. "The
idea of a stag party. I'm invited to one in two weeks. A New
Jersey highway patrolman." Diana still believed that Nick
worked on the Jersey docks. "An arrogant son-of-a-bitch,
and from what I hear, sadistic. Hates colored people."
Louella's eyes flashed.

"What's the grudge?" I asked.

Nick couldn't meet anyone's eyes. "He dated my sister.
The day after he took Connie's . . . he deflowered her,
Harry and his fiancée announced their engagement. My sis-
ter cried for two months."

"The guests at the party?"

"About sixty. Mostly cops."

Diana had a thing about men wearing blue. "Darling, I'm
breathless at the prospect, but wouldn't those celestial policemen arrest us should we perform our little vignette?"

Nick shook his head. "Not at a private party, so long as no
pandering is involved."

The actress hesitated. "I'd hate to appear in *Confidential*.
I am a public figure."

"Believe me, jugs, the common herd is as likely to recognize an Off-Broadway actress as it is the author of an article

190

in an educational journal."

"I'd forgotten how irritating you can be. All right, I'm in. Louella?"

The Negress spoke with loathing in her voice. "Only people I hate worse than honkie lawyers and society types is police." Nick blanched. "I'll cover that pig with turds outta my black ass."

I hoped she spoke metaphorically. Diana waxed with enthusiasm. "I can still fit into my high school cheerleader's uniform. Louella, you'd be a striking majorette. Kurt could be a football player, and Nick could be the coach."

Nick declined the part. "I know too many of those guys."

A little hitch couldn't stop Diana. "A divine young man lives in my basement, unbeknownst to the landlord. I feed him occasionally and let him use my shower. Wants to be an actor. Much too macho for an affair; he would never accept my denying him la pénètration. If we made it worth his while . . ."

Nick's brother was on the entertainment committee. "A hundred bucks?"

"He could use it."

I interrupted. "Another scenario comes to mind. A sailor, a hooker, a policewoman, and a state trooper."

Diana gazed at me with admiration. "Love it! I could wear glasses and pin up my hair. Louella, you could wear that sleazy pink number with the slits to your pudenda. Show off your mahogany skin and those gorgeous long legs."

Nick preferred Diana's idea. "Hits too close to home, cops watching other cops getting it on."

Nick left to check with his brother, Louella for a voice lesson, and Diana for God-Only-Knows. I called Francisco the Model. "Any parties tonight?"

He gave me three addresses. "I'm driving to Boston tomorrow. Will you come with me?"

"Checking buns at Harvard's pool or have you a new lover?"

191

"You must meet him. A linguist at MIT. This is it, Kurt. I've finally found true love." I gave it three weeks. "Come by the flat at eleven. We'll brunch with friends and dine tomorrow night with Morris."

"Morris!"

As ugly a number as I'd met since attending a music festival in Wewa, Arkansas. Morris looked like an unshelled turtle. He and Francisco held each other's hands and gazed into one another's eyes. I left them after brandy and considered what remained of the weekend.

I resolved to enter Sporters Bar only as a last resort. Nor would I attend a play or a concert, as I'd done so often while stationed in Boston. I had viewed objets d'arte at museums and walked along historic streets. I had grown as cultured as a pearl.

I hired a taxi and propositioned the butch Irish cabbie. He snarled. To avoid repercussions, I disembarked several blocks past the Miles Standish Memorial and walked back to the Farmington YMCA. I rented a single room. I took a lonely shower. I prowled empty halls.

In the basement restroom, a foreign gentleman unrolled a sausage; its thickness exceeded Scarlet O'Hara's waist. He grinned and made pumping motions. Unwilling to be disemboweled, I hurried into the city.

I decided to make my debut at the Punch Bowl. Harvard students, military officers, professional athletes, and movie stars were reputed to mill about the huge interior of this legendary bar in gay profusion. It turned out to be a case of "You should have been here last night." Fairies of a bygone era simpered under heavy make-up. Corsets elicited groans. The sawdust smelled of urine.

I drank a beer and left for a section of Boston haunted by hustlers. Several appeared appetizing. No matter. Suspecting my lack of ready cash, the boys ignored me.

As a frequent guest of Paul when he lived in The Hub, I'd met many gay men at his house. Paul remarked on their intelligence and their charm, and I'm sure they could have professed other good qualities, but most were homely and I never bothered to remember any names. Paul gone, it was a city of strangers.

I ventured into a bar catering to sadists and masochists. Several denizens expressed interest, but each asked, "What are you into?" How ever would I know until I tried it? I could be all things to all men. The little games they proposed sounded insipid and unimaginative. I returned to Farmington.

A mild-mannered man cruised me under the showerheads. We went to his room, where he pulled two packages of prophylactics from his wallet. "Put this on. I don't want to catch any diseases." Slightly affronted, yet willing to try anything, I obliged the man, who enjoyed only dry humping, belly-to-belly. A future free of bubules seemed assured.

Sunday morning, I explored the YMCA from cellar to attic. On the fifth floor, I found three rooms filled with disheveled cots. A sailor sat on one, holding his head.

"Who sleeps here?"

He looked up through bloodshot eyes. "Reserved for active military."

"I'm Navy. Could I sleep here?"

"Two dollars a night."

I'd slept alone for six dollars!

That afternoon, I cheered the Red Sox against the Yankees. In the men's restroom at the Greyhound terminal, I peered through a gloryhole and watched helplessly as a sublime soldier abused himself. During the bus ride to Newport, I completed the second volume of Gibbon's *The Decline and Fall of the Roman Empire*.

At the hospital, I drew blood and analyzed urine. The SEAL never mentioned our relations with Moscow, apparently considering the affair with Diana as a bad dream; we exercised together and ran the seven miles of Ocean Drive. The actor joined me for evening strolls along

193

Cliff Walk. I attended to my correspondence and cruised the streets. I read.

My co-workers seemed satisfied with unadventurous lives. The lab absorbed them. Ninety-five percent of their extraneous chatter concerned television programs. All professed lumps in their throats while listening to the song "Honey."

Everyone tolerated me, but despite our spending long duty hours together, none knew anything about my personal life. They argued endlessly about the major league pennant race, but no one knew I'd played in the minors for Detroit, the year's top team. They rhapsodized over girlfriends or complained about wives who sounded as bland and dreary as themselves; no one asked about Jane or my family. I was made party to the most trifling details of their existence. Despite innumerable comments about Vietnam, including their views on how the war should be won, no one asked about my experiences. I was neither shy nor secretive; I just saw no reason to intrude upon such disinterest.

My isolation extended to the barracks. Over the years, I'd had my fill of the talk about cars and chicks so vital to adolescent heterosexuals. I smiled and kept my distance.

One evening, I strolled through the Jewish cemetery in a light rain, which suddenly turned into a downpour. I ran through the gate and took refuge in a recessed doorway. A car passed by. A few minutes later, it passed by again. A middle-aged man drove. I knew no middle-aged men in Newport nor did I wish to meet any, but if this one invited me to his place so I could get out of my wet clothes and into a dry martini . . .

On the third pass, he stopped and beckoned. "Do you need a ride?" No, I got my rocks off wrestling pneumonia. He drove a few blocks before asking abruptly, "Would you like a home-cooked meal?" I assented, surprised that he's summoned the nerve to issue the invitation.

He had decorated his apartment with Latin American tourist products. "A friend working in Panama sends them."

194

A lover? I doubted it. The man sported a sun-lamp tan and a trim body, but seemed desperately lonely. His library was comprised of technical manuals, uncut reference tomes, and a few fad books. Two chairs stood in alignment along one wall of the living room, each focused on a large color television set that he turned on immediately upon our entering the apartment.

While he bustled happily about the kitchen, I showered. As I toweled off, he called, "There's a robe on my bed." About twenty dollars lay atop his dresser; no experienced queer would permit an unfamiliar sailor to lurk unattended near so much cash. Several gay paperbacks stood upon his bedside table; three framed photographs of an athletic young man hung on the wall.

I carried one of the photographs into the kitchen. "This your friend?" He nodded. "Good-looking kid." The man wriggled with delight.

He served a delicious dinner: hamburger steaks, brussels sprouts, and creamed potatoes; before sitting down to the repast, he hung my wet clothes in front of an electric heater and set up an ironing board. "I've seen you in the bar."

That's why he had summoned the nerve to pick me up. "You should have spoken."

He appeared startled. "I never talk to anyone. Too shy, I guess."

"My old pal, Paul, prefers to cruise by staring. He's left bars with many a trick with whom he hasn't exchanged a word."

"I never leave with anyone."

"Oh?"

"I don't like bars. The music's too loud and everyone belongs to cliques." He grimaced effeminitely. "They're always filled with cigarette smoke."

"Your friend. What does he do in Panama?"

"Electronics. Like me." Asking about his work, I endured a precise interminable lecture about a field as interesting as

195

the art of skinning reindeer. "Would you like a glass of anisette?"

I needed it badly. "How long have you known your friend?"

"Seven years."

"Are you lovers?" He shook his head negatively. "He's straight?" An affirmative. "Have you made it with him?"

"We messed around a couple of times."

"Like how?"

"I rubbed his back. The second time, he took his shirt off."

"Don't be bashful. I've sucked more cocks than a porcupine has quills."

"That's all." I learned that the man, now forty-four, had enjoyed only one sexual experience in his life, a furtive handjob on a sailboat ten years earlier. "A guy I worked with. He was fat."

My host had rounded shoulders and held his elbows against his sides; he slid his feet along the floor instead of lifting them. He whined, forcing a high-pitched voice through his upper nasal cavity. He stocked the medicine chest in the bathroom with remedies for stomach aches and constipation. He was almost bald.

Nevertheless, I felt obliged to pay for services rendered; perhaps I could brighten someone's day. As he ironed my clothes, I stood, letting the bathrobe fall to the floor. He giggled, a hand covering his nose and mouth. "You interested?" His eyes slid down my body with longing. "At the risk of sounding narcissistic, sex with me is a step up from a handjob by a fat guy." He stared at Precious. "Want to make it?"

He looked at me through pale blue eyes. He resembled a rabbit. "I'd have to know you better." I dressed, and he drove me to the hospital, complaining again of his boredom. As I got out of the car, he asked timidly, "Will you be my friend?" I thanked him for supper and walked through the hospital gate.

I should have liked another go at Tiernan, O'Hara, and the other corpsmen who underwent the "Melbourne Method," but felt no overwhelming desire to work up a gig; after all, I'd had them. I should have liked to caress the SEAL's powerful muscles at my leisure; I could live nicely without the pleasure. I considered the doctors and other officers off-limits, admiring a few pretties without lust. Several attractive body builders at the gym caught my eye; unfortunately, they stayed in tight pairs and none could compare with the SEAL. No one among the unsullied corpsmen at the hospital tickled my fancy.

I had no patience to read a book or sit through a movie. I derived no pleasure in trading badinage in a gay bar. The snow had melted and flowers bloomed. Perhaps I had spring fever.

The porcine WAVE shared weekend duty with me. A nice girl, she read books, Gothic romances, to be sure, but in this man's Navy, a person willing to read fiction was as rare as a gay garbage collector.

Shortly after supper, the Shore Patrol carried in a tall black man found dead alongside a road across the bay. Until the authorities identified him as Navy, no autopsy could be performed to determine cause of death. He would refrigerate overnight in Pathology.

At eleven, Petunia left for the WAVE barrack. I closed down the lab and checked the Negro's body: cold and still. I picked up *Dead Souls*. At midnight, I switched on the Saturday Night "Creature Feature." *Night of the Zombies.* A terrible film, but I'd clutched my crotch at worse. The zombies were tall black men who rose from the dead. I braced a chair against the knob of a locked door. Wild horses couldn't have dragged me into Pathology.

Work . . . exercise . . . cruising . . . I could find no antidote for the poison within. Nick called to say that the hosts of the stag party contracted for our stage show, so I dabbled

197

at a script. In spite of good intentions, I replied to none of Jane's letters.

Friday evening, passive with depression, I tried to read against the volume of a television in an adjoining cubicle. Would I wallow in lassitude through an empty weekend? A newscaster reported the week's casualties in Vietnam. I packed an overnight bag and caught a bus to Boston.

I sat across the aisle from the only other passenger, a sailor who bore the name of a famous watchmaking company; his family owned a cottage along Cliff Walk. During the course of our conversation, I mentioned the break-up with Jane and my subsequent depression. "I'm determined to get laid in Boston. Trouble is, when I'm this horny, I push too hard and the ladies back off. If I get rid of my wad before reaching Boston, I'll be cool." I pulled out a handkerchief.

He seemed amused. "You're going to do it on the bus?"

"Why not? It's dark. Nobody to see. If it bothers you, I'll move further back."

He shrugged. "Enjoy." At first, he stared out the window; eventually, he watched. I tucked Precious away before getting rid of my wad and buttoned my bellbottoms. "You cool now?"

I stood, straightened my uniform, and sat next to him. "No, dammit! I got embarrassed, you aware of what I was doing."

"Didn't bother me."

"Guess I lost my manners in Nam. One of the marines would start whacking his dong, the rest of us would raise sympathetic hards and pull out ours. Tell me, if you don't mind, did you raise a sympathetic hard?"

A brief silence. "I guess so."

"Damn! If I'd known that, I wouldn't have stopped. So you're horny, too?"

He laughed shakily. "I guess so."

"Then you have no objection to my finishing what I

started?" He said nothing, so still sitting next to him, I indulged. He watched. "Got a sympathetic hard yet?" He looked in my face and at what I did to Precious; he turned to look out the window. "I'll bet you do." My hand covered his lap. He did. I quickly unbuttoned his bellbottoms.

Like an idiot, I told Paul, who decried such tomfoolery. "I'm willing to overlook your mania for anonymous sex, the immediacy precluding passion, and your Caesarian mentality of 'Veni vidi vici.' But to make it with someone because he bears a famous name. Shame!"

"He had clear skin, white teeth, broad shoulders, a flat belly, and long legs. He could have been named John Smith for all I cared. I wanted him."

"You attempt to define these furtive little fumblings as epiphanies for your partners, most of whom consider them no more meaningful than munching a jellyroll during a coffee break. I held such hopes for you and the state trooper."

"You would allow me a straight proletarian?"

"He stirred you to something approaching affection. These dismal little episodes with strangers are so meaningless."

"I feel desire in varying degrees for everyone I bed. I have lots of fun."

"You're such a whore, I wonder that you've never performed for money."

"Hustling? Where's the fun in bedding the old, the fat, and the wrinkled? Someone paying a few pennies for the use of my body would not bolster my ego. My 'Uncle' Ralph patronizes hustler bars. The boys to whom he introduces me seem dull, lazy and pitiable, haunted by the passing years that continually introduce other boys who are younger and prettier."

"I'm not talking about street hustlers. For two years, a very nice man provided me with luxuries and introduced me to the haut monde of New York and Paris."

"I should prefer meeting the giants of this earth with

199

something more to offer than shallow youth."

"Many 'giants' appreciate beautiful youths."

"So what? If you weren't there, some other boy would have been. You hate the perversity within you, Paul. That's why you drink so much and take so many pills. Instead of reveling in the brilliance of what you can do, you castigate yourself for what you can't. You're trying to destroy the mind and body that have betrayed you. Being kept was a fancy way to abase yourself."

"I loved him."

"Romantic love is a panacea for loneliness nurtured by advertisers, film-makers, and inferior novelists to sell their products. It's an antidote for adventure, a catering to an effeminite need for security. Romance fulfills a woman's needs for pornography. I've learned much from the joys and sufferings of my infatuations, but I prefer a friendship such as ours, colored by the patina of age and use."

"Friends say good night in the parlor."

"I have an active imagination and a ready hand."

"You're play-acting cynicism, Kurt. Deep down . . ."

"Deep down, I'm really shallow. Men have died from time to time, and worms have eaten them, but not for love."

"You love Nick. Your misery is palpable."

"I'll get over it."

"If you weren't so goddam proud . . ."

"Nick has a bourgeois mentality better served by marriage and family. Could it be called love if I tried to deny him happiness? I must be content with the good feeling our limited relationship provides."

"You're heading for a lonely old age."

"Memories will sustain me."

Paul sighed with exasperation. I decided that he would never hear any more about my sexual escapades. Too bad for him. I enjoyed an interesting weekend.

The scion and I exchanged cordial farewells in Providence, and I boarded the Boston bus with several other

200

passengers. Everyone sat near the front except a tall good-looking sailor, who stretched across the last seat. I sat in the next-to-last seat. The bus roared along a dark highway. I covered the light under the seat with my peacoat and dangled my arm against the sailor's leg. He noticed, sitting up to light a cigarette. Muted conversation drifted back from the front. The bus vibrated.

The sailor ground out his cigarette with his shoe and reclined again. I stroked his bellbottoms. I felt a strong hairy calf. I moved to the end of his seat.

At the Greyhound terminal in Boston, I watched the sailor stride athletically into the darkness. I would never see him again. I would never know his story. I suffered another little death.

I worried that the dormitories at the Farmington YMCA would be filled, but no one else had checked in. I explored the accommodations. Rooms A and B had five beds in a line and two head-to-toe along the wall. Room C held twelve beds. I could take my choice from among twenty-five sailors.

Lurking in dark corners, I watched them enter, usually intoxicated and innocent of my designs. Room A seemed the most promising: two cute little drunks, a sleek well-bred type, a lean blond redneck, and three drearies. I crawled into a bed near the door of Room C and waited.

Within an hour, young men slept trustfully on every bed. I went first for the little drunks. The floor between their coats was slick with vomit. Strike One!

The handsome redneck recoiled from my touch. I checked the sleek type, who slept upon his stomach, so I went back to Lil Abner. His teeth gleamed in the faint light: a grin anticipating pleasure or a grimace foreboding combat? Ready for battle, I caressed his groin. He sighed and surrendered. My first success! I knelt beside his cot and eased a long uncircumcized unmentionable through the fly of navy boxer shorts. I pulled back the foreskin. A tangy odor of stale urine pervaded the room. Strike Two!

I hated passing up such a sexy dude, but I preferred clean peewees. I returned to my bed in Room C. The unremarkable man in the next cot had exuded pomposity, which left my libido unstirred; still, he had good biceps. I reached across the gap between our cots and slipped my hand under. . . .

"What the hell are you doing?" he roared. I withdrew my hand and froze. "Goddam faggot's trying to play with my dick!" His diatribe resounded in the otherwise silent room and shook buildings across Boston Harbor; every reasonably sober man in the building must have awakened. I feared no single man, but a dozen. . . . Could this be the way the world ends? My pulse accelerated threefold. The roars eventually diminished into empty threats. Finally, he rolled over, grumbling, and pulled a blanket around his body. The rest was silence.

I lay absolutely still for half an hour while making several resolutions. 1. I would stash my gear in the basement. Few white men could outrun me; I'd dash down the fire stairs to hide in a warren of dark spooky rooms under the building. 2. The desk clerk had glanced at my military I.D., but failed to match it against my registration. I could switch the numerals of my seven-digit service number and scribble a "William K. Strom" that only God could decipher. 3. Never again would I try for a man unless I grooved on him. 4. I would never, ever try anything in a room that I shared with more than one man.

I was soon up and about, wondering if the torrent of abuse would keep the boys wakeful and defensive; during the next few hours, I learned that three sailors considered it an advertisement.

I spent Saturday afternoon sleeping through two double features. That night, Room B held the beauties. One had appeared neat and compact in his uniform. I'd barely touched him when he sat up with a startled air. I fled the room.

Minutes later, I crept back in. The sailor waited for me, flipping the sheet away from his body. Tentatively, I approached him. A rigid thickness stretched the fabric of clean white jockey shorts. Soft dark hair covered his chest and legs. Afterwards, a voice from an adjoining cot said, "How could you let him do that, McFerrin?"

"Shut up, Nolan."

I offered my services to Nolan.

"No way, faggot. Get lost!"

The next morning, I shaved while a handsome sailor, bronzed from outdoor duty, sat on the throne while talking to a couple of buddies. "I dreamed this beautiful chick was giving me head. A blonde, and she did fine. It felt better and better, but I woke up and dadblamed if some ole sissy wasn't gobbling my joint. I sure wisht I hadn't woke up, but I had to stop him." (To my great regret.)

"Why?" asked a lean redhead, who hadn't stopped me.

"Don't know. Didn't seem right, somehow."

The hairy McFerrin had departed immediately after our session; Nolan didn't leave until morning. The only fellow left in Room B, a good ole country boy, slept in a bed across from McFerrin's, whose cot I usurped. A long skinny kid with a big nose, he hadn't seemed worth the effort, but his twanging masculinity turned me on. We lay in our respective beds and chatted. "I dreamed this beautiful chick was giving me head. A blonde, and she did fine. It felt better and better, but I woke up and dadblamed if some ole sissy wasn't gobbling my joint. I sure wisht I hadn't woke up, but I had to stop him."

The country boy nodded sagely. "I know who it was."

My heart skipped a beat. "Who?"

"The Phantom Cocksucker. He's stationed aboard our ship." I relaxed. "Goes from bunk to bunk. 'Least twenty guys I know of woke up getting blowed."

I chuckled. "He get you?"

"Hell, no! I'd kill the old cocksucker, he tries anything with me."

I sat up and examined myself. "Better see if the sissy left any teeth marks." Precious responded to the examination. "Damn, I'm horny! Sure wisht I hadn't stopped him." The good ole boy's eyes widened as I lay back with Precious in hand. "That hot mouth sucking like a vacuum, that hot tongue . . ." The good ole boy rubbed himself; then he threw off his sheet. I droned on, each of us watching the other until white pools collected upon our bellies.

He dressed quickly and left, so I made final rounds. A lone man remained, the sleek well-bred type from Friday night. I attained rapture, but the janitor's clattering wagon frightened me onto an empty cot. I watched in frustration as the sailor finished himself under the covers.

Deeds let escape are never to be done.

These little sordidities made me feel alive, but I recognized their unimportance when two corpsmen, driving in a thunderstorm, skidded on wet pavement and ran into a telephone pole. The passenger was killed. My mentor, the Yellow Yeti, tried to convince everyone that we should vilify the driver. "He's a killer! Murdered his best friend! They should kick him out of the Navy! Lock him in jail and throw away the key!"

"It was an accident, for crissake!"

"He was drunk! Stoned on drugs!"

"The authorities hold a different opinion. They didn't even charge him with reckless driving."

"Nobody should talk to him!"

"The dude has a broken collarbone. I'm certain that he feels enough pain and guilt to satisfy the Furies."

"He's a killer!"

The victim had lived in a cubicle adjoining mine; a brief exchange of conversation had immediately determined me to avoid his company. Loud, pimpled, and bitchily effeminate, he would have few mourners besides his mother and the

Yeti.

I entered Pathology, opened the reefer, and pulled out a tray. A sheet lay draped over the corpse: hardly enough to ward off the chill. I uncovered the head. Dried blood encrusted his face.

I conjectured about his friendship with the driver. Did the queen harbor an unnatural desire for the attractive Latin? Did they consummate their friendship? Was it the ultimate thrill to die at the hands of one's beloved? I closed the tray and left the room.

The sudden death of an acquaintance shocked me. To die before one's time seemed careless and unfair to the survivors.

Daddy withered away from cancer, weighing less than seventy pounds at death. We'd known for a year of his inevitable demise. I felt nothing but relief when he died at thirty-three. His children suffered from Mother's unchecked neuroticism and her remarriage to a pussywhipped tyrant. My brother, Neil, suffered the most. Five at Daddy's death, his pet and very like him, Neil missed a real father. They would have been good friends.

While Daddy served in the South Pacific during World War II, we stayed with Mother's parents; Mom and Dad lavished attention upon me, the son they never had. They promised Daddy on his deathbed to help Mother raise us, buying a ranch in Montana so we could live with them. My grandfather believed that incessant manual labor would make a man of me and rid me of such crazy ideas as reading books. I resented his slave driving, and our close relationship faltered. Dad turned his adoration upon my youngest brother, who reciprocated. When Dad died, having wasted away from cancer like my father, Ricky was devastated. I felt nothing.

Mother died of cancer while I served in Nam. Kept in ignorance about her illness, I was shocked. I'd despised the grasping virago she had become, but I recalled her courage during Daddy's illness, the tenderness toward a sensitive

205

little boy before spasmodic rages and a brooding self-pity estranged us. The gentle contralto. The comforting lap. Since her death, except for occasional and unwelcome memories of good and bad times, I've felt nothing.

The hollow man filled his headpiece with straw and boarded a bus for New York. Diana greeted me with steaks and a salad. During dessert—cheese and a pear—she perused my script for the stag show. "You're hardly Shakespeare, darling, but it will certainly do. How ever did you divine that I'm a raving exhibitionist!"

"My dear, seven blind Hindoos . . ."

"The presence of all those celestial policemen might shatter me, but I do worry about sweet Nicky's destructive impulses. In retrospect, I rather regret our pushing that yummy attorney over the edge, and I'll probably feel the same about tonight's infernal bridegroom. Do you think as an old lady I'll feel shame?"

"I can't refuse Nick after he's fulfilled my fantasies."

"We enjoy these games because they challenge our intellects, prove the force of our personalities and the power of our beauty, and are fun. We're modern bourgeois descendants of the characters in *Les Liaisons Dangereuses;* Heaven forbid that we become as vicious and competitive as they. What I'm trying to say, darling, is that Nicky and Louella entertain brooding hatreds. You and I don't wish to humiliate people."

"We expand their horizons."

"Mmm. We like our victims. Darling, I wonder if your influence upon Nicky is unhealthy?"

"I think it ends with tonight's performance. Nick's mother is dying, his wife is due any day now, and my hamming in this peep show should gross him out."

"You want the affair to end?"

" 'The time has come,' the Walrus said."

"How is your walrus?"

"My SEAL! Fine. We exercise together three times a week

206

and speak sparingly, never of you." I sipped red wine. "However we rationalize, our seductions would strike most people as pitiless."

"You're a chevalier without peer and I . . ."

"La Belle Dame Sans Merci." Diana like the role. "Do you want to call off or tone down tonight's show?"

"Not at all. I'm curious and excited and we promised Nicky. And I revel in tawdriness."

"What about your introducing this aspiring actor to the public in a perverted orgy?"

"I've spent years studying and have acted in over a hundred plays to reach the point where several unfluential critics consider me as one of Off-Broadway's top five actresses. This youth expects immediate stardom without paying his dues. By the way, he thinks you're the star of a television pilot, "The Shoshone Kid." The producers are looking for a contrasting type to play your sidekick, Rattlesnake Reilly."

"I hate horses."

"You're unlikely to ride one in Newark, darling, unless a few mounted police urge their steeds onto the stage."

"You'd probably take on all of them."

"The Mounties or their steeds? Oh God!" Diana had just expanded her fantasy world. "Guess who I play in the series."

"Nympho Nell. Is the would-be actor straight?"

"He'd kill a lavender lad for winking at him. I play Sally, the dance-hall hostess with a past."

"It took more than one cowpoke to change your name to Spearfish Sal. Will he perform the perversions in the script?"

"He's ruthlessly ambitious and terribly stupid. And it will be his only chance to touch his fingertips to my glorious body. He'll perform." Diana brushed long blond hair from her face; she knew that Precious wouldn't cooperate unless a sexy butch beast promised bliss. "To assuage guilt, I've written letters of introduction to a director friend making commercials and a hot new photographer in men's fashions."

207

The budding thespian arrived early, a small intense package of energy. He devoured the script as if it were rare sirloin and uttered no objection. Louella, the Negress, blew in from a voice lesson; while she showered, Nick knocked at the door. We loaded costumes and props into his van. When Louella dressed, we drove to a seedy night club in downtown Newark.

Eighty guests had emptied a dozen kegs of beer before the host blew a police whistle three times to quiet them. Wearing Nick's high school football jersey and one of my old baseball caps, hands sweating and knees shaking, I walked onto the tiny stage. I'd adapted the introduction used on Nick's lawyer to fit proles, bidding several to drag the bridegroom and his best man to the stage. Nick obviously had a thing about sexy blonds; the two men had well-knit bodies, hard blue eyes, and thick drooping mustaches, and both were staggeringly drunk.

Diana entered the hall from the rear, bouncing down the aisle while waving pom poms, her enormous breasts jiggling within a white sweater.

"Joystick High School's the team to beat!
They got great big balls and their dicks taste sweet!
Jam it in their mouths! Ram it up their seat!
Joystick players never beat their meat!
Stick 'em for Joy, boy!"

I waved down the applause. "Okay, bridegroom! Gotta show you where to stick 'em for Joy." The aspiring actor entered from the wings dressed as a football player. I slapped the top of his helmet. "Head!"

Diana flounced up to us. "You call that head?" She pushed me to my knees, lifted her skirt, and pulled my face into her honeypot. "That's head!" The crowd roared. I lapped at that well-worn hairpie until Diana shuddered. She collected herself and jerked down the football player's

208

knickers. "Head!" She knelt and performed until the actor erected. "Okay, Jocko, show me what you learned. "Head!" The actor performed cunnilingus upon Diana. The crowd roared. Diana pulled away and jerked down my sweatpants. "Jocko. Head!" The actor engulfed Precious. The crowd became silent. A few boos.

A whistle blew and the dusky majorette pranced on stage, executing strange double-time maneuvers apparently taught at Booker T Junior High. "Head!" I announced. Diana and the actor performed upon Louella, who returned the favor. The bridegroom, grinning foolishly, split his attention between the crowd, his best man, and the show.

I took command again and plunked the actor's jersey. "Chest!"

The girls pulled off the jersey and a pair of shoulder pads. They agreed. "Chest!" They pulled off my jersey. "Chest!" The majorette unbuttoned her sleeveless gold blouse. "Tits!"

Diana pulled off her sweater, exhibiting two huge melons. She caressed them and smiled. "Balookas!" The audience cheered.

Diana placed the bridegroom's hands on her breasts. As he squeezed those enormous mammaries, the actress unbuttoned his shirt; as she unbuckled his belt, the bridegroom kissed her deeply, obviously forgetting that her mouth had recently held the actor's unmentionable. Noting the best man becoming restless, I bade a pair of his buddies onto the stage to hold him while Louella stripped off his clothes.

"Ass" followed "Groin," the ladies using our victims as examples. Soon, neither man wore a stitch. While the actor and I carried a long sofa onto the stage, the girls fellated the groom and best man into hardness. My co-stars led them to the sofa, where the men lay, a head on each armrest, their legs intermingling; the girls positioned themselves to receive "Head." I knelt on the floor and alternated rapture between the men. Bedlam. When the best man ejaculated, the actor closed a bedraggled curtain.

The best man freed himself from between Louella's legs. While he dressed, the girls lifted the bridegroom's legs and I spit on my hand. Pumping the struggling groom, I looked up to see Nick, his brother, and several other men watching from off-stage. Diana manipulated the groom to a climax.

After I washed and dressed, Nick handed me two hundred dollars. "Nobody expected you to screw in public for free."

"Split it between Louella and the little stud. Where are they?"

"She's turning tricks in a churchyard across the street. Ten bucks a throw. The actor's getting a percentage for collecting the money."

Diana agreed to divide the gratuity between our fellow performers. "We did it for fun, darling. Accepting money would literally make us whores. Now use the apartment whenever you like. I gave you a set of keys, didn't I? And don't forget your appointment with the little stud. Sunday at one, and write me all the details. Dream up seven rip-roaring plots. Oh, Kurt! Have a marvelous summer." She hugged Nick and me before joining a pair of husky men waiting by a car.

"Celestial policemen?"

Nick grinned. "Dumb flatfeet."

We sat on the front steps of a church overlooking the cemetery, hearkening to raucous laughter among the tombstones. It didn't come from ghosts. "What a night!"

Nick shook his head. "You amaze me!"

"Isn't it what you wanted?"

"I guess. Christ! Never thought you'd get so far."

"Surprised me, too. Booze and momentum."

"Too bad everybody didn't see you plug old Harry."

"You wanted to embarrass the guy, not destroy him." We sat in silence, pondering that last statement. "If old Harry really loved his fiancée, he wouldn't have been dating your sister on the eve of their engagement; he's probably giving up his bachelorhood for no better reason than to get regular

210

snatch. Resentful of being trapped, he had an unconscious urge to get even. Too inebriated to worry about repercussions. . . ."

Nick squeezed my knee. "I'm gonna miss this." Oh, shit! "Nothing to do with you, Kurt. The doctors say Ma's got two months at the most; I want to spend as much time with her as possible. Dad, too. He needs me." He sighed. "Rosemary, too. This has been her worst pregnancy." We listened to shouts from the cemetery. "You gonna look for somebody else to play games with?"

"I wasn't looking for you, buddy. A thunderbolt blasted through the Jersey smog and fell upon a crippled hitchhiker standing in the snow. A pitiless north wind blasted a cold lonely Godforsaken spawn of the devil. A black night . . ."

Nick laughed. "I've got a 'Wait for a couple of months' present. One of the guys standing off-stage. Harry's future brother-in-law."

"Jesus! Will the wedding be cancelled?"

"Don't think so. The brother-in-law is putting you up tonight." He grinned. "His duty as an usher."

"He a cop, too."

"A longshoreman. Was an army ranger. Mean dude. A killer."

I digested this information. "Tell me about the best man."

"A fireman. The bridegroom's brother."

"You're kidding! He watched me. . . ."

"Sure did. I had a boner that about split my britches."

"How about *your* brother?"

"Mike's square. Probably shook him up."

"He knows we're friends."

"Yeah. Well, takes all kinds. He'll keep it to himself."

"What was the audience reaction to my public blowjob."

"You could have come down off that stage and sucked off half of them." He stood. "Guess I'll mosey over and check on Louella."

"You gonna ball her?"

"Gimme a break! Mike and me are gonna take her and the little stud into Manhattan."

"What's my excuse for staying in Jersey?"

"You have an appointment tomorrow in Newark at a certain carpet shop."

"Nice. Is the brother-in-law part of the gangbang in the cemetery?"

"No. Him and Mike are using the van to carry the beer kegs to my place."

"Are you setting me up?"

"You musta been too busy to get a gander at him."

A tall rangy redhead with chiseled good looks and magnificent long legs. He said nothing until we entered a small furnished apartment in Elizabeth. "Want to shower?"

I emerged from the bathroom clad in a towel and accepted his offer of a beer, my first of the evening. I wondered how many he had drunk. "Should I apologize for what you saw after the curtain closed."

He glanced at me, surprised that I would mention the exhibition. He looked down at his can. "I still can't believe Harry's a queer."

"He isn't. I took advantage of the situation."

"Harry let you cornhole him!"

"The dude was drunk. Maybe he wanted to see how it felt for a woman."

"I'll never be able to look him in the face again."

"You going to tell your sister?"

"Never! I just hope nobody else does. That was disgusting!"

"I couldn't help noticing you had a boner." I hadn't even picked him out of the crowd.

He glanced at his crotch. "No! We . . . I. . . . Well, who wouldn't after watching them two broads?"

"You looked so horny, I almost offered you some relief."

"I'd have knocked your teeth in."

"You saw me giving head to Harry's brother?" He nodded.

212

"Didn't bother you?"

"He ain't marrying my sister."

"Getting head feels real good."

"Sure. When a female does it."

"Feels good when anybody does it."

The redhead went to the bedroom and returned with sheets and a pillow. "Make yourself a bed on the couch." He returned to the bedroom and closed the door. As I made up the couch, I heard the shower run. Shit! Why hadn't I watched the gangbang in the cemetery, perhaps priming a few hunks? I could be cruising. Wondering how I would seduce the little stud at Diana's. (Sunday, Precious rode his ambition into every orifice.)

I awakened when the bedroom door opened. The springs of an armchair squeaked as someone sat down across from me. A lighter flared. The glowing tip of a cigarette made scarlet arcs. The glow disappeared in an ashtray. Silence. I lifted my sheet, moved across the room, and fell to my knees. My hands moved up lean, slightly-hairy legs. They slid under a towel.

In mid-act, a strong hand grabbed a shank of my hair and pulled back my head. A hard voice came out of the darkness. "You ever tell anybody, I'll kill you."

I owe God a death.

June 1968

A corpsman on the Medical Intensive Care Unit accosted me in the mess hall. "We need another guy to share our apartment. Rent's six dollars a week."

The ramshackle white frame house stood halfway between the naval hospital and the Newport town green. Several sailors stationed aboard a destroyer in dry-dock rented a garage behind the tall narrow house for their motorcycles. An ancient crone lived on the ground floor.

We climbed steep stairs to the second floor. Dirty dishes cluttered the kitchen; splatters of grease covered the stove, walls, and ceiling. Grit crackled underfoot. A pair of stained chairs and a grimy sofa filled most of the small living room; no one had swept the carpet for months. At the top of another narrow flight of stairs were two small bedrooms and a filthy bathroom. A homely corpsman shared one bedroom with a WAVE who had been booted out of the Navy after a nervous breakdown caused by her refusal to accept the death of a newborn. Three men slept in the other bedroom.

I'd wearied of the barracks' sterility. Why not?

Slim extended the invitation. Although he could boast of ascetic good looks, I kept a distance, having never trusted those with mouths that curled in perpetual sneers. The Puppy had a short stocky body, dreamy blond looks, and a contagious smile; I suspected that his constant cheerfulness hid a simple mind. The squat ugly Toad doggedly attempted to provoke serious discussions every evening in the parlor, despite his lacking humor, intellect, originality, and bonhomie. The couple kept to themselves. Ah well! It was home.

I kept my bunk and my locker at the hospital, moving only a change of clothes to put in the shallow drawer allotted me. Perhaps enforced camaraderie would make me normal.

The lab pathologist considered my appointment a success and added two more regular corpsmen to the roster: Tiernan of the green eyes, and the Duck. I would now stand duty every sixth weekend.

The Duck's incompetence almost made me regret such easy duty. A vacant-looking ash blond with big hips and a narrow chest, he waddled about the lab quacking incessantly, feigning interest in everyone's duties while patients waited in the Leeching Room, which became a torture chamber that Torquemada would have found excessive. So busy quacking that he couldn't concentrate on the business at hand, the Duck missed the easiest veins. After fruitlessly stabbing a patient several times, he would waddle back to Urinalysis. "Another tough one." He had slyly recognized my pity for his victims; I made twenty trips a day out front. (During my three-month tour in the Leeching Room, I had difficulty with just three veins, each of which I stabbed only once before calling for Petunia, the laboratory expert.) The patients regarded me fearfully, blood oozing from several punctures. I would locate a vein that hadn't collapsed, fill the necessary tubes, and look up to learn the Duck had waddled off to trade repartee in X-ray or Physical Therapy. Patients in the overflowing waiting room gazed at me so beseechingly, I drew their blood before going in search of Old Quack Quack. Bloodletting trips to the wards that should have lasted ten minutes stretched into hours. Enough complaints trickled down to the lab that the pathologists assigned Tiernan to man the Leeching Room and sent the

Duck back to Urinalysis.

I despaired of teaching him. The Duck mixed up chits and bottles. He mixed up bottles and tubes. He scribbled gibberish on the Urinalysis chits. Doctors screamed. "How could a bedridden man with cancer of the esophagus have Kotex strings in his urine?"

The head pathologist came down on me. "Too many mistakes from your station."

"The Duck has no business working in the lab."

"His ward nurse recommended him highly, praising his rapport with patients."

"Did any live?"

The Duck and I would sit side by side in front of the microscope. I'd interrupt a gush of gabble. "Describe the slide." Cells and crystals became Rorschach tests suggesting associations dredged from the shallow wastes of his unconscious. I would describe the slide. "Look again. Tell me what you see." He would peer through the microscope and look at me blankly. I'd describe the slide again.

"Oh, yeah."

"Look once more. Tell me what you see."

He'd try to recall my description, but it had drifted into a labyrinth filled with television programs, hospital gossip, and fuzzy bunnies. I dreaded calls to draw blood on the wards; I would return to preposterous test results and the Duck quacking in another department of the lab. Near murder and headed for a nervous breakdown, I begged for a change. Everyone else, enamoured of the Duck's perpetual affability, thought me neurotically unjust. The Yellow Yeti, an eager instructor, offered to switch jobs, and I moved to Hematology.

As I counted blood cells one day, my buddy Babich dropped by the lab to visit. We had served together at Hospital Corps School near Chicago, the Chelsea Naval Hospital in Boston, and Combat Training School at Camp Lejeune, North Carolina, only to be separated in Vietnam;

216

completing military service, he pursued a career in pharmacy at a college in Minnesota. "It's terrible, Kurt! Just terrible! The girls are of Scandinavian descent and look like Ann-Margret. They protest the Vietnam war and hate veterans. They'd hate me anyway, ugly as I am."

"How is school?"

"Okay. I made straight A's last semester, but I took easy courses. It gets hard next year."

"What easy courses did you take?"

"Biochemistry, Biophyics, Microbiology, and Calculus. Listen, Kurt, you gotta come to dinner. Mom didn't hear anything for a month after I was wounded except for your letter, so I gotta drag you over so she can thank you in person. My family's real depressing, as you might of guessed from knowing me."

I expected denizens from the lower depths, but Mrs. Babich was trim, chic, and attractive. After supper, Babich and I explored the night life of New Bedford. His eternal depression no longer seemed amusing, and we had little to talk about except the past. He vowed that we would renew our friendship by spending much of the summer together. The prospect left me cold.

I continued to work out in the gym three times a week with the SEAL. I enjoyed holding down his rock-hard legs for a thousand sit-ups. We left the gym to run ten miles. Our bodies tanned.

The SEAL's taciturnity seemed inherent. One day in the shower room, he shocked me by speaking unnecessarily. "Where do you go now?"

"Back to the hospital for chow."

We toweled off and dressed. He watched me comb my hair. "Where do you go after chow?"

"A stroll along Cliff Walk. Maybe a movie and a couple of beers."

During a workout two days later, we stopped for a breather. The SEAL dusted his hands with chalk. "I'm

217

leaving for the Med next month." (The Mediterranean Fleet)

"I'll be sorry to see you go."

As we left the gym, he stopped abruptly. "Wanna have a beer sometime?"

"Sure."

I walked out of the chow hall to find the SEAL waiting for me. "Wanna have that beer?"

"Sure." I braced myself for a dull evening.

He drove twenty miles to Fall River. I made desultory conversation that he gave no indication of hearing. We stopped at an uninteresting bar. When I'd finished my beer, he ordered two more. I drank the second in silence. He glanced at my near-empty bottle. "Want another?"

"Not really."

He nodded. Five minutes of silence. "Wanna walk on the beach?"

"Sure."

He drove thirty miles to an uninhabited cove along Buzzards Bay. We walked along a deserted stretch of beach without talking. We watched the sunset and returned to the car. He pulled out his keys, but didn't turn the ignition. Fifteen minutes of deafening quiet followed. He cleared his throat. "You're my best friend."

I felt woefully inadequate. "I've enjoyed knowing you, too."

Five minutes of unbearable silence. "We should of done more things together." I agreed, although so much vivacity might have aged me before my time. His confessions piled atop one another. "I wish I had your body." I could truthfully declare that the desire was mutual. "No, I look like I lift weights. You look natural." Mother had considered me a natural.

Prurience seemed out of order, but nothing ventured, nothing gained. "I've thought a lot about that Russian spy. What we did to each other—I'm glad it was you."

He nodded. Time passed. "Wanna go swimming?"

A misspent youth by the Gulf of Mexico had developed a partiality for warm water. Cold water neither refreshed nor invigorated me. Jellyfish, sharks, cottonmouths—I preferred the danger of each to a brisk five minutes in the North Atlantic. But I'd trek barefoot across Penguin Island if I suspected good sex in some igloo or another. The SEAL grabbed a blanket from the back seat and we gamboled among the icebergs. After running along the beach to dry off, we flopped upon the blanket. In the dim moonlight, I reached over to run my hand down that magnificent chest. The weight lifter groaned from his toes and rolled towards me.

Despite his sexual inexperience, the SEAL proved a sensualist. I had suspected as much, although he'd been stiff with Diana and What's-His-Name. Under their relaxed exteriors, sensual people seethed with intensity. Like a dancer, the SEAL appeared stupid, but at home with his body. Awkward in domestic surroundings, he was grace itself in the open air. Diana, Nick, Montchanin, Darby the soldier . . . I'd met others in the past. Too few.

I wondered how many of my victims at the Farmington YMCA were sensualists. My "modus operandi" precluded research. Friday: seven raptures. Saturday: six raptures. I slept through movies during the day, cruised Sporters Bar in the evening, and prowled the Y at night.

I'd delighted in Boston since my old pal, Paul, invited me up from New York five years earlier. I spent an idyllic autumn weekend with Paul and his lover in their flat on Beacon Hill. Stewie was a brilliant and attractive blond with a sunny disposition and a huge unmentionable. I went from his bed to Paul's and there and back again.

Two years later, they bought an apartment house in Back Bay, tearing out five floors of partitions and over-extending themselves financially. I visited after a trip to Montreal and ate cabbage soup for breakfast, lunch, and dinner.

It was very good cabbage soup, but I made a decision.

"I'm enlisting in the Navy."

"Why?" Stewie stared at me, appalled. "They'll shave you bald and deny your individuality. Don't waste your youth. Tell them you're queer. It's never come back to haunt me." The physicist retired to the library.

Paul poured more wine. "After Army boot camp, my company rode a troop train from Georgia to Seattle. Five days and nights. I shared a berth with a dumb country boy from Alabama. Sweet kid. First time away from home. Have you ever slept in an upper berth? Too small for one person, much less two. We'd wake up in the morning, our arms and legs intertwined." Paul smiled to himself, rapt with the memory of splendor in the grass.

"And?"

"And what?"

"Did you get it on?"

"Of course not!"

"Oh, Paul!"

"He liked me. He trusted me."

That's the time to strike, for crissake. The next day, I visited the Navy recruiting center. "I'll sign up for two years."

The recruiter shook his head. "We offer only four-year enlistments."

"My father and my uncles served two-year hitches during World War Two."

"That was twenty years ago."

I had no choice. The Army and the Marine Corps offered two-year enlistments, but I didn't yearn to become a grunt; the Air Force accepted a high caliber of men, but demanded four years from their lives. All three branches had built bases in Godforsaken prairies, deserts, and swamps; I preferred large cities situated on coastlines. Family tradition pointed at the Navy. Of course, I could admit my deviance. That seemed cowardly. Disloyal. I could never claim manhood were I to avoid serving my country.

I carried a bag of groceries and a bottle of gin to Back Bay, where Paul whipped up beef Stroganoff. Stewie shook his head. "Four years! By the time you get out, you'll have sagging tits and a wrinkled ass." He retired to the library.

Paul mixed Martinis. "During a war game in Alaska, I played a Russian spy. The 'Americans' caught me. The sergeant said, 'We need this spy for questioning, but we gotta move on and can't take him with us.' He assigned a member of his platoon to guard me. For an hour, we sat and stared at each other. I said, 'I'm thirsty. Let's go back to camp and get a drink.' The soldier glared at me, hate in his eyes. 'Sarge said not to move from this spot and you ain't supposed to talk English.' Another twenty minutes passed, and I grew thirstier. I said, 'This is silly. I'm leaving.' The soldier aimed his rifle at me. 'I'll shoot you.' I said, 'It's a game, for God's sake. You don't even have any bullets. I'm thirsty. Goodbye.' I got up and started towards camp. The soldier stopped me with a flying tackle and pinned me to the ground. Until the platoon returned two hours later, he lay on top of me. Wouldn't let me talk because I was a Russian spy. For two hours, I stared into unwavering blue eyes. His lips weren't six inches from mine."

Paul stopped. I waited for him to continue. He looked at me expectantly, proud of his little anecdote. "Nothing else happened?"

"Isn't that enough?"

"You would try the patience of Job. Have you no happy endings?"

"That was a happy ending."

"It rivals the denouement of a Jacobean tragedy!"

"Someday, perhaps, you'll mature into the realization that sex is more than writhing, sweating bodies. Sex can be poetic, a pure and abstract experience." Paul put on the pompous condescending face that his students must have known well and ended the discussion.

The next morning, I returned to the recruiting station. A

different man handled my case. "You'll be released from active duty in four years."

"The recruiter who interviewed me yesterday offered a three-year hitch."

"He wasn't supposed to. Those billets are filled for the next six months."

Resigning myself to the additional year, I leaned back in my chair and absently adjusted my crotch. The recruiter watched. I'll be damned! "Could I think about it over lunch?" He nodded. I liked his narrow foxy face. "Any good places to eat around here?" Precious snaked down my leg and bulged against my slacks.

The recruiter tore his gaze upward. "I usually grab a hoagie on the corner."

"Good?"

He shrugged. "Okay."

"I know a place where you could feast on a giant salami without cheese." I brushed Precious with my knuckles.

He stared. "Give me fifteen minutes."

Who got the advantage? He enjoyed a midday amourette and I signed up for three years.

Some of the men at the Farmington Y must have resented my ever enlisting. Nights spent ransacking the Y proved tiring, but catnaps at the USO revived me. Sunday, I strolled through the spring sunshine to Sporters Bar for a free brunch. The natural aristocrat from Greenland stood in a corner. I lacked interest in bedding the handsome young man—after all, I'd already had him—but good manners decreed that we exchange salutations. As I approached, he turned away. I veered in another direction.

Had I offended him? Had his tremulousness been an act? Did I hope for true love and recognize me for a tramp? He stood staring into space. I considered neither him nor anyone else worth an effort, so I returned to Newport.

Three men worked in Hematology. Every hour, I picked up dozens of blue-topped tubes filled with fresh blood from the Leeching Room. (Tubes with green, pink, violet, gray, and black tops went to Chemistry, those with red and yellow tops to Serology.) I decanted the blood onto slides, poured purple dye over the samples, and set them on a rack to dry.

An average specimen included ninety to ninety-five red cells per hundred (they appeared blue under a microscope), three to five eosinophil cells (red), and two to five white cells (very light blue and larger than red cells). An abundance of white cells signified infections or leukemia.

I spun down tiny capillary tubes of blood to check for anemia and answered calls from the wards. I took pride that the children on Pediatrics would allow no one else to draw their blood. The nurses on SICU asked for me by name; the doctors called for me to start bottles of intravenous fluids on different veins. As the other techs disliked leaving the lab, such partiality aroused no jealousy; each had instructed me, and I never hesitated to ask their opinions. Nor did any seem to mind taking the time to explain the theories behind my deductions.

I'd wondered how the SEAL would disport himself after our one-on-one intimacy; he waited for me at the gym, as usual, and our workout proceeded normally. As we dressed in the locker room, he casually asked, "What are you doing tonight?"

"No plans."

"Want to go for a beer after chow?"

"Sure."

He waited in my cubicle. We drove to that same bar in Fall River for two bottles of beer. We drove to that same beach on Buzzards Bay for a swim. I reached. He rolled. I thanked Diana inwardly for needing a variety of contortions to make her "da hottest."

One major difference: He never stopped talking. I learned of every victory and every defeat in his life. I learned about his relationships with his father, mother, sister, buddies, and girl friends. His hopes and fears. His loves and hates. His agonies and ecstasies.

He considered two subjects taboo: the patriotic orgy with Nick and Diana, and our subsequent couplings. Twice, I alluded to perversity; both times, he answered me with silence. I let him talk as he would.

My new roommates reacted against the continual mopping, waxing, and polishing that the Navy demanded by never cleaning the apartment. Sheets, pillowcases, and underwear turned a grotty gray. Tired of listening to cockroaches skitter across dirty dishes left in the sink, I scrubbed the kitchen from top to bottom, only to find it filthy three days later. I slept in a bed used by whichever roommate worked the night shift; none of them washed or changed the sheets. My mother kept a clean house. This was slumming.

I continued to wash and iron my clothes on base. I showered in the barrack. I ate in the hospital mess hall. I enjoyed no privacy. What was I paying for?

The Puppy. His smile could make a cesspool smell sweet.

The saccharine little redhead from the lab came by one day to find a date for his sister, who planned a visit. I could think of few greater ordeals, but felt offended when he passed me by to ask the Puppy. "I wouldn't trust Strom with my pet turtle." I despised the redhead, but envied his sister. The Puppy had great looks and a big basket.

I despaired of getting him alone, what with the gregarious Toad and the watchful Slim, but late one night, I returned from yet another rendezvous at Buzzards Bay to find the Puppy asleep on the couch. All else was still. It took fifteen bone-chilling minutes to inch down the zipper of his trousers. The discrepancy between how well he appeared to fill his jockey shorts and the actual size of his apparatus might have dismayed me had his blond looks not hurdled the shortcoming. I carefully denied the Puppy orgasm, which would have awakened him and probably diminished my reputation.

I would have preferred his orgasm. I would have preferred him to awaken. I would have preferred reciprocity, his hitherto undeveloped sensualism overwhelming a heterosexual predisposition and years of moral training. I wanted his everlasting desire for my body, at my convenience. I wanted magic words that would hypnotize hunky straights into performing whatever acts I bade. I wanted my seductions made easier by a ring that would glow in different colors according to a man's availability: green—full speed ahead, yellow—proceed with caution, red—no way, José. I wanted a pocket television that I could plug into a straight's memory bank in order to view the sexual exploits of his past. Fate, however, denied me supernatural powers, so I made do with what I had. If that meant a revolting tendency to take advantage of a man's need for sleep to satisfy my curiosity, I would continue to invade his dreams. It passed the time.

So did the sailors at the Farmington Y. Lifting a sheet off a comely, clean-limbed young man and the warm musty smell of his nether regions almost excited me enough to forego caution, which meant touching no part of his body except the penis; all other parts of a man's body seemed to be excessively sensitive during slumber, especially the lower abdomen, the inner thighs, and the testicles. I craved the intimacy, passing beyond the knowledge that his best friend might have of my prey's genitals. I relished odor, texture, and shape. I delighted in awakening a softness into rigidity. I loved a straight man's purity.

Saturday morning, two men remained abed in Room C, awake but reluctant to rise. I stroked Precious for their benefit. The further man began stroking his long member, and I recognized a sister. The tanned sexy sailor between us lay on his side, watching me through half-closed eyes; then he sat up quickly and noted the activity of my sister. Falling back on his bed, he pushed down his sheet with a well-muscled arm. An erection poked through the fly of his navy

225

drawers. I was beside his bed and on my knees like a sworn companion to the wind. A considerate young man, he turned on his back so my sister could view the encounter. Later, as the handsome sailor dressed, he watched my sister attack Precious. He smiled, winked, and left.

My sister and I spent the day together. Lack of sleep loosened my tongue; I bragged of sexual exploits, enthralling the giddy queen. That night, I stalked and brought down several desirables in Rooms A and C while my sister spent three hours approaching a stud in Room B. I'd given up the chase and settled on my cot when I heard indistinguishable bawling. The queen fled past the doorway. A minute later, another man marched purposefully down the hall. The stud intended to report my sister.

I slunk to the queen's cot and gathered her belongings, which I hid under my cot. Fifteen minutes later, two policemen entered the room and shone flashlights in everyone's face. They paused at the empty cot. "Does anybody know the man who slept in this bed?" The clothes below me glimmered with the white radiance of eternity. No one answered the policeman, so he and his buddy checked the other dorms and left.

The man in the next cot murmured, "Your buddy try to steal someone's wallet?"

"No, he was drunk and horny. Heard there was a cocksucker in that room. Guess he tried to cram his wang in the wrong mouth."

The sailor digested this information. "Is there a cocksucker in that room?"

"He hangs out in the john."

A few minutes later, the sailor rose and padded down the hall. He had a butch walk. I followed with alacrity.

Rustling sounds awakened me in the morning. Bleary-eyed mariners carried shaving kits into the restroom. I rolled my sister's uniform into a ball and descended the fire stairs. The poor queen, bloody and bruised, crouched in a dark corner of the cellar. I cajoled her into a washroom.

She looked at herself in a mirror and screamed. "I can't walk out the front door with a black eye. They'll arrest me."

"You won't be the first sailor involved in a brawl, and I seriously doubt the management suspected the others to be queers."

"I'll never do that again."

"Can't say I blame you. Come on. I'll walk between you and the desk clerk."

After breakfast, the queen returned to her ship, and I strolled towards Boston Common. A dead ringer for Sidney Poitier, the black actor, cruised me. As willing as a shopgirl to fantasize about movie stars and capable of transferring a smouldering intensity from the silver screen into the soul of a mild law student, I accepted an invitation to the look-a-like's apartment.

My fantasy dissolved upon contact; the law student's soft body and his powerful cologne nauseated me. Manners decreed that I stay until his climax, which I tried to bring about quickly. Dead Ringer refused to cooperate, apparently thinking that we'd just begun a long day's journey into night. Precious drooped. After forty minutes of unbearable activity, I ignored his protests and left for Sporters.

I'd experienced a limited social and sexual contact with Negroes. In the fourth grade, I competed with a colored girl for class domination. Esther was older than the rest of us, held back the previous year because of a bout with rheumatic fever. Our teacher, just out of college, was determined to encourage the skills and talents of all her students through athletic events, panel discussions, and art projects. Esther and I improvised plays. She always played the mother, I the father, no more conscious of the difference in race than our integrated children.

We decided to collaborate on a full-length play. I suggested using fairy-tale characters in a mystery set in Toyland; Esther had a religious turn of mind and demanded

227

that we dramatize the story of Joseph and his brethren. Carrying empty tablets, I accompanied Esther home from school one day, but before a word was written, a violent argument broke out over who would play Joseph.

"I'm a boy. You can be Potiphar's wife. That's the best girl's part."

"I ain't gonna be no whore. I'll be Joseph."

"We'll have to call him Josephine."

"Ain't nothing wrong with Josephine. That's Mama's name."

Before we could stun the theater world with our epic, Esther completed the work she'd missed during her illness and advanced to the fifth grade.

We moved from Pennsylvania to Montana, where no Negroes attended our consolidated school and Indians constituted the most despised minority, and from Montana to Louisiana, where segregation still existed.

I never met the middle-class and professional blacks who shopped and socialized in New Orleans and limited themselves to three or four children they sent to Negro colleges throughout the South; my acquaintance was limited to unskilled laborers and the fat black women who slapped into town on Saturdays wearing tattered shapeless dresses, their toes and heels sticking out of slashed shoes.

Several dozen blacks worked for my stepfather. A few were sober family men, but must drifted from job to job and from woman to woman, serving periodic terms in jail; when free, they spent hours everyday lounging outside little grocery stores in Euclid Hummock, loud raillery interrupted by swigs from bottles wrapped in paper bags. As Mother forced me to work at menial jobs on the plantation, I knew many of the lower-class Negroes in the area and understood their language. When they realized I was no talebearer and could work with the best of them, they talked freely in my presence. Their conversation seldom extended beyond pussy and crime. Every evening, I drove a truckload home to their unpainted two-room shacks standing in yards with no grass.

Idella had worked as a weedpuller in the ferneries for fifty years. Ten different men, none of whom she married, had fathered her twelve children; to the best of her knowledge, she had sixty or so grandchildren and innumerable great-grandchildren: her female descendants augmented welfare checks by casual labor. None had completed high school. Idella's seventeen-year-old great-granddaughter, Lutie Mae, already had four children by four different men.

For five years after Daddy died, Mother raised the four of us on one hundred and sixty dollars a month. We lived in a neat two-bedroom house with a large well-maintained yard. We dressed well, did without nothing that we really wanted, and drove about in a nice car. How could we respect people who lived so badly on more money? Negroes suggested only venality, stupidity, and sloth.

No blacks attended Prairie Dog Flats Junior College in Oklahoma; my first close encounters occurred during my sojourns in the minor leagues. I enjoyed a few beers with my darker teammates, but I had no more in common with them than I did with most of my white teammates, raw country boys with little interest in anything beyond baseball, pussy, and their rustic pursuits back home. I kept company with a pair of bright attractive fellows owning college educations, which inhibited intimacy with anyone else, especially the blacks, who had segregated themselves into cliques.

During my first winter in Manhattan, I was stunned by the natty black men and lovely exotic black women who hung around Times Square. Several effeminate white acquaintances numbered Negresses in their social circles. The women spoke with intelligence, and I wondered at their friendships with silly queens.

Each off-season, I worked as a waiter or a clerk, meeting witty black girls with whom I enjoyed banter. The older women kept to themselves; the men—cooks and dishwashers—seemed remote, downtrodden, or belligerent.

229

I'd never felt the slightest desire to bed a Negro, but late one night in 1962, I passed a black with light skin and fine features while strolling down a deserted Second Avenue. He boasted a mustache, seldom seen among young whites at that time, and walked with dapper masculinity. He must have noted my admiration, because he stopped, turned, and stared. So did I. Instinct sounded no alarm when he stepped in a recessed doorway, so I followed and fell to my knees. We never spoke a word.

A second bit of miscegenation occurred when I played ball with Mobile in the Southern League. After a night game in New Orleans against the Pelicans, I decided to thumb home and spend the following off-day with my family. A handsome young black picked me up. A senior majoring in Business while playing football at an athletically-outstanding Negro college, he spoke intelligently and our conversation flowed easily. We recognized each other's names; we had graduated from different Bonifay high schools the same year. He had received publicity as valedictorian and football captain at Euclid Hummocks High; his grandfather had worked as a laborer on my family's plantation. Somehow, I eased into the role of an aristocratic planter; the football player fell into a mushmouth servility. In spite of his mounting anger, I couldn't stop, and neither could he. Finally, he pulled off the road and forced my head into his lap. (Negroes, like convicts, seemed to recognize homosexuals with what appeared to be a sixth sense.) Our union climaxed when he threw me over the hood of his car and fucked me silly.

Still shaking with rage, he drove towards Bonifay in silence. "How ever did that happen?" I wondered.

"I don't know," he replied shortly.

"You ever done that before?"

He sighed deeply. "No."

"A beautiful panther loathed me enough to drop the veneer of civilization and commit a savage act of destruction."

"You dig getting buttfucked by colored boys?"

"Actually, it's a first. Too bad. I'll probably never again be violated so explosively."

"You fucked with me, and I still don't know how you done it. I ain't got no use for faggots."

"Has to be envy, but I've hardly achieved renown as a professional athlete."

"No, I admire you for getting as far as you have."

"Okay. How about . . . you determined early upon attending college. Pride demanded that you didn't burden your family financially, so you studied hard, winning scholarships, and worked summers and weekends, giving up a carefree youth to follow a dream. Am I right?"

"As rain."

"I would hazard to guess that you performed unskilled labor that used a minuscule amount of your mind."

"I did shit jobs in a sawmill."

"Dull work breeds resentment. What group of people do you most envy?"

"I don't envy no man."

"We're playing 'Truth.' "

He stared ahead at the road. "Rich white boys with yellow hair and soft hands. They get everything without working for it." He glanced at me. "You're cool, man."

"As penguin shit. And you, my friend, are very hot."

And he didn't reek with cologne. I partook of Sporters' brunch, but the odor lingered, eroding my confidence. I returned to Newport on an early bus.

A letter lay on my bunk. My stepfather had fallen in love and asked my permission to marry. His delicacy amused me; after all, Mother had died a year earlier. I didn't like the man, but he had treated my mother well, giving her wealth, prestige, and adoration. He offered plane fare if I would attend the wedding, to be held a week before my stepsister's marriage the end of September. I agreed to go.

231

If I lived that long. Accidents happened in the lab, and I'd twice had to wash my eyes of chemicals. While siphoning blood, I got a mouthful of stale vile liquid. (Dracula's eternal life could have been bearable only without taste buds.) I spit it out immediately and rinsed my mouth, but I'd swallowed some. The test was for serum hepatitus.

One night, I returned from more lust in the sand with the SEAL to find the Toad pontificating before a ward corpsman whom I had desired since walking into the shower room and catching him with erection in hand; he had looked up, flashed a sheepish smile, and turned a pretty posterior toward me. The following week, a carousing clutch of corpsmen had crashed into the barrack, the cutie among them. He staggered past my cubicle and collapsed upon his bunk. I ambled over for a chat; he mumbled incoherently and passed out. I stripped off his uniform and covered him with a sheet; too many men remained awake in the barrack for me to do more than cop a quick feel. Although he feigned unconsciousness, his sex responded immediately. I've never been disgusted by lewd fellows of the baser sort.

He had a short wiry body, a rough complexion, a hard-bitten Bronx accent, and a butch streetwise toughness, a type of man that women seldom preferred, so I figured him available. To the Toad's delight, I plastered a smile on my face and hearkened to his philosophy, which made Rod McKuen seem like Aristotle. Several centuries later, the Frog Prince stumbled up the stairs and Toughie stretched across the sofa. Within fifteen minutes, I attained rapture. I'd hoped for a response, but settled for corpse-like trade.

My sister, Karen, wrote, describing an anguished telephone call from Jane, who had not heard from me since her drunken exhibition. We'd enjoyed a pleasant little romance; now it was over. Why couldn't she understand that? I pulled out a letter that I'd received while languishing in that Louisiana hospital. It had followed me from DaNang.

232

Dear, dear Kurt,

Please forgive me—I really thought that you would be home by now. I didn't know where to write. I thought that your last letter indicated that you were leaving Vietnam in a matter of days.

When I didn't hear from you, I really got worried. Last night, I called your home in Bonifay. Your step-father answered and said that you were still in Vietnam. So I am writing now and I am so sorry—I would have written long ago if I'd had any idea that you were still there.

I can't wait for you to come. I even look for you in subways. Every evening when I come home from work as I turn the corner of 8th Ave. and 45th St., I start looking for you—silly when I know you won't be there. I did think you were in Louisiana though. I couldn't remember your address there—I don't know your step-father's last name and Karen didn't answer her phone and I felt as though I might *never* find you.

Will you be going home soon? Did you have to stay longer in Vietnam than you thought or did I misunderstand? I keep hugging the sweatshirt you left and hoping.

Things are going along—no luck with the costume business. I am still working 3–4 days a week for the American Jewish Committee. I am registered with a good employment agency and they send me to interview for a more permanent job. I *wish* you were here—I need advice. So far I interviewed for a clerk-typist position with Newberry Stores. $76.00 per week—I was over-qualified. Also the assistant to the head of fashion promotion of Simplicity Patterns—high class job, much $—. I was not qualified enough in retail work. Monday I will go see Coats & Clark (thread). They need a designer for promotion ideas—you know, stuffed animals, pillows, etc. *Then* the Milwaukee Rep wrote and asked me to please apply as a costumer—they need a shop supervisor—December through April—

233

they are waiting to hear from me. I do not really want to leave N.Y. yet but I *do* want to work in theatre. So I need you to help me. Also—I need you to come because of a dear Australian boy named John who I have been going out with and who is getting *too* fond of me. When you come, it will dampen his spirits. He is nice so I hope he doesn't get too unhappy. However, even if you weren't what you are to me—he would not be my type for anything other than a friend. There are lots of reasons—even more important as to why I need you—but as you once wrote to me—"I won't bore you by enumerating them."

Do *please* let me know where you are and when you will be back in the States—if you know. I drive the lady at the desk crazy checking for letters and sometimes I think it would be better if I didn't know you were coming—I get so distracted. However, do give me a little notice if you can. However, if you should pop in unexpectedly—I will not be too unhappy—not at all!

I must go to bed as I have to go to work in the morning—So—wish you were here and know you will be soon.

Bye for now
Love,
Jane

Tell your step-father that it was me that called—The operator spoke to him—he sounded very surprised.

I don't want to stop writing because I feel as though I will lose you again having just found out where you are—but I must—This is an awful letter I know—But I have been so worried and have been waiting to talk to you about so many things and now I can't seem to make much sense.

Soon?
Love again—much of it,
Jane

Gay life was more simple; one merely dropped a lover and

picked up another. Troubled, nevertheless, by a feeling of inadequacy, I lost myself in work and play.

I stood weekend duty with the porcine WAVE. Saturday afternoon, an ambulance brought the dead body of a good-looking sailor crushed between two pipes. He had suffocated before co-workers could free him. I stripped off his working blues and stuck him in the reefer.

I'd heard rumors of a funeral parlor in New York that put out calls to necrophiliacs around the world whenever the body of a beautiful woman or an athletic man arrived for disposal. As I preferred my tricks to remember our acquaintance, I doubted this particular aberration to be among my idiosyncracies. The Bible, however, says "Know Thyself."

When the WAVE left at eleven for her barrack, I closed down the lab. I entered Pathology, pulled out the man's tray, and lifted the sheet from his body. Only a scratch on his chest marred the perfection of his physique. "What a waste," as Mother said of her attractive gay beautician. The man appeared to be sleeping. I touched his arm. Cold. I knew without experimentation that I felt no lust for a corpse. What a relief! A lot of hurly-burly would have gone into scratching that itch.

Every morning, I jerked off, titillating Slim, who watched with half-closed eyes from his bed. (His sneer, his pale skinny body, and his dirty underwear protected him from my machinations.) Two or three evenings a week, I visited Buzzards Bay with the SEAL, whose passion, physique, and latent ruthlessness kept One-Time Kurt intrigued; then, too, I'd always been a sucker for people who liked me. Every free night, I strolled downtown to stalk sexy men. I bagged several in taverns and movie palaces. I dirtied my knees at the bus station, in a copse of trees, and under a dock. I seduced an aristocrat on Cliff Walk and a prole in a cemetery. I enjoyed debauchery with horny youths picked up in a restaurant, at the library, and outside a laundromat. I subjected two more corpsmen to the "Melbourne Method."

235

"Something's gone haywire," worried Paul. "I've never known you to be so recklessly aggressive nor so willing to sacrifice quality for quantity."

"None was less than a 'B' on the 'A' to 'F' scale. Check my trick book."

Paul pretended to disbelieve my stories, declaring that I embellished those that I didn't make up, so I let him read my trick book (names and ratings of all the men with whom I'd had sex, along with descriptions of each encounter); he knew it to be as accurate as I could make it.

Paul looked up horrified. While in Vietnam, I had my way with a wounded marine who died the next day. "You gave him a 'B.'"

"That's what he was."

"He died the next day!"

"I couldn't help that. He was a 'B.'"

"Can't you give him an 'A' for dying?"

"I'd have liked to, but I couldn't. He was only a 'B.'"

"You are the least sentimental person I've ever known." Paul read voraciously, shaking his head from time to time. "Your insistence upon flirting with danger is one of your greatest charms. Inviting exposure is not."

"Gambling is a principle inherent in human nature."

"Stop with the quotes!"

"The sea hath bounds, but deep desire has none."

"How about 'Reckless youth makes rueful age'? You must get to the bottom of this rashness before you wind up in the brig."

"Mother and Daddy worked hard and pinched pennies with the dream that they could travel and enjoy life after we'd grown; during the seven years after Daddy's return from the war to his death, they never traveled more than thirty miles from home. When Mother married money, she spoke of visiting Paris. The West Indies. California. For no good reason other than inertia, she never went. Throughout my sojourn in Nam, I heard to satiety about the hopes and

236

plans of marines who had no future."

"I understand that, but . . ."

"The stream of time glides smoothly on and is past before we know. I must flourish in my youth."

"These temporary attachments are soon consigned to oblivion. One day, even you won't remember them."

"Just what would you have me do? I'm a stupid queer, Paul, unable to teach or practice medicine or raise children. Of no use to anyone, I must have been put on earth to amuse myself. What else good am I?"

"Your eyes light up whenever you speak of the trooper. You've established rapport with the SEAL, the NP tech, and the soldier from North Carolina. Can't you settle down with one of them? Adventures await during the exploration of another's mind."

"Nick hates with a passion that frightens me. The man has begun manipulating me to achieve revenge; I don't like that. He thrives on danger and has a blacker soul than mine."

"Then you should be as transported as a masochist on a chain gang."

"He doesn't like our tricks. He uses them. That bothers me."

"I hear the righteous voice of hypocrisy. What about the SEAL?"

"Other than sharing his body, he just gives his surface. He tries, God knows! 'How I felt when I scored the winning touchdown,' 'How I felt when the head cheerleader let me take her to Prom,' 'How I felt when I earned an "A" in World History,' 'How I felt during my first dive.' I listen and add such revelations to my knowledge of the man, but . . ."

"My God, Kurt! The man allows you access to his body and his mind. What do you want?"

"An interest in me. In anyone but himself. He just recites experiences common to many people."

"Your description of his muscular physique hardly sets

him up as common."

"He lacks a sense of humor."

"Enough said. The others?'

"Montchanin writes lengthy letters from Camp Lejeune. Only I among his friends can sympathize with his present disposition. Montchanin is handsome, lovable, intelligent, curious— a man deserving of appreciation and I appreciate him. Unfortunately, he would drop me flat for the first twitching cunt that comes along."

"The soldier?"

"Sweet but dumb. If I cleaved unto a single man, I risk not only abandonment, but regret for missed opportunities. The unknown draws me onward."

"Downward, you mean. These brief encounters are so temporary. Man must aspire to immortality."

"Posthumous fame could hardly match the pleasures of carnality and revenge."

"Revenge?"

"I am one among a despised minority and must sit silently when those around me denigrate homosexuals. I feel no pride in my deviance, nor do I consider myself special because of it. Nonetheless, I loathe those who make me feel repellent."

"Ignore them."

"You jest! I attain satisfaction by teaching attractive straights the felicity of the very same man-to-man sex that they ridicule queers for enjoying. I gain revenge upon unattractive heterosexuals by denying them such refreshment."

"They must cry into their pillows every night."

"By opening my orifices to men, I make women unnecessary except as servants."

"They wallow in blissful ignorance of your little successes."

"So what? It's my movie. Women consider queers as despicable inferior creatures. At best, we're allowed the rank of pets."

"Women can respect excellence, too."

"Bullshit! They wonder only 'What's in it for me.'"

"Are men different?"

"Does gonorrhea cramp one's style? Men will do things out of curiosity, for the adventure of it. Women don't. Mostly they just sit around blaming men for not making their dreams come true, like Negroes blaming Whitey for dead-end lives caused by their own sloth. A woman thinks subjectively, brooding upon her emotions and thrusting away reason with both hands. Nine-tenths of them lack competence at any task beyond home economics and should be exterminated after menopause."

"Do you hate women so much?"

"Not at all. I love my sister and feel affection for Diana and several other ladies. Although each has girl friends, they despise the bulk of womanhood as much as I. Most women exist only to propagate, and they must rob man of his freedom to provide security for the wee ones. Generally, they capture and dominate men with their pussies, aware that a plethora of holes abound; they must diminish their mates so the men will lack the confidence necessary for philandering. Women hate competition, insecure creatures that they are, not having been brought up like men, who experience competition in sports, in the military, on the job. . . . Homosexuals are pale substitutes for 'the other woman,' but we can service men denied sex by circumstance or by those bitches who punish or goad their husbands by refusing conjugal rights."

"How did you develop this theory?"

"As a child, I could hear my mother in the kitchen with her friends enumerating their husbands' weaknesses; while visiting my own friends, I could hear their tired washed-out mothers screaming at their fathers for not making them rich and beautiful. Playing ball in the minors, I attended local social functions. Even the most successful man talks to a professional athlete with difficulty, perhaps because I embodied a fantasy. Women would notice their men's discomfort, either boldly playing up to me or publicly disparaging the poor guys, who couldn't compete with the archetype I represented. Men get together to talk about business or sports or adventures or pussy. Women get together to manbash. I've met some nasty men, but none so vicious as the average American woman."

Paul furrowed his brow. "I'm trying to think of an example to contradict you, but I can't."

"My mother is a case in point. I can recall her contemptuously spitting out the names of several famous entertainers rumored to be gay and laughing derisively about her nellie beautician. Whatever had those men done to deserve contempt? What lofty heights had Mother reached that she could sneer at anyone? She couldn't cook, lacked job skills, nagged Daddy into an early grave, screamed and ridiculed her children into neurotic wrecks, and died friendless."

"A man should never judge all women by his mother."

"She embarrassed and abused each of us before our friends, who shrugged off her frenzies. After all, their mothers had peculiarities, too."

"What has this misogyny to do with your current flirtation with self-destruction?"

"How the hell would I know?"

"Poor Kurt. Abhorred by women, real men, and God."

"That's why I kneel before a demi-god: Priapus. Did you know that 'Cock' and 'Gism' are Anglo-Saxon corruptions of the words 'God' and 'Jesus'?"

Back in the lab, I could hardly deny the porcine WAVE's competence, although I suspected her of Sapphic leanings, which was a different kettle of fish altogether. Like the other techs, I'd learned to ignore nurses, although a couple of ladies in white could have been charged with competence. I considered them as exceptions that proved the rule.

Sailboats crowded the Newport harbor. While enjoying the colorful display, I struck up a conversation with a pleasant fellow who pointed out a heavily-pregnant Lynda Bird Johnson Robb diving from a yacht. I wondered whether Janet Auchincloss disported herself nearby.

My new friend served aboard an LST in dry-dock. After walking me home, Lenny asked if he could stay the night, willing to philosophize three hours with the Toad for the privilege. He slept on the couch; I played 'Creepy Fingers' to overwhelming reciprocation. (I marveled at those who say they can always identify a homosexual; I sure couldn't.) The next evening, I returned from wrestling behind a tavern with a brutal sailor in aviation ordnance to find Lenny discussing the upcoming presidential nominations with the Toad. My lust had been slaked, and I resented Lenny's using the Toad to remain within my orbit. After the ugly creature trolled off to bed, I declined a rematch. The yeoman tried to turn me on with a tale about a handsome friend who feigned sleep while accepting fellatio. Not wanting to mortify my guest, I, too, accepted fellatio and went to bed.

The weekend loomed before me. Boston was off-limits since my sister's debacle in the Farmington YMCA, and it would sadden me to see the Enlisted Man's Club overrun by Asian hordes. I did, however, have the keys to Diana's apartment.

Long irritated by the sand of Buzzards Bay sifting into my Vaseline, I offered to show the SEAL around Manhattan. He accepted. The following day, I received a letter from Darby accepting an earlier invitation to spend the weekend at Diana's. This would be the soldier's last liberty before embarking for Vietnam; the SEAL would leave in a week for Europe. I refused to consider any logistical catastrophe.

During the drive from Newport, the SEAL told me about his family's trip to Yosemite Park and his rebuilding of a Model-T Ford and his attending a Boy Scout Jamboree in North Bay, Canada; nevertheless, he had muscles, and I wanted to examine them under a strong light. How ever could I with Darby in attendance? Each man assumed our binding to be as unique in my life as it was in his; it wouldn't do to suggest a partouze.

Darby waited on the corner of Third Avenue and 54th Street. When we walked through the door of Diana's apartment, the SEAL stopped short before a full-length nude portrait of the actress. "Who painted this?"

"I did." Photographs of Diana stood in frames on end tables at either side of the sofa. As Darby and the SEAL studied the painting, I slipped the photographs atop a secretary.

"Why?"

I eased into the bedroom, where a collage of Diana in performance covered six square feet of wall. "I'd never met such a strange woman."

"You aren't just whistling 'Dixie.' Why did you hang it here?" I had told both men that this was my new girl friend's apartment.

"Diana's best friend dates an art critic who will be coming by to judge my work." I thrust the collage behind a bureau. "I have always dreamed of being an artist." Did Diana make good her threat to have a friend tile the bathroom with miniature replicas of the nude portrait?

"You sure remembered her good."

Ah! The bathroom was still papered with scenes from 'A Rake's Progress.' "I have a photographic memory."

"Those sure are big tits," observed Darby. "Who is she?"

I could trust the SEAL's discretion. In spite of our intimate acquaintance, I knew nothing about his normal sex life. "A Russian spy Strom and me fucked."

If all went well, the SEAL would have another girl to fuck that night and Darby one the following night. Or vice-versa. I'd called Francisco the Model before he left for his cottage on Fire Island and wrangled three invitations to a party given by a gay fashion editor of old acquaintance. A dozen models attended, skinny girls wearing too much make-up; they chattered inanely while glancing sideways at

242

the photographer and a couple of dikey fashion editors. They resembled tropical birds and seemed to have as much intelligence.

Even had my buddies dressed with more chic and not huddled in a corner terrified by several leering fairies, they would have found it impossible to break through the narcissistic models' cold hard ambitions. We left the party after gulping two drinks and walked down Madison Avenue. "Okay, Strom. Lead us to your happy hunting grounds."

"Huh?"

"You must know a lot of places where chicks hang out."

I hadn't an inkling of where sluts cruised. "I'm out of touch, what with Jane and Vietnam and Diana and my elbow and being stationed in Newport . . ."

The SEAL had heard wild stories about Times Square. "We could pick up chicks there."

"Diseases, too, and a knife in the gut. If your wallet isn't stolen, you'll have to pay for a tired piece of ass that's soggy from today's quota of forty tricks. Let me make a few phone calls."

We stopped at a telephone booth and I called several friends. Stupid! All my friends were gay. What did faggots know about promiscuous cunts? Torn between wanting the boys to have a good time and wanting them to myself, I emerged from the booth with no plan. The SEAL was deep in conversation with Darby. "It made me sick to think the spy was going to slide his pecker up my ass, but we had to give the intelligence man downstairs time to photograph the dossier."

I suggested that we stroll over to Times Square so the SEAL could check out pussy. Scumbags of all races and sexes loitered outside squalid shops and cafes portending ptomaine and salmonella. We trekked up Broadway to Central Park; my friends rejoiced in the area's exoticism, so we crossed the street and trekked back down. On Second Avenue, long lines of young people waited to enter smart discotheques. The

243

females seemed to have dates. Strolling through the wolfpacks of gays who lurked on Third Avenue made the boys uneasy, so I suggested buying a fifth of Scotch and returning to the apartment. The boys agreed.

I walked out of the kitchen with a bucket of ice as Darby said, "The dude had a knife to my throat, so I let him."

My buddies were seducing each other for me! All I had to do was get out of the way. "Hey, guys! Gotta run down to the deli and buy some things for breakfast. I'll be back in a few minutes."

A sexy number wearing jeans and a black t-shirt exchanged glances with me in the delicatessen; he had decorated his apartment on First Avenue in Early Acid. Two hours later, I returned to Diana's. Deep in their cups, my buddies conversed earnestly. I led them into the bedroom and pointed at Diana's king-size bed. It was the work of a minute to inaugurate proceedings. Darby and the SEAL liked each other.

We spent Saturday afternoon cheering the Tigers at Yankee Stadium, where I led the awed servicemen into the visitor's clubhouse to greet a couple of my old teammates. The former Mud Hens invited us for dinner and a few drinks, after which we attended a musical about a Greek whore who enjoyed nearly as much sex as I did. I took my comrades by the restaurant where "Uncle" Ralph worked as a short-order cook. He would serve as a reliable witness to their desirability.

The men seemed uninterested in looking for women. "Maybe buy a couple bottles of hooch and watch some television. Feels good to get out of the barracks." And into bed, where we frolicked until dawn.

We spent Sunday afternoon exploring Central Park. In the Ramble, "Uncle" Vince and Aida turned a corner and confronted us. Vince's usual pattern was to pass by without recognizing me, ostensibly to save me embarrassment. Aida betrayed his discretion by lunging at me with a joyful bark.

"What a friendly dog!" I exclaimed. "How old is she?"

"Ten years next month."

"She looks a lot younger. Say, maybe you could help us find a theater near here that puts on open-air productions of Shakespeare. Can you tell us where it is?"

"Better yet, I could show you. Aida and I just happen to be walking that way."

Vince led us past several benches holding park denizens who would envy him forever; he dined out on the story for weeks.

When the SEAL dropped me off in Newport that evening, Lenny the yeoman waited on the front steps; I snarled so violently that he left in tears. The sailors who kept their motorcycles in the garage behind the house sat cross-legged on the living room floor, surrounding a poncho piled high with marijuana. I packed the few belongings I kept in the apartment and returned to the barracks. I had no intention of getting kicked out of the Navy four months from an honorable discharge because of dorks selling dope.

He's sudden if a thing comes in his head.

July 1968

A throng of people descended upon Newport for the Bermuda Race and the first of a series of week-long music festivals: Jazz, Rock, Folk, and Opera. Crowds milled in the streets; navy personnel who lived off-base reported that their usual ten or fifteen-minute drive home now took over an hour.

Babich, my buddy from pre-Vietnam days, dropped by the hospital during supper, insisting that I accompany him to one of the concerts.

"Jazz ain't my bag, buddy."

"You just need to listen, Kurt. It's the greatest music in the world."

"All I hear is a cacophany of squalling saxophones and squeaking clarinets. I prefer songs from musical comedies."

Babich groaned. "Let's go for a beer. Maybe find some snatch. Heh, heh, heh!"

We drank that beer in a huge bar packed with attractive young people, the men outnumbering the women by ten to one. After a second round, Babich and I retired to the restroom, where thirty men waited nuts-to-butts in a double line. As the line crept forward, I felt something prod my backside. I looked behind me. A good-looking blond grinned devilishly. Worried that the dude couldn't wait for his turn at the urinal and might, accidently or intentionally, piss on my pants, I protected my behind with a hand. A semierection poked my palm. I tugged it obligingly. The blond didn't repulse me. But so many people! And Babich, brooding in the other line, might have glanced our way. I dropped my hand, ending a bizarre encounter.

Babich left for home, so I ambled along the waterfront. Although I had my heart set on one of the bronzed young men who crewed the hundreds of boats in the harbor, I settled for a schoolteacher from New Hampshire; he did have a tan and a room at the Navy YMCA. We got along well, so after ado, he decided to walk me to the hospital. As he dropped off his key at the front desk, I peered into the lounge. Two dozen sailors sprawled on couches, chairs, and the floor, using the room for a free crashpad. An attractive fellow reached from his perch on a sofa to grope a sailor sleeping on the floor. A pickpocket? No, few sailors carried small pink wallets in their crotches. I should have enjoyed seeing what happened next, but the schoolteacher joined me and we left the Y.

The following day, having worked up a sweat running along Ocean Drive, I stopped at the fag joint for a beer. A tall, lean, good-looking youth wearing swimming trunks suddenly slumped over the bar. When he slid onto the floor, I helped a fat middle-aged man pick him up. The Fat Man sighed. "It's four blocks to the house. I'll never get him there alone." I threw the drunk over my shoulder and followed the Fat Man to a renovated saltbox. I set the youth upon a chair in the hall. Jumbo blocked the door. "You must have left your drink in the bar. How about a fresh one?"

"Thanks, but I should be running along."

Refusing to take "no" for an answer, the Behemoth led me into the kitchen, where a skinny man with a ferret's face prepared supper. "Junior's in the hall." The Weasel glared at me before leaving the room. "Navy?"

"Gimme a break! I'm working as a yard boy for some rich people."

"You have short hair."

247

"They wouldn't hire me otherwise. You live here year round?"

The Fat Man hesitated; I expected a lie. "We're visiting from Baltimore. A friend loaned us the house." A stupid lie. The cars in the driveway had New York license plates. As he added ingredients to boiling pots, we chatted about Newport. The Weasel rejoined us, nodding to Jumbo when he entered the kitchen. "My friend has a bad back. Would you mind carrying Junior upstairs?"

I hauled the unconscious youth upstairs and dropped him onto a double bed. The Fat Man stripped off the youth's swim suit. "Like him!" I nodded. He flipped the boy onto his stomach. "Fuck him."

As I cornholed the boy, the Fat Man sat on the edge of the bed and stroked my back; eventually, he took my place while I bathed in a sunken tub. Jumbo entered the bathroom to wash. "Who is he?"

The Fat Man shrugged. "Haven't the faintest."

"He's not your guest?"

"Never saw him before. Probably off one of the yachts."

"Gay?"

"What difference does it make?"

I wallowed in the tub a few more minutes before toweling off, pulling on my shorts, and returning to the bedroom for my shoes and socks. The Weasel plunged roughly into the boy while Jumbo snapped pictures with a flash camera. The Fat Man smiled. A shark's smile. "Memories." When they'd completed the photography session, the Weasel left for the bathroom. "Come downstairs for a drink," ordered Jumbo.

"As soon as I tie my shoes." He nodded and lumbered down the stairs. The youth breathed raggedly. I felt his pulse: Slow, intermittent, and thready. I shook him. "Hey! Wake up!" No response.

A screwdriver awaited me in the parlor. Jumbo smiled smugly. "Beautiful ass, huh?"

I agreed. "I've always considered heavy drinkers as easy

pickings, but raising and maintaining their erections can be exasperating. Attempting to bring them to orgasms can be futile."

The Fat Man shrugged. "We're only into fucking them."

"I played minor league baseball for several years. Small towns. Difficult to find gay action. Risking exposure, I patronized straight bars. Made out royally. Drinkers seem to need affection. They want to be liked, even by a stranger. Their total passivity amazes me. Those few who reciprocate invariably lack technique, which I ascribe to religious or moral guilt and feelings of sexual inadequacy."

"I don't care why they do it. We just want to fuck them." He showed me out the door. "Come for dinner tomorrow. Six."

"Fine." I hurried to the barracks and changed into whites, barely making the mess hall before it closed; then I changed into civvies and waited for Babich, who was to come by with two tickets for the night's jazz concert. He showed up with three tickets and an old friend, Kipp Stokes, who had served with us in Boston and Lejeune. I'd never liked him.

Untrue. I liked his lithe golden grace plenty. I just mistrusted his knowing glances and took umbrage at the slumming rich boy who peeped from behind a "regular guy" exterior to sneer at the proletariat.

Stokes was wounded three times in Nam, the last wound sending him Stateside. Simultaneously discharged from the hospital and the Navy, he immediately married a fifteen-year-old from the wrong side of the bay. She expected their first child in a month. They summered at his family's cottage on Cape Cod while Stokes considered his future. "College, I guess. Business at Brown, probably. Seems tame after Nam. Christ, I miss the action. Don't you?"

Absolutely not. I'd enjoyed my hours of leisure far more than those spent on patrol and ambush, and Babich had feared for his existence from the moment he received orders for Vietnam. Seven purple hearts among the three of us.

249

Somehow, we'd survived.

Stokes's bright eyes appeared dotted with pinpoints of madness. A residue of mutual unspoken hostility kept us on either side of Babich, who blithely assumed that his two best friends must like one another. We sat among thousands of jazz devotees, so far from the stage that we couldn't make out the performers' features. Babich tried to attain enthusiasm, but he would have preferred the intimacy of a small smoky club. Stifled by the crowd and bored by the music, I waxed nostalgically for ambushes and firefights.

Returning to the hospital, we had little to say. The concert had depressed Babich; the company oppressed me. As we pulled up to the barracks, Stokes fixed glittering eyes upon us. "Wanna drive up to the Cape and watch me fuck my wife?"

Babich demurred, and the evening ended.

The next morning, Stokes dropped by the lab. "A friend is flying me to Hyannis. Want to come along?"

I had declined several friendly overtures by Stokes during our sojourn in Boston because he enjoyed the sophistication to suspect that I might succumb to the exposure of his long elegant pecker, and a competitive sort, would describe the intimacy to Babich. But now, to whom would he declare his victory? And why? "I have a dinner engagement and won't be free till seven-thirty."

"Fine."

That afternoon, I dropped off a change of clothes at the saltbox and went running. (Alone. The SEAL never came to the gym again after our weekend in New York.) At my return, the Fat Man said brusquely, "Go upstairs and take a bath. Your sweat will stain my furniture."

Dirty jeans, a torn t-shirt, and ragged sneakers littered the floor of the master bedroom. A young man lay sprawled on the bed. Long greasy hair, filthy feet, and a bloody asshole. Very unappetizing. Jumbo appeared in the doorway. "Want him?"

"Not my type."

"Why?"

"He looks like he might have scabies."

Jumbo studied the youth, absently scratching his chest. "Think so?"

"Crabs. Head lice. Clap. Where did you find him?"

"Hitchhiker. Coming for the Rock Festival." We gazed at the comatose boy. "Take your bath. Dinner's ready in ten minutes."

When I entered the kitchen, the Fat Man handed me a banana daiquiri. "You like the boy we had yesterday?"

"I couldn't recommend his personality."

"He looked good, right? The All-American type?" I nodded. "You must meet a lot of good-looking studs."

"Too few allow me fun, like your sleepy friend."

"How would you like to fuck a handsome stud every night?"

"You've pushed my button."

"We'll talk about it after dinner."

A delicious dinner: double servings of rare roast beef, little new potatoes, steamed broccoli, corn on the cob, a garden salad, and strawberry shortcake. The Weasel served coffee in the parlor and Jumbo revealed his plan. "You meet a stud. Promise him anything: drugs, booze, women. . . . Call us, anytime, day or night. We'll pick you up."

"Will you have whatever I promise ready to hand?"

"Don't worry about that."

"Why bring me into it?"

"What would you think if a middle-aged stranger offered you drugs or a woman?"

"I'd figure he was after my body. A lot of dudes will make the exchange."

"Hustlers. Bums. Punks. Losers. We want boys with class. You get many like that?"

"A few."

Jumbo wondered how to share in my winnings. "Here in

Newport?"

"Some. Mostly quickies. I have no place to take them. Gets frustrating."

"You could bring them here."

"Why ever should I share them?"

Jumbo turned to the Weasel. "Get the pictures." The Weasel protested, looking suspiciously at me. "Get them!" The whey-faced ferret climbed the stairs to fetch a thick folio. Jumbo pulled out thirty-odd folders, each holding several photographs of a different young man. Full-length nudes, fore and aft. Close-ups of the genitals. Every series included snaps of the Weasel penetrating the youths anally and orally. "Aren't they beautiful? Check the asses."

"Difficult to judge a man's looks with his eyes closed. Are all of them unconscious?"

"Doesn't matter. We just fuck them."

I held little inclination to participate in such smarmy doings, but ever one to keep his options open. . . . "You won't take pictures of me?"

"Only if you want us to."

"I don't."

"You like the set-up?"

"If it gets me hunky guys."

"It will. How about tonight?"

"Already have a date."

"With a classy guy?"

"Yes, but he's an old friend."

"Tomorrow?"

"I'll try."

At seven-thirty, a powder-blue Aston Martin pulled in front of the hospital gates, an imperially slim blond of thirty-five behind the wheel. Stokes waved me over. "Rush Brede—Kurt Strom." Rush drove to the airport, where we climbed into a four-passenger plane and flew to Hyannis. Stokes disembarked. "See you next week."

Rush beckoned me into the co-pilot's seat. "Care to fly up

252

to Provincetown for a drink?"

"Usually, ah must oblige Uncle Sam with mah presence by the dawn's uhley light, but as tomorrah is the annivuhsary of America's Independence . . ." When I was around rich folk, I tended to affect the drawl of a Louisiana planter. (A true-life Louisiana planter would protest the drawl, claiming it sounded more like the besotted groanings of low-life swamp trash.)

"Good." Rush dressed simply: a silk skirt, fawn trousers, and Gucci loafers. Appraising a watch, a ring, and a gold chain, I estimated his exterior worth at twelve thousand dollars, excluding the plane.

"Ah'm moah accustomed to hacks and gilded chariots."

Rush smiled. "I'll just bet you are."

He landed outside P-town and hired a taxi. We strolled about the crowded resort, eventually settling in a bar filled with lavender lads; Rush seemed completely at ease amidst the preening and the screeching. I'd worked up a mild lech for him as a wealthy pilot with a fabulous name, although I would not have noticed him in a crowd. We chatted; he had enjoyed a good education at Groton and Princeton (B.A. in History), had traveled extensively, conversed easily. . . . My lech grew. "Why did you bring me here."

"You're uncomfortable?"

"Not at all."

"Kipp thought I should meet the most mysterious man of his acquaintance."

"Why?"

"Need one have a reason?"

"I've learned that one usually has a reason."

"What could I possibly want besides the pleasure of your company?"

A dyke wearing a tux announced the floor show, a series of bawdy songs and precious skits. We applauded the finale. "I've never trusted Stokes."

"The boy has a troubling tendency to provoke people."

253

"He's tempted me."

"No doubt. Kipp's quite attractive."

"At the risk of seeming rude, may I ask if you . . ."

"No. Kipp's like a little brother. Besides, I prefer women."

"Then, why. . . ?"

"You weren't listening. I merely prefer women."

"Then this is dangerous, Rush." He raised an eyebrow. "Prolonging the pleasure of anticipation."

"I dislike sex with strangers, no matter how attractive."

"Under close scrutiny, an Olympian god could become bland and ordinary. The mystery dissipates."

"Have I lost my mystery?"

"You've let me see nothing but your impeccable manners."

"They hide a cornucopia of imperfections."

"What if one of us should see somebody more desirable?"

"You could never worry about that."

"As I'm a sucker for casual elegance, you have no competition either."

During the flight back to Newport, Rush asked if I would be his guest at a Fourth of July barbecue at Strawberry Hill, summer home to some other rich folk. My mind ransacked my meager wardrobe. Thank God, I let Francisco and my sister, Karen, choose my clothes. "Sure. Will Janet Auchincloss be there?"

Rush laughed. "I shouldn't be surprised."

"I wondered how much time would pass before you infiltrated the monied Newport," snapped Paul. "Don't plan to outwit them as you do your plebeian tricks. The rich are masters at using up people and discarding them without compunction."

"What ever could I want from the wealthy? I have a comfortable bed, ample food, pleasant working conditions, and a healthy body. I enjoy sex with desirable men and enough free time to indulge other interests."

Paul melted. "I've always loved you for two reasons: You succumb to the moment without watching yourself, and you envy no one."

"Why should I? The rich enjoy greater mobility than I and can buy bigger toys. That's all. They catch colds. They suffer toothaches and heartaches. They age and die."

"You don't feel the rich are different from you and I?"

"Despite my family's poverty during our adolescence, my sister, Karen, attained prominence and popularity during high school because of her brains, beauty, and talent. As a gangling doofus who wore eyeglasses, I lacked such attributes and cut a more narrow swath, earning less-than-average grades and dating less-than-pretty girls. When Mother married money, popular and pretty girls let it be known that they considered me an acceptable date. I received invitations to attend fashionable parties and to join the better clubs. I was no different from the nerd living in a small house with a coal miner's widow on the dole."

"Few people are more vulgar than the nouveaux rich."

"Don't judge my family by me! My stepfather's ancestors founded the plantation over a hundred years before John Jacob Astor trapped beaver on the Columbia. Most of the great families of Newport are descended from tradesmen; the Kennedys are only two or three generations from shanty Irish. My stepsister represents the twelfth generation of Landreaux to live at Belle Ombre."

"The South shall rise again!"

"With the advent of air conditioning, I shouldn't be surprised. But seriously, Paul, those old plantation masters, with their hundreds of slaves and thousands of acres, might have been America's only true aristocrats."

"You sound chauvinistic."

"Hardly. Without the trappings of money and lineage, my stepfather's family is indistinguishable from some of the white trash that lives on the plantation."

"Why this obsession with the wealthy Mr. Brede?"

"Obsession? I've met a nice guy who seems to enjoy my company."

"You desire him, in spite of his ranking below your physical ideal."

"Racial memory. I descend from farmers and company-town coal miners. Deep in my heart, I believe the rich to be cleaner than the rest of us."

Paul shook his head. "Poor little match girl."

Despite my mammy's dark warning that white gentlemen have no use for a lady who eats too much in public, I gorged myself at the barbecue. I assumed that the other guests were members of the haut monde, but recognized no one: Suzy Knickerbocker didn't illustrate her column. My croquet playing probably embarrassed Rush; I sported a low-life exhuberance when blackballing.

Late that evening, I entered one of the sailor bars along Thames Street. A lean, dangerous machinist's mate admitted an interest in fulfilling the beautiful young wife of an impotent rich man. I called Jumbo, who picked us up. On the way to the saltbox, the Fat Man offered the machinist a slug of brandy. Within a minute, the sailor lapsed into unconsciousness. I carried him into the saltbox and up the stairs.

After the Fat Man and I finished with the youth, the Weasel performed for the camera. I dressed the sailor and carried him to the car; Jumbo drove to a secluded spot along Ocean Drive and pulled the car over. "Put him out." The Weasel dragged the machinist behind a large rock.

I was appalled. "Here!"

"He'll be all right."

"People can die from ingesting knockout drops."

Jumbo's eyes narrowed. "He'll be all right."

"Someone should stay with him in case he needs medical care."

"Too dangerous."

"It's chilly by the ocean. He could go into shock."

"He'll be all right. Get in the car."

"Let me stay with him until he recovers."

"What if he turns mean?"

"I can run faster than any white man you've ever known."

"All right." The Weasel climbed inside the car and closed the doors.

"Wait! Drop us off near town!"

The Fat Man drove away. I lifted the sailor to my shoulders and walked three miles to a telephone. A taxi took us to the back gate of the hospital. I checked the night barrack. Empty. I carried the sailor inside, undressed him, and went to my locker for a towel. The holiday shift slept, so I hauled the sailor to the shower room, where I held him under lukewarm water, wondering if I did the wrong thing, and washed him thoroughly. Carrying him back to the night barrack, I lay him in a bunk and crawled beside him. An hour later, I awakened when he began moving restlessly. Jesus! Had anyone come in and seen us. . . .

"Where am I?"

"Safe. You passed out."

He tried to push my roving hand away. "Didn't drink so much."

"Someone slipped you a mickey."

"Feel like shit."

"Don't doubt it."

"What're you doin'? Hey! What're you. . . ?" For the first time that night, he attained an erection. Half-an-hour later, immediately upon his climax, I left.

I ran the next morning, treating myself afterwards with a stroll along Cliff Walk. At a jumble of rocks near its end, a skin diver emerged from the ocean. Hair burnished by the sun, he stripped off a black wet suit and sat on a big slab of rock. Joining him, I initiated a conversation that led to tales about bisexual ladies. He stared, bemused, when I pulled out Precious. He watched uncertainly as I nuzzled his leg. I slid my hand under his red swim suit. He primed his spear gun. I scuttled over the rocks like a startled crab. He could have killed me. Precious dripped with excitement.

On my way back to base, I passed the YMCA. I liked its

location, downtown near the docks and across the street from the town's gay bar. I rented a room for ten dollars a week.

I made immediate contact with a slim little sailor who lay nude in a room with the door open. I stood in the doorway and asked what so many people have asked me, a question I equated to fingernails scraping a blackboard. "What'cha readin'?" A book on nutrition. "What do you plan to do after your Navy hitch?" He held aspirations to become a jockey. I stroked his leg. A description of his diet gave me sufficient time to close his door and remove my clothes. "I've never done this with a man," he murmured, as his tongue swirled around my bunghole.

Sin has many tools, but a lie is the handle that fits them all.

Leaving the prospective jockey's room, I passed a sexy blond headed for the shower room. I grabbed my towel and a bar of soap. Old Yellowhair showered under the second of three nozzles. We chatted. I bent to wash my foot, my head level with his crotch. I maneuvered closer when I washed the other foot. My lips were inches from his unmentionable, which stirred and lifted. During rapture, he reached down to feel Precious's heft. I stood to give him access, should he wish to reverse our positions. The blond jumped back, frightened. I cajoled him into finishing what we'd started. When I returned to the Y from supper, I saw Old Yellowhair enter the gymnasium on the second floor with a pretty girl on his arm.

Every Friday and Saturday night, the YMCA held dances in the gym. I boogied in my own way, cruising the sailors that used the second floor john. After relieving a bemused hunk in the last booth, I stood at the sink, brushing my teeth while watching the reflection of a little sailor who sat on one of the toilets. Suddenly, he twisted his head to vomit. Never dependant on the proper setting for l'amour, I streaked across the tiles. He looked down at my bobbing

258

head and said, serious as leprosy, "I don't feel so good."

I dragged him into the shower room, stripped off his uniform, and scrubbed him thoroughly. I wrapped my towel around the boy and pulled him up to my room on the fourth floor. He seemed grateful that someone would take care of him.

This episode gave me the idea of operating a little hotel in my room. Every night, the lounge held sailors unable or unwilling to return to their ships. Most had drunk too much. Others had missed the last bus to the piers or the ferry boat across the bay. A few wanted an early start on the beach.

Before I could put my plan into operation, I attended a party at the Brede's summer cottage on Cliff Walk. (The "cottage" had forty rooms.) Rush played host for a week to a British group that opened and closed the Rock Festival. The party was to welcome the five musicians.

The group's leader held court in the ballroom, several girls at his feet adoring his pasty-face splendor; I elbowed my way through the rest of the group and its entourage, all gorging tapeworms in the dining room. As I ate, a skinny little musician with long straggly hair, a spotted face, bad teeth, and stick arms engaged me in conversation. A Limey accept muffled by incessant mastication proved incomprehensible, so I excused myself and walked outside.

Several couples danced on the terrace; others strolled about the grounds, including the scion of the watchmaking family whom I'd met on the bus to Providence. He nodded and turned away. My buddy, Stokes, introduced me to a pale, pregnant redhead; we traded insincere badinage. I wandered towards the cliff and watched the breakers; the little stick figure followed at a distance. Moving back to the house, I found an atrium on the second floor, its centerpiece a jacuzzi that held three nude girls. They looked past me and screamed. I turned around. Uncomely Clive from the buffet. The girls wrapped large bath towels around themselves and pulled the musician onto a dark balcony.

Left alone, I stripped and submerged myself in the jacuzzi. Rush and Stokes appeared, Stokes leaning against a wall, Rush sitting on his heels beside me. "Having a good time, seafood?"

I indicated the balcony. "Those girls look awfully young."

"Thirteen . . . fourteen. . . ."

"Go Directly To Jail. Do Not Pass 'Go.'"

"Groupies. They want to bang the rock stars."

"No accounting for taste. Won't a mass of them overrun the estate?"

"I've hired guards for the rest of the week. Your name will be on their list." I looked at him quizzically. "There's a party every night. You're invited to all of them."

"Such an invitation would overwhelm me if I didn't have five AM calls everyday."

"Come when you can." He stood. Stokes walked over and stuck his hand in the water. "Stay in the chauffeur's quarters if you need sleep. The noise shouldn't carry."

"I might take you up on that."

"Please do. I'll be up all night and can drive you to base."

"Where's the chauffeur?"

"Driving Mother around Scandinavia." Kipp left to rejoin his wife; I toweled off and dressed. Rush led me to the butler's pantry. "Here's a key to the garage. Keep it. You might meet someone and need a place to do dirty."

"Thanks a lot, buddy."

"I'll take it out in trade."

"What a wonderful way to pay debts!"

Four glasses of wine convinced me to accept Rush's offer. At two AM, I awakened when someone climbed the stairs of the chauffeur's quarters. Footsteps crossed the floor. A hand touched my chest. The sound of a zipper. Shoes kicked off. Pants falling to the floor. Shirt. Briefs. A lean body knelt at my head. Smelled good—couldn't be one of the musicians. I stroked a long elegant unmentionable—couldn't be Rush. Always one to take a gift horse in the mouth . . . My demon

260

lover entered me from the rear. Lovely technique. A grunt, a shudder, and a sudden stillness. The wraith jumped up and groped its way to the bathroom. I turned on the bedside lamp. The bathroom door opened. Stokes!

I watched him dress. "Did you know how hot I was for you at Lejeune?" No reply. "You've fulfilled a fantasy, buddy. Sure wish I'd known it was you." He tied his shoes. "We've had this date for a long time." He glared at me and left.

Rush seemed amused by the encounter. "The lad has always preferred to hobnob with the working classes."

"I'd thought he considered me a peer."

"Kipp envies you, the glorious barbarian he'd hoped to become. As a boy, he refused to attend a private school, insisted upon taking a paper route to earn pocket money. Entered the military as an enlisted man, apparently hurling himself at the guns of the Cong. Married a common girl." Rush shook his head. "He's coming around now."

"And in copious amounts."

The rich man raised his eyebrows. "You allowed him a victory."

"Who cares? It finally happened! Actually, he seemed to regret it."

"What a silly boy!"

I longed for a rematch with the silly boy, but he didn't attend Monday's party; I returned to the YMCA at midnight. A gorgeous sailor stirred restlessly on a chair in the main hall. He looked up as the front door opened.

I nodded. "Bitch of a place to sleep. Miss the last bus?"

"Wanted to get an early start on the beach."

"You'll be sleeping on the sand all day, ending up with third-degree burns and no girl." He sighed. "Where you from?"

"Chicago."

"As a teenager, my mother lived on Clark Street, a few blocks away from the St. Valentine's Day Massacre." We

261

talked about the Second City—I had relatives there and had served six months of my hitch at Great Lakes Naval Base, a few miles to the north. "Hey, no use you being miserable all night. I've got a room upstairs."

He shifted again in the wooden armchair. "I'd hate to put you out."

"No problem."

The desk clerk watched the locked door that led upstairs to the rooms, but I'd found a door on the fifth floor that opened onto a circular iron staircase down to the gym, which had an access door to a fire escape leading to a walled yard behind the Y. I opened a gate in the wall and the sailor entered. As he walked into my room, he saw the narrow bed we would share. He stiffened, then relaxed. "Give me a blanket, and I'll sleep on the floor."

"That would be my duty as host. There's room for both of us on the bed." I stripped to my skin and picked up a towel. "It's up to you. I'm heading for the shower."

When I returned, his clothes hung over a chair and he lay in the bed, scrunched against the wall. I stuck my wallet in a shoe, draped my towel over the end of the bed, and crawled under the sheet. He must have appreciated the comfort of the bed and the safety of my room; he made only a token objection when my hands roved. Eventually, he allowed me to turn him on his back and remove his skivvies.

A British diplomat had learned the art of Fang-Chung in Hong Kong and taught it to Diana, who taught it to me: mouth, hands, and fingertips massaged a man's erogenous zones for some time before centering on the genitals. A bisexual Italian architect whose wealthy father had sent him to the great bordellos of Egypt taught Francisco the art of Imsak, a variation of the Chinese technique. The kept boy of a Manhattan socialite knew how to drive men up the wall merely by using his lips, tongue, and teeth on kneecaps. A butch carpenter hitchhiking home to his wife and children in Arkansas had spent the winter in Miami with a French couple and a night at my family's beach house near Mobile; he used his throat and a twisting hand to slowly bring on the aurora borealis.

My simple sailor didn't stand a chance.

After half-an-hour of foreplay, I got up to turn on the light and knelt at the young man's head. Shocked into full consciousness, he realized that I demanded (and deserved) reciprocation. After a few seconds of hesitation, he sighed and reached for Precious. He held the rigid pole between his fingers and gazed at it, lifting it to examine the undershaft; then without tactile or lingual exploration, he popped the bulb into his mouth. Ten seconds later, he withdrew and looked up hopefully. I stared unrelenting. He closed his eyes and returned to work, one hand encircling the base of the shaft. A novice couldn't possibly bring me off, so I rewarded the boy with another half-hour of my technique. His powerful climax was my reward.

Following ado and the light switched off, the sailor backed against me spoon-fashion, and with my arm encircling his chest, drifted into slumber. I never could sleep in that position; I left to prowl the halls and bathrooms. Nothing. I returned to my room, greased Precious with K-Y, and eased into my bedmate's posterior. The drowsy boy accepted me, and wonder of wonders, gently returned my kisses.

The memory of seducing such a beautiful man glowed within me through duty on Tuesday. Stokes failed to show again at Wednesday's revels for the British musicians; an admirer kept me from feeling forsaken—Uncomely Clive, who gazed at me with sorrowful eyes. I took Rush aside. "Tell me about Uncomely Clive."

"Who?"

"One of the musicians."

"They're all uncomely." I described my shadow. Rush provided a name that meant nothing to me. "It does to millions of screaming fans."

"Could you screw up his courage? I'd prefer a

confrontation so I can turn him down. His watchdogging has become a trial."

Rush obliged, and Uncomely Clive finally made his pitch. "I'm mad for that great white bum of yours."

"Flattering, ace, but my lover owns every acre."

He gazed at me wistfully. "I haven't tossed it off with anyone for two months."

I reported the proposition to Rush, who expressed surprise. "I'd heard no rumors. He's nellie, but all of them are. You've impassioned him, Kurt. As far as I know, he hasn't approached anyone else."

"Lucky me. You interested?" I asked hopefully.

"It's your great white bum he's mad for."

"Has he bathed this month?"

"Not since Boxing Day."

"Bad teeth, no chin . . ."

"Hasn't taken off that red velvet suit since his arrival."

". . . a chicken chest, knobby little legs . . ."

"Rumor reports eleven thick inches."

"There's some good to be said about everyone. Well, perhaps through pity."

"Little Orphan Annie would cry her eyes out."

"He is a haunted, driven little creature."

"Depressing."

"Hordes of screaming fans allowing him no privacy."

"The tribulations of a star."

"It's not as if I'm a trembling virgin."

"Hardly."

"Eleven thick inches, huh?"

I joined Uncomely Clive at the buffet, where he sucked up food like a vacuum cleaner. "You really want this great white bum?" He garbled something in Limey through three Swedish meatballs. I assumed an affirmative. "Thing is, I'm turned on solely by blokes who prefer dollies. May I be blunt?" Swallowing one of the meatballs, he looked like a pale snake ingesting a frog. "If you chat me up with a pair

264

of good-looking groupies of the masculine gender, Moby Butt is yours."

"How do I chat you up?"

"Tell them that I'm a rock musician, a drummer for the hottest new group in England. The Turquoise Toads. No! The Stars of Bethlehem. Mick Jagger's me mate. The Beatles, too."

"Your moniker?"

I thought a moment. "Dandy Lyons. Just introduce us and I'll take it from there."

Clive swallowed the last meatball. "I don't fancy looking the fool."

"Then no one gets shafted."

I left soon after. A very drunk sailor with very good legs staggered down Thames Street. "Want me to call you a cab?"

"Only if you pay the driver. I'm broke."

Hmm. "Where you planning to crash tonight?"

"My ship."

"Last bus has already left."

He backed against a wall to hold himself up. "A park?"

"Not a chance. The Shore Patrol will take you in." He looked very sad. "I have a room at the Y."

He thought about it. "You Navy?" I pulled out my I.D. More thought. "Okay."

I loved sharing a bed with nifty sailors.

Thursday evening, Rush flew to Boston, leaving me to wander listlessly about the grounds of the estate. Other than playing trombone and tuba in my high school band, I had little in common with professional musicians and nothing in common with their groupies. I listened to the musicians' spiels. Homely, undereducated, lower middle class boys thrust into sudden fame—they alternated between pomposity and silliness. The fame, the money, the easy sex: everything depended upon fickle fans. Rush could utter the proper clichés that made him sound respectful of their noise.

I hadn't the knack.

Bored, I left and walked to town. Looking through the window of a dockside bar, I saw two attractive lieutenants, bright and shiny as new pennies in their uniforms and tanned to the same color. Within ten minutes, they accepted invitations to meet a famous rock group at a famous mansion.

I showed the officers around and left them to fend for themselves while I parboiled in the jacuzzi. Uncomely Clive entered the atrium. "Our bargain still hold?" I nodded, and he led two cute teenagers forward. They gazed at me with adulation; Clive had evidently chatted me up very well.

I invited the youths to join me. Overwhelmingly grateful, they stripped, revealing unblemished bodies. They shared a joint with Clive, who knelt by the edge of the jacuzzi, and waited for pearls of wisdom to pour from my lips. What to talk about? I knew nothing about the current rock scene. I had never bought a record nor had I ever seen an Elvis Presley movie. Long trips by car with Mother had given me an enviable repertoire of songs from the Thirties and Forties. During my teens, our band director immersed us in Sousa marches and semi-classical pieces; I listened with only half-an-ear to current pop hits. In the Sixties, "Uncle" Vince introduced me to opera, which almost turned me off music altogether. The British rock scene, huh? "Did I blurt out that the Ugly Plugs are ragging me to divulge the secret of me cymbal banging on 'Dodie Dum.' Ahh, Clive! Ye must hear our new side: 'She Laughed, She Cried, She Died.'"

One of the teenagers bravely, if tactlessly, interrupted. "You talk different from Clive and the others."

"I'm Welsh. Have you chaps tried the new fad? It started on Carnaby Street and is sweeping Merrie Old England. Be over here directly."

"What's that?" asked a youth eager to be in the know.

"A chap balls a jolly dolly while another bloke buggers him." The youths couldn't understand my Limey slang.

"Rams it up his arse." Quizzical looks. "A dude balls a chick while another dude fucks him." They understood. Disgust marred their good looks. "Great way to pop off. Everyone who's 'IN' does it. Mick, John, Paul, Amos, Andy. . . . I've always said, says I, 'Try everything twice.' You chaps ready for a shower? Hot jacuzzi, cold shower. Follow me, mates." I led them to Chase's bedroom, which had a bathroom with a regiment-size shower stall. The boys followed me into it. "Listen, mates, I need a favor." The awe-struck boys could deny me nothing. "I've got a date with _____ and _____ (a couple of television stars). They want to experience the new fad, but I've never done it and me bunghole needs stretching. Would you mind?"

They might have minded, had they not had been too stoned to stand. I led them to the bed, where they needed considerable rapture to achieve the hardness for bunghole-stretching. Uncomely Clive watched from a dark corner.

As the boys dozed, I arose and bent over an ottoman. Uncomely Clive charged, pulling out much less than the rumored eleven inches. Ah well! At least, I wouldn't have to look at him while he did it. Unfortunately, Clive spent his money on dope instead of lessons in Cairo's brothels; before finding the hole, he ejaculated all over Moby Butt. Breathing shallowly, I held the sobbing rock star; minutes later, he left, a broken man. I showered and rejoined my fans, stretching a couple of bungholes myself.

Downstairs, the Navy lieutenants had succumbed to the environment; they sprawled on the lawn, completely stoned. I led them to the chauffeur's quarters and stretched two more bungholes.

I'd had more than enough sex, but a stocky little sailor with crinkly blue eyes and a merry smile played pool by himself in the Y's game room. He had no place to stay. I stretched my fifth bunghole of the night.

Friday, I took my aching Precious to New York, where Paul and I ate dinner at the Lion's Head. Just a month of his

267

sabbatical remained; he would return in September to his teaching job in Colorado after a year of studying modern American art. Francisco entered the restaurant. I introduced my old friends and invited the model to join us.

"I'm meeting my lover."

"So have a drink while you're waiting. How is Morris?"

"Morris?"

Ahh! "Tell us about your new paragon."

A doctor from Wilkes-Barre with innumerable stellar qualities. I'd never been able to pinpoint Francisco's taste, so the young physician's healthy good looks shouldn't have surprised me. The doctor liked my looks, too. Never one to intrude upon another's love affair, I took care to throw out no signals, but we were left to chat about medical conditions in Vietnam while my old friends gossiped like village spinsters about mutual acquaintances. Paul swallowed another bite of eggplant and said, "I make it a rule never to believe a word that Kurt utters."

Francisco looked at me reproachfully. "Do you lie?"

"Never to my friends."

Paul sniffed. "No one ever turns him down. Kurt snaps his fingers and the world drops its pants."

"Battalions of men have spurned my advances. Entire armies."

"Only veterans of the First World War. According to your embroidered exaggerations, Napoleon commandeered fewer troops than you've sucked off. Kurt's the Baron Munchausen of the twilight world." Paul wiped his lips with a napkin and sipped his wine. "Last night, for instance, he fucked five so-called straight men. No one has done that since Alcibiades."

Francisco smiled. "You must remember that Kurt is like Santa Claus. He comes just once a year."

The doctor frowned. "That's not good."

"After I ejaculate, I lose all interest in my partner. Better to show him a good time and recall the episode at my leisure."

Paul growled. "Five straight men!"

Francisco defended me. "Kurt says that you seduce men with your intensity and the deep mellifluity of your voice, and I can see that you have the bearing of a Middle-European aristocrat. You are most attractive, but do you understand the power wielded by the truly beautiful?"

"All my lovers have been beautiful."

I laughed. "Each could have stepped out of a painting by Fragonard."

Paul glared at me and turned to Francisco. "I defy you to acclaim Kurt's beauty."

"He photographs well. Fine facial bones. Clear skin. Perfect teeth."

The doctor exclaimed, "He's the healthiest-looking person I've ever seen."

"That's it!" cried Paul. "I'm a teacher and see him as a diamond in the rough. No beauty. He's a chameleon, able to look or act any part needed to seduce his victims. If you see him as beautiful, it's what he wants you to see. The selfish bastard also has the knack of making people want to please him."

Francisco knit his perfect brow. "Then why do so many people dislike the boy."

"Because if he's not sexually interested in a person, Kurt withdraws and gives nothing of himself."

"Aren't we all like that?"

"No! Most people judge others by several criteria. If they don't turn on Kurt, he can't hide his disdain. He's the rudest person I've ever met."

"I've always thought Kurt had lovely manners."

"Exactly. That's why his rudeness is so insulting. He's an amoral animal, stupid as Quasimodo, running on instinct. He's straight out of Pandora's box."

Francisco nodded. "You're right."

I winked at the doctor. "These are two of my best

269

friends."

The doctor shook his head. Francisco chuckled. "We love him."

Paul threw back his head and laughed heartily. "He's outrageous, a wonderful mixture of wide-eyed innocence in this best of all possible worlds and the cynicism of a Nazi storm trooper."

Francisco poured more wine for each of us. "Someone told me about a Viking king called Harold the Fair, 'the wildest, most beautifullest man who ever lived.' I thought immediately of Kurt."

Paul grinned slyly. "I can picture an effeminate little monk transcribing those words, squirming ecstatically within his cum-stained woolen underwear." The disagreeable Brahmin changed the subject and began talking about a young artist whose work he found fascinating. "His paintings show such depth and subtlety. Amazing tactile value." On our way to the restaurant, we had stopped by a gallery to view the artist's work. I recalled a painting labeled "Man's Soul." It looked like a decayed olive.

We accompanied Francisco and the doctor to a party on Gramercy Square. Paul left within minutes on the arm of an affected little queen. The doctor invited me to Wilkes-Barre for the weekend; when I declined, he told Francisco that I'd made a pass. The model and I had been through this before; the affair would not last its accorded month. I stayed until the end of the party because a lovely boy hung upon me, moaning over my desirability; as the last stragglers said goodbye, he left with a rotund little bald man. His sugar daddy. The wildest, most beautifullest man since King Harold the Fair went home alone.

Saturday morning, I called "Uncle" Vince. "Baby! Come up this moment!"

Throughout the winter, the softhearted Sicilian had opened his small railroad apartment to the homeless, which limited our contact; the dismal derelicts stank and their babbling nonsense allowed us no privacy for chat. Despite Vince's admonitions, the bums lacked any discretion about throwing their scungy bodies at me, so whenever I visited, I held a growling poodle in my lap; Aida loathed the pariahs even more than I.

A perennial guest prepared lunch. An artist, Dazzy had moved to Tangier with a rich lover after the Second World War. Twenty years later, the lover threw Dazzy out and the destitute painter returned to New York, where he moved in with Vince, the two of them having been young girls together, until he got his feet on the ground. Two years later, Dazzy remained ensconced on a couch in the cluttered living room. He had yet to find a job. He had yet to open his paintbox.

The rich lover had recently returned from Morocco. To Vince's chagrin, Dazzy declared the man a friend and insisted that I meet him. Vince and I listened as Dazzy begged over the phone for an audience.

We trekked to a penthouse in the East Fifties. Dazzy's portraits of Arabs decorated the living room—thick swirls of yellow, orange, and brown. The heavy-set lover didn't offer drinks and treated us as Mother did a house she considered buying: she sniffed the air as if she smelled doody. I braced myself for an interrogation. "What do you do?"

When I'd first arrived in New York, a sexy dancer told me never to ask that question; too many aspiring artistes lacked employment in their chosen professions and admitting to menial work performed in the interim before success embarrassed them. "I'm in the Navy."

"Officer?"

"Enlisted."

He sniffed and turned to Vince. "Do you still live on unemployment?"

"I've been working for a talent agency the past five years."

The lover sighed and told us about skiing in Switzerland.

He glanced so sharply at me that the dead furry animal atop his head nearly flew across the room. He adjusted his toupee and asked, "Do you ski?"

"Water and snow." He shrugged off water skiing and asked where I had first hit the slopes. "My grandparents' farm outside Pittsburgh."

He lifted his eyebrows. Hovering over him, the new kept boy smiled disparagingly. "What does your father do?"

My stepfather owned forty thousand acres of Louisiana and employed several hundred men and women in his ferneries, canefields, sawmills, and shrimp boats. "He's a farmer." Vince's mouth twitched. The man pleaded another engagement and dismissed us.

I'd endured a similar interrogation several years before when Vince took me to meet his ex-lover, an actor supported by a plump man of no occupation. The two queens uttered vicious sarcasms designed to diminish the Sicilian. The unprovoked attack disconcerted me, but I had not yet developed the weapons to combat a pair of waspish tongues. My warm generous flamboyant friend meekly accepted the insults. We returned in silence to his apartment, where I sat on a chair and scratched Aida's ears. "Why do you take it?"

"I still love him."

"Was he always this way?"

"Baby, everyday for eight years, we rushed home from work to hop in the sack. We spent every free moment together. He came close to getting good parts that would have made him, that did make other actors, only to lose out at the final audition. I suffered with him. For eight years, it was beautiful; I'll always love him for that. Epstein's nearly fifty now. He'll never make it as an actor. I show up with a glorious twenty-year-old. Tonight was hard for him. I don't mind."

Leaving Dazzy to beg his ex-lover for an allowance, Vince, Aida, and I meandered through Central Park's Ramble, eventually meeting up with a piece of human wreckage that had spent the winter in Vince's apartment. "Uncle" Ralph had ceased his visits because of the derelict. "It's bad enough Miss Dazlan's always there, moaning over her lost fortune, but Joe is so dreary. He depresses me. Now, how about giving your old Uncle Ralphie one of those super-deluxe back rubs you do so well."

During the summer, Dreary Joe lived in Central Park, having dug out a hole beneath a boulder that he lined with newspapers. "Rats is bad dis year. Kilt tree in my hole last week." No sooner did a friend distract Vince than Dreary Joe propositioned me, describing his expertise. He accepted my refusal philosophically and gave me advice on cruising. "You gotta try da meat rack on Central Park West. Beautiful men on every bench."

"Joe, the same sagging buns have squatted upon those benches since Hamilton shot off on Burr. The only difference is that the buns are older, darker, or fart chili beans."

"No, dey's some really nice stuff dere."

Vince and I joined a line of people waiting for free tickets to Shakespeare-in-the-Park. Joe stood with us and told tales of the city. "I read in *Screw* magazine dat sailors just off de boats is always horny, so I walked over to da Brooklyn Navy yards. Dint see nobody, so I was walking back to Manhattan when dis guy comes up alongside me and asks if I want some sex. I says, 'Sure,' so we goes to his apartment. Da dump reeks a cat shit. He musta had twenty a da little fuckers. We're making it, I starts hearing dese screams from da kitchen. I says, 'What's dat noise?' He says, 'Ain't dis good sex?' I says, 'What's dat noise?' Da screaming gets louder and louder, da guy's getting more and more excited. Finally, da screaming stops and he cums. We're laying dere, I says, 'What was dat noise?' He says 'Wasn't dat da greatest sex of your life?' I says, 'It was all right, you know. What was dat noise?' Da guy smiles and says, 'I was baking a cat in da oven.'"

Behind us in line, a girl gagged and ran towards the lake

below Belvedere Castle.

Joe continued to rhapsodize over the meat rack, so after the play and against my better judgment, I said good night to Vince and the derelict, who planned to do dirty among nearby bushes, and strolled down Central Park West. To my immense relief, I recognized no one; those dismal faces and tired bodies haunted someone else's memory. I retraced my steps just in case Joe America had made a late appearance. He hadn't, but I reached the north end of the gay section in a quandary. Diana's apartment lay on the east side of the park; bands of hoodlums roved through the trees and across the meadows, robbing, beating, and sometimes murdering those foolish enough to wander about its environs after dark.

Cars cruised up and down Eighth Avenue, their drivers staring at those hanging on the meat rack. I would sacrifice only a little integrity by succumbing to a blowjob that would get me across the park. A *little* integrity! One had it or one didn't. I walked down to Times Square, where "Uncle" Ralph worked evenings at a greasy spoon.

He was just getting off and suggested that we grab a cab to Sammy's Bowery Follies. Zaftig blonds of indeterminate age dressed as Diamond Lil and sang songs from the Gay Nineties. Thanks to Mother, I knew every lyric.

We walked up the Bowery to Ralph's "Very Favorite Bar." Filthy bums crouched in doorways and sprawled in garbage-strewn gutters. Other bums dashed into the street with greasy rags to wipe the windshields of cars stopped for red lights. Horrified drivers objected, but unless they parted with change, their windshields were smeared with slime.

We entered a well-lit bar filled with wobbly tables, mismatched chairs, and society's dregs. Two derelicts threw ineffective punches at each other. Neither received a hit, but throwing the punches sent them reeling into those sitting at tables, knocking over chairs and their occupants, who were too drunk to get back up. The owner, an ex-prizefighter named Pinky, grabbed the combatants' necks, banged their

274

heads together, and threw them out the door. He blinked, a large mole on each eyelid. "Only way to make the dumb fucks happy is to shove nightsticks up their assholes." The heavyweight brought me a glass of cheap wine. "On the house."

As I inspected the glass distrustfully, an old tramp too drunk to stand crawled through the open doorway. "Please, Pinky! Just one more."

Pinky looked down wearily. "Got any money to pay for it?"

"Give it you 'morrow. Promise."

"Get the hell outta here, you stinking old fart." Pinky kicked the drunk in the side until he crawled out the door.

Ralph basked in the ambience. "Isn't this an amusing little bar? Do you find the barmaid attractive?"

"She's toothless!"

"That's why she is no longer a geek."

"What ever is a geek?"

"Every carnival used to have one. A geek sits in a cage. Someone throws a chicken in the cage. The geek chases it down and bites off the head. A high-class geek plucks the chicken before eating it." The barmaid collected thirty-five cents from a bum and poured him a beer. "Pinky locks her in the back room after the bar closes. He got mad with her last week. Wouldn't let her out for two days."

"What did she eat? Rats?"

"Pinky threw her a sandwich now and then." And she gummed them down. "Would you like another glass of wine, baby?"

Two of New York's finest entered the bar. Several youths of the Latin persuasion had robbed a bum of his pennies in front of the building next door, stabbing him in the process. The cops asked Pinky if any of his clientele had witnessed the assault. Pinky gestured at derelicts lolling on chairs and lying unconscious on the floor. "Are you kidding?" The cops left in disgust.

I felt the need to urinate. Picturing a giant spirochetes leaping at me from the toilet seat, I was almost glad to find a crowd surrounding the bar's sole restroom. Pinky suggested that I elbow my way through the reeking dregs to check the cause of the commotion. A drunken woman sat on the toilet. She hadn't bothered to close the door, and an old geezer waiting to use the facility had dropped to his knees upon that indescribable floor to perform an act of cunnilingus.

Ralph shrugged his shoulders with world-weary disdain. "I realize that it's not a high-class establishment and that the old broad probably sells her rotten pussy for a dime, but this is a gay bar."

I'd wondered what happened to elderly fruit flies.

Pinky never concealed his disdain while talking to the bums, but he treated Ralph as a peer, laughing together at the human debris surrounding us; then, Ralph tippled one too many and passed his limit. Pinky continued to talk pleasantly with me, but spoke to my old friend as if he were another piece of refuse.

Ralph's "Very Favorite Nephew" joined us. (I was now his "Very Oldest Nephew.") A hustler with bad teeth, he divided his time between bullying those unhappy souls in the bar and telling me what sexual acts we would perform at Ralph's apartment. I felt certain that we wouldn't.

A nice-looking waiter from Sammy's Bowery Follies passed the bar and caught my eye through a window. He entered the dump and bought a beer. I waved him over to our table. Ignoring the hustler's disparaging comments about faggots, the waiter said, "I saw you at the Follies with Auntie Ralph."

My old friend emerged from a bleary-eyed stupor to take umbrage. "I'm 'Uncle' Ralph. Not Auntie! Uncle. I'm nobody's auntie. Certainly not yours. Please leave our table." I made my apologies and followed the waiter outside.

The next morning, I called Vince to gossip about Ralph's

new hangout. He laughed. "You haven't experienced squalor until you visit the_____ _____Bathhouse on Coney Island."

I wanted to experience squalor, so I rode the subway to the end of the line and rented a locker at the bathhouse. Dozens of elderly men crowded the steam room, conjuring up images of Dante's *Inferno*. One fossil sat on a bench and fellated a dozen wrinkled ancients with sagging stomachs, withered buns, and varicose veins; he spit the consequences into a corner. An ugly pockmarked Negro stepped in the gummy puddle. Another old man fell to his knees, picked up the sticky brown foot, and sucked each toe. I caught the next subway to Manhattan and the next bus to Newport.

Entering the YMCA with no thoughts of ever having sex again, I saw a lanky SeaBee buying a Coke. I spoke of my admiration for the SeaBees of Vietnam, who worked long dirty hours building bases along the coast. My new friend had Monday off and disliked spending the night aboard his ship, only to return to town the following day. I offered a bed; he accepted. I had another success on my hands.

I'd read that a predator picks his victim among a herd of grazers and runs it down. Something snaps in the captured animal's brain; it accepts death, and in shock, feels no pain. While living at the Y, I invited twenty-one sailors to share my room. Twenty accepted. One insisted upon sleeping on the floor; nineteen shared my bed. I never used force, nor did I threaten to evict them should they prove uncooperative. None showed enthusiasm. Each succumbed.

I could develop no theories. I initiated contact. The sailors effected no effeminate mannerisms nor did they exhibit the fear and hostility of the closet queen. Several years older than most enlisted men, I used an amiable paternal tone. During the week, the YMCA always had a few vacancies and the rooms rented for a pittance. Were the boys so lonely, far from home, that they would oblige anyone who showed an interest? Had constant proximity to attractive young men aboard ship awakened homoerotic longings? Did

277

I represent an officer that they wanted to please? Did I feel an affinity for the "victim" type?

I saw a few queers in the halls of the Y, but they were sailors and we avoided each other carefully. A handsome lieutenant, however, approached me Monday afternoon as I stepped out of the shower room. He smiled. "Hi."

Okay! "Hi!"

"How are you?"

"Fine. And you?"

"Fine."

Apparently, someone had recommended my talents. "Come to my room. We can talk there."

His smile reached from ear to ear. "Okay."

We sat on the bed. He wore a uniform; I wore a towel. I was seconds away from whisking it off when he asked, "Will you be able to make it home for the wedding?"

I crossed my legs. "I'm not sure. What's that date again?"

"September twenty-ninth."

"My hitch isn't up till the middle of October."

"Gosh, that's too bad. Lorelei will be disappointed."

My stepsister? Ohmigod! This was her fiancé. What the fuck was his name? It began with an "O." Onan? Surely not. "She's written a lot of nice things about you." He smiled. Omar? Lorelei had dated dozens of boys and finally narrowed her choices down to three. This was the "Blah" one. Better than the beau who kept me riveted for half-an-hour with a description of the new seat covers he'd just installed in his '63 Chevy and far better than the one with boils on his balls. Oscar? I tied the towel tightly around my waist and pulled a stack of letters from the table. Ollie? "What did you major in?"

"Abnormal Psychology."

That gave me a start. Octavius? Obadiah? Ogbert? I riffled through the letters. "What will you do with such a degree?"

"I plan to be a church counselor."

278

What better place to meet abnormal people? Lorelei dear, what ever were you bringing into the family? Oswald? Osric? Obie? I scanned Lorelei's latest letters. "What church?"

"The Primitive Evangelist."

"I'm sure you'll do well, Orin." I set the letters aside. "I was just perusing *Numbers* the other day. Well worth rereading."

"I prefer the New Testament."

Could have prophesied that. "How long will you be in Newport?"

"I leave tomorrow for Key West."

I'd had enough revelations for one day. "Damn! We could have downed a couple of brews and enjoyed a good talk. Unfortunately, I have duty tonight. Holy cow! I'm late!"

"Maybe I'd better go."

"What a bummer! Well, you know the Navy. See you in September. Like the song."

Orin looked at me blankly. "Huh?"

With my future brother-in-law in the neighborhood, I couldn't cruise the lobby. What to do? I descended the stairs; Orin stood by the Coke machine, smiling. I continued down to the basement, where sailors aboard ships kept lockers for their civilian clothes. Previous visits had convinced me that traffic moved too slowly through the locker room to be worth my while, but Orin's presence confined me for the evening.

Two men finished dressing and went upstairs. I checked the shower room; an attractive nude sailor had passed out on a bench. I awakened him with my ministrations; he looked at me reproachfully and went to his locker. I ran upstairs for a towel and a book.

A couple of drearies returned from the beach, showered, and left; I read two chapters of *Sense and Sensibility*. An appealing sunburned young man came down the stairs. I hurried to the shower room and primed Precious. The sailor entered the shower room "unnoticed," saw me in action, watched for a few moments, and turned on his shower. Hearing the water, I "realized" I wasn't alone and feigned embarrassment. After a brief chat, I left. When the man returned to his locker, he could see my reflection in a floor-to-ceiling mirror along the front wall. Believing himself unseen, he watched me abuse Precious while I viewed his reaction in the tiny mirror of my contact lens case. To my amazement, he raised an erection.

I decided to spend an hour every afternoon in the locker room, despite a busy schedule. For instance, Rush called me at work the next day. "Dinner tonight?"

"Ah'd love to, but ah jest washed mah hayuh."

"Eight?"

"I'll be there with bells on."

After work, I exercised at the gym and ran seven miles, ending up at the Y; I grabbed a towel and ran down to the locker room. An obliging sailor watched Precious explode.

As Rush and I sipped brandy on the terrace, I apologized again for seducing Uncomely Clive. "After all, he was your guest."

"You humiliated him. Forced him to pander."

Waves crashed against the cliff before us. "My stepfather flew fighter planes at Guadalcanal and the Carolines. Whether courageous or foolhardy, he knew dozens of men who flew to their deaths, yet he kept climbing into his cockpit. I consider that courageous, yet DT shrugs off acclaim; instead, he points at those men who flew hopelessly into the Japanese Fleet at Midway, every one knowing he would be killed. DT saves his respect for those gallant young flyboys." Tears came to my eyes; I was more sentimental than Paul suspected. "Now they lie in watery graves, forgotten by everyone except a handful of middle-aged men, while our youth considers silly little musicians and self-important actors as their heroes."

"We live in a decadent age, Kurt."

"When you aren't giving parties and clipping coupons . . ."

"Nothing. I do absolutely nothing." He shrugged. "I visit friends and enjoy myself. Father wants me to run for Congress."

"Will you?"

"Have you any idea how few relatives of congressmen serve in Vietnam? An infinitesimal percentage. Abhorring hypocrisy, I prefer the sweet life." He coughed. "Now that you're no longer surrounded by uncomely rock stars, could you acquire a taste for wealthy wastrels?"

"Quicker than I could for caviar or anchovies."

He stood. "Let's go upstairs."

Rush proved a disappointment in bed. As Precious pulled out of the old dirt chute, the rich man evacuated his bowels, soiling both of us. So much for racial memory.

His cynicism troubled me, so I benumbed myself that night with a handsome young seaman from Missouri. The next day, after my run, I dropped by the saltbox. The Weasel told me to wait for Jumbo, who had gone to the grocery store, and suggested that I bathe while waiting. As I soaked, I heard the doorbell and an adolescent voice. A minute later, the Weasel led a fourteen-year-old into the bathroom. The paperboy! They smoked a joint together; I stepped out of the tub and began toweling off. The Weasel unzipped the teenager's jeans and pulled out a small unmentionable. "Suck it!" He pulled down the boy's pants and began rubbing his own penis against those smooth buttocks.

Suddenly, Jumbo ran into the bathroom, slammed me against a wall, and shrieked, "I'm not running a whorehouse!" The paperboy scooted down the stairs. I dressed and followed.

I missed supper again at the mess hall because of cruising the locker room. Over the next weeks, twelve of twenty attractive sailors raised sympathetic erections while watching my exhibitions. Seven masturbated to climax.

281

Why ever would my self-abuse turn on a normal heterosexual? A masturbating woman, an ugly straight, an effeminate gay—none of these would light *my* fire.

In a wonderful book, *Animal Kitabu,* the author describes the mating ritual of the rhinoceros, which involves considerable grunting, snorting, and crashing about, the rhino being quite shortsighted. Other animals of the veldt gather in a large circle to watch, particularly the gnu. Why ever would the gnu express curiosity? What ever does the gnu think about while watching the courtship? Does the ritual make it hot? Twice, I made passes at these human gnus, but each bleated and hurried from the locker room.

"You tried only twice?" asked Paul sarcastically.

"Discretion."

"You showing discretion! I'd sooner expect mercy from the Beast of Belsen."

"In the military, always surrounded by others, one has difficulty finding the privacy to masturbate. I've interrupted men jacking off a dozen times; I doubt if that is remarkable. In Corps School, a good ole country boy publicly stroked a gigantic appendage while playing cards. Everyone noticed; no one said anything. Masturbation is normal, if gauche. But to make a blatant pass at a man watching my gaucheness while manipulating himself. . . . The dude has already dipped into the darker recesses of his mind. He might be shocked into reporting me."

"I thought you thrived on danger."

Paul never forgot any goddam thing I said. "I abhor foolishness. To achieve gratification, I'll court danger, but I prefer comfort and safety."

"So many men, Kurt. So little depth."

"I would love furthering my acquaintance with some of these dudes, but we're unlikely to meet again. Should I refrain from seducing an available man merely because a relationship between us is impossible?"

"They're interchangable. You hardly bother to describe

282

them anymore."

"As you say, they're of a breed. My libido demands only youth, vitality, and sexiness."

"What about intelligence, personality, and character?"

"My time with them is limited. How can I judge those traits?"

"Those are the first things I look for in a man."

"You don't even speak to half your tricks before you crawl into bed with them." Paul pursed his mouth. "A young healthy man has hundreds of possible lives before him. Heredity, environment, and circumstances have already narrowed his choices, and because a normal man must provide security for his family, he usually chooses a safe life; nevertheless, deep in the caves of a mind, the upper levels of which are dulled by routine, lurk wolves and panthers. I like to open shafts to the mind's darker recesses and creep down to face fierce yellow eyes."

Paul stared. "Wolves! Panthers! These silly twerps you seduce are sheep."

"All with golden fleeces. Like every other living thing, a man exists to procreate. Most social animals strive for power; the strongest will gather harems to impregnate as many females as possible. Procreation. Nothing else truly matters."

"What about teachers expanding young minds? Doctors saving lives? Artists creating beauty?"

"Abstract procreation."

"Your philosophy would baffle anyone not addicted to comic books."

"When I seduce a man, I am a god. I control his immediate destiny. I have defeated him in battle. I can hang his head in my trophy room."

"The spoils exist only in your mind."

"And in my stomach. For several hours, I carry the man's essence, his sperm, within me, millions of his replicas, one of whom might have been the lover without mercy who would accompany me along the perilous road to Wisdom."

"I should have thought the state trooper to be such a companion."

"He is."

"You both have criminal minds."

"That's not true! A criminal cares nothing about inflicting pain and loss."

"You damage a man's esteem and rob him of innocence."

"Perhaps. I do try to show him a good time."

"A rapist with a conscience!"

"Faulkner said 'An Ode to a Grecian Urn' is worth any number of old ladies."

"I wouldn't touch that one with a ten-foot pole. Whatever happened to Nick?"

"Another son—Michael Angelo Esoldi. And his mother just died."

"The affair is over?"

"I want it to be, but I miss him."

"He fulfills your need for a buddy."

"I'm sterile, figuratively speaking, and the world loses nothing by my expending energy upon little adventures. Nick bears responsibility as a husband and father. It stifles adventure to offer hostages to fortune."

"To keep his affection, couldn't you suppress this lust for strangers and just enjoy a pleasant love affair."

"Hardly my style."

"You're using self-mockery to cover up your natural bent of pushing away happiness with both hands."

"Of all people, Paul, you should sympathize with such a bent."

My old friend shriveled into his chair. We sat in uneasy silence. "Why do I make myself unhappy?"

"Against all reason, you believe sentimentally in romantic love. You demand that your current amour fulfill the mercurial needs of the various facets of your brilliance. As you usually choose partners with artistic temperaments and superficial understanding, you become bored and irritated, faulting yourself for the growing estrangement and despising yourself for the inevitable ending."

"That's nonsense!"

"Your masochistic longings manifest themselves by your insistence upon bedding mannered young queens. I know from bitter experience that you give short shrift to affectation."

"I've been cruel to you at times. I'm sorry."

"I'm grateful. Strip me of any affectations you notice. I have no yearning to be a faggot."

We hate most in others what we see in ourselves.

I hardly needed Paul to tell me that my current rampage made little sense. I had only to show availability for quick uprights. I had only to rent a room, and I could bed a succession of sleepy sailors. Twice, I met bright, handsome, sober young straights who responded to me as a person. Safely wrapped in anonymity, they adapted my technique with creative touches of their own. They asked questions, wanting to know me. Each was worth further pursuit and let me know he would welcome it, but seeking quantity, I let them slip away. Their grace and curiosity, those fabulous faces and bodies—two young men should have been indelibly stamped in my memory; instead, they became blurs in a crowd.

Most of the lab techs took thirty-day leaves during the summer, which involved exchanging duty with one another; through no maneuvering on my part, I shared weekend duty with Tiernan, the long-legged redhead who first underwent the "Melbourne Method." We'd seen each other every weekday, yet seldom spoke and never of anything besides laboratory procedures. Tiernan expected to spend two days and three nights with the Yellow Yeti; I wondered what he thought when the Saffron Snowman left Friday afternoon, and I stayed. He obviously thought something, appearing reserved and keeping his distance. Friday evening, he lay in the upper bunk and watched television beyond my endurance. After the Late Late Show, I turned down the volume to near-mute and slept.

At two AM someone tapped at the door. I got up and pulled on my whites; a fully-dressed Tiernan slept on the top bunk. A WAVE stood in the hall. "We have a woman in labor."

I went to Maternity and drew the woman's blood; back in the lab, I typed-and-crossmatched the russet liquid. O Positive. To my disbelief, the reefer held none in stock. Should the woman hemorrhage during delivery, she might have bled to death. The most common type of blood, O Positive ran through my common veins. I awakened Tiernan and asked him to draw a pint from me. His touch was cool, his hand steady. I stared into those green eyes. He glanced at me, frowned, and turned his attention to the blood bag.

I lay recovering on the bunk. "It's a weekend. Gonna be difficult to find anyone off-duty."

"Why do we have to?"

"Should have two pints ready to hand."

"I have O Pos."

"Call Maternity. Ask how close the woman is to delivery."

He made the call. "Least another hour."

"How about going to the kitchen and bringing back a couple quarts of orange juice. We'll need our body fluids replenished."

Ten minutes later, Tiernan lay on the lower bunk while I prepared for his leeching. Golden hairs gleamed along his sinewed forearm. I sat on a chair, watching his blood drip into the bag. "You ever think about what we did?"

Tiernan glanced at me, startled, before turning his gaze to the bag. "Sometimes."

"You feel bad about doing it?" He shrugged. "What do you think about when we're together?"

"I don't get you."

"Do you think about having my cock in your mouth? Up

286

your ass?"

"I don't want to talk about it."

"C'mon, Tiernan, I'm curious. I did things with you and that captain that I've never done with another man. I sure think about it."

Silence. "What do you think about?"

"I suppose if I had to do those things, I was damn lucky to do them with a handsome intelligent man whom I respected."

The blood dripped. "I guess I feel the same."

"I never thought I'd have sex with anybody except a woman, but a couple of times with you . . . I lost my head."

He nodded solemnly. "I remember. The bag's full."

I carried it to the Blood Bank, typed-and-crossmatched it, labeled the bag, and stuck it in the reefer. In the bunk room, Tiernan lay as I'd left him. I sat on the edge of the bed and handed him a glass of orange juice. "Feeling okay?" He nodded. We stared at each other. I traced the flap of his bellbottoms with my forefinger. He watched, a frightened look in his eyes. I unbuttoned the bellbottoms. He lifted his hips as I pulled them off.

We spent a lovely weekend that sustained me during a rainy week. A sailor who lived down the hall in the Navy YMCA met a girl at a nearby laundromat. While their clothes tumbled in dryers, they drove to the Point to watch a thunderstorm roll in from the ocean. A huge wave crashed over the rocks and swept them out to sea. Both drowned.

The weekend dances in the gym ended at ten-thirty. After the dancers left, a couple of janitors set out cots for those sailors who preferred staying in town. By midnight, young men filled nearly all of the two hundred cots.

An elderly guard stood watch at the entrance of the large airless room, but I knew the secret of the spiral staircase. Friday night, I left a sweet seaman from Appalachia in my room and went downstairs to check out the lobby. The desk clerk told three sailors that the trio had rented the last cots.

Two of the sailors looked good; the third was magnificent.

I ran upstairs and cuddled with the hillbilly for half-an-hour; then, I descended the iron staircase. All of the two hundred sailors had thrown off their sheets. Most wore navy shorts; some lay nude. The elderly guard sat beyond a closed door. A dim light gave sufficient illumination for me to trip merrily, if warily, on a wild voyeuristic tour through the room.

The magnificent sailor lay on a cot near the door, the tip of his unmentionable peeking through his drawers. I attained rapture immediately; when I realized the sailor didn't sleep, I gave him the gift of my best technique. Either the stuffy room or the beautiful man made me giddy: I pulled off my shorts and crawled aboard, riding that sailor like a bronco. While impaled, I ejaculated upon his chest and stomach, which brought me to my senses. I nodded at his buddies, who had watched, and quickly climbed the circular staircase.

Before reaching my room, I felt guilt at leaving the magnificent sailor despoiled, so I doused a towel under hot water and returned to the gym. He had gone. I checked the restroom. Empty. I returned to his cot and sat down. One of his buddies watched me brood. The room was quiet. He nodded. I slipped to the floor. The second buddy also proved agreeable. So did twelve other sailors. I swallowed enough protein to feed a Pakistani village for a week.

Appalled by my recklessness, I grabbed the morning bus to Manhattan, caught a train at Grand Central headed for Sayville, Long Island, and boarded a boat destined for Fire Island. After years of hearing about the depravity to be found there, I would finally experience it.

Francisco the Model had extended an open invitation to stay at his beach house and seemed delighted by my arrival. He mixed a huge Bloody Mary while I looked over his other guests. None held appeal. Francisco suggested that I visit "The Snake Pit." I changed into swim trunks and headed for a sandy clearing in the wood between Cherry Grove and The Pines, two predominately gay resort communities. A deeply-tanned "A+" from St. Louis convinced me to make public ado. After he'd gone, another "A+" accepted an invitation to join me. Scores of men watched both encounters.

Sated, I returned to Francisco's cottage for "Cocktail Hour." The sun and surf seemed to have turned the brains of his other guests into fluff. Everyone drank too much. Butch types became nellie and effeminate types became raving queens. The witty became malicious, the eager grew desperate. This is midafternoon!

I undertook a solitary stroll along the beach. Thousands of homosexuals sunbathed on the sand. I became deeply depressed. Apologizing to Francisco, I caught the last ferry to the mainland.

Disturbed without knowing why, I called Nick, castigating myself for involving him again in my life. "I'm sorry to bother you, buddy. Christ, I hate coming to you out of weakness."

"You're at Diana's? I'll be over first thing in the morning. Whatever's bothering you . . . can it wait that long?"

"I'm fine, Nick. Thanks."

An hour later, the doorbell rang. Vince and Aida! "Nick called, asked me to spend the night with you. Who's the cunt with the knockers?"

Nick arrived at nine AM. The sun shone again. "Mom died last month."

Vince clucked over him sympathetically and said the appropriate words. "No one will ever care so passionately about your happiness."

The trooper brushed tears from his eyes. "My wife's supposed to."

"She has five children to nurture. Occasionally, a husband must be satisfied with bed and board."

"Bed's been as cold as my dinners."

"Say what?"

289

"Rosemary don't want any more kids."

Vince had been thinking of his own mother. "And the Church forbids your using birth control." Nick nodded. "Can't you use the 'Rhythm Method'?"

"We tried that." He looked away, embarrassed. "Her periods are irregular."

"Voila!" I cried. "Little Michael Angelo."

"Little Peter Dominic, too. We wanted to stop with three."

"What about the cold dinners? Hardly sounds like Rosemary."

"Not her fault. I got assigned to investigating a burglary ring. Late hours. Never knew when I'd get home." His mouth worked bitterly.

"How goes the investigation?"

"Came close to cracking it. Might have earned me a promotion."

"What happened?"

"Fucking FBI moved in. Said it was Interstate."

"Was it?"

"No, but they broke the ring. I laid the groundwork and got evidence against everyone involved, all the way to the top. The FBI asks to see what I've got and takes all the credit."

"I thought they cooperated with the local police."

"In an ideal world. Two eager beavers trying to make their mark." Nick shook his head sadly. "With the new baby and trying to help Dad pay Mom's medical bills, I sure could have used the extra pay. Dammit!"

He asked about my call. "I missed you. Sorry."

"My pleasure. We got till six. Tonight, the family visits Dad. Can't let him down. We could hit the beach for a few hours."

"Sounds good."

"Plenty of room in the van for you and Aida, Vince."

"It's tempting, but the two of you in bathing suits would

ruin my day."

"Nick probably looks splendid in a bathing suit."

"After seeing him so attired, everyone else will look like dog meat." Vince scooped up Aida, hugged her, and gazed into those adoring eyes. "Pardon the expression."

On the way to the beach, I told Nick about Jumbo and the Weasel. Curiosity piqued, he asked, "What do they use: Ativan, Diazepam, or Scopelamine?"

"Haven't an inkling."

"People die from ingesting knock-out drops."

"No kidding! I asked a doctor in the Emergency Room. Mixed with certain medications. . . ."

"Why the pictures? Blackmail?"

"Perhaps. Maybe just an illustrated trick book."

At Jones Beach, we set our blanket near a family disporting themselves on the sand. The mother led her three children down the beach to look for shells; the handsome blond father, whose muscular masculinity I admired, cast a quick glance our way and disappeared into the dunes.

I smiled at Nick. "Interested?"

"If that dude's queer, I'll let you fuck me." He shook his head. "Go for it."

The man waited in a hollow between two dunes. As I performed, he kept watch. "Someone's coming."

Nick! "It's my buddy."

My buddy caressed the man's hard buns. "Hey! I'm just here to get done."

Nick jerked down his swim suit and grabbed the man in a choke hold. "You're going to get done to a turn, ace." They ejaculated at the same time.

We watched the man jog down the beach towards his family. Nick sighed. "Wild!"

"I love big broad hairy chests. The ultimate 'Humpy Daddy.'"

We ran to the water, washed off, and returned to the blanket. Nick mused on social diseases. "I figure plugging straight dudes, I'm safe."

"I prefer fellatio, also fairly safe. Refrain from fucking gay men and straight women, a person will catch few germs."

We lay absorbing the sun. His eyes seemingly closed, Nick said, "It's not for sale."

"Huh?"

"You've been staring at me for almost an hour."

"Fruitlessly examining you for imperfections." Nick grinned. "To my dismay, you continue to enter my thoughts unbidden. You star in my reveries. I lie beside you content, ready to hand over my soul to the devil for five more minutes. Am I making a fool of myself?"

Nick cleared his throat. "No."

"When we met, I considered you a sexy hunk, a handsome state trooper to be seduced and chalked in my trick book with an 'A+' beside his name. When we first made it and I saw you nude . . . touched and smelled you . . . I thought, 'This man is physically perfect.' When you refused to discard me and played my games, I thought, 'How lucky I am to wake up and find my dream a reality.'"

Nick leaned on his elbow and traced a pattern in the sand. "Why do you keep all this to yourself?"

"Because love is a lie. A bubble. It touches the ground and dies."

"I'd like a chance to prove you're wrong." I lay on my back with a defeated sigh. "Diana thinks you're like some dame called Lilith, leading men to their doom."

"I couldn't bear to hurt you, Nick."

The trooper looked me in the eye. "I made a commitment."

You can take me now, Mephistopheles; this is the moment I want to last forever. Gulls swooped above us, squawking over a piece of flotsam. "What do you say, we go back to Diana's where I'll give you an 'Around-the-World' like you wouldn't believe."

Nick stood and picked up the hamper. "I wonder some-times how this will end."

I shook sand from the blanket. "To judge from the omens, I'd say with a bang."

August 1968

The laboratory officers trusted me. When duty rosters for August came down, I was listed as senior man four times, including two more nights with Tiernan. As several departments remained riddles wrapped in enigmas surrounded by a mystery, I felt elevated beyond my competence.

I entered Bacteriology only on duty nights and then to scratch late deliveries of spit and shit onto red pads within small plastic cases. The ex-lifer in charge welcomed visits, and I should have watched the samples grow. I didn't. And learned nothing.

Two first class corpsmen ran Serology (venereal diseases) and Cytology (cancer of the pussy). Unsocial fellows, they would nonetheless have answered any questions. I asked no questions; besides, I considered their affinities for such departments as perverted.

Perhaps if I had studied my co-workers' textbooks. I knew how to perform the tests; I didn't know what the results meant. Instead of overcoming such ignorance, I let a feeling of inadequacy make me apathetic.

Assigned to a role of leadership, however, I decided to do the best I could, so borrowing several textbooks from Petunia, I caught a bus on Friday afternoon for New York. That evening, a cocky state trooper swaggered into Diana's apartment carrying an overnight bag. "Wanna mess around with a couple of good-looking FBI agents?"

"Sure."

"I told you about the assholes who took credit for the burglary ring I cracked."

"What are you up to?"

"I called one. Told him about the Fat Man. We could kill two birds with one stone."

"The FBI! Are you crazy!"

"Ever watch the TV show? The agent I called looks just like the main man's sidekick." Lean. Clean-cut. Goodlooking.

"Enjoy yourself. I'll bake a cake and send it to Leavenworth."

"The other agent has blond hair and lots of muscles. They're both macho, Kurt. You'd like them a lot."

"Even were I to go along with this, a dubious assumption at best, what do you get out of it? They know you."

He explained his plan. "Like it?"

"Nick, good buddy, you've gone along with my schemes, and I've appreciated it, but FBI agents! I could never leave the base again."

"Sure you could. I'd like to pit our skills against experts."

"They'll beat me up! They'll lock me in jail and throw away the key."

"The Fat Man's got to be stopped."

"Well . . . pain builds character."

"They look real good."

"Stone walls to not a prison make."

Nick appeared satisfied. "Could be a nasty business."

"I can be nasty. A serpent's heart is hidden by this flowering face."

"Okay. I already set up an appointment at eleven."

"You bastard!"

He grinned. "I knew you'd go for it. We gotta disguise you." The trooper set the overnight bag on a coffee table and opened it. "Used this when I worked Vice." He pulled articles from the bag. "Red rinse for your hair. A bushy red moustache. Thick eyebrows. Cowboy boots."

"Cowboy boots!"

"Make you walk different. They remember things like that. Have anything with long sleeves?"

"A sweat shirt."

"Have to do. Hide the scars on your arm." He smiled. "No way to hide those muscles. Can you make up a good story?"

"Can you doubt it?"

"That's my boy!"

We met the agents on a hillside in Central Park near the Metropolitan Museum of Art. The lights of Fifth Avenue shone dimly upon us; Nick had me sit with my face in shadow. It seemed odd, talking with two strangers wearing business suits who had no idea that I might become acquainted with every part of their bodies. Nick introduced them as Raven and Saffron. Using a pleasant tenor voice, Raven asked how I had met the criminals.

"I hitched into Newport for the Tuesday night performance of the Jazz Festival. Got there early, so I stopped for a beer."

"Where?"

"Sailor hangout on the main drag."

"Know the name?"

"I could point it out. Anyway, the place is packed. I'm looking around, happened to notice a fat man slip something into the glass of a young dude who'd just left for the john. Wasn't thirty seconds after the kid takes a swallow than he falls to the floor. I'm curious, so I goes over to help him up. Jumbo says the kid's his guest. An alcoholic. Would I mind helping them home? I carries the kid to their apartment . . ."

"What's the address?"

". . . and lays the kid on a bed. Jumbo strips him, looks at me, and says, 'Wanna fuck him?' "

"Any idea why he thought you might?"

"Might what?"

296

Raven drew a deep breath. "Fuck him?"

"I wondered about that myself, until a chick in show biz laughed about the handkerchief I always used to carry in my back pocket. Blue with white polka dots. Seems fags put handkerchiefs in their back pockets for signals. Blue in one pocket means I dig cocksucking, which I don't. The other pocket means I dig getting head, which I do. Brown hankies means the fairies dig eating shit, for crissake!"

"The Fat Man asked if you'd like to . . . fuck the young man."

"Yeah, how did you know?"

"You just told us."

"Oh? Yeah. Okay, I says, 'I'd like to take my time with something this nice, and I'm on my way to a concert. You go ahead.' Damned if that old dinosaur didn't cornhole the poor kid."

"Did the young man regain consciousness?"

"Not while I was there. Anyway, Tubby's boyfriend comes in the room and gets ready to take his turn. That's more than my stomach can stand, so I excuse myself and make as to leave. Tubby smiles, squeezes my crotch, and invites me to dinner the next night."

"Did you watch the second man . . . consummate. . . ?"

"Punkfuck the kid? Nah! I'd had my fill of that duo, but then I got to thinking—they might kill somebody with that stuff."

"What stuff?"

"The knockout drops, so after the concert, I slept on the beach. Next evening, I went for dinner, worried that the oven was turned up to HIGH for Little Hansel here. I mean, the Human Hippo could chomp me up in two bites."

"Was the boy still there?"

"No, and I figured the dynamic duo planned to play 'Hide the Sausage' with *my* hiney."

"Why did you go back?"

"I seen too many nice kids get raped in stir. I got

297

brothers. Cousins. Made me sick to think of the Weasel sullying their bodies."

"The Weasel?"

"The Fat Man's buddy. I lead sort of a crummy life, but I got principles. Figured if I helped shut these guys down, it might make up for some bad shit in my past. Know what I mean?" They nodded. "Anyway, I turn on the charm, told them I jumped ship off one of the yachts and could use a little bread. Hint at pandering for them—you know, promise a guy pussy and he'll follow you anywhere. They offer me ten dollars for any good-looking stud I pick up. I want to check out their act, and figuring it might help nail them if they carried someone over a state line for immoral purposes, I went up to Fall River, Massachusetts, and talks up a fisherman interested in slick pussy. I calls the Fat Man. He shows up half-an-hour later, we gets in the car; the fisherman takes a swig of Tubby's brandy and keels over. We carry him into the house. Everybody fucks him. . . ."

"You, too?"

"Had to fake it, man. I couldn't get up no boner for a dude."

"How did you fake it?" asked Saffron in a gruff voice.

"Told them I was shy, but that didn't cut no ice. They were bound and determined to watch. I crawled under the sheet and hunched the dude like I was getting his ass. After the two of them had finished with him, who could tell the difference?"

"The fisherman is unconscious throughout?"

"Dead to the world. Afterwards, we drop him on a deserted beach. That seemed real cold, so I stayed behind till the kid regained consciousness. About an hour."

"Get a name?"

"Smith. Bubba Smith."

"Where he lived?"

"Fall River. Jumbo wrote the address down after he took the pictures."

"What pictures."

"The pictures he took while the Weasel pronged the dude in the mouth and the ass. They got an album full of pictures of the guys they fuck. Thirty or so. Names and addresses written under the pictures."

"Just one album?"

"That's all I saw. The Fat Man said they had friends did the same thing."

"In Newport?"

"Washington, D.C." The G-men glanced sharply at each other. "Jumbo said the other dudes picked up military officers and government employees." Nick coughed. Raven asked for the Fat Man's address. "No way, man."

"Why not?"

"This is my gig."

"What do you want? A reward?"

"No, man. I want to work with the FBI. Jeez! You guys got your own TV show."

"We're trained to handle situations like kidnapping. You could get hurt."

"I discovered these creeps and I wanna help the G-men."

"We'll find them whether or not you tell us the address."

"Newport has over thirty thousand people. Dudes might kill some kids before you find them."

Raven sighed. "Okay, you can come with us. What's the address?"

"I wasn't born yesterday."

The FBI agents got up to confer several yards away. When they came back, Raven asked "What do you want?"

"I got a plan. When the Fat Man sent me looking for suckers, he said to call anytime except between eight PM and eleven-thirty. I did some undercover work—just like you guys." Saffron grunted. "I hung around Newport, kinda watching their house. Tubby goes out every evening for some reason—I didn't have a car to follow him. Suppose I call while he's gone, tell the Weasel I've got a couple of studs stoned out of their minds. The two of you. Queers can't resist studs; he'll tell me to bring you by. Once inside, we can tie the Weasel up and search the place for the knockout drops and the photo albums while we wait for the Fat Man."

The G-men looked at each other. "All right. Where do we meet?"

"Newport. Thursday. Ten PM. The south end of Cliff Walk. Nick will work back-up."

The trooper demurred. "Out of my jurisdiction."

"I don't think Sergeant Esoldi is needed for this operation."

"He goes or no deal."

Raven turned to Nick. "We could get you from New Jersey for a few days."

My buddy protested, but allowed himself to be drawn into the posse. The agents left, heading west across the park; they had great walks. Nick and I strolled towards the Central Park Zoo. "Obviously, I'm to be dumped as soon as they know the address."

"You did good, Kurt."

"These boots are killing me."

"Can't help it your feet are big enough to walk across snowdrifts. I liked that touch about Washington, D.C."

"Think they'll come up alone?"

"These are hot shots, Kurt. They want the glory of the bust."

"Get promotions for handing over nude pictures of pretty boys to old J. Edgar."

Nick spent the night; we enjoyed pleasing each other. "Uncle" Vince and I spent Saturday in the Ramble; that evening, "Uncle" Ralph and I attended a W.C. Fields' double-feature. Sunday, I brunched with Paul and joined Francisco for supper. All that conviviality, and I finished one of the textbooks.

Thursday at seven, I met Nick on the Newport green. We

300

drove past the saltbox; the Weasel's car sat in the driveway by itself. "I suspect the Fat Man of working on the business end of the festivals."

"Thought the concerts were over."

"A ballet this weekend."

Nick drove around the block. "Houses are close together."

"The neighbors must be accustomed to a stream of unconscious youths moved in and out like something from *The Body Snatchers*."

"One nosy old lady . . ."

We put the rinse in my hair at the YMCA. Nick pasted the red moustache above my lip and handed me a pair of horn-rim glasses. "Let's get going."

The FBI agents waited at the end of Bellevue Avenue. Both wore business suits. "The Weasel will meet us in twenty minutes. I didn't know what type of car you'd be driving, so he's expecting two guys in swim trunks passed out in the back of Nick's van."

"We'd prefer to take our car." The possibility existed of the FBI assigning extra men as back-ups for Raven and Saffron who would follow the car by radio.

"No way. Nick will follow in your car." They agreed without much argument. "Put these on." I handed each a pair of sheer colored briefs. They refused. "I told the Weasel you would be wearing swim trunks."

"How about just doffing our shirts?"

"Goodbye."

Saffron handed Nick the keys to a '67 Ford; both men crawled into the back of the van and changed into the briefs.

"We're practically naked," moaned Raven.

"We look like fairies," growled Saffron.

I switched on the overhead light. "You look great!" And they did. Saffron had a puglike face of no distinction, but could brag of a smooth muscular body. Raven had a hairy chest and sensational legs. Neither filled their briefs with

301

large baskets; I didn't care—I was almost sick from anticipation. "You'll pass for Navy lieutenants cruising for chicks and damned certain of finding them. Nick, you better get in the other car. If we get separated, I'll come back and meet you at the town green." The trooper winked at the G-men and followed my orders. I crawled into the van with the agents. "The Weasel's nervous, me bringing two dudes at once. I had to tell him that I stopped at an Army-Navy store to buy a couple pairs of handcuffs."

"Nobody cuffs us!"

"Toys." I reached into a paper sack and pulled out two pairs of children's aluminum handcuffs. "You could break them with a dandelion. Here, try them."

They examined the cuffs and tried them on. Satisfied with the toys, they allowed me to turn off the overhead light. I grabbed two pairs of Nick's official handcuffs that he'd hidden under the front seat. "Let me put them on before we go."

"No need."

"I'm running this show and I want no slip-ups. You don't know the rendezvous point."

Sighs. "Okay." I slipped the regulation cuffs around their wrists and looped a piece of clothesline around Saffron's ankles before they realized what was up. I tied Raven's kicking legs and stuck socks in their mouths. I put tape over the socks. After blindfolding them, I drove to the saltbox.

The Weasel opened the door. "Thought we'd seen the last of you."

"No such luck. I have two hot numbers in the van."

The Weasel checked them out. "They're older than the Fat Man likes."

"They have great bodies."

"Yeah."

"They got class and tight assholes. Help me carry them inside, for crissake."

The squirming agents made the transferral from van to

302

living room difficult. We lay them side by side on the floor. The Weasel went to the kitchen for a butcher knife and cut off their briefs. "Let's juice 'em."

"Fine."

While the Weasel padded upstairs to fetch the "juice," I ran to the car for another length of rope that I tied into a slip knot, returning to the living room before the Weasel descended the stairs carrying a mason jar full of yellowish liquid and a small syringe. He knelt beside Raven and drew up liquid in the syringe; as he prepared to remove the man's gag, I dropped the rope around his neck. When he blacked out, I carried him down to the cellar, emptied the syringe down his throat, and tied him to a couple of pipes; then I carried each of the G-men upstairs and lay them atop blankets I spread on the bedroom floor.

I looked through closets and dresser drawers, finding two more mason jars filled with juice, six folios of photographs, several journals, and four hundred dollars in cash. I carried everything downstairs, where Nick had come up empty during his search. Loading our spoils in the van, I drove it around the block and parked. I returned to the saltbox and talked softly with Nick for half-an-hour until the Fat Man pulled into the driveway. He offered no resistance to our ambush, so we tied him up, shot him full of juice, and dumped him in the cellar.

Nick started up the stairs, speaking in a normal voice. "I still can't believe those FBI jerks let the Weasel get away. Three of you and. . . ." He entered the bedroom and saw the G-men. "What the hell!"

I stood in the doorway, holding his revolver on the trooper. "Strip!"

"What?"

"Take off your clothes or I'll shoot your nuts off. Now!"

"You're kidding!"

"Try me, pig. Strip!"

Nick obeyed. "Why are you doing this? I thought we were

303

friends."

"I ain't friends with no oink-oinks. You put my lover in stir, pig. The spades there are making him take turkey cock in the mouth."

"What's his name?"

"You don't need to know that. What you need to know is what it's like to suck dick."

"I'm married! I don't swing that way."

"Tough shit! Turn around and put your hands behind you."

"This is a joke, right?"

"Turn around!" I slipped a pair of handcuffs around his wrists and pushed him to the floor; then I removed the blindfolds and gags from the FBI agents. "Any of you yell, I slit your throats." I pulled the butcher knife from my belt. "The feds put me in prison when I was eighteen. Do you know what happens to nice-looking white boys in prison? Now it's happening to my boy. You're going to learn how that feels."

"Oh, no! Please! We're friends, Scrub."

I sighed. "Yeah, you've helped out a couple of times. Okay, I'll give you a chance." So far, I had adhered to Nick's plan, but I was about to depart from it with my own scenario. "If you guys have already had queer experiences, I'll let it go. Otherwise, you're gonna get dorked. You gotta know what me and my baby went through." I grabbed a hank of Nick's hair and put the point of the knife to his throat. "You first, wop. Tell us about a queer experience."

"Never had one."

"I ain't kiddin' around, wop. You been thinking we're friends, huh! I've been using you, you fucking goddam guinea!" I lightly sliced his skin from neck to tits, drawing blood. "Tell me about being queer." Nick looked at me uncertainly. The knife made a red line down his belly. "I'm gonna keep going and slice open your prick."

Nick shook his head, bewildered. The knife blade

304

continued down his abdomen. Tears came to his eyes. "My brother. I fucked my brother."

"When?"

"Kids. Fifteen . . . sixteen. . . . We slept in the same bed. Couple of times, I come home from a date . . . hunched Mike."

"How many times? The truth."

"Maybe twenty times."

"Was he asleep?"

"Asleep. I only hunched him."

"You said you fucked him."

"Twice. Just twice. Pulled down his underwear."

"You came inside him." Nick nodded. "He wake up?"

"No."

"He blow you?"

"No."

"Has any dude ever blown you?"

"No."

"You've saved yourself from getting dorked up the ass, but you're going to suck some dick." I pulled out Precious. "Get down on it." Nick looked at my crotch with revulsion. "You want sliced deeper?" I pulled his head down. "Bite it and you're dead." Nick worked on Precious for a few minutes. "Stop! I don't want to cum yet. Saffron, tell me about your queer experiences."

The blond stared at me with hatred. "Never had one."

"You'd better make one up."

"Fuck you!"

"Wanna suck on me a while?"

"I'll bite it off."

I believed him. "Straddle his face, Nick. Do it!" The trooper obeyed. I took his penis in hand and rubbed it against Saffron's tight lips. "Open your mouth." Lips stayed tight. I grabbed Saffron's testicles and squeezed. "Want me to crush them? Open up." I squeezed harder. The agent opened his mouth. Nick grew hard quickly and pumped as

305

ordered. I stopped him before ejaculation. "Okay, Raven. Your turn. Tell me about a cocksucking experience."

The dark-haired agent had watched his partner perform. "High school. Guy on the basketball team."

"How did it happen?"

"District finals. We lost. Long trip home in a bus. Ray and I sat in the last seat talking about a cheerleader we both wanted. Old school bus vibrating, we developed erections." He sighed. "Felt each other's. Joking around. Pulled them out." He threw a glance at his partner. "It was night. Everybody sleeping. We . . . masturbated each other. Ray leaned over. Took me in his mouth."

"You return the favor?"

He shook his head. "Jacked him off. That was all."

"So you've never blown a guy?"

"No."

"Okay, your mouth remains virgin. Now we're gonna talk about dorking ass. Raven?"

He shook his head sadly. "Never." I flipped him onto his stomach and worked up Nick; then, I guided his unmentionable towards Raven's asshole. The agent clenched his sphincter muscle, so I went to the bathroom for Vaseline. Before I could apply it, Raven spoke. "Ray and me made love."

"When?"

"Two weeks after the incident in the bus."

"How did it happen?"

"We spent the night at his house. I wanted him to . . . repeat what he had done, so I promised. . . ."

"What?"

"Uh, to jack him off."

"Bullshit! You offered to blow him, too, didn't you?"

Raven snuck a glance at Saffron, who stared at the ceiling. "Yes."

"You like it?" He shook his head negatively. "Nick here could make you like it."

306

He closed his eyes. "Ray was my best friend. I liked making him feel good."

"Which of you was the first to fuck each other?"

"Ray did. He penetrated me before I penetrated him."

"Did you lie on your back or your stomach?"

"My back."

"Then you kissed?" He nodded miserably. "Did he cum inside you?" An affirmative. "Did you cum inside him?" Another affirmative. "You sucked and fucked each other at least a dozen times, didn't you?" No response. "Okay, you've saved yourself a dorking. Saffron?" Silence. I took his balls in hand.

"Never!"

"You're a virgin!" I worked Nick up again and covered his unmentionable with Vaseline; then I positioned him atop Saffron. The Vaseline made futile his sphincter's resistance. Nick had a good time. I broke my promise to Raven, enjoying him anally. I worked on each man's unmentionable; then put them in a '69 position and had each blow the other. Continuing to threaten them with the butcher knife, I forced each to achieve a climax in his partner's anus. I used the Fat Man's camera to take pictures of their coupling.

I gagged and blindfolded the three men, carried them to the Fat Man's car, and drove to a woods just past the city beach. "I'm leaving a pair of Nick's pants with the keys to the handcuffs in the pockets." I set each man on the ground and unlocked Nick's handcuffs. "See you later, pigs."

I drove back to the Fat Man's saltbox, wiped down everything I'd touched, and carried the camera and the money to the hospital, where I slept for two short hours before duty called.

At three-thirty PM, I boarded the ferry and slipped into Nick's van; we drove towards New York. My buddy had perused the folios and journals that I'd hidden in his van. "I kept running across two guys called M&M and another called A. I checked the Fat Man's address book. M&M could

307

be Mitch and Marty. Address is in Chelsea. Only A is an Alec Daffin in Washington. You might have been right, Kurt."

"How many boys had they picked up?"

"The machinist's mate was #310, if you are R."

"I combined my brothers' names: Rick O'Neill."

"Look at picture #303." A nice-looking sailor. "Notice the 'x' by his name? Same 'x' is in the journal. Last summer, they worked out of Revere Beach near Boston. #237 has an 'x' by his name. Three summers ago, they worked in Atlantic City. #120 has an 'x.' What do you think?"

"The boys died?"

Nick nodded. "I'll check. Far as I could tell, they used you so they wouldn't be recognized by the dead sailor's buddies."

I chewed on that thoughtfully. "Wonder if they planned to off me? No witnesses."

"They weren't killers. Just selfish. They wanted the kids, did what they had to so as to bed them. If the kids couldn't handle it . . ."

"Sounds like what I do."

"Sure. Sometimes you call the dudes we get 'victims.' We're criminals, too. Nastier than the Fat Man, actually. Their victims don't know what happened. Ours do."

I didn't want to think about that. "I mark an 'x' by the men in my trickbook who saw me with a hard-on, but with whom I didn't have sex."

"Why did you cut me?"

"Didn't want the G-men to suspect that we were in cahoots."

"Maybe you're too good, Kurt. You scared me. Thought you might have gone off the deep end." He drove in silence. "I wanted to tell you about Mike. Couldn't. I've always felt guilty. Tried to tell myself he was asleep. Couldn't have been."

"Unlikely." I waited for more, but Nick apparently had no desire to pursue the subject. "What did the G-men say when they removed the gags?"

"Saffron was madder'n a wet hen. Wanted to know how much I knew about you. Raven didn't say much. I said you called from time to time with information; I dropped a few bucks on you in return. Never knew your name other than Scrub."

"They believe you?"

"Why not? Everybody has informants."

"Think they'll look for me?"

"Not after you threatened to spread those pictures around if they did. The case will be written up as a crank call."

"I developed an interest in Raven's buddy, Ray."

"Raven's from Delaware. Shouldn't be hard to find out his buddy's whereabouts."

Arriving in New York, we drove to Chelsea and checked M&M's address. A photography studio: passport pictures and the like. The shop was closed, but the proprietors' names were embossed on the window. We drove to Diana's apartment and called them at home. "Hello, my name is Rick O'Neill. Francisco Avila suggested that I call you about making a portfolio."

"Francisco Avila! We've never photographed him." No second-rate shutter-snapper ever had.

"He knows your work. Suggested me and my buddy get our portfolios done by you."

"Quite a compliment! Why us?"

"Mr. Avila says his usual people are busy with the winter fashions. He thinks my buddy and me got the looks to make it big as models and should start making the rounds as soon as possible."

"I see. Could you come in Thursday?"

"Gosh, we're lifeguards at Seaside Heights and have to work every day till dusk. Another lifeguard's driving us up tonight." Silence. "We'll pay double. Mr. Avila said if we give him the portfolios right away, he could get us some underwear ads. He says we're real handsome and got great

309

bodies. Maybe move up quick to swim suits."

"One minute, please." A hand over the mouthpiece. A minute passed. Two. "Hello."

"Yes sir."

"Would you be willing to trade favors?"

"How's that?"

"We're shooting a series of perfume ads. We've already snapped the ladies, but we need to superimpose a few pictures of men to go along with a change of layout."

"Sure!"

"You and your friend will pose as Tarzan, Indian braves, castaways . . ."

"Sure!"

"You'll have to show your bare behinds."

"Uhh . . . Nothing like porno?"

"A few nudes."

"I don't know."

"Look, do you want the portfolios or not?"

"Yes sir. Okay. Tonight?"

"About nine?"

"Great!"

At nine-fifteen, I held the photographers at gunpoint in the back room while Nick searched their studio. He found two cartons filled with pictures of nude youths in a closet and three cartons of negatives; he showed them to the men lying spread-eagled on the floor. "Tell me about these pictures." Neither of the soft middle-aged men spoke. Nick slammed the head of one against a wooden floor. Blood streamed from the man's nose and mouth. "Tell me!"

The uninjured man looked at his partner with horror. He whimpered. "A friend. They belong to a friend. He asked us to look at them."

"Bullshit!" Nick grabbed a handful of hair and lifted the man's head. "Want your face smashed in, too?"

"We took them at orgies."

Nick slammed the man's face against the floor. Bones

310

crunched. Teeth broke. "Tell me the truth."

The man spat out blood. "Hustlers we picked up." His partner moaned. "They posed for us. Men's magazines."

"Bullshit!"

"Truth! Truth!"

"You drugged these kids and raped them. Why?"

"Sex. Hustlers."

"You don't have to drug hustlers for sex."

"Straight guys."

"Why the drugs?"

"Only way to get them."

"A lot of hustlers are straight. You can buy them all over the city."

"Dangerous. Rob us. Blackmail."

"Why the pictures?"

"Remember them."

"Blackmail, you mean."

"No! Remember them."

"Why attach their names and addresses to the pictures?"

"No reason."

"Why?"

"Later. For later. Do it again. Too hard to get the good ones."

"You do this with other old fags. Name them."

"Nobody else."

"You're lying!"

"Nobody! Nobody! Just us!"

Nick pulled a hunting knife from its sheath and straddled the sobbing man's back, tickling his throat with the blade. "Who else?"

The photographer gasped the names of the Fat Man and the man in D.C. "That's all!"

We carried the pictures and negatives to the van, which Nick had parked three blocks away. I waited while Nick went back to the studio with a jar of "juice." "Give them a taste of their own medicine." He returned with two large

311

sacks of camera equipment, including two miniature cameras shaped like cigarette lighters and six dozen tiny rolls of film. Stopping by the men's apartment, we found nothing of interest. At Diana's, I wanted to pore over the pictures and journals, but Nick suggested that we sleep. "Gotta drive to D.C. tomorrow."

The next day at noon, we parked four blocks from a pretty town house in Georgetown. Dressed collegiate in a T-shirt, jeans, and sneakers and carrying a clipboard, I rang the doorbell. A squatty man in his forties answered the door; I recognized him from the negatives we'd found in the box marked A. He was the Weasel of the D.C. arrangement. "Yes?"

"Hello, my name is Rick O'Neill. I'm a student at the University of Maryland, making a survey about the opinions of people in Washington about the Vietnamese conflict. I wonder if I might have ten minutes of your time."

"Come in." He beckoned me enter a small hall and shut the door behind me. "I'll get the master." As soon as he'd gone, I unlatched the door, leaving it open a crack, and moved to the archway between the hall and a large parlor.

The butler was speaking to a man who sat at a desk near French doors overlooking a garden. The man turned toward the archway, gave me a quick once-over, and nodded. "Come in." He murmured something to the butler, who left for the back of the house. "Won't you sit down?" I sat. "What sort of questions do you have for me?"

"Whether you approve of the war, the escalation of troops, the bombing of Hanoi, draft dodgers. . . . That sort of thing."

"Why?"

"I served in Vietnam with the Marine Corps, but had no opinions. They sent me there; I served. I feel that I performed honorably and don't regret my service. I wonder about the protests. Is there a right or wrong to this war?"

"Will you slant the answers because of your service?"

"I hope not. That I served there is immaterial."

The butler returned with two glasses of lemonade on a tray. He handed a glass to master. I wondered about the other glass. Suddenly, Nick stood in the archway with a gun in his hand. "Put 'em up!" The two men obeyed. "Check his wallet."

I glanced at the master's drivers' license. "Alexander Daffin."

Nick threw two lengths of rope at me. "Tie 'em up." After searching the house for anyone else, he interrogated the two men, but neither said anything, not even after the trooper manhandled the butler. Nick poured a pint of "juice" down the unconscious butler's throat. "He's gonna die, Alex. You wanna die that way, too? Where are the pictures?"

"In the safe."

"Where is it?"

"Under a potting shed behind the garage."

"What's the combination?"

Nick found the pictures of five hundred young men and diaries covering the past six years. A search of the house turned up nothing more. Nick pocketed two hundred dollars from the man's wallet, forced him to drink a pint of juice, and we carried the pictures and diaries to the car.

Returning to New York, I browsed through the pictures. "A lot of students, but most of these guys are military."

"Think old Alex was a spy?"

"No. These are enlisted men for the most part—grunts from Quantico, sailors from Norfolk. . . . The old fuckers probably just wanted illustrated trick books. Never know for sure; maybe some aging fairies together for dinner started talking about sexy young straights being difficult to bed. Alex was a professor—expressed a yearning for some of his students. The Fat Man mentioned his majoring in chemistry. The photographers developed the pictures. Did you feed that much juice to all of them?" Nick nodded. "They're all dead, then?"

313

"Couldn't arrest them without dragging a lot of those kids through the dirt, the publicity maybe fucking up their lives. Most of them don't even know what happened." He looked at me sharply. "You're okay about it?"

"I've lived a long time with the secret of my queerness; I can handle this. I don't much like the idea of looking over my shoulder for the rest of my life."

"They were murdering young kids, Kurt. No matter if they got caught, even served time in jail . . . they wouldn't have stopped. People don't change their spots. Believe me on that." I stared out the side window. "Nobody's going to make you. I think you're special, but there's a lot of handsome blonds walking around. Even if they do make you, nobody can lie better." I said nothing. "Kurt, I ain't going to let anything happen to you."

"I know that. I'm trying to figure out how I feel about being a murderer."

"You didn't kill anybody. I did."

"We're in this together, stem to stern."

"Who could make you?"

"The actor. The paperboy."

"Who saw you with the actor?"

"The bartender at the fagjoint in Newport."

"Same dude see you with Jumbo?"

I thought a moment. "No. Different shift."

"The paperboy?"

"Saw me naked. The scars."

"None of them show that much except to someone looking hard."

"He was stoned and scared to death."

"Unless you fall apart, you're safe. Are you going to fall apart?"

"No. They had to be stopped. I saw better men die in Nam for less reason." I pulled out of myself and thought of my friend. "Are you all right, Nick?"

"I've seen men go free or serve just a little time after

314

raping kids; some of the little girls will never be able to have babies because of their injuries. I've seen mobsters go free after terrorizing and hurting nice people. I've seen murderers put back on the street because of technicalities or lack of evidence. An arsonist set fire to an apartment house, killing seven children; we knew who it was, but couldn't prove it. Do you know how much satisfaction I get offing these sick sons-of-bitches?"

I lay my head in my friend's lap and gave him pleasure. What else could I do?

We stopped in Newark to attend a family fish fry. "The FBI agents might suspect our collusion, Nick, and be watching your place."

"They won't be watching Dad's place."

Nick's beautiful brother, Mike, had brought his family to the cook-out. As his wife and Rosemary cooed over their babies, six children whooped and hollered. Nick helped his father at the grill, so Mike and I made conversation, enlivened by my asking if he'd enjoyed the stag show. He looked away. "I didn't know people did things like that."

"Nick thought it weird to watch a buddy perform public perversions."

"It was weird all right."

I shrugged. "Navy doesn't pay worth shit; I needed the money. Sure was fun." Mike gazed at a smoggy sky. "Remember the blonde? She's an actress. Loaned me her apartment while she plays summer stock. I'm there every weekend. If you're ever in the city, drop by." I gave him the address. Nick smiled at us, appreciating my attempt to draw blood from a turnip. What ever was I doing?

The next morning, worried that I might unload my troubled soul on Vince or Ralph, I boarded a bus to Newport, carrying the journals with me. As I walked towards the hospital, I passed a wedding party as it erupted from a church. People in pretty clothes threw rice at the bride and groom. Monday's paper reported the bride to be Janet Auchincloss.

315

I tried to define my participation in the murders. The criminals deserved no pity; their victims deserved vengeance. The important fact was that six men could no longer hurt innocent youths. I did feel that Nick was drawing me into a web.

All that week, I expected the FBI agents to walk into the lab and arrest me. Nothing in the Newport daily newspaper about a double-murder. Hadn't the Fat Man and the Weasel been found? Were they dead? I moved back to base from the YMCA and no longer undertook my daily run. I returned from exercising in the base gym to study the journals, trying to reconstruct the juicers' seductions.

Public juicings, such as the one in the fagjoint that introduced me to the Fat Man, seldom occurred. The Fat Man preferred hitchhikers, who succumbed to his brandy. The photographers traveled about the countryside, looking for workers—telephone linemen, railroad hands, farm boys— who would pose for the camera, accepting drugged drinks as payment; on a week's vacation on the Appalachian Trail, the pair drugged and molested twenty attractive hikers. The D.C. duo offered poorly-paid servicemen two hundred dollars to perform with a woman in front of a camera; the boys awakened with no money and very sore assholes. These dastardly deeds titillated me, so Friday, I hurried to Manhattan so I could match diary entries to photographs.

Nick arrived at Diana's apartment to find me surrounded by pictures. "Learn anything new?"

"Didn't come across any more deaths, although the D.C. duo crossed out a pair of entries without adjusting the numbers, which leads me to suspect that they were protecting their asses, should they ever get caught."

The trooper shook his head. "A damn shame."

I pulled a set from the photographers' New Jersey file. "Know this guy?"

"Kevin Savage. He's been with the patrol for a couple of years. How. . . ?"

"At an all-nite doughnut shop. While the waitress baked doughnuts in the back, Savage went to the restroom; he returned to a spiked cup of coffee. The juicers carried him to their van and drove down the road, where they did dirty."

"I'll be damned."

"Wouldn't doubt it. He's an attractive guy. A blond."

"Yeah. So how are you?"

"Nostalgic. Sure wish I had pictures of all my tricks. They would give permanence to shadows."

"Safer to keep them in your memory."

"Lonely, though. No way to share their good looks with anyone else except by using words."

"Isn't that one of the reasons we do it together—so we can share memories?"

"You certainly know how to lift a heavy spirit!"

My trooper grinned. "Wanna lift it higher?"

"I'm afraid to answer."

He indicated the piles of photographs. "Pick your ten favorites in the metropolitan area." A tough choice. Thirty per cent of the victims lived within an hour's drive.

I spent half-an-hour choosing my favorites. "Shuffle the pictures." I closed my eyes and plucked one of the snaps from Nick. A snubnose, good-looking, and well-hung Jewish law student of twenty-two. We read the account of his seduction in the diary. Nick dialed the number printed on the youth's folder. "Stephen Greenfield? We're federal investigators. We'd like to talk with you as soon as possible. No, I can't tell you over the phone. Forty-five minutes? Fine." He checked the address again. "Let's go."

"What about the I.D. cards and the shields I lifted from the G-men?"

Nick looked at me in surprise. "Good man!"

I dug into my travel bag. "I look nothing like Saffron."

"Just flash the shield. We'll have him on the defensive right away."

The tanned Greenfield had dark curly hair and a compact

317

body. Our shields satisfied him; he invited us into a tiny studio apartment. "What's the problem?"

"Your father's a dress manufacturer on Seventh Avenue?"

"Correct."

"On October fifteenth, 1967, you visited your father's office."

"Could have. I don't remember."

"Do you remember waking up in a strange place with a splitting headache and no idea of how you spent the previous two or three hours?"

Greenfield's face closed. "I don't take drugs."

"This has nothing to do with street drugs. On the fifteenth of October, you left your father's office. Somebody gave you something to drink. You woke up in the doorway of an abandoned office building on West 20th Street a couple of hours later."

"I don't take drugs."

"But this happened?"

He lowered his eyes. "Yeah. One day, I got dizzy. Thought I must have blacked out and walked to 20th Street. A kind of amnesia. I worried that I might have had a stroke. Went to a specialist. Took a battery of tests. Brain scan, EEKG, couple of others. You want the doctor's name?"

"Unnecessary. We're after the dudes who slipped you the mickey." The student stared. "That's right. Somewhere between your dad's office and West 20th Street, you ingested something." The youth shook his head. "Did you meet two short middle-aged faggots that day?"

"No! You must have the wrong man."

"Hey! A dressmaker associates with designers, models, photographers, many of whom are gay."

"I don't remember."

"You ever stop for an egg cream across the street from Macy's?"

"Sometimes. It's around the corner from Dad's office." Nick pulled the snapshots from their folder and handed the student a picture of his being cornholed. "Oh my God!" He stared at it. I handed over the others. "Oh my God!" He looked up in horror. "This can't be me!"

"Your name and address is attached to the photograph."

"I've never done anything like that. Never!"

"Sure resembles you."

"It can't be!"

I took over the investigation. "We could find out right now."

"How?"

"A digital test. The prostate gland swells permanently after anal penetration."

"Who knows about this?"

Nick spoke. "The three of us. Our supervisor. The perpetrators. No need for anyone else to know. My buddy here could perform the test in five minutes. Up for it?"

"Will I have to appear in court?"

"No. We have other victims willing to testify. We do have to know whether you were assaulted. If you don't go along with the test, we turn the evidence over to the city police and you'll have to explain these pictures in court."

"Oh my God! Sure. Go ahead. I want to put all this behind me."

I looked at Nick. "Have you ever been fucked in the ass?"

"What do you think?"

"Then you'll act as the control subject?"

"What do I do?"

"Strip. Completely. You too, Greenfield." The dazed student followed Nick's lead. "Both of you lie on the bed." They lay side by side on the narrow daybed. I pulled out a tube of K-Y petroleum jelly. "Lie on your sides facing each other." The two men lay inches apart. "If you were anally abused, your prostrate will be much larger than his." I pulled on rubber gloves and greased both forefingers, gently inserting the left into Nick's anus and the right into Greenfield's. Each forefinger stroked a prostrate gland.

319

Nick protested. "Hurry up with this. You're giving me a hard-on." His erection brushed against Greenfield's belly. The student looked down, his own member swelling. My thumb caressed the bulge between the testicles and the anal cavity. "Goddam! You're got me hotter'n hell." Nick stroked his unmentionable, his hand brushing Greenfield's dingaling. "Hurry up!"

"Just a few more seconds."

"It don't take this long, bastard. You're fucking with us." He grabbed Greenfield's member with one hand and pulled my head down with the other. My lips parted. The young man watched incredulously. Forty minutes later, we walked out the door, leaving behind a law student with a firm memory of being had.

Before driving home, Nick stopped by Diana's for a shower. He emerged, toweling his hair. I sat on the floor perusing pictures. He grinned. Not one of those twelve hundred good-looking youths could compare with my sexy Italian.

Saturday evening, Nick called and asked me to grab a bus headed for Newark. "Bring Savage's pictures." We drove to the suburb of Nutley. "Pick out two. Savage will probably tear them up."

"So what? We have all the negatives."

"Who would develop them?"

"Vince. He has a darkroom in the corner of his kitchen."

"Hate anyone knowing about this."

"Vince wouldn't even ask."

"Maybe he won't tear them up."

Savage expected us. Nick suggested that we drive to the carpet shop. "Best to talk about this in private." The trim well-muscled trooper said goodbye to a pretty wife and walked to the van. The two highway patrolmen talked shop until we arrived at Mike's establishment; the younger man obviously respected my buddy. When we entered the room upstairs, Nick indicated the bed, where he and Savage sat,

320

while I took the chair. "Kevin, we have a problem. A few months ago, I went fishing in the south part of the state. I didn't have any luck and went back to where I'd parked my car. A pair of photographers were snapping pictures. Asked if I'd pose for a couple of shots. I'm a little too old to be vain, but what the hell! They offered me a shot of bourbon for payment. Next thing I know, I'm stretched out on the back seat of my car with one hell of a headache. The photographers were gone." A troubled look clouded the young man's face. "Worried me a little, but my money was still in my wallet—maybe the heat got to me. Yesterday evening, I learned it hadn't." He looked at me. "You'd better explain."

Explain what? Nothing if not game, I cleared my throat. "Two dudes in New York slip mickeys to unsuspecting young men, photograph them in compromising positions, and put the pictures and negatives up for auction. I paid four thousand dollars for the two of you."

Savage turned to Nick. "What the hell is this?" I handed him the pictures. He studied each carefully and looked up, his face white.

"Apparently, you stopped for coffee at a doughnut . . ."

"I know when it happened. If you expect to make a profit on that four thousand. . . ." He shook his head. "I ain't giving up my house."

Nick put his hand on the young trooper's shoulder. "He doesn't want money."

"How many people looked at these?"

"The photographers. The auctioneer. Me. You."

"The auctioneer!"

"He announced a handsome highway patrolman. Thirty-five. Italo-American extraction. Sergeant Esoldi went for fifteen hundred. A handsome highway patrolman of twenty-two with blond hair went for twenty-five hundred."

"These ain't worth money like that."

"No, but sex with you is."

321

"Huh?"

"This game has rules. I buy all the pictures and negatives, using them to blackmail you into bed. If I succeed, the pictures and negatives are destroyed. If I fail, I can try to sell them to someone else; should no one buy them, I am allowed to distribute copies of these pictures among your family, friends, and co-workers."

"You couldn't if you were dead."

"A friend who holds the the key to my safety deposit box could. And would."

The young trooper restrained himself from leaping up and throttling me; his hands tried to wipe rage from his face. Nick and I waited silently until the man calmed down. He turned to Nick. "You, too?"

"Afraid so."

"What do you think?"

"I asked around, learned that this club has been in existence for over seventy years. At least two dozen men have gone to the police, but nobody could crack it. They're careful. Twenty men paid the price and never heard another word. Four men refused and had their lives shattered. I like my life, Kevin; I don't want it ruined."

Savage glared at me. "What a piece of scum you are." I shrugged. "What do you expect?"

"Complete access to your and Nick's bodies for the next couple of hours."

"Shit!"

"Look at it this way," said Nick. "I've never known a call girl worth twenty-five hundred a trick."

"This is crazy!"

Nick watched the handsome young man bury his face in his hands. "Just out of curiosity, do cops always cost this much?"

"No, they usually go for five hundred to seven-fifty. Young congressmen sell for three thousand. A pro football quarterback sold for ten."

322

Savage looked up. "He . . . let it happen?"

"Must have. I've never heard a scandal about one."

"You gonna do it, Nick?" My buddy nodded. The troopers gazed at each other. "What exactly do you want."

"I have a fantasy about being arrested by two cops who force me into blowing them and getting fucked. The second hour, I want to be one of the cops and you be the guy we arrest."

Savage stared at nothing for nearly a minute; then he glared at me and stood in a crouch, moving sideways with his forefinger pointed at me. "Stick 'em up, shitass." I obeyed. "Throw him against the wall, Nick, and frisk him."

Two hours later, Nick and I dropped the ravished young trooper at his house and drove to a diner to discuss our success; I didn't get to Diana's until two AM. At three, the doorbell rang. I pulled on a pair of jeans and padded downstairs. Nick's brother swayed on the doorstep. "Mike! Come up!"

"Late."

"Not for sailors on liberty."

"Mebbe better go," he mumbled, looking away from me.

"You're too drunk to drive. Come upstairs and I'll brew some coffee."

Within minutes, he fell asleep on the couch. I took off his shoes. Well-formed feet. I wished my "Uncles" Vince and Ralph could see this man's inhuman beauty. I grabbed one of the confiscated cameras and took pictures of the sleeping man. I eased off his clothes and took more pictures. My "Uncles" would marvel. A juicy dago cock lay draped over Mike's thigh. I rummaged through the bags of spoils from the photographers' studio and pulled out a miniature camera which, when set on automatic, took pictures every thirty seconds for eight minutes. I knelt beside the couch and worked Mike into an erection. Two strong hands grabbed my head. "Lick my ass!" I obeyed. "Fuck me!"

At eight AM, the phone rang. Nick. "I'll be by in an hour. We got an appointment in Stamford, Connecticut. Numbers

323

248 and 249." I thought about Mike still asleep on the couch. I thought about my own need for sleep. Hell, I could sleep when I got old.

I showered, dressed, and perused the photographers' journal over coffee. #248: James Nordzey, twenty-five, would-be actor/model who dropped out of Cornell. #249: James' brother, Thomas, nineteen, student at Amherst, brought to the studio by his older sibling. I studied the pictures with amazement, rinsed my coffee cup, and ran down to wait on the sidewalk for Nick.

At eleven, we knocked at the door of a large colonial on a lovely tree-lined street. A tall handsome strawberry-blond opened the door. We showed our credentials and stepped inside. "It would be best to speak of this in private."

"Everybody's gone to church except my brother. He's upstairs sleeping."

"James?"

"Yeah." He led us into a den furnished, like the rest of the house, in Early American.

"On the eighth of June, James took you to a photographers' studio on West 14th Street in the Chelsea section of Manhattan."

The youth regarded us warily. "Maybe."

"Our objective has nothing to do with the drugs you ingested that day. We're after those men for something very different."

"What?"

"Take a look at these." Nick pulled out a folio of pictures. Tom studied them. Glancing at us, stricken, he cried, "I'll kill the fucker!" He ran out of the room and up the stairs. We followed him to a bedroom at the end of the second floor hall. "Wake up, you fucker! Look at these!"

"Whass matter?" An older, bearded version of Tom looked up at his brother.

"Look at these!" James glanced at the pictures and blanched. "You fucker! You goddam asshole! You set me up!"

"No, bro. No way."

"You got me stoned and fucked me in front of people. You fucked me! Your own brother!"

"Not me."

"Look at the pictures! That's you and me! Why?"

"Out of my head. They got me stoned, too."

Tommy dropped into a chair, head in hands. Nick asked, "Did the photographers request that you bring Tom to the studio?"

James looked miserably at the pictures. "I ran into them at an audition. They'd just moved to Manhattan and were trying to build up a reputation. Offered to shoot a portfolio for free if they could use it for advertising. Maybe get me a modeling job. When they shot the pictures, I got stiff. Uptight. I was broke. Really needed the work."

"How did they talk you into bringing Tommy to the studio?"

James sat up to light a cigarette, revealing heavy shoulders and a broad chest. "They'd asked me to bring by any other pictures I'd had taken. One was a snap of Tom and me." He reached for an ashtray. "They had a fashion layout using those sisters on 'The Biddles of Boston'. They wanted brothers for the layout. Thought Tom and I might do. At least, his presence might loosen me up for some good pictures."

Tommy raised his head, his eyes filled with tears. "I remember thinking, 'What a great summer job!' Those sisters were fine."

"I still photographed stiff, so they passed around some reefer. The main guy thought costumes might help. They had another modeling gig. Something about Tarzan and some Indian braves."

"For which you had to show your bare behinds."

"Yeah." James glanced at Nick. "This a regular scam for them?" Nick nodded. "Jeez! I guess we were really stoned. We posed nude."

325

Tommy interrupted. "I didn't want to, but we smoked some more reefer. Then I drank some wine and passed out. Slept most of the day. That's when you did it!"

James said nothing. Nick spoke. "Might be best if you tell us everything."

"Who are you?"

"FBI agents." We flashed our badges. "We're gonna get those guys. What happened next?"

"They kept taking nude shots. Wanted a couple with me hard. Oh, shit! I feel so dumb."

"What happened?"

"I couldn't get it up with anybody watching, so the assistant went down on me. Then they wanted some shots of me pretending to . . . mess around with Tommy. Just pretend! I don't know what happened."

Tommy cried, "Did all of you do it? Did all of you stick your peters in my mouth? Up my ass?"

"Oh, Tommy, I'm so sorry."

"God damn you, James! I though we loved each other. How can we ever be brothers again?"

James hung his head. "I dunno." Both boys cried. "I'd do anything to make it up with you, bro."

Tommy jumped up. "You never could." He ran out of the room and disappeared into a room down the hall.

I turned to James. "You mean that? You'd do anything to make it up with him?"

"Absolutely."

"Those perverts got their kicks seducing brothers. You're the fifth pair we've tracked down."

"I feel like such a fool."

"Drugs and booze make anybody foolish. Two pairs of brothers suffered total estrangement after falling for the routine. The other two pairs have worked it out."

"How?"

"The victim watched his brother perform fellatio and accept anal penetration, same as he had."

326

"I couldn't do that. Believe it or not, I don't go the gay route."

"You pulled a tough gay act on your brother."

Silence. "That's so heavy, man." We allowed him time. "You think Tommy would forgive me?"

"That's how it worked out."

James considered this option. "I've never . . . I wouldn't be much good at it."

"The thought is what counts. You're willing?"

He considered. "I don't think so." He shook his head. "No, I'm not."

I tapped at Tommy's door and entered his room. He lay on a bed, staring at the ceiling. I told him about the other sets of brothers. "James is willing to humiliate himself in front of you with the hope of forgiveness."

"I'll never forgive him. Never!"

I returned to James' room. "Tommy said that if you're willing to have done to you what was done to him, the rupture might be mended." James nodded. "C'mon in his room."

The man stared incredulously. "I'm supposed to . . . Tommy!"

"And us."

Nick sputtered. "What do you mean 'us?' This ain't my problem."

"Aw shit, buddy. We can help out these dudes. It isn't gonna send us to hell."

Nick conceded. "Maybe. But you first."

"C'mon, James." He reached for a pair of shorts. "Better if you enter the room nude. Shows more humility." Nick's mouth twitched. The young man heeded my sage advice. Tommy watched us enter without speaking. As we stood beside his bed, I pushed James to his knees and pulled out Precious. The man looked at his younger brother and took Precious in hand. Five minute later, Nick took his turn. "Now take care of Tommy." James crawled on the bed between Tommy's legs and looked earnestly at his brother. The youth nodded slightly. James pulled down the zipper of his brother's jeans.

I handed Nick a tube of K-Y. Within a minute, he had mounted James. Twenty minutes later, Nick eased into Tommy, who plugged his brother. I favored the older youth with my best technique.

Driving back to Manhattan, I asked Nick if watching the brothers do it had turned him on.

"Goddam right! That James is a full-fledged loser. It may sound hypocritical but if anybody messed with my brother, I'd kill him. Wanna pick up some Chinese food and take it to Diana's?"

"Uhh. . . . I'm tasting pizza. Let's go to 'Uncle' Ralph's 'Very Favorite Pizza Joint' on 14th and First."

Okay with Nick. I kept him away from the apartment until he returned to Newark.

The pictures and diaries obsessed me. Schemes to seduce those luckless young men whirled in my brain. The three-hour bus ride to Newport passed in a flash. Eight-hour workdays whizzed by. I strolled along the three miles of Cliff Walk in an instant.

Restlessly prowling Thames Street for sailors, I ran into the machinist's mate drugged by the Fat Man. He stared at me quizzically; then, leaving two buddies to approach me, asked, "Did what I think really happen?"

"Can't read your mind, ace."

"I shit blood for three days. I ought to kill you."

"Maybe you'd better hear the entire story. Let me buy you a beer, and I'll tell you all about it."

"Can't leave my buddies."

Stalwart sailors glared at me with dangerous intensity. "Bring them along if you don't mind their knowing."

"Why should I care?"

I stopped at a bar and bought a six-pack of beer before leading them to the public library, an isolated building surrounded by large trees. As we sat on the front steps drinking, I explained how I had run into the Fat Man and the Weasel, and after informing the Newport Police Department, had agreed to help catch the villains in mid-act. Unfortunately, the police lost the Fat Man's car in traffic and the sailor had got gangbanged. "I ended up carrying you for three miles over my shoulder, so pissed by police incompetence that I refused to help them again. I read in Monday's paper that the two assholes had apparently picked up a guy who killed them both."

The machinist's mate shook his head. "You fucked me, too?"

"What else could I do?"

"No wonder my ass hurt."

"I felt real bad. Tried to make it up by giving you head."

"I remember that part. They're dead, huh?"

"Read Monday's paper."

"Somehow, I ought to get even with you."

"Cripple him," advised one of his buddies. "Smash his face against these steps."

I affected nonchalance, although my feet made ready to run. "I sucked your prick, ace. I've never before done anything like that."

The second buddy uttered an ideal solution. "Fuck *him*, Bevis."

"That's a hard way to get revenge, but I feel bad enough about pronging you to believe that turnabout is fair play." I stood and dropped my pants.

"You don't turn me on, mac."

"I did the other night when I blew you."

The machinist's mate denied himself the satisfaction of revenge. His lecherous buddy said, "Bevis, how about if he blows me and I'll owe you."

Bevis chuckled. "Sure."

The buddy undid the thirteen buttons of his bellbottoms. "Go to it."

329

As I offered up my expertise, someone rubbed my ass with his hand. The second buddy, who would eventually get his turn, laughed. "Gonna get revenge, after all, huh, Bevis?"

Paul's accusation that I lived for sex seemed correct. Did I? Was it wrong?

My co-workers spent their hours away from the lab watching television, pulling up crabgrass, or getting drunk. I borrowed two or three books a week from the base library; I spent countless evenings exploring Newport and the psyches of its inhabitants. If there was a Heaven, my guardian angel would not keep a boring account book.

St. Priapus might have run out of ink the following weekend, when I outdid myself. First, I stopped by the Enlisted Man's Club to say hello to my friend, the desk clerk.

"Sorry, Kurt. We're filled already. Ninety percent gook."

"I'm house-sitting. This is a social call."

"Nice to see you, too. Any room at the inn?"

"Sure. Should a couple of dazzlers appear, send them up."

"Will do."

Certain that the desk clerk would oblige a sister, I stocked up on groceries. Good thing I did. At seven-thirty, a hunky soldier from Fort Dix rang the bell. Fifteen minutes later, a sexy air jockey stationed in upstate New York joined us. I sent them to the USO for free movie tickets and called Nick. "Bring your captain's uniform."

"Sorry, Kurt. Told Dad that I'd play cards tonight."

Unwilling to endure solitude, I strolled across town to visit a tough straight bar near the docks. Two butch French sailors agreed to accompany me back to Diana's for booze, grub, and a place to crash. Before I filled their bellies, I insisted that they shower. The second returned to the living room squeaky-clean and caught the first enjoying my expertise. He flopped upon a chair and awaited his turn.

They retired to Diana's king-size bed before my military guests reappeared. Hard on their heels came a bogus captain. "Some of Dad's friends invited him to an all-nite poker

330

game." As always, Nick exuded authority and told outrageous tales about his duty in Nam as captain of a sampan
cruising the Mekong Delta; I poured large drinks for his
wide-eyed listeners. At two AM, I led Nick into the bedroom;
he studied the sleeping Frenchmen. "Not my type. Take a
quick shower and come into the living room naked."

I carried linen to the military men and pulled out the sofa
bed. Saying goodnight, I took a shower, emerging as I
toweled off. Nick walked past me, nude, and sat down in a
chair by the sofa bed. "Couldn't sleep. Looking at that ass of
yours, I doubt I will."

"Beg pardon?"

"I sleep nude. Four men in a bed, I'd have to rub against
those pretty buns. Next thing you know . . ."

"Are you queer, sir?"

"Not at all, but living on ships without women, a man
learns to take sex where he finds it." He fingered that thick
unmentionable.

"You make your crew suck on that?"

"Everybody takes his turn in the barrel."

The air jockey spoke. "What does that mean?"

"Got a big barrel on the stern with a hole cut into the side
about crotch-high. One of the men draws the short straw,
crawls in the barrel, and the rest of the crew line up to stick
their pricks through the hole. Old Short Straw sucks them
off."

The soldier laughed. "I heard that story in boot camp."

Both men watched as Nick caressed himself into hardness.
Precious responded. "Like this, swabbie?"

"I've never seen an officer with a hard-on."

"Want a closer look?"

"That's all right. Thank you anyway, sir."

"Want to make an officer happy?"

"Sorry, sir, but it's not my bag."

"Your dong says it is." Nick stood and moved next to me.
"Taste it. Just a little."

I indicated my other guests. "Kind of public."

"Shit! I'll bet you five dollars they're both hard, too." He pulled down their sheet; their shorts bulged. "Pull 'em out. Let him see." The airman nervously declined; the soldier snickered and obliged. Nick reached down and worked the soldier with one hand while stroking himself with the other. "Get over here, swabbie."

Eventually, the airman made it a quartet. Nick took two anal cherries before he left.

After breakfast, I sent everyone on his way and called "Uncle" Vince, who invited me to accompany him for the day. "My new playground. A strip of beach along the Hudson just above the George Washington Bridge. You can watch New York burning across the river and there's marvelous cruising. Queens sunbathe nude, baby, and the action in the trees climbing the hill is fantastic."

Vince asked only that a man be amply endowed. I flattered myself that I preferred more. Pleasure emanated from none of the middle-aged men patrolling the strip—just desperation. I spread a blanket and napped.

"Uncle" Ralph dropped by Diana's for dinner. The two servicemen ate with us; I'd half-expected them to find another place to stay, considering what had happened, but they intended to return after a night on the town. Ralph and I attended a Marlene Dietrich double-feature and patronized his "Second Most Favorite Bar," a hustlers' hangout near Times Square.

One tough cutie appealed to me. Nick had insisted upon dividing the nine hundred dollars we'd picked off the juicers, so, flushed with cash, I offered Toughie twenty for the night. Despite his swearing to no previous customers that evening, I insisted that he shower. As running water increased my anticipation, the doorbell rang—the French sailors had brought two shipmates: one older and homely, the other a handsome blond beast. It was an embarrassment of riches.

The Frenchies had come to rob me; their hostile attitude, their reluctance to bathe, the way they watched the hustler's and my every move pointed to a ransacking of Diana's apartment and the maiming of my body. Toughie knew the score. When I went to the kitchen for more ice, he followed. "I know two guys. Deliver furniture. Always need money. Maybe for a hundred, they'll come over."

"Call from the bedroom. Tell them to pick up a couple of bottles. Scotch and gin. And tell them to hurry. The frogs might be anxious."

Twenty minutes later, the delivery men rang the bell. Neither was especially attractive, but they were butch, muscular, and mean-looking. I should have preferred squandering my money on finer models, but Toughie assured me that the men were novices, which turned me on. I performed first with the hustler; then with the delivery men. The two sailors of the night before allowed a repeat performance; their shipmates could only capitulate, although the blond protested and proved difficult to arouse. Despite aching jaws, I met the challenge.

The Sons of Gaul indicated a desire to spend the night, but I sent them back to their ship. Sweetening the pot with another fifty, I asked each of the delivery men to penetrate my little rosebud. As I let them out the door, my military guests walked down the sidewalk. They watched the hustler and I perform; then they performed a little themselves.

While everyone slept, I went out to buy the Sunday edition of *The New York Times*. An hour later, recovered, I joined my three guests in Diana's king-size bed.

Thursday afternoon, the Medical Service lieutenant interrupted my work. "You're to report to the O.D.'s office."

The Officer of the Day! Oh, no! Only a month and a half from an honorable discharge. Wondering which of my tricks had reported me could have led to madness. I squared my shoulders and prepared to meet my doom. The O.D. smiled at me. "Your request for an early out to attend college has

333

been approved. You are discharged from active duty as of noon tomorrow. Good luck, sailor."

I felt hurt that I'd not been asked to re-enlist, although I would never have done it. Perhaps someone had penned a notation in my record: F.A.G.

I returned to the lab, where my co-workers had set up a going-away party with a cake, gag gifts, and a card signed by everyone. The surprise party touched me, especially as several techs had left for other parts with nothing more than casual handshakes. The best present came from the head honcho, who handed me a certificate: "HM3 William Kurt Strom has qualified through on-the-job training as a medical laboratory technician." I could practice the vocation almost anywhere in these United States. I'd had no idea that I could do so without schooling.

My early discharge depressed Nick. "I'd counted on another month. Christ, we haven't even decided what we're going to do with these photos."

"We can't leave them here at Diana's."

"That dizzy broad would use the pictures as playing cards. Unless you got a better idea, I could buy a trunk and put it in Dad's attic. Nobody ever goes up there."

"I'd hoped to file them, but Diana comes back next week-end."

"Do it in Newark. Stay with Dad. He'd love the company and I'd have a chance to spend more time with you." I agreed. "Okay, I got a going-away present for you. Tell me again what type of dudes you think are sexiest."

"Canadian mounties . . . airplane pilots . . . medical interns . . . Irish firemen . . . Italian state troopers. . . ."

"Guess again. You musta told me a dozen times."

"Humpy daddies!"

"I've spent a week fixing us up with a couple."

"Let's go."

"Not till ten. What do you want to do in the meantime?"

"Carry the pictures and the camera equipment to the

van."

"We can do that just before we leave."

"In that case, I'm rather content lounging here with you."

Nick sighed, kicked off his shoes, and lay his marvelous head in my lap. "The photographers set up a fake shoot in Teaneck. Used the promise of modeling careers to get girls for the session. According to their journal, a pair of young hoods watched the proceedings. The photographers asked them to pose for one of the shots. Raved over the kids' looks, said they'd be naturals. Great way to meet beautiful girls and make some money on the side. The kids dig it. After the chicks leave in a taxi, the kids accept paper cups full of brandy. They wake up two or three hours later in the park. Numbers 386 and 387."

Included with the usual nasty pictures were some of the snaps taken in the park. Handsome, vital, athletic-looking teenagers around seventeen.

"Sleazeballs," said Nick. "A friend of mine works that precinct. The kids sell dope to high school students. They're suspected of raping four junior high girls. They've burglarized a stereo shop. They come to Manhattan for fagbashing; put maybe three queers in the hospital. Each offense, their fathers used connections to get the kids off and keep their records clean."

"The fathers?"

"Well-to-do lawyers. Around forty, in good shape. Pilot fish for Mafia sharks. One's a city councilman, the other's up for a spot on the bench."

"What's the plan?"

"I'm banking on the kids being liars, never admitting guilt, even to their dads."

"Who wouldn't believe the truth when they hear it."

"Not from their sleazeball sons."

We stopped by Newark to unload the pictures and equipment; Mr. Esoldi seemed delighted by my moving in for a week. Nick drove to a "safe" house near the Palisades.

335

"What's a safe house?"

"Place where they hide witnesses and informers who are in danger. This one's empty."

Twenty minutes later, a car pulled into the driveway. Four men got out: two stayed by the car; two approached the front door. "The fathers," murmured Nick.

The men entered in a dudgeon. "This better be serious."

"Murder is always serious."

"Where's your identification?" (Nick had used the facilities of the Highway Patrol to attach our pictures to the G-men's identification cards.) The cards passed examination. "What's this about?"

Nick described the meeting between their sons and the photographers. "After the shoot, your sons got stoned and had sex with the men."

"That's a lie!" Nick showed them the pictures. The men sat.

"Your sons apparently suffered regrets. Last night, both photographers were beaten to death."

"Frankie was home from dinner to breakfast."

"Al, too. He's grounded for bad grades."

"School doesn't start for two weeks." Nick had spent Thursday night following the youths, who had driven into Manhattan and wandered aimlessly about the Village, spending the better part of an hour tormenting an unfortunate little fairy. "Their fingerprints are all over the faggots' studio."

Neither man seemed surprised by his son's violence. "Why is the FBI on the case?" asked the lawyer.

"The photographers dealt in drugs as a sideline. We'd arranged a buy. As we approached the studio, your sons came stumbling out the door and ran to their car. A gray '64 Mercury, right? I followed them back to Teaneck; Saffron here entered the studio and found the faggots. One gave your sons' names before he died."

The men's bravado crumbled a bit. "Why hasn't anyone

arrested them yet?"

"We haven't informed the city police."

"Why not?"

Nick paused. "G-men don't earn a lot." He sighed. "I still owe ten thousand on my house."

The lawyers had too much savvy to offer a bribe to a federal agent. The councilman looked at me and sneered. "I suppose you could use ten grand, too."

"I'm in no need of money."

The men turned their attention back to Nick. "So all you're worried about is a mortgage. You'll have that paid off in no time."

"Actually, there's two things about my partner you should know. One—he saved my life, and two—he's gay."

The men's mouths twisted. "So?"

"Well," I said, "I've long held an unfulfilled fantasy. A voyeuristic fantasy. I've always wanted to look on as a straight father and his straight son watch each other have sex with other men." The lawyers glanced at each other incredulously. "We could destroy the evidence and save those boys from prison if I can watch the two of you balling each other's sons."

Nick broke into their outraged expostulations. "You do as my partner says, and I'll destroy the evidence on the murder and on a couple of investigations." Nick described two business affairs in which the lawyers were involved—dubious ventures, especially for men in politics. "From what I hear, you've been protecting the kids, but the Mafia can't cover up these murders. Those boys are headed for prison. You have five minutes to decide."

"Fuck you!" The men walked to the door. We watched from a window as they strode furiously to the handsome teenagers who leaned against their car. The quartet conversed with wild gesticulations. The fathers pulled their sons into the house. "Show them the pictures."

The boys looked, their eyes widening. "That's not us!"

337

Big mistake! The boys could have denied everything but the pictures. Nick pulled out a snap of two bodies he'd taken from the police morgue, two men lying with their heads in pools of blood and their mouths gaping, beaten beyond recognition. "Remember them?"

The boys screamed their innocence. The councilman asked, "Where were you last night?"

"Here! In Jersey! At the bowling alley!"

Nick showed them another snap. "This little faggot fingered the two of you for beating him up in Greenwich Village an hour before the murders. You weren't five blocks away from the photography studio."

"No! Wasn't us! Here! At the bowling alley!"

"We ought to let them hang," said the prospective judge. "They aren't any good."

The councilman shook his head sadly. "They're our sons, Frank." He asked for a few more minutes and the quartet stepped outside.

My heart beat furiously. "Nick, I haven't been this excited since the first time with you."

Nick smiled. "Stick with me, kid."

"Think they'll bite?"

"Who knows? Maybe have to settle for just the boys. Gives you something to jack off over even if they don't."

The two men returned. "We can't get that much money this weekend. Will you take a check?" Nick refused. "If you'll meet us somewhere Monday night, we'll bring the boys and the cash."

Nick shook his head. "I'll trust you for the money. The sex goes down now."

The men looked at each other. "Can you give us the weekend to think it over?"

"Five minutes, or you better figure on weekly trips to Attica." The lawyers shook their heads. "Better that you prong the kids than them serving as punks for a hundred or so niggers in prison. Let's go, Saffron."

338

"Wait!" We stopped at the door of the motel room. "Five more minutes."

Nick grimaced. "All right."

The two men argued outside the door. "Nick, you aren't coming back Monday for the money?"

"They'd have hired guns waiting." The councilman returned with an offer of fifty thousand if we'd omit the sex. Nick shook his head. "I don't like people associated with the Mafia. My grandfather could hardly raise the rent on his store; still, he had to pay those fuckers protection. I don't need more than ten grand, so shit or get off the pot."

"It'll take a few minutes to talk the boys into it. Maybe we got to a coffee shop. . . ."

"So you can call some goons. Where's your buddy? This goes down now."

I glanced out the window. The other man ranted at the two youths. The councilman spoke. "How do we know you won't cross us?"

"I brought a camera. You can take pictures of Saffron blowing your boys."

"Better if we had pictures of you both."

"Anybody sees them, I lose my job. Forget it."

"Pictures of both of you with the boys or no deal."

"I don't give head."

"Then you can fuck them." Nick assented reluctantly. The councilman turned on an oily charm. "Why don't we forget about the pictures and the sex and just keep it to money?" The man pushed himself between Nick and me. "Nobody but the fairy wants this perverse shit. We could introduce you to some beautiful women." Nick shook his head. "What kind of hold does this faggot have on you?"

My buddy stiffened. "Two minutes! Stripped and ready for action. Otherwise your sons go to prison, your wives know you could have kept them out, and your careers are destroyed."

Breathing hard, the councilor returned to the others. "I

thought the Mafia was like the Marine Corps: Death Before Dishonor."

"It is. These guys aren't members of the family. They're Romans. Good for show, but nothing much inside. Hey! They're all coming."

Nick ordered me to pat each for weapons before they entered the house. The shuffling, shamefaced youths carried switchblades. Nick opened a door to a small bedroom with one large double bed and bade everyone enter. The men stared at Nick, the boys at me. The prospective judge spoke. "How about if the boys do whatever you want and leave us out. We're old men. You can't be perverted enough to find us juicy."

"Saffron has a fantasy."

The judge turned to me. "You want to blow us? You can blow us."

"I'd like that. I'd like you to fuck me, too."

He breathed deeply. The boys watched him intently. "Okay."

"The boys will take care of Raven."

He closed his eyes. "Yeah." He opened them. "When we do it . . . can the others wait in the other room?"

"That kills the whole idea of the thing."

"How can we be sure there's no further blackmail?"

Nick held up the camera. "You'll have pictures of us with the boys. Our careers are worth more than money."

"You won't take a raincheck?"

"Now or never! I suggest you start taking off your clothes."

The man gazed at his son and removed his tie. "Dad, we didn't do it! We ain't lying!"

The man slipped out of his jacket. "Do what the pig says."

"Dad!"

"Shut up! Do you realize what Frank and I are doing to keep you out of jail? This sickens me! I hear one more god-dam lie and I'll hand you over myself."

340

"D-a-a-d!"

The jurist backhanded his son. "Get your clothes off like the man said."

A trickle of blood ran down from a corner of the boy's mouth. His buddy, ashen-faced, unbuckled a fancy leather belt. Soon, the quartet and I stood nude.

Nick pulled out the camera. "Both men on the bed. Saffron's gonna show your boys how it's done." He dropped his pants. "Then they're gonna show me what they learned."

An hour later, the lawyer exploded inside me as Nick rammed the councilor's son. The councilor and the lawyer's son watched. After we washed off and dressed, Nick handed the lawyer the camera and we said goodbye. The men gazed at us with hatred. What a turn-on! As the car drove away, Nick gathered the soiled linen and locked up the house. We crawled over a fence and strolled down a back road to where we'd parked the van. "Aren't you worried about their tracing you through the pictures?"

Nick smiled. "I'd already exposed the film."

"Ahh! Too bad we don't have any snaps. That little episode will rank among the highlights of my carnal life."

My thoughtful buddy pulled one of the miniature cameras from his pocket. "This clicked through some of the action. Will Vince develop them?"

"Sure." We climbed into the van. "Somebody, we'll have to watch a father and son do dirty with each other."

Nick grinned. "Stick with me, kid."

The next day, I carried my sea bag and a travel bag to Newark. Mr. Esoldi worked as a supervisor in a factory from nine AM to six PM, which gave me the house to myself. I prepared supper every night; he seemed to enjoy my plain cooking and a couple of forays into Cajun cuisine. His friends dropped by most evenings to play cards, so I disappeared upstairs to read or cross-index the pictures.

A couple of times, Nick and I chanced sex in his old room, where I slept. Late one night, I awakened when someone

341

entered the bedroom, undressed, and lay on the bed. I knew that smell. "Mike?" He grunted. I waited a few minutes, so he could pretend to sleep, and proceeded to enjoy him. Two hours passed befores I allowed him release. He lay shaking for some time before rising, dressing, and leaving.

Thursday, Nick and I took his three older children to the Bronx Zoo. A lovely day. That evening, we dropped the tired kids at the trooper's house and treated Mr. Esoldi to supper at an oyster bar. Mike joined us for a couple of games of hearts; then Nick and I drove to the Palisades and parked. The trooper spoke with embarrassment. "Mom always had a lot of people around." He pulled a cigarette from the pack in his pocket. "Dad really likes you." The hand shook that held his lighter. "A lot of room in the old house. You could stay there and go to college in the city."

"Nick . . ."

"Or you could join the force. I checked your record. It's clean."

"Nick . . ."

"Dad would give you privacy. Nobody would interfere with you going into Manhattan and having fun."

"Nick . . ."

"We got over a thousand folders to go through. Take years. Stick with me, kid."

"If I stayed in New York, I'd end up living in a dingy little apartment and working at meaningless jobs like Vince and Ralph. You'd lose respect for me and gradually withdraw. I'd pound the pavement, staring into the eyes of strangers in a hopeless search for another you."

"It needn't be that way."

"There's a good chance it would."

"I want you to be part of my life."

"That's all I'd be—part of someone else's life."

"I've never met anybody who's more his own man."

"God, I wish that were so." I took his hand and explored those elegant fingers. "In my daydreams, I longed for a sexy

342

lover with whom to share adventures, but I knew life didn't work that way. Along comes as beautiful and intelligent a man as I could ever hope for, with a thirst for danger and a willingness to explore the deepest, darkest recesses of the human mind. And he cares for me. Dear Christ!" Nick's hand clenched mine with a fierce strength. "From now on, wherever I go in the world, I won't be lonely, knowing you're alive. I'll never again believe myself incapable of love."

Nick released his grip and rubbed his palm lightly over my thigh. "If you love me . . . how can you leave?"

"I gotta be a man."

My trooper sat very still, his glistening eyes reflecting the lights of Manhattan. I watched the moon turn black.

Epilogue

Francisco urged me to work in New York as a model. "You don't wear clothes well, but your face and hands could earn you a small fortune."

"Money is not to be sneezed at, baby," opined Vince. "Make it while you're young."

"And you'll be able to buy beauty when you're old." Ralph toasted beauty with a glass of raspberry wine.

Aida sighed, my finger scratching her ear. "I want to travel."

"Baby, in Manhattan, you can meet people from every part of the world, eat all sorts of ethnic food. . . . Buy some *National Geographics* if you want scenery."

Paul understood my quandary. "The gods have blessed you, Kurt, but youth and beauty fade. Wit becomes viciousness, and charm grotesque affectation. You don't want to become an old man removing his teeth to suck off pimpled boys in public toilets."

"What do you advise?"

"You could travel while you have energy and no ties. You could attend college, which might funnel your mental ability into creative channels. You could stay in New Jersey with Nick; you're too young to know how seldom Eros brushes a lover's heart with the same colors as your own."

And the gods might frown should I spurn their gifts. I spent Friday cleaning Diana's apartment in expectation of her return from Cleveland. "Darling, you're so nice to come home to. Goodness gracious! What a summer! Toil and trouble!"

"I'll run a bath. Would you like a martini as you soak or afterwards?"

"Both. I'm yearning to hear about your sizzling summer with the divine Nicky. Your letters were so cryptic."

I perched atop the toilet seat and told Diana about several enchanted evenings. "A couple of sessions were filled with violence, which seems to turn Nick on."

"Only Nick?"

"The pupil has surpassed the master."

"Not yet."

"He's bewitched me, Diana. I'm giving thought to staying in New York."

"Oh, darling! Do! You can sublet the apartment this fall. My agent, Doris the Dyke, has secured two film roles: madam of a joyhouse and an alcoholic chanteuse. Meager parts to be sure, and very little substance, but lots and lots of lovely money."

"Nick and I are bad for each other."

"Yet you love him?"

"Something like that."

Diana lathered her breasts tenderly. "I've never known you to be indecisive."

"I could leave only if Nick spurned me."

"Would he do such a thing?"

"If I made him hate me. The best way out of this valley of indecision is to burn all my bridges."

"What do your friends say?"

"Everyone seems to agree with my 'Uncle' Ralphie, who says 'You're a fool to leave such a cute boy.' "

"We do what we must."

"Not only should I leave, I must stop Nick from solitary flings. Our exploits have unleashed a frightful sadism in both of us."

She rinsed her breasts with a sponge. "Hand me that lemon." Yellow juice streamed down those fleshy dugs. "Scare him. Show him that everything eventually comes around." I told her about Nick's brother, Mike. "Does Nicky know?"

"I've thought of writing about his visits and leaving a copy in Nick's van, along with the pictures I took."

"What good will that do?"

"Nick is capable of destroying anyone who hurts a member of his family, if you recall the infernal bridegroom."

"Hmm." Diana stood and closed the shower curtain. I went to the kitchen, where a towel baked at low heat in the oven. I dried the actress off, covered her body with coconut oil, and placed a robe around her shoulders. I refilled the martini glasses when she joined me on the sofa. "His sons?"

"They promise great beauty, but the oldest is twelve."

Diana agreed on the seaminess of despoiling those in prepuberty. "Only as a last resort. What does his father look like?"

"A handsome man. Nick in twenty years. Lean solid body. Thick iron-gray hair. Walks with a good-natured swagger. Lonely since his wife died. Utterly masculine."

"Nick cares for him?"

"Very much."

Diana's eyebrows lifted. I understood her drift. "Did I tell you that the Portland Rep offered me Imogene in *Cymbeline* and Isabella in *Measure for Measure* next summer? Imogene dresses as a boy." Diana absently stroked those huge balookas and looked at me worriedly. "Isabella's a virgin."

"So were you, once upon a time."

"Long, long ago."

"When the world was young and dinosaurs ruled the planet."

"Shut up!"

"Ransack your memory. Find a hypnotist who will take

346

you back to your third birthday."

"Darling, she is willing to let her brother die rather than give up her silly maidenhead. I could never portray such a twit."

"You could play any female role ever written, except maybe Peter Pan and Little Eva."

Diana laughed. "Did I ever tell you about playing Topsy in grammar school?"

I returned to Newark, where I had spent the week filing pictures and journals. Despite nightly debauches with Nick in the carpet shop and two more visits by Mike, I was in a state of perpetual horniness. The pictures turned me on, of course, but so did Mr. Esoldi.

During the past few years, I'd never had sex with a man more than ten years older than myself, and uncircumcised penis seldom intrigued me. Mr. Esoldi was fifty-four and his hefty unmentionable marked him as an infidel.

His morning routine allowed me the pleasure of viewing that unmentionable. Upon awakening, he shit, showered, and shaved, the bathroom door ajar; afterward, still nude, he padded downstairs and sat at the kitchen table with his morning coffee. We both awakened early, so, nude myself, I joined him at the table; we usually talked for a couple of hours, chairs back from the table and facing each other. Once, I told the Lesbian story. Precious erected; so did he. I admired it openly. "It isn't often that I meet a man with a prick as big as mine, but damned if yours isn't bigger."

"No, I think yours is bigger."

There was nothing to do but pull out a measuring tape. My fingers touching his shaft, I came damn near to making a pass; his fingers touching mine, I came damn near to ejaculating. "You beat me by a quarter of an inch, Kurt. My boys got big ones, though." I knew that. "They'd probably beat you." Only in girth. Lengthwise, I had an inch on both.

Saturday morning, I awakened to the sound of rushing

347

water in the bathroom. I hurried downstairs, plugged in the coffeepot, and set the automatic camera on a shelf facing Mr. Esoldi's favorite chair. Ten minutes later, as we sipped our coffee, I asked his advice.

"I love two women. Would marry both if I could. But I can't. Gotta marry just one." The older man nodded. "Jane's a sweet girl. Designs costumes for plays. Very good at it. She was a virgin when we met." I held up three decorous photographs of Jane.

Mr. Esoldi looked at them. "Lovely girl. Lovely. Marry her."

I handed over several erotic nudes of Diana that she had lent me. "Diana's an actress. Witty. Fun company. Great in bed. Loves to suck my whopper for hours. Gives me a hard-on just to look at those pictures." Mr. Esoldi glanced at Precious, which stood at half-mast; he nodded, his own unmentionable stiffening as he studied the snaps. "Trouble is, I wasn't the first." I handed over several pornographic snaps of Diana with an ex-boyfriend and three others with an ex-girlfriend. I arose and moved to the cabinet, where I started the automatic camera. "I never planned on marrying, having witnessed my parents' unhappiness, but Nick has often told me how content you were with Mrs. Esoldi. How you worked together to instill decency and ambition in your children. Everyone knew when you were due home from work, because your wife's face beamed with joy. How you forewent a long-planned trip to Italy so your daughter could attend college, neither of you regretting your unselfishness."

Tears ran down Mr. Esoldi's cheeks, blinding him to the pictures he still held in his hand. His unmentionable began to droop. I stood next to him, my arm around his shoulders. "Don't, Joe. She'll always be alive for you." I knelt between his legs and hugged him. "You'll never forget her voice. Her smile. Her smell." My hands stroked his back; my chest pressed against his stirring pride. "Your children will remember her, too. And their children." I eased my head

348

down his chest to his belly. One hand caressed his back, the other a thigh. "She bore three bright handsome children. Loved them and you. Made you happy." My cheek rested against pubic hair. Mr. Esoldi stroked my head. "Her pain is over." My lips nuzzled a velvet rigidity.

It passed the time.